THE STRAVINSKY INTRIGUE

THE STRAVINSKY INTRIGUE

FUGUE & FABLE BOOK II

DARIN KENNEDY

*For I consider that music is, by its very nature, essentially powerless
to express anything at all, whether a feeling, an attitude of mind,
a psychological mood, a phenomenon of nature, etc.
Expression has never been an inherent property of music.
That is by no means the purpose of its existence.
If, as is nearly always the case, music appears to express something,
this is only an illusion and not a reality.*
Igor Fyodorovich Stravinsky

intrigue:
noun
1 - The secret planning of something illicit or detrimental to another
2 - A secret love affair
3 - A mysterious or fascinating quality
Oxford Dictionary

1
___

PRELUDE

It begins as it did the first time.

With a simple melody.

Invisible bows drawn across the ethereal strings of the cellos and basses of some unseen orchestra create tones deep, rich, and resonant that shake me to my very core. Soon, the brass of this phantom symphony joins in, filling my mind with the same six notes, over and over, repeated in perpetuity. A blink, and the dim around me shifts into a dark wood, the trees surrounding me thick, close, and ancient. A single flap of mighty wings sounds from directly above my head, and I jerk my eyes upward just in time to see a flash of orange flame disappear into the forest's canopy. While my eyes are directed skyward, something soft brushes past my leg, its touch silky smooth and as ephemeral as the music that fills my senses.

Then, a voice I prayed I'd never hear again permeates the spaces between the notes and fills my heart with a dread I thought I'd left far behind.

"Come, Scheherazade." A rough whisper punctuated by the clang of iron on iron. I have no doubt as to the owner of the voice. "You are needed once more."

"Stop it," I grunt at the pitch-black sky. "You don't exist. The Exhibition doesn't exist." I fall to my knees onto the soft forest floor. "It's all gone."

I

The touch of sadness in my voice at those last three words surprises me more than I'd care to admit.

"Regardless, storyteller, you are needed. More so now than ever before."

"I can't." Acid tears sting my eyes. "Scheherazade is no more."

"Oh, really?" A quiet chuckle freezes the marrow in my bones. "Then what is that weight hanging at your side?"

A glance down reveals my body wrapped in Scheherazade's green sarong. The familiar bracelets dangle at my wrists like golden manacles. The bejeweled dagger that saved my life and freed a boy from the dungeon of his own mind rests again at my waist.

As if it's supposed to be there.

As if it never left.

This can't be happening again.

Oh, God. There's blood on my hands. Warm, dark, and sticky.

Is it mine?

And if it isn't, then whose?

"No…" I awake to a darkened room. The white-blue glow of the mercury streetlight filters through two slats of the drawn blind and bounces off the mirror, hitting me square in the face. A familiar snore rises and falls every couple of seconds from the other side of the bed. I reach out in the darkness and encircle Thomas' warm wrist with fingers that must feel like ice.

"Mira?" Shaking his head to get rid of the cobwebs, he rolls toward me from his usual perch at the edge of his king-size mattress and comes nose-to-nose with me. "Everything okay?"

"I'm not sure." I let go of his wrist and bring my hand to my face where I find hot tears rolling down my cheeks.

I'm crying. Dammit, I'm crying.

"Bad dream?" he asks, the sleep already trickling back into his voice.

"If only."

"Was it the Exhibition again?"

"Yes." I wipe away the tears with my pillowcase. "Well, not exactly."

"Hmm." Thomas sits up in the darkness, his voice sliding effortlessly into therapist mode. "What was it then?"

A chill steals through me. "There was nothing… then a dark wood… then music, like before… and then, *her*."

"The witch?"

I swallow back the bile in my throat. "She said I was needed."

"Needed?" Thomas looks down at me in the dim light of the room. "What does that mean?"

"Like I have any idea." I roll away and feel around the nightstand until I find my phone. Ripping it from its charger, I pull it up, squinting as the backlit screen burns into my retinas.

"Who are you calling?" Thomas asks. "It's three o'clock in the morning."

"Who do you think?" Though nine months have passed since I've had to use it for anything other than pleasantries, I keep this particular number on speed dial. It rings once, twice, three times. I'm about to hang up and call again when a subtle click lets me know she's picked up the phone.

"Caroline, it's Mira."

"Mira?" She coughs. "Do you have any idea what time… Wait. What's wrong?"

"I just needed to know." I choose my next words carefully. "Is Anthony… okay?"

"Anthony?" Caroline is awake in a second. "Why are you calling me, Mira?"

My stomach twists itself into a tangle of knots. "It's happening again."

A sharp intake of air echoes in my ear, followed by the sound of a half-asleep Caroline clambering out of bed and rushing down the hall. A knock comes across the line followed by a gentle voice Caroline Faircloth reserves for her children and her children alone.

"Anthony?" Her call is answered with silence. "Anthony?"

"Mom?" A muffled squeak that can be none but Anthony Faircloth. "What's wrong?"

Nine months, and I still can't get used to hearing the boy talk. When we first met, he was all but comatose. Couldn't say a word.

Who would have guessed he'd end up being such a little chatterbox?

Mythological beasties? Obscure composers? The latest superhero movie?

A few months hanging around with Anthony Faircloth and even my pitiful mid-thirties brain is bordering on becoming an encyclopedia of pop culture.

"Nothing's wrong, sweetie." The normal singsong quality in Caroline's voice is undercut with fear. "Everything's fine." Her relief comes across the line loud and clear, though the distance in her voice suggests she's forgotten I'm even part of the conversation. "I just wanted to know if you were all right."

"I'm fine, Mom." A moment of silence. "Who's on the phone?"

"Nothing for you to worry about, honey. We'll talk about it in the morning. Now, go back to sleep." A door clicks shut as Caroline comes back on the line.

"Well?" I can almost see Caroline's exasperated stare. "Anthony says he's fine."

"Good." I bite my lip hard enough it hurts. "Maybe I'm overreacting. You know." I let out a yawn for dramatic effect. "Probably all just a dream."

"Now, Mira Tejedor," Caroline comes back, her gentle motherly tone replaced with the voice that once inspired an iron-toothed witch. "You and I both know you wouldn't have called me in the middle of the night if you thought whatever happened was simply a dream."

"You've got me there." A real yawn comes this time. "Drop by in the morning?"

"You want a little hazelnut in your coffee?" Though weary and frightened, Caroline remains, as ever, the model hostess. "And just a splash of creamer?"

"See you at eight." Hoping to lighten the mood, I let out a quick laugh. "I'll drop by the store and grab some banana bread."

I end the call and rest the phone back on the nightstand. Thomas snakes an arm across my belly and pulls me into him. The familiar lilac rush of his nearness fills my mind.

"So?" he breathes into my ear. "What happened? What did you see?"

"It's more about what I heard." I shiver in his arms. "There was a voice, just like before. The witch's voice."

"You're sure?"

"You've never heard the voice of Baba Yaga, Thomas. Trust me. It's not something you easily forget."

He gives me a squeeze. "What did the witch say?"

"She called me Scheherazade. Said I was needed again." I swallow away the bile at the back of my throat. "I think she was calling me back to the Exhibition."

"There is no Exhibition." Thomas inhales, the cool air tickling my ear. "You nearly died making sure of that."

"And yet, here we are."

"Are you sure it wasn't just a dream?" Thomas kisses my neck, a move that usually sends goosebumps down my arm. This time, however, they're already there. "You've had nightmares off and on about the Exhibition for months."

A pain blossoms above my left eye. "This was different."

"Not to mention, there are a lot of changes coming up next week." Thomas' voice downshifts into therapist gear even as the black pepper of his skepticism floods my senses.

Sometimes, it sucks being a Geiger counter for emotions.

"The big move to Charlotte. Isabella coming down to stay." His warm hand caresses my shoulder. "Maybe your brain just needed an escape valve."

"I've had more than my share of stress nightmares, Thomas. Believe me." I take his hand in mine, letting our fingers intertwine despite the fact he's starting to piss me off. "This was not the same thing. Not by a long shot."

"But, Mira—"

"No. I spent almost two weeks last year traipsing around inside Anthony Faircloth's head. By the time it was over, sliding into his mind was like putting on a well-worn pair of shoes. I'll never forget what that felt like. Looked like. Sounded like. Smelled like." I disengage from Thomas, sit up in the bed, and stare into the mirror across the room. The reflected brightness from the streetlight outside sends the headache above my eye spiraling out of control. "Wherever I went just now may not have been the Exhibition, but it was definitely not a dream."

"He's sleeping in?" I pull my coffee close to my nose, the deep hazelnut aroma a welcome addition to the cool July morning.

"School's out for summer. For all his differences, Anthony's just another fourteen-year-old boy." Caroline glances down the hall, a hint of dark circles below her eyes. "I'll be lucky to see him by noon."

I cross my arms, my gaze dropping to my lap. "Not to mention I hear someone called your house at three in the morning last night and woke him from a dead sleep."

"Now, don't you worry about that, Mira. He was snoring again in minutes." Caroline takes a sip of her coffee and shoots me a wink. "Too bad his mother couldn't do the same."

"Oh, Caroline—"

She stops me with a raised hand. "It's fine. You were worried about my son." She scoots closer on the couch and pats my knee. "Like I've told you a thousand times, my family owes you everything. You can call anytime."

"All right." I take a gulp of bittersweet hazelnut and set the mug on the table. "So. Anthony. I haven't seen him in a couple weeks. He's been acting… normal?"

"As normal as Anthony gets. No changes I've noticed, and believe me, I'd know." Caroline's eyes flash with mild amusement. "He's been underfoot for weeks now."

The patter of quiet footsteps from the hallway pulls my attention. Rachel Faircloth, dressed in Disney Princess pajamas and mismatched socks, wanders into the room, wiping the sleep from her eyes.

I shoot her a big grin. "Good morning, Rachel."

"Miss Mira!" She rushes to me and throws her arms around my neck. I haven't seen her since her ninth birthday party back in April. Just a few weeks have passed, and she's already grown another inch. She'll be taller than Caroline before we know it.

As Rachel does her best to squeeze the life out of me, an image of Isabella's face filters through my mind. It's been hard, being away from her so much this last month, but getting ready for the move to Charlotte has taken way more time and energy than I would have dreamed.

Thank God for Mom.

"All right, Rachel." Caroline pulls her daughter onto her lap. "Let's let Mira get some air."

Rachel yawns. "Can I have pancakes this morning?"

Caroline strokes her daughter's hair. "I'll make you some pancakes in a minute. Why don't you go pour yourself a bowl of Cheerios for now? Later on, I'll let you help me make the batter."

"Cheerios!" Rachel scuttles off to the kitchen, and Caroline's smile fades immediately back to her game face.

"It's good to see her so perky this morning. She hasn't been sleeping well lately."

"I'm sorry to hear that."

"Oh, she'll be okay." Caroline's eyes narrow. "And speaking of people that aren't sleeping well, you never told me exactly what it was that prompted you to call last night."

"I'm not sure what to tell you." I grab my coffee, more to have something to hold on to than anything else. The warmth of the mug feels heavenly between my fingers. "I was sleeping. Dreaming. And then… I wasn't."

"You woke up?"

"Not exactly. One second, normal dreams, at least normal for me. The next, I'm in a dark place filled with music." My gaze locks with Caroline's. "Orchestral music I've never heard before."

Caroline's eyes grow wide. "Something from before? *Pictures? Scheherazade?*"

My heart skips at that last word. "Neither, but it was strangely familiar."

I take a deep breath and return in my mind to the dark forest, trying to recreate the melody that haunted me last night. Six notes, running up and down some kind of scale, the tone of the music deep and ominous. I'm barely through the second run when Caroline blanches.

"It *is* happening again."

"What?" I take Caroline's hand. "What is it?"

"You've never heard that tune before?" Her fingers clamp down on mine.

"No." I pull my hand away and shake out my crushed hand. "Should I have?"

"That's Stravinsky. *The Firebird.*" She looks away, her lip trembling. "It's all Anthony's been listening to lately."

"*The Firebird?*" Another set of images trickles through my mind. A flicker of orange flame disappearing among the gnarled branches of the imaginary forest. The solitary beat of wings as the unseen creature flies to avoid my curious gaze. The gentle brush of silk along my legs while my attention is directed upward.

And the last measure of this terrifying new melody.

The voice from the darkness, Baba Yaga. The witch was formed from a potent mixture of Anthony's respect, awe, and fear of the most important woman in his life, the woman who currently sits beside me on the couch.

She can't be back. Yaga is Anthony. And his mother. And me. The situation that created Yaga, necessitated her existence, is over. Anthony's mind is healed.

And yet, there's no mistaking that it was the witch's voice I heard last night, the sharp whisper no different than nine months ago when I first heard it echoing down from the Exhibition's stormy ceiling.

"So, Mira." Caroline picks up her coffee with trembling fingers. "What do we do now?"

I flick my eyes in the direction of the hallway leading to the bedrooms.

"It may be a bit early for him, but the two of us should really speak with Anthony."

~

"Mira."

Anthony steps into the room and heads in my direction, a slight shuffle in his steps as he tries to come awake. Caroline, hot on his heels, tries with minimal success to run a brush through his usual unkempt hair, made all the worse today by a severe case of bedhead.

"Good morning, Anthony."

"I didn't know you were coming by today." Anthony glances back at his mother before returning his earnest gaze in my direction. "What are you doing here?"

Ah, Anthony. Always to the point.

"I needed to come by and chat with you and your mother about something." At his blank stare, I add, "Something important."

Anthony sits down next to me and adjusts his glasses.

"Is something wrong?" His voice comes out a bit on the squeaky side as his vocal cords continue to adjust to the ravages of puberty. "Mom?"

"Nothing's wrong." Caroline clears her throat. "Mira just had one of her… feelings and wanted to make sure you were doing all right."

Anthony's gaze shoots back to mine, and I give him a subtle nod. "You were on my mind last night, kiddo. Thought there might be something you wanted to talk about."

Anthony looks back at his mother. "Am I in trouble? Did I do something? If I did, I didn't mean—"

"No, Anthony." Caroline strokes his hair and slides into her most soothing motherly voice. "You're not in any trouble."

"At least, we don't think so." I grab my coffee and take another sip, allowing the earthy tang to center my thoughts. "What can you tell us about *The Firebird*?"

"*The Firebird*?" Anthony stares at me with an odd sneer. "The Stravinsky piece?"

I give Anthony a cautious smile. "Your mother says you've been listening to it nonstop the last few weeks."

Anthony's eyes shift out of focus, a look I've seen dozens of times before.

He's going into lecture mode.

This should be educational.

"*The Firebird* was Stravinsky's breakthrough composition." At my puzzled gaze, Anthony adds, "You know. Igor Stravinsky."

"Oh." I fight to keep a sarcastic grin from my lips, though I don't really need to bother. In my experience, that kind of social subtlety goes right over Anthony's head. "*That* Stravinsky."

"Stravinsky composed *The Firebird* for Sergei Diaghilev way back in 1910. In modern times, it's usually played as a symphonic suite, but in its original form, it was actually a ballet."

"A ballet, you say?" I shudder as images of Anthony's sister, Rachel, literally dance across my mind's eye. Trapped in Anthony's Exhibition as part of Mussorgsky's "Ballet of Unhatched Chicks," some small part of Rachel's psyche was held against her will and forced to dance, an unwitting victim of her brother's trauma.

A dance that was forced on me as well.

From the look on Caroline's face, it's clear our thoughts are flowing in similar directions.

"Go on," Caroline whispers. "Let's hear it."

"Yes, Anthony." I rest a hand on his shoulder. "Tell us. What is this ballet about?"

Never happier than when he's the expert on a subject, Anthony breaks into a wide smile.

I gulp down the last dregs of coffee from my cup and settle in for the long haul.

"*The Firebird* portrays a tale of good versus evil." Anthony's eyes glaze over as he focuses his thoughts. "The hero, Prince Ivan Tsarevich, dares enter the magical realm of Koschei the Deathless, an immortal being protected by an army of enchanted creatures."

"Koschei the Deathless." Shaking my head, I take a breath. "And an army of monsters?"

At Anthony's enthusiastic nod, my stomach turns.

And here I thought facing a witch was bad.

"Early on in the story," Anthony continues, "Prince Ivan captures one of the enchanted creatures, the majestic Firebird, which in turn offers Ivan its allegiance in exchange for its life and freedom."

I somehow maintain my beatific smile. "And then what happens?"

Anthony's eyes turn up and to one side. "As I remember it, Ivan falls in love with the most beautiful of thirteen princesses he meets in Koschei's kingdom. He and Koschei argue over Ivan's plans to marry her, and the

Immortal sends his army of magical creatures to destroy the young prince."

This keeps getting better.

And by better, I mean worse.

Dammit.

"Dare I ask how the story turns out?"

Anthony raises an eyebrow, oblivious as to why I'm going down this particular rabbit hole. "The Firebird returns and casts a spell over all the creatures of the realm, including Koschei himself, forcing them into this insane dance that ends with them all falling into a deep sleep. The Firebird then reveals to Prince Ivan Koschei's big secret, that his immortal soul is contained within a magical egg kept within his home. Ivan breaks into the palace, steals the egg, and destroys it in front of Koschei, bringing death to the Deathless and an end to his enchantment over the land. Koschei, his palace, and all the creatures of the magical realm fade into nothingness and Ivan's princess awakes."

Caroline and I stare at each other across her very special son.

"Any particular reason you've been listening to this piece so much lately?" Caroline asks.

"I don't know." Anthony shrugs. "Because it's beautiful?"

"One more question." I peer deep into Anthony's eyes. "Have you been... dreaming about *The Firebird*?"

"Why do you ask?" Anthony's brow furrows even as fear crosses his gaze. "I'm not going away again. I promise."

"Of course not, honey." Caroline puts an arm around Anthony and pulls his trembling form into her. He accepts this act of love far more graciously than he ever would have when we first met. "Of course not."

We haven't discussed it in months, but once we all agreed Anthony was as out of the woods as he was going to be, Thomas, Caroline, and I did our best to explain to Anthony what happened to him last fall. Between his mother, his therapist, and me, not to mention the better part of two pepperoni pizzas, he finally seemed to get it. Funny thing, though? Before we even started, I got the impression he already knew what we were going to say.

Kid plays his cards so close to the chest, I wonder sometimes if even he knows what he has in his hand.

"Anthony," I whisper. "No one's going anywhere, but I felt something last night. Something I haven't felt since everything we went through last fall. If you start having bad dreams or notice anything else strange, I need you to let me know, understand?"

Anthony's gaze flits to his mother then back to me. "I'm afraid."

Caroline squeezes Anthony even tighter. "We're not going to let anything happen to you, honey." She shoots me a pointed glance. "Right, Mira?"

"Everything is going to be fine, Anthony." My heart races as I pray Caroline and I aren't writing checks we can't cash. "Promise."

INTRODUCTION

"And that's not all." I rest my glass on the restaurant table. "This time, it seems there's an evil immortal with a legion of monsters waiting for me."

"Now, Mira. Don't go freaking yourself out." Thomas peers across both our lunches at me. Amusement flirts at the edge of his otherwise serious stare. "What happened last fall was a once in a lifetime event, an event you yourself brought to an end."

"But what happened last night felt exactly the same."

Thomas tilts his head to one side. "I'm still seeing Anthony on a monthly basis, at Caroline's insistence, and I have to say, I haven't noted anything like what was happening before. In fact, I've actually been planning to drop our visits back to quarterly." Thomas takes a bite of his sandwich and chews it thoughtfully before continuing. "He's doing well in school. His grades are excellent. Hell, kid's even making some friends outside his family." His shoulders rise in a subtle shrug. "Quite frankly, he's proving to be one of my success stories."

As Thomas drones on, I zone out. He's trying to reassure me, but each passing moment makes me more certain something isn't right. Something just on the edge of my memory.

Mom and Grandma both had intuition you could set a clock by, and as I always say, I am my mother's daughter.

"Look, Mira." Thomas brushes his fingertips across my wrist, sending a pleasant shiver up my arm. "If it will make you feel better, I'll have Caroline bring Anthony for an extra session this month. I should have an opening on Wednesday."

A measure of relief washes over me. "Thanks, Thomas."

Two days. I hope Anthony can wait that long.

More importantly, I hope I can wait that long.

"So, the apartment is supposed to be ready Saturday?" Thomas asks, clearly trying to lighten the conversation.

"That's what the management company keeps telling me." I force a smile. "After the thing with the dishwasher, I guess I'll believe it when I see it."

It's funny. Till last night, getting the new apartment set up for the big move had been the main thing on my mind. Work has been pretty steady lately. Mom's got Isabella for a couple of weeks, and the two of them have been having a great time checking out all the museums in D.C. before she brings Isabella down this weekend to stay. Thomas has been working a reduced schedule so he can help me get everything ready, and the time together has been pretty fantastic. I've got my website all updated to reflect my new information and even have a couple of emails from potential clients. Life is good for the first time in a really long time.

Like the punch line of some cruel joke, my phone buzzes in my purse. Though the only people who call me these days are Thomas, Mom, or Isabella, the gentle buzzing sets the hairs on my arm on end.

I check the number and what do you know? Intuition wins again.

I press the answer button and hold the phone to my ear, pained that I still remember these particular seven digits.

"Detective Sterling. Surprised to see your number on the screen."

"Hello, Mira." Detective Calvin Sterling, his deep voice all business with just a hint of contrition. Looks like I'm not the only one with a long memory. "How are you?"

"You tell me." I excuse myself from the table and step out of the restaurant into the early afternoon heat. "To what do I owe the pleasure?"

"The proverbial bad penny, I suppose." I can almost see him stroking his chin the way he does when he thinks he's being clever. "Noticed you've changed your number."

"I'm moving." A fact I wish Calvin Sterling, of all people, didn't know. "I'm assuming this is a business call?"

"Actually, yes." He clears his throat. "Something's come up. Something up your alley. I wanted to pick your brain, excuse the pun, and when I couldn't get through to you by phone, I looked you up online. Imagine my surprise when I came upon your new website."

I breathe a quiet sigh. "Girl's got to make a living."

Sterling huffs, somewhere between a cough and a laugh. "You should've told me you were heading this direction. I've seen what you can do. CMPD could definitely use a 'consultant' with your skills."

"I'm keeping my involvement in police matters to a minimum for the time being. I hope you understand."

I glance through the restaurant's bay window at Thomas. He's at the table picking at his food and pretending he isn't bothered that I took this call. I don't have to be psychic to see through all that, though the aroma of rotting apples wafting across my consciousness confirms what his body language is screaming.

"But, Mira." Sterling's voice takes on just a hint of desperation. "What you did last fall—"

"Almost killed me." I take a deep breath through my nose. "So, Detective, unless there's something else you need, I'm going to get back to my lunch date."

Sterling holds off a couple seconds before answering, the swagger in his voice still intact. "And how is the good Dr. Archer?"

"And people wonder how you made Detective."

I can almost hear Sterling's wheels turn between his quiet breaths. "All right. Sorry to have disturbed you. I won't bother you again." Another pause. "Take care, Mira."

I murmur a frustrated pleasantry in return, step back into the restaurant, and return to our table. As Thomas takes the last bite of his sandwich, I sit and try to catch his eye in apology, but he's engrossed in whatever is showing on the TV mounted on the wall across my shoulder.

No. More than engrossed. He's upset, the rotting fruit scent from before replaced with the cool chlorine of worry.

And something tells me his anxiety has little to do with Sterling's call. "What is it?"

"I know that child." Thomas points to the screen. "She was one of my regulars till about a year ago."

I turn to catch the newscast. A picture of a little girl with bright blonde hair, not much older than Isabella, stares out of the TV at me. Her ebullient smile is in sharp contrast to the words flashing across the ticker at the bottom of the screen.

NINE-YEAR-OLD HANNAH ABRAMS MISSING SINCE THIS MORNING

"A good kid." Thomas shakes his head. "Why her? Poor thing has already been through enough."

"I don't know, honey." A realization dawns on me as Thomas turns back in my direction.

"So, what did Detective Sterling want?" he asks.

"I didn't let him get that far." My phone already half out of my purse, I excuse myself from the table a second time. "But I've suddenly got a pretty good idea."

"**I**f we're going to try this again, we're going to need to set some ground rules."

"Agreed." Sterling matches my steady gaze from across his desk at the station. "I'm assuming the first rule is that this is strictly professional?"

My lips turn up in an ironic smile. "Strictly."

He answers in kind, his dark lips pulling back to reveal an even set of white teeth. "And the second? I'm guessing that it's your way or the highway?"

I actually laugh at that last bit. "So, you got the memo."

"Mira." Sterling massages his neck, avoiding my gaze for the moment. "I've had a lot of time to think about what went down last year. I want you to know if I had it to do again, I would handle a lot of things differently."

"Good to hear." I shoot him a raised eyebrow. "Though you're already stepping all over the first rule."

"Right." Sterling turns and flips through a filing cabinet to his rear, his jacket stretching across his broad shoulders.

Damn. The man can fill out a suit.

A few seconds later, he rests an open folder on the desk before me. The top document is a large photograph of Hannah Abrams, the girl from the newscast. I flip through the papers and find a couple more photos, a few school records showing top marks, and an adoption certificate.

"Not much to go on." Sterling picks up the eight by ten and studies the photograph. "Nine years old. Disappeared from her bed early this morning without a trace. No note. No sign of a break-in. No witnesses to anything funny. Her mother last checked in on her a little after midnight." Sterling leans across the desk, crossing his arms and resting on his elbows. "Any thoughts?"

"Runaway, maybe?"

"Hannah is a model student. Won last year's science fair. No issues with her folks. In fact, she and her parents were leaving for Disney World tomorrow morning." He hands me the picture. "Does this… help at all?"

"Sorry." I scan the various items from the folder. "Nothing here of the girl's personal effects. Nothing to read."

Sterling leans across the desk. "What do you need, then?"

"To see her space. Like… last year." I grab my purse. "The sooner the better."

My mind tracks back to the last time I came into a missing girl's room for a reading. Julianna Wagner, dead for days before I even entered the picture. At least Hannah was still alive as recently as twelve hours ago.

Sterling escorts me to the back of the station where a line of police cruisers awaits. The ride to the Abrams house is shockingly quiet as the radio is off and neither of us knows quite what to say to the other.

"How is Detective Bolger?" I eventually offer in an attempt to break the silence.

"Mitch?" Sterling lets out a chuckle. "Taking a long overdue vacation with his new girlfriend. About five years too late, if you ask me, but unless I miss my guess, he's probably burnt to a crisp on a boat in the Caribbean right now."

"New girlfriend?" I laugh as well. "She must go for the tall, not so dark, and pasty type."

"Hey, cut him some slack." Sterling turns left onto a suburban avenue. "You caught him during a particularly rough time."

"You mean his forties?" At Sterling's earnest stare, I raise my hands in surrender. "Fine. Tell him I said hi."

"Oh, I'm sure he'd *love* to hear that." Sterling's eyes return to the road as he retreats into his thoughts.

We continue our drive in silence. I stare out the window at the passing houses. Alternating between old one-story bungalows and brand-spanking-new three-story craftsman style mini-mansions, the neighborhood is clearly going through a big renewal. We stop at a house a block or so down from a tavern where Thomas and I grabbed a drink a few weeks back. The front yard is marked off with the obligatory police tape. One patrol car is parked at the corner with two officers inside. One's head is down, working on something, while the other watches me like a hawk as I step out of Sterling's ride.

The house is one of the smaller bungalows, but it's well maintained and the yard is immaculate. A bicycle with training wheels rests on the sidewalk and a pink and white soccer ball lies wedged beneath a holly bush by the front door. A balsamic tang mixed with a scent of sulfur permeates the space, grief warring with fear.

Hannah's parents already dread the worst.

I grasp the yellow-and-black-striped tape. "May I?"

"Of course." Sterling gestures toward the front lawn. "All yours."

I step into the yard, glad I opted to wear jeans and sneakers rather than the heels and skirt I considered this morning. My first stop is the overturned bicycle, but other than the zesty lemon scent of freedom and speed, I don't pick up anything of consequence. The soccer ball, on the other hand, is another story altogether.

As I rest my fingers on the pink and white synthetic leather, the fearful reek of sulfur grows exponentially in my mind. Fighting the urge to retch, I motion for Sterling to join me.

"Find something?" His brow furrows the way most people's do when they watch me working.

"I don't know what happened to this girl…" I swallow back the bile at the back of my throat. "But whatever it was, she was holding this ball when it happened."

Sterling kneels beside me. "Any clue as to where she might be?"

My eyes slide shut as my mind searches for anything that might help. "No. I sense nothing but terror and sudden loneliness."

"And what is it she's afraid of?"

I raise a hand. "Quiet."

Sterling clams up, and there it is. Breaking through the sulfur stench. Another aroma, this one far more pleasant.

Cut grass coupled with fresh rain.

And then, a sound. The gentle lapping of water against stone. The honking of geese. The sound of children playing. And along with this collection of sounds, a feeling of peace. Of safety.

"Water on stone. Geese. Children." I catch Sterling's eye. "Where is the nearest park?"

"Park." He pulls himself up to his full height and scratches his chin. "Freedom Park is a little over a mile from here. You think she was taken there?"

"Not taken, at least not in the way you mean." Leaving Sterling in the yard, I head for the front door. "It's somewhere Hannah thinks of as a safe haven."

I ring the bell and wait for a few seconds. When no one answers, I knock.

Something tells me we don't have a lot of time to spare.

After another few seconds, a short, balding man, late thirties at most, opens the door. The rings under his eyes tell me everything I need to know.

This is Hannah's father.

"Can I help you?"

Sterling steps onto the doorstep beside me. "Mr. Abrams. We met earlier."

"I remember." Abrams' gaze shifts to Sterling for half a second before landing back on me. "Who's this?"

I extend my hand. "My name is Mira Tejedor. I'm a consultant for the police department. Detective Sterling asked me to come and see if I can help."

"And what skills do you bring to the situation, Miss Tejedor?" Abrams crosses his arms in a huff. "Hannah's been missing for hours and not one of the dozen cops that have come by my house seems to have a damn clue of where she is or what the hell to do next."

"Honey?" comes a woman's voice from inside. "Who's at the door?"

"It's the police." Abrams surveys Sterling and me with a withering look. "Again."

Mrs. Abrams comes to the door, her eyes red and swollen. "Do you have any news about my daughter?"

"Not yet, ma'am," Sterling murmurs, his game face not betraying any emotion.

Her eyes narrow in cold anger. "Well, shouldn't you be out there looking, then?"

"Ma'am, most of CMPD is out looking for your daughter right now."

Her shoulders drop. "I know."

"Mr. and Mrs. Abrams," I butt in. "It may sound strange, but I need to know something." Nauseated by the fear and anxiety wafting off Hannah's parents, I suck in a quick breath in an effort to keep my composure. "Does Hannah like to go to the park?"

Mr. Abrams' eyes narrow. "She's a nine-year-old girl. What do you think?"

"Where do you take her when you go?" I ask, breathless as I struggle to keep my lunch down. "Detective Sterling mentioned a place called Freedom Park?"

Hannah Abrams' parents lock gazes and a silent message passes between them.

"Go," Mrs. Abrams says. "I'll wait here in case Hannah calls."

Though his car is parked across the street, Abrams hits the driver's seat in five seconds flat and motions us to hurry up. Sterling ushers me back to the patrol car, and my seatbelt is barely fastened before he pulls back onto the road and flips on the lights and siren. The traffic is pretty light, and most cars wisely get out of our way. A look back reveals Mr. Abrams close on our bumper. I don't know exactly what he thinks is going on, but I salute anyone who trusts their intuition to this degree.

You don't have to be psychic to hear that little voice inside as long as you bother to listen.

We're three minutes into the trip before I realize I'm still holding Hannah's pink soccer ball in my hands. Images flash in my mind—a man-made lake created from stone and masonry, a cement running path, an island amphitheater.

"Is there a bridge?" I ask.

Sterling doesn't answer, but the engine roars as he steps on the accelerator.

I take that as a yes.

≈

Though the parking lot is packed, Sterling finds a spot in seconds and wastes no time climbing out of the police cruiser. I've barely had a chance to shut my door when Abrams whips into the next space and leaps from his car.

"I know who you are," he grunts as he takes off for the park entrance. "You're that psychic, the one from Virginia." He shoots me a sharp glance across his shoulder. "You found that Sarah Goode girl."

"Yep," I mutter. "That would be me."

For someone who works really hard to stay under the radar, I get recognized a hell of a lot more than I'd like.

I race to catch up to Abrams, Sterling hot on both our heels. At first, it's all playgrounds and picnic shelters, but as we round the corner of a small hill, the park I so recently saw in my mind unfolds before us.

The manmade lake stretching on for a quarter mile.

The concrete path surrounding the water.

The stone bridge leading to the lake's lone island.

"Mr. Abrams," I shout. "Where are you taking us?"

"Her favorite spot," he yells across his shoulder, heading straight for the bridge. "It's where we go to feed the geese."

Abrams is across the bridge and scouring the miniature island before I can say another word. Screaming Hannah's name and scaring people on either side of the lake, he searches every square inch of the place before falling to his knees behind the large amphitheater that serves as the island's focal point.

"Not here," he sobs. "She's not here."

I rest a hand on his shoulder. "Mr. Abrams—"

He brushes my hand away. "You said she was here."

"Actually, I got an image off a soccer ball." I kneel beside Hannah's father and peer deep into his tear-filled eyes. "There's a reason for that. Help me." I drop my voice to a low whisper. "Help Hannah."

He considers for all of two seconds before taking my hand, his intuition miraculously kicking in for a second time that day. "What do I do?" His pleading eyes yank my heartstrings. "Tell me."

"I need you to call for her. As loud as you can."

As he inhales to shout, I place a finger over his mouth.

"Not here." I bring the same finger to his temple. "Here."

Abrams stares at me, incredulous. "You want me to… think at her?"

Sterling, who has just finished sweeping the island, comes up on Abrams' other side. "Trust her, Mr. Abrams. Mira knows what she's doing."

"Call to her with your mind. I'll do the same, as will Detective Sterling." I squeeze Abrams fingers. "If she answers, I may be able to hear her."

Through the eye-watering onion scent of desperation and the ever-present sulfur, a new aroma pushes through to the top.

One that means hope.

Or, to my tricked-out brain, marshmallows toasting over an open fire.

"Hannah," Abrams whispers. "Hear me." His hand trembles in mine. "Hannah."

"Hannah," I reach out and grasp Sterling's hand. "Where are you?"

It takes him a few cycles, but Sterling catches on quick, showing a surprising bit of intuition himself. As the three of us stand in a half-circle performing our hushed chant, a crowd gathers and generates a murmur all its own.

But none of that matters.

I'm only listening for one voice.

Hannah's.

Seconds pass into minutes. The sun shifts behind a cloud. A cool breeze wafts across the pond, bringing the scent of summer grass. A baby cries in the distance.

And there it is.

Above the psychic static of Abrams' desperation, Sterling's raw determination, and the mixed confusion and awe of the mob of rubberneckers, a melody. And a voice.

A little girl. Singing. Her choice of tune more than a bit surprising.

"Lucy in the Sky with Diamonds?"

Abrams looks up at me. "What did you say?"

I meet his gaze. "Your daughter a fan of The Beatles?"

"Hannah." Abrams shoots to his feet, the scent of roasted marshmallows almost knocking me over. "Where is she?"

I release his hand and shut my eyes, trying to hone in on the quiet voice warbling about tangerine trees and marmalade skies.

Skies.

"Sterling, you've looked everywhere, right?"

He shakes his head. "She's nowhere I can see. I checked under all the trees, the bridge, the stage, everywhere."

My eyes track up the rear wall of the amphitheater. "What about up there?"

Sterling's brows knit together. "On the roof?"

"She came here to get away from something." I walk the three steps to the rear of the structure and step up onto a large box that no doubt holds the amphitheater electronics. "Maybe she went to higher ground."

It takes some doing, but with an assist from Sterling, I'm able to clamber up the wall. The roof scorches my fingers and forearms as I pull myself up onto the pitched surface, the heat radiating off the metal as if I've fallen inside an enormous frying pan. I can't make out anything at first, the blinding sun beating down on me as if it bears a grudge. I raise a hand to shield my eyes, and that's when I see her. Near one of the front corners, Hannah's crumpled form flirts with the edge of the roof.

"She's here," I shout as I rush across uneven metal and kneel by her side.

Still in her nightgown, her bare feet bleeding from the mile-long trek from her bedroom, Hannah Abrams is, thank God, still breathing. Her bare skin red from sun exposure, her face is drawn as if she's in the middle of a fitful dream. Her eyes, however, are open.

I reach down and touch her feverish cheek.

And that's when I hear it.

The music from last night.

The same six notes, deep and resonant, repeating over and over and over.

I try to pull away, but my hand refuses to move.

Somewhere in the distance, Sterling shouts my name.

And then… I am somewhere else.

3

―――――

THE ENCHANTED GARDEN

The only similarity to the last time is the sensation of falling. Everything else is different. The rainbow maelstrom of Anthony Faircloth's fractured mind, filled with blaring music and booming percussion, seems almost pleasant compared to the impenetrable darkness of this place. Not a glimmer of light intrudes as those six notes continue to cycle for what seems forever.

I attempt to check for the familiar presence of the Sultan's dagger at my waist, but I have no hand with which to reach and no body to examine. I try to scream, but no sound comes.

I am a wraith, alone in the darkness. Directionless. Formless. Hopeless.

Left with nothing but my own silent thoughts for companionship, I succumb momentarily to the rising panic in my chest. The no-longer-missing girl may be the catalyst, but only one person I've encountered in all my years has such power in the world of dream, and only he would wield it with such orchestral accompaniment.

But why would he do such a thing?

On the other hand, the son of William and Caroline Faircloth had no intention of hurting me last time, and we saw how that turned out.

With every iota of willpower I can muster, I try again to speak, to say the one name that might free me from my prison. Though in this place I

23

have no mouth, throat, or lungs, eventually a single word fills the darkness.

A whisper.

My voice, and yet not my voice.

"Anthony."

Like the curtain rising on a play, the darkness retreats, leaving me stranded once again, a stranger in a strange land.

A twilight garden forms around me. Emerging first from the mist is a tree of brass-colored bark, twice my height and curved so its canopy shades a flat sitting rock. Golden fruit hangs from its branches, each glistening apple more perfect than the next. Atop the rock and beneath the shade of the tree, Hannah Abrams lies trembling uncontrollably, as if sleeping through the most horrible of nightmares. Her brow furrowed, a low whimper passes her lips with every breath.

What is it she's so afraid of?

I'm not left wondering for long.

As the bizarre garden continues to expand and overtake the darkness, the thing that has left Hannah so terrified rears its ugly head from the edge of a stagnant pool. The size of a full-grown Rottweiler and twice as broad, the toad-like creature with gnarled horns and yellow eyes drags its six-legged form from the muddy water. Slime-covered lips pull back from a double row of jagged teeth. I silently thank my unseen host for leaving me an invisible wraith.

That is until one of the creature's slit-like yellow eyes turns to gape at me.

A quick glance down confirms my worst fears. Suddenly embodied, my form is again covered in green, though gone is Scheherazade's sarong, replaced with a finely tailored tunic with pearl and gold accents and embroidered pantaloons tucked into knee-high black boots. Black bracers decorated with inlaid gold in the shape of treble clefs guard my forearms.

Somewhere in the distance, the high-pitched violin of Scheherazade's theme echoes through the trees.

No doubt about it.

This is Anthony's doing.

And if this is indeed Anthony, the danger is very real.

In an instant, the thing from the pool leaps at me, and I'm paralyzed by its rage-filled bellow. Barely able to get my feet to move, I dodge to one side and land in the spongy blue grass of this peculiar garden. Remembering painful lessons from the Exhibition, I search this new body for weapons but find nothing. The toad-thing wastes no time, lowering its gnarled horns and rushing at me with all the speed its six legs can muster.

Praying my abilities as the storyteller somehow apply in this new dreamscape, I hold out my hand and cry out for the Sultan's dagger. With a flash of golden light, a weapon materializes.

But this is no dagger.

In my palm rests a recurve bow, intricately carved and well worn. A moment later, the weight of a full quiver hits my shoulder. With instincts I would never possess in the real world, I roll to one side, narrowly avoiding being impaled on the creature's horns, and leap back to my feet with an arrow nocked and trained on the thing's head.

"I don't know if you can understand me, creature," I shout, "but stand down, or I will slay you where you stand."

Another bellow and the thing rushes me again. I let the arrow fly, but the razor tip ricochets off the creature's horn. I leap to one side, spinning again from the monster's path, but the thing shifts its head at the last second and extends its squat neck. A searing pain rips through my side as the tip of its curved horn tears into my side.

I pull myself back to my feet and turn to face the creature, drawing another arrow, nocking it, and leveling the bow at the thing's midsection in one fluid movement. The fletching soft against my cheek, I do my best to appear strong and confident, but cannot suppress a shudder as the thing's tongue shoots up its gnarled horn to lap at the blood at its jagged tip.

I chance a glance down and find a quickly spreading pool of deep crimson staining my verdant tunic.

One fact is certain. I will not survive many blows like that.

I spare a quick look in Hannah's direction. Still in the throes of a fitful sleep, she appears safe for the moment, the toad-thing's attention fully directed at me.

Narrowing its pale yellow eyes, the creature paws at the ground with the front pair of its six legs like a bull preparing to charge. First blood has been drawn and tasted, and this thing is hungry for more.

The toad-thing and I don't move for several seconds, each of our gazes fixed on the other's in a determined glare. I fear our temporary stalemate has far more to do with the creature enjoying the moment than any fear it might have of my little bow and arrow. Then, as I sense it about to attack again, an ear-shattering screech fills the air. The sound makes the toad-thing's bellow seem like the peaceful burble of a stream.

Together, our gazes shoot skyward, the twilight darkness fading into morning as this dreamworld's sun peeks above the tree line. Out of this flare of orange comes a majestic bird unlike any I've ever seen. As large as a pony with a wingspan that seems to stretch from horizon to horizon, a creature that can only be the Firebird flaps its golden wings once, twice, three times as it rises in the sky. A golden gleam crosses its eyes as it peers down upon this garden made battlefield, and a very different spark flits across the toad-thing's wicked gaze.

A spark of fear.

The creature spins and scurries for the water, but not before the Firebird falls from the sky like an avenging angel and impales it on its sword-like beak. The toad-thing roars in agony, a roar that quickly fades into a quiet gurgle. Once the creature ceases its struggling, the Firebird pulls its dark beak from the creature's back and proceeds to rip off first one horn and then the other with its mighty talons. Then, without so much as a pause, the majestic bird scoops the carcass up in its beak, eyes me with a quick appraising gaze, and takes to the sky, disappearing into the blinding sun.

Clutching my side, I run to the flat rock beneath the tree of golden apples. Hannah still sleeps, though her brow smooths, as if she somehow knows the danger has passed. I kneel by her side, as I did in the real world before—How long has it been? Minutes? Hours? Days?—and caress her forehead.

"Hannah?" I whisper. "Can you hear me?"

"She is lost to you." Like rumbling thunder, the venom-filled voice comes from everywhere and nowhere at once. "Careful, or I may arrange for you to join the girl in her eternal slumber."

Leaping to my feet, I nock another arrow and step from beneath the apple tree. "Wow. Scary surroundings. Mysterious voice from the sky. Barely veiled threats." I cock my head to one side. "Never experienced this before."

A low chuckle fills the air. "You believe your storied experiences have prepared you for this, Ivanovna, but you have never faced dangers like those that grow in my garden."

"Ivanovna?" I raise an eyebrow and inject a healthy bit of sarcasm into my voice as I smooth the silky green fabric of my tunic and try not to wince at the pain in my side. "Am I no longer Scheherazade?"

A single laugh this time, amused, yet impatient. "You may be unmatched in certain realms, storyteller, but mere tales and invocations will not save you here."

"I know where I am." Fighting to keep myself from shivering, I raise the bow to the sky. "And I am not afraid." I pull in a deep breath. "Now, show yourself."

"As you wish, Ivanovna."

The remainder of the garden, till now shrouded in shadow and mist, paints itself into existence around me. At its center, the bent tree filled with golden apples arches across the flat hunk of granite, shading Hannah Abrams from the cresting sun. Everything radiates with the ambience of a place once beautiful that has fallen into ruin.

The murky pool that held the toad-thing, currently spoiled and dilapidated, was clearly in the past a thing of elegance. A statue of a cherub at one end likely once served as a fountain and the intricate stonework fashioned of dark granite and white marble still retains some of its previous glory. The statue, however, stands headless, and only half the stonework remains intact.

The grass at my feet, no doubt lush and full when this garden was created, has been trampled by years of traffic, the work of the toad-thing and whatever other creatures hide among the shadows of this blighted place.

All trees but the curved apple stand leafless and bare as though winter has come, though the air suffocates me with the muggy heat of a Charlotte summer. As if in answer to an unspoken wish, a blast of frigid air hits me from behind, though I find the sudden cool anything but refreshing.

I know it's there before I even begin to turn. The cold stone and drafty halls twist my marrow as sheer malevolence assaults my senses. I spin around, arrow nocked and bow raised.

Before me looms the palace of the Immortal, more enormous than I could have imagined. Its facade a grinning skull with stone stairs the color of midnight issuing from its mouth, the structure reminds me of a cartoon I watched as a child. Mixed with elements of various other fortresses, castles, and palaces from popular culture, the edifice is no doubt an amalgamation of every movie, show, and comic book a certain fourteen-year-old boy has ever seen.

Oh, Anthony. Yours has truly been a misspent youth.

A subtle glow emanates from the empty sockets, a sickly yellow, as if the stony skull stares at me through jaundiced eyes. The spires of the twin towers framing the palace disappear into the mists above. The stairs leading up to the main gate ooze with slime that shifts, bubbles, and heaves as if it were alive.

"Very impressive, Immortal, but I asked to see you, not your hovel."

Another fit of laughter chills me to my bones. "Very well. I merely thought you would appreciate a taste of what lies before you, brave Ivanovna, should you pursue this quest."

The pale phosphorescence fades from the skull's eyes, only to reappear at the mouth of the palace. Swirling faster and faster, the color shifts briefly through a putrid green and a deep blue before settling on a dusky plum.

"Welcome, fair Ivanovna, to the Enchanted Garden of Koschei the Deathless." Ancient and scarred, Koschei steps out of the light and onto the top step of his morbid home. In one long-fingered hand, he holds a black staff that terminates on an orb of obsidian glass. His other hand strokes a scraggly beard the color of dishwater. His ornate robes and voluminous cape alternate between black and deep purple and are decorated with silver accents that in the shadow of his palace make him appear skeletal. Cold blue eyes stare out at me from sockets that have looked upon centuries of pain and misfortune, while his lips are turned up in a knowing smirk. "Now, what is it you would like to talk about?"

"Anthony?" I ask. "Is that… you?"

Koschei's smug grin blossoms into a full-blown smile. "No Anthony here, my dear."

"Bullshit." I wave my arm in a wide arc. "This *is* Anthony. The music. The landscape. Me. You. All of this."

"This is my garden, lovely Ivanovna, and you are trespassing here."

"What about the girl?" I gesture in Hannah's direction. "Why is she here?"

"You expect me to reveal all within seconds of our first meeting? How quaint." Koschei vanishes from the mouth of his dark palace only to reappear standing over Hannah beneath the tree of apples. "Suffice to say I need her, as I will soon need the remaining twelve."

A pang I don't fully understand rips through my midsection. "Twelve?"

"Princesses. Thirteen in all." He kneels by Hannah's side and strokes her cheek, his fingers long, black, and gaunt, like the legs of a spider. "I see from your eyes you understand of what I speak. Who have you been speaking with, fair Ivanovna?"

I try to banish any expression from my face, but Koschei's right, and he knows it. All of this is exactly as Anthony told me.

A magical garden filled with monsters. The Firebird. Koschei the Immortal. Prince Ivan and his thirteen princesses.

Wait.

Koschei called me Ivanovna.

I suppose that means I've been cast as the Prince in this piece.

Fantastic.

"This girl is no princess." I take a step in Koschei's direction. "Hannah Abrams is an innocent little girl. Lives in the suburbs. Rides a pink bike. What could you possibly want with her?"

"Innocent." A serpent couldn't hiss more saying the word. "Splendid."

I take another step. "Answer me. Why have you brought her here?"

"Come no closer, Ivanovna." Koschei brings one of his dagger-like nails to Hannah's throat. "Though both of us would prefer this child to continue breathing, there are plenty more where she came from." He casts his opposite hand to the sky, his gleaming grin making a return appearance. "An entire city from which to choose, in fact."

"Leave her alone," I shout. "She's done nothing to deserve this."

"Was she not born into sin just like every other child?" he spits. "Do not speak to me of innocence. I know your thoughts, Ivanovna. Where you think you are. Who you suspect me to be. Is this Anthony you carry so close to your heart not an innocent as well?"

"Is that what this is all about?" I look up to the threatening sky. "Are you trying to get my attention, Anthony? Because, trust me. You've got it."

"Scream all you want, Ivanovna." Koschei scoops Hannah up into his bony arms and heads back for his palace's gaping maw. "The boy cannot hear you here."

Raising the bow, I rush at the Immortal only to pull up short as a dozen toad-things leap from the brush and form a line to Koschei's rear. My heart pounds as twelve sets of yellow slits converge on me, each creature's gaze hungrier than the next.

"My apologies." He glances across his shoulder at me. "Were you under the impression your wishes hold any sway in this place?" He steps beneath the incisors of the palace's mouth and turns to face me, Hannah Abrams hanging limp in his arms like a rag doll. "Farewell, Ivanovna. May you enjoy the company of the *bukavacs*." The smile disappears from his face. "At least for the last few moments of your life."

As Koschei retreats into the darkness of his palace, the *bukavacs* form a semicircle around me and force me back toward the pool from where their brother attacked me. My bow drawn, I work to keep all twelve in my field of vision, though they and I both know I'm quickly running out of room. Keeping their line, the horned toad-monsters draw closer and closer, their slow shuffle more unnerving than the previous one's charge. No idea how smart these things are, but at some level, they must collectively know the first to leap will be the first to taste an arrow.

My right heel impacts the pool's raised rock edge. Game over. The *bukavacs* surround me on three sides with the pool to my rear, and for all I know, there are more of them in the water. First one, then another, tests my resolution with a cautious step forward. All along the line, the creatures take turns letting out terrifying bellows that leave my knees weak. Our impasse lasts almost a minute until, as my attention is focused on one end of their line, I catch movement in my peripheral vision.

I spin to find one of the horned toad-things from my opposite flank flying at me. Before I can complete another thought, the arrow leaves my bow and flies into its head. A second leaps at me, and I dispatch it with another arrow drawn and fired with skill I've only seen in movies. A third meets a similar fate before my luck finally runs out. I'm spinning to fire at my fourth attacker when it hits me full in the chest and knocks me across the stone lip of the pool and into the murky water. Pounded by the thing's six webbed feet, I lose my breath, gagging as the silty, lukewarm liquid passes my throat and fills my lungs.

No. It can't end this way. Not now.

Faces flash across my mind's eye.

Hannah Abrams.

Anthony.

Thomas.

Isabella.

"No!" My eyes fly open to find the blurred outline of Detective Sterling looking down on me. Back beneath a Carolina blue sky, I tremble despite the full sun beating down on me. I bring a weak hand to my chest and come to a startling realization. I'm back in the real world, but I'm still wet. I run a forearm across my eyes to wipe away the muddy water and attempt to sit up.

Not happening.

Boy, am I out of shape. At least for this kind of action.

"Sterling?"

He leans over me, blocking out the sun. "Mira. Are you all right?"

"I think so." My voice reminiscent of one of the toad-things that just tried to kill me, I clear my throat. "Why am I all wet?'

Sterling brings a pail into my line of sight. "By the time we got up here, both you and Hannah were unconscious. I tried to wake you, but nothing worked."

Mr. Abrams leans over me. "I spotted a bucket by the edge of the pond. Filled it with water and got back up here as fast as I could." His eyes shift to one side. "Sorry about your clothes."

"No apologies needed, Mr. Abrams." On my second try, I manage to sit up. "I think you just saved my bacon big time."

"Saved you?"

I don't bother to answer Abrams' question, turning my attention instead to the little girl that lies in the fetal position at my side, her nightgown soaked with the same pond water that just shocked me awake. "Hannah?"

"She's still unconscious."

Sterling pulls me to my feet even as Mr. Abrams drops to his knees and pulls his daughter into a one-sided embrace. Unsteady, I grasp Sterling's shoulder. As strong as I remember it.

"I don't think we're going to be able to wake her," I whisper, "but we need to get her down from here quick. She's exposed. Sunburned. And who knows what else?"

"What next, then?" Sterling asks.

"We get her to a hospital."

"And what about you?"

"I'm fine." I suppress a cough as the sensation of silty water flowing into my lungs echoes through my nervous system. "But I need to talk to Thomas right away."

"Archer?" Sterling asks. "What does he have to do with this?"

His patient.

Hannah Abrams used to be his patient.

Just like Anthony.

The girl's entire body begins to shake uncontrollably, and I don't believe for a second it's just the chill from the water.

4

THE SHROVE-TIDE FAIR

"It has to be Anthony." I cross my arms and recline on the couch, the scene just like every cartoon of a psychologist's office ever drawn. "There's no other explanation."

In the corner of my vision, Thomas leans back in his big leather swivel chair. "You're sure?"

"My fingers brush an unconscious girl's skin for like half a second and the next thing I know, I'm sucked into a magical land where monsters and demons do their level best to kill me while a soundtrack of classical music plays in the background." I massage the bridge of my nose where it feels like someone is hammering an ice pick between my eyebrows. "If you have a better explanation, I'm dying to hear it."

"I just spoke with Caroline on the phone. She said Anthony has been sitting in the living room for the last two hours watching a movie with Rachel." He rolls his chair over to the couch and takes my hand. "No falling into a coma. No humming. Nothing out of the ordinary. Anthony is fine."

"It's not exactly Anthony I'm worried about at the moment." At Thomas' stern gaze, I add, "Come on. You know what I mean."

"I'm worried about Hannah too." Thomas squeezes my fingers gently. "She used to be a client, remember."

"Unresponsive. In the hospital, undergoing every test under the sun.

Seriously creepy dude running around between her ears." I pull myself up to a seated position. "Sound familiar?"

"I have to admit, the similarities are uncanny." Thomas shakes his head subtly. "Still, if it's Anthony, don't you think he'd know?"

A centipede with stickpins for legs begins a slow march up my spine. "Honestly, that's what worries me most."

"You can't be suggesting he'd do something like this on purpose." Thomas peers at me from beneath a furrowed brow. "If this is, in fact, Anthony in the first place."

"Good God, Thomas. Get your head out of the sand." Heat rushes into my cheeks. "Last time, the kid reached out and grabbed my brain from clear across town at least twice. It's him."

"Fine, Mira." Thomas pulls his hand away and rests it in his lap. "I'll concede the whole thing stinks of last fall." He crosses his arms before his chest as his expression shifts into clinical mode. "Now what do you suggest we do about it?"

～

"You can't be serious." The fury in Caroline Faircloth's face makes it easy to understand her role as Baba Yaga in Anthony's Exhibition. "You're insinuating my son is responsible for what happened to this Hannah Abrams girl who's all over the news?"

I raise my hands, palms out, and take a step back. "You saw what the Exhibition did to me. To Rachel." My hands ball into fists. "To Veronica Sayles."

"In case you're forgetting, Anthony was the victim of what happened last fall." The color continues to rise in Caroline's cheeks. "Not to mention, I seem to remember you telling me he was better. That the whole thing was over."

"That's what I believed, right up until last night. But in the last twenty-four hours, I've had dreams of the Exhibition, heard the voice of Baba Yaga, fought monsters in another realm, and argued with a god who lives in a skull, all of it set to the music you're telling me your son has been listening to non-stop for weeks."

Caroline's eyes shoot past me. "Thomas? You know my son as well as anyone. What do you think?" Her eyes narrow. "Is Mira right?"

Thomas clears his throat. "I hate to say it, Caroline, but I'm having trouble imagining a scenario where Anthony isn't somehow involved."

"Involved in what?" Anthony wanders into the room, nibbling on a grilled cheese sandwich as his concerned gaze passes from one of us to the next. "What's going on?"

"Anthony." Caroline's words come out sharper than I suspect she intends. "I thought I asked you to stay in the kitchen."

"I'm not stupid." Anthony washes down the bite of sandwich with a slug of milk. "I know you're all out here talking about me." He retreats beneath his mother's wing as his gaze shoots to me. "It's about *The Firebird*, isn't it?"

"Caroline?" I raise a questioning eyebrow in her direction.

Deflated, she lets out a rough sigh. "Go ahead."

I venture over to the couch and pat the cushion by my hip. "Anthony, come over here and sit with me."

"Mom?" Anthony looks up into Caroline's eyes, tears forming at the corners of his own. "Am I in trouble?"

"I hope not, Anthony." She smooths his unkempt hair. "Now, go sit with Mira and see what she has to say."

Sheepish, Anthony trudges over and plops down next to me on the same couch where he and I explored his labyrinthine imagination just nine months ago.

Unless I miss my guess, I'm due for one hell of a return trip.

"Anthony." I rest a hand on his knee and try not to take offense when he jumps. "There's a little girl. Her name is Hannah. She's in a bad way." When the boy doesn't say a word, I add, "Like you were last year."

Anthony's gaze shifts to his mother and then to Thomas, who subtly nods.

"Can you help her?" he asks eventually. "Like you did with me?"

The kid is breaking my heart. "I'm not sure, Anthony."

He bites his lip. "Why not?"

"Remember when Dr. Archer, your mother, and I told you about everything that happened last fall?"

Anthony nods.

"And how nothing like that had ever happened to me before?"

He nods again, brushing away the tears with a pillow he's pulled into his lap. "I remember."

"Well." I squeeze his knee. "It's happening again."

"What's happening again?" Rachel wanders into the room, a purple My Little Pony with a rainbow tail tucked under her arm. "What's wrong, Anthony?"

"Come on, honey." Caroline pulls Rachel tight to her and escorts her toward the kitchen. "Let's get you a cookie."

"But—" Rachel gets out before the two of them disappear from view.

Thomas catches my eye, and at my quick nod, joins Anthony and me on the couch. "Hey, champ. I know it's scary, but listen to Mira. I think she might—"

"Where is she?" Anthony's eyes flick back and forth from me to Thomas. "This Hannah girl you were talking about. Did they have to put her in the hospital?"

I take the boy's hand and squeeze his trembling fingers. "They don't know what's wrong with her. For now, it's best."

"And what's happening to her is what happened to me?" His entire body shudders. "Has she become… like me?"

"Not exactly." I take a breath. "I touched her temple and was transported to a mysterious garden filled with monsters, a majestic orange bird, and an evil sorcerer calling himself Koschei the Deathless." I meet Anthony's gaze. "Sound familiar?"

His face goes pale. "*The Firebird.*"

"I hate to ask, Anthony, but think about it." I look him dead in the eye. "A girl falls into a deep sleep not all that different from what happened to you last fall. She's got creatures and demons and magical birds swirling around in her head and Stravinsky booming down from the sky. That's quite a bit of coincidence, don't you think?" I let go of his hand and turn to face him. "Lately, has anything strange been happening with you? Anything… different?"

"It's not me." He buries his head in the pillow. "I didn't do it. I promise."

"Enough." Caroline has stepped back into the room, her face twisted into an expression I haven't seen in months. "Mira, a word?"

"Of course." I stroke Anthony's cheek. "Sorry, kiddo. I just needed to…"

The trill of a flute fills my senses.

A high-pitched melody, the tune unknown to me, yet strangely familiar.

String arpeggios alternate with woodwinds, then brass.

"Thomas, can you hear it?"

His eyes grow wide. "Hear what?"

"The music." The melody builds and builds until a fanfare blares, deafening in its power. "Thomas?"

No sooner does the word leave my lips than everything goes gray.

A blink, and for the second time that day, I am somewhere else. Neither maelstrom of light nor eternity of darkness surrounds me this time, but a collection of brightly colored balloons. A cloaked man carries the balloons away and a vibrant fair opens up before me, the various stalls and games inscribed with Cyrillic letters. Merchants and stalls and games and people materialize around me three and four at a time, like pieces being set on a game board by some giant, invisible child. I stand at the center of the carnival, the crossed thoroughfares packed with peasants and noblemen, revelers and children, musicians and dancers. In the distance, a grand cathedral stands, its base obscured by a low fog.

And all the while, the music swells, mysterious interspersed with triumphant.

In period attire reminiscent of Russian clothing from two centuries past, the mob circulates the fair with choreographed precision, their individual stories playing out under the watchful eye of a constable dressed in a long brown cloak and a silver helmet and badge and carrying an eight-foot pike. To my right, a simple carousel turns, the boys and girls on the wooden pigs, goats, and unicorns all squealing with delight with each rotation. To my left, a huckster spins a wheel of fortune to the amazement of the passing rubes.

Before me, a two-story theater stands, the second-floor balcony occupied by two Gypsy fortunetellers and an old man I take to be the Master of Ceremonies. Like a rail-thin Santa Claus with a knee-length beard and a long robe of midnight blue, he plucks the strings of a golden lute in time with the ambient music. Yellow lace plays at his wrists like wisps of flame and a shimmering orange feather adorns his gray fur cap. Catching my stare, the barker shoots me a wink and a smile before returning his attention to his Gypsy companions.

"Anthony?" I take a step toward the theater and nearly get bowled over by the sweeping kicks of a quartet of drunkards dancing arm in arm. My second attempt is blocked as well as a row of dancing women all decked out in full-length pink gowns and bonnets run by in a line, their hands across their hearts as if they have each felt the sting of spurned love.

Oh, Anthony. What fresh hell have you created this time?

Melting into the crowd, I glance down to see who or what I have become in this place. For once, I'm not clothed in green. Neither sarong nor tunic covers my form, but a simple dress with long white sleeves, a pink skirt with purple stripes, and a red vest with dark trim. I pull the skirt close to my legs and find pointe shoes on my feet.

Unbidden, images of *The Ballet of Unhatched Chicks*, my forced performance from Anthony's Exhibition, flit across my memory. No more than a puppet, while on that stage I was unable to so much as breathe unless told to do so, captive to a witch's whim.

I don't like where this is headed.

Not one bit.

A young girl in a rainbow dress runs to the center of the square followed by a boy carrying a brightly painted organ grinder. Cavorting about the space, she plays the triangle in perfect time with the music. No sooner has a crowd gathered around her than she gains some competition.

From the opposite direction, a second girl joins the fray, this one also accompanied by a boy carrying an intricately carved music box. Hiking up her plain orange skirt, this new girl throws herself into a dance. Though their styles couldn't be more different, the first girl's classical and poised and the second's more provocative and contortionist, the two performances are each compelling in their own right, and soon, the onlookers' attention is split.

Their dances grow increasingly intricate by the measure, the skills portrayed more and more impressive with every step. As the music hits its climax, the two dancers spin in concert, their simultaneous pirouettes going faster and faster into what seems like infinity, and only the crude advances of the quartet of revelers from before brings the mystifying spectacle to an end.

No sooner has the constable dispatched the four than the music shifts to a martial beat.

Out of nowhere, a pair of soldiers in blue uniforms marches past me on either side, beating on snare drums. Arriving at either side of a structure I hadn't noticed before, they each perform a crisp about-face and divide the crowd so all gathered can see the enormous wooden box with a thick blue curtain hanging across its face. Above the curtain, three half-circles decorate the arch of what I'm guessing is some sort of stage. The first is decorated with an image of a merman dragging a young girl into the sea; the second, a demon's face with eyes that glow red like hot coals; and the third, a beautiful bird, its plumage orange and gold, its long dark beak like a blade.

The Firebird.

Before I can begin to process what the Firebird's appearance in this place might mean, a face pops out from between the curtains to a gut-wrenching orchestral hit.

A very familiar face.

Mussorgsky, the composer from Anthony's Exhibition, his black hair and beard now as white as freshly fallen snow, stares out from beneath a tall wizard's hat. Mysterious woodwind tones fill the air as the bizarre little man peers first at one side of the gathered horde and then the other.

My heart fills with dread.

If the composer is here, can the others be far behind? Can the Exhibition?

Stepping from behind the curtains, Mussorgsky has traded in his trademark dark suit for a bright blue magician's cape embroidered all along its length with silver stars and crescent moons. Beneath his cape, a floor-length robe spun from gold thread and covered in various runes and sigils glistens in the midsummer's light of this place. Holding up first one arm and then the other with the flourishes of a trained illusionist, this Mussorgsky magician grins mysteriously at the crowd. Gone is the kindness in the composer's gaze, replaced by the conniving eyes of a master showman.

His spindly fingers disappear into his cape and reappear with a golden flute. The magician shifts his eyes left and right and brings the shining instrument to his lips. Faltering on the first few notes, he taps the flute against his palm and begins anew. This time, a beautiful melody pours from the instrument and within seconds the entire host is swaying in time with the magician's tune.

A lone girl in a dress the color of a pale buttercup and a coat fashioned of gold cloth steps away from her family, her eyes blank. Ensorcelled by the flute's haunting tones, she walks in a daze toward the center of the square. I circle behind the crowd in an attempt to get a better look at her as something about the girl's hair triggers a flicker of memory. Seconds later, the magician takes a breath, and the momentary break in the music allows the girl to look away. Terror fills her eyes as she locks gazes with me.

My suspicion is confirmed.

The girl is Hannah Abrams.

The magician resumes his hypnotic tune, bringing the enchanted girl nearly to the center of the square before finally releasing her. As her father, a bearded version of the Mr. Abrams I met hours before, comes to lead her back, the magician takes a not-quite-humble bow and begins to search the crowd for another victim.

From the heart of the mob, the constable I saw before steps out and heads straight for the magician. The wizard catches him out of the corner of his eye, and before the brown-cloaked officer can so much as say a word, the white-bearded Mussorgsky sorcerer slips a bribe into his coat pocket. As the constable smiles, I suddenly recognize the gaunt, pock-marked face beneath the fur cap.

It's Mitch Bolger, Sterling's partner.

Or in this place, I suppose, Schmuÿle.

"Anthony. Stop this." Diving past the constable's pike, I rush at the magician. "Stop this now."

The magician shifts his eyes in my direction and without so much as a word, points the flute at me as if it were a magic wand. In a swirl of silver mist, everything goes away. After being booted from Anthony's mind by Baba Yaga so many times I can't remember, I fully expect to wake up a moment later, back in my own body with Thomas and Caroline looking down on me.

Instead, I find myself hanging limp by my armpits surrounded by muted darkness. My legs dangle beneath me, useless hunks of meat, and my arms and hands won't so much as twitch at my command. Even my eyes refuse to move.

Helpless, I stare straight ahead at a thick curtain that barely muffles the music and roar of the crowd of which I was a part moments before.

A thick *blue* curtain.

I have no doubt as to where I am. My only question is what happens next.

God help me.

5
———

THE CHARLATAN'S BOOTH

The curtains draw back, revealing my limp form to the laughing mob. Somehow, the magician's flute has transported me inside his mysterious cabinet. In this realm of dream, however, questions of how aren't nearly as important as questions of why.

My head lolls to one side like a chicken's whose neck has been wrung. Try as I might to raise my chin from my chest, I can't move a muscle, a marionette with no strings. Two blurred shapes flank me inside the box, the barest hints of green and blue to my right and white and orange to my left confirming I am not alone.

The crowd that moments earlier seemed unable to see me now stares and points as if they stand before the main event at some carnival sideshow. Half a dozen children, their faces turned up with expectant grins, await something intently, while the adults surrounding them share knowing glances as if each understands fully what comes next.

Just within my field of vision, I catch a glimpse of the magician's blue and silver cape. A distant piccolo whistles as he waves his golden flute, and in answer, the green and blue form to my right springs to life. The magician comes to me next, again waving his flute as another two-tone whistle sounds. Strength flows into my extremities and my entire body assumes a dancer's position *en pointe*. The magician steps past me and waves his flute a third time, the orange and white form to my left obediently snapping to attention as the third piccolo whistle hits my ears.

40

Before I can take a breath, a quick-paced melody of brass and woodwind fills the air and my feet begin to move. My legs kick and step in perfect time with each jubilant note as if I've become a life-sized wind-up doll. My peripheral vision reveals the other two forms similarly keeping time with the happy tune. Terrified as I am, I can't seem to banish my exuberant grin as I perform for this bizarre fair that only exists between the ears of a fourteen-year-old boy.

The music grows increasingly frenetic with every measure, as if building up to something. Terror fills my heart even as my legs scissor-kick beneath me again and again. Then, as if on silent cue, my feet touch the wooden floor, and I, along with my two mysterious counterparts, rush from the booth. To both the delight and terror of the surrounding mob, we continue our dance, each of us under the sway of the magician and his golden flute-wand. As I spin through what seems an endless set of pirouettes, I finally get a look at my bizarre companions.

On my right, in a costume straight out of *Arabian Nights*, dances a man in blackface, his naturally dark skin accentuated with broad white circles around the eyes and exaggerated red lips. Atop his head rests an elaborate turban fashioned of blue and gold silk and decorated with pearls and a fluffy blue feather. Rich royal robes of shimmering blue and green drape his torso while gold pantaloons tucked into silver boots cover his legs. His every movement confident and sure, an image of a male lion flits across my consciousness even as an unmistakable attraction to the power on display burns at my core.

The figure to my left, on the other hand, fills me with nothing but revulsion. A clown in a white silk top, orange-and-red-checkered pants, and blue leather boots, his dancing style reminds me of the Scarecrow from The Wizard of Oz. His every movement clumsy and disjointed, the funny little man appears small and insignificant compared to the Arabian. His hands covered in orange mittens, the clown keeps his head turned down and away from me as he limply dances along. Or so it seems. He takes every opportunity to glance up at me when he thinks I'm not looking, only to again hide his face every time I peer back. An eternity seems to pass before my gaze and his intersect. My heart freezes as I finally peer into the clown's steely blue eyes.

A particularly familiar set of steely blue eyes.

Beneath the floppy orange hat and the half-smile, half-frown makeup lies the face of Thomas Archer.

And yet, not Thomas.

Gone are the confidence, sensitivity, and understanding I've almost come to take for granted there, and in their place, all I find is the pitiable stare of spurned love. How the gaze of the man I'm moving four hundred miles to be with can fill me with such disgust is mystery, and yet, it's there as plain as the unmitigated lust I felt for the Arabian.

As the magician directs our strange dance with his golden flute-wand, the musical accompaniment solidifies my initial impressions of the bizarre trio into which I've been conscripted. When the Arabian dances, it's all smooth, rich woodwinds, while my various spins and pirouettes are accompanied by the precision and power of a team of violins. Most telling, however, is the ridiculous piano that rings out in time with each of the clown's clumsy steps.

Oh, Anthony. Is this really how you see the man that has worked with you for years?

Wait. If the clown is Thomas…

I fight against the forced contortions in an effort to get a look at the man beneath the turban. His every step sure, his every turn powerful, the Arabian finally turns in my direction as I complete a long sequence of spins.

How did I not see it before? Beneath the ridiculous blackface reside the piercing gaze and strong jawline of Detective Calvin Sterling.

In that moment, the music shifts to something that sounds like a high-pitched xylophone, and the three of us twirl in tandem, the footwork beyond anything I could replicate outside of Anthony's world of dream. Then, as the music dips to a somber solo clarinet, my feet turn *en pointe*, and a flaccid pair of hands encircles my left arm. I glance down to find the clown hanging off my wrist like a lovesick puppy. My revulsion doubles. No sooner does he look up into my face than the magician rushes over and pulls us apart. I lose sight of the clown, but a part of me doesn't care a whit as a compulsion to join the Arabian overwhelms my every thought.

There the two of us stand: the Arabian, the confident master of all he surveys, and me, the demure ballerina—that is, until the clown attacks us from behind with some sort of cudgel. The Arabian and I dance away in lockstep to escape having our heads bashed in. Strangely, the clown holds the club between his arms rather than in his grip, almost as if he were a hand puppet rather than this place's version of the man I love.

He strikes the Arabian once, twice, three times, losing his cudgel on the fourth attack. Disarmed, he runs from the Arabian who chases him through the crowd. Just as he's about to escape, the clown trips over the foot of one of the children at the edge of the mob and falls flat on his face. The Arabian, in turn, trips over the clown and is sent sprawling. As they rise from the ground, I muster the will to leap between them and keep them from fighting, only to have the magician choose that moment to reassert full control. And just like that, the three of us dance hand in hand as if nothing untoward has occurred, our legs kicking in synchrony like the three strangest Rockettes in history, even as my vision goes red at the indignity.

What is going on in Anthony's mind? He's set up Thomas, one of his most trusted friends, as the fool of the piece and has cast Sterling, a man he's never met, as the alpha male?

And that's the thing.

As before with this dreamscape world of his, Anthony has never met Sterling. Or Bolger, for that matter.

Of all the pictures that made up the Exhibition last year, the home of Samuel Goldenberg and Schmuÿle, aka Sterling and Bolger, was the one place that was as much me as it was Anthony. If that's the case, what does this scene say about me? About my choices in this insane dance? About my clear preference for the Arabian?

I was, after all, cast as Scheherazade for a reason.

As if in response, the music of the movement comes to its last note, a long peal of brass, and the three of us all fall to the floor. The Arabian assumes a graceful lotus position, I a long ballet stretch, while the clown merely crumples like a rag doll cast aside by a petulant child.

His pointed shoe just visible from the corner of my vision, the master of puppets laughs as the carnival-goers pay him for the entertaining performance.

And then? Back into the cabinet we go like toys to their box at the end of the day.

"I think she's coming around." The first voice I've heard besides my own in what seems like a millennium. "Mira? Can you hear me?"

"Thomas?" My eyes blink open and my distorted vision perceives Thomas' mouth as the half-smile, half-frown of the clown from the fair. "What happened?" Much like the first time I entered Anthony's mind, my voice resembles a toad's with one of its vocal cords ripped out. "Is Anthony—"

"He's fine." Thomas stares down at me, concern etched in his features. "Are you?"

"I've been better." The pleasant smell of baked bread mixes with the pungent aroma of rotting eggs as Thomas' concern and fear war in the recesses of his mind. It's all I can do not to gag. "Help me sit up?"

"That's twice in one morning," Thomas notes as he pulls me up off the floor and sets me on the couch. "Can your brain take that kind of punishment?"

"We'll see." Caroline's wary gaze slams into me, a barely conscious Anthony held in her arms. "Caroline? Is he—"

"It was just like before." A bitterness encroaches on Caroline's tone, a bitterness I haven't heard in months. "He couldn't speak. Couldn't see."

"Caroline, I'm sorry, but..."

She pulls Anthony into her chest. "I can't go through this again."

"But—"

"I know how walking in Anthony's mind leaves you, Mira. I'll give you a few minutes, but when you feel well enough, I think you'd better go."

Thomas steps in. "Now, Caroline. Mira is just trying to—"

"I know what she's trying to do. I get it. But I almost lost my son last year, and everything has been fine since. I'm not putting him through that again."

"But everything isn't fine." I bite my lip, doing my best to tread carefully. "First *The Firebird* erupted out of that little girl's head, and now, Anthony's mind is home to a bearded street magician and his big box of freaky dancing puppets."

Caroline's face blanches at that last word. "Enough." She grabs Anthony's hand. "I'm going to go put my son to bed. You two can show yourselves out."

"Hey." Rachel appears from the hall. "Why is everyone shouting?"

"Back to your room, Rachel." Caroline barrels straight for her daughter. "Now."

As the Faircloth family disappears into the dim hallway, Thomas shakes his head. "Looks like you two are back to square one."

I rest my forehead in my palms. "What else could I say? Last year, Anthony's Exhibition almost killed me half a dozen times, and now, here we are again." I stretch my back and try to massage the mother of all cricks out of my neck. "And that's on top of everything that happened earlier with Hannah Abrams..."

"This street magician." Thomas sits beside me and pulls me close. "Who—"

"It was Mussorgsky, the composer from the Exhibition, though older. Grayer. And evil."

Thomas' eyebrows knit together. "But Mussorgsky was a representation of Anthony's father, not to mention one of your staunchest allies among the various characters pulled from Anthony's psyche. Why would he suddenly be cast as the villain?"

I squeeze Thomas' knee. "If we knew that, we'd be well on our way to figuring this whole thing out. All I can tell you is I was powerless against his spell." I swallow. "He made me… dance."

"And the puppets you were talking about." A calming half-smile flits across his face. "Anybody we know?"

My heart freezes in my chest. "They were just puppets." A fresh headache flares as the lie leaves my lips. "An Arabian in blackface and a sad sack clown." My voice goes quiet at that last word, as if I'm ashamed to say it aloud with the clown's doppelgänger sitting opposite me, looking on with nothing but love and concern in his eyes.

Visions of Anthony's dreamworld flow through me anew, and I shiver as an emotion I've never felt before for this man I'm about to move hundreds of miles to be close to hits me square in the chest.

Disgust.

"I don't feel well." I look away, unable to gaze into those crystal blue eyes for another second. My stomach turns as my love for Thomas and the unmistakable revulsion coursing through my veins at his very presence vie for supremacy. "Can you get me some water?"

"Of course." Thomas stands, looking down on me confused and maybe a little hurt. A psychologist's intuition can be a two-edged sword. "Be right back."

He walks away, a slight gimp in his gait. No doubt his foot has simply gone to sleep from sitting cross-legged on the floor with me, but with each step, I imagine his legs clothed in red-and-orange-checkered pants. The disquieting contempt at my core goes white hot.

Why settle for the fool when you can have the sultan?

Scheherazade's voice, as if from directly behind me.

I jerk my head around. Not surprisingly, I find I'm still all alone.

Not to mention, one simple fact.

I am Scheherazade.

Not to mention, Ivanovna, the Ballerina, and, somewhere in there, Mira Tejedor.

Lost in my thoughts, I almost scream when the glass of cool water appears in my hand.

"Drink up." Doing his best to cover up the hurt, Thomas' caring smile sits at odds with the smell of old cheese filling my senses. "If you're going to run a marathon, you'd best stay hydrated."

"Thanks." I bring the glass to my lips, resisting the urge to retch as I allow the icy liquid to coat my throat. I down the water in four huge gulps and rest the glass on the carpet. "Just what I needed." My voice a shade closer to its normal tone, I ask a simple question. "So, what next?"

Thomas shakes his head. "You know Caroline. She's been through a lot, but I suspect she'll calm down once the initial shock wears off." He sits by me and rests a hand on my knee. "It's got to be hard, seeing your son go through something like this twice."

"What about the Abrams family? They were supposed to be headed to Orlando this weekend, not the hospital."

"I know, I know." Thomas' grimace brings back images of the clown, and a wave of nausea hits me like a tsunami. "Hard to know what to do."

"One thing for certain." I force myself to lock gazes with Thomas. "Regardless of Caroline's objections, Anthony is once again at the center of things." I glance in the direction of the darkened hallway, and images of the Exhibition dance before my mind's eye. "I'm not sure how or why, but this is only beginning."

6

DANCE OF THE FIREBIRD

My sore muscles unknot in the scalding water of Thomas' garden tub. Whirlpool jets hammer at my back as the lavender scent and bubbles tickle my nose. My body as exhausted as it's been in months, the back-to-back forced excursions into the world of dream have left my every muscle aching and tense. Though a good night's sleep is exactly what the doctor ordered, I fight with every fiber of my being to stay awake. Part of it is simple self-preservation. I don't want to drown a week before my daughter and I change our address and get the fresh start we've both needed for over a year. More than that, though, I dread what I might see if I allow myself to dream.

I fear my little trip through the Russian fair was nothing but a taste of what's to come.

"Thomas?" Wow. That's not good. Just saying his name makes my toes curl. "Can you come here a minute?"

A few seconds pass before the man I profess to love pokes his head into the bathroom. "Hey. Everything okay?"

"Nothing a little wine and bubble bath can't clear away." I tap the wine glass sitting on the tiled edge of the tub. "Pour me another?"

Thomas holds up the bottle and peers through the bottom as he swirls the dregs. "Only about half a glass left. You sure?"

A not so subtle way of asking if I intend to drink an entire bottle of wine by myself tonight. The clever psychologist's tone may work on most people, but I went to school just like he did. I know the tricks. I've seen the man behind the curtain.

Or in this case, unfortunately, the clown.

"Just hand me the bottle then."

"No, I've got it." Thomas takes the glass and pours me the last remnants of the Malbec. "Might as well finish it off." He sets the wine glass back at the edge of the tub. "Don't stay in there too long. Prune isn't your look."

I allow myself a lone chuckle. "One big bowl of Mira soup coming up." I pull a hand up through the suds and study my wrinkled digits before grabbing the glass and downing its contents. "Another dash of vino for taste."

Thomas peeks out into the hall in the direction of the bedroom. "At least you'll rest well."

The thought of sharing a bed with Thomas tonight sends a shiver through me despite the heat of the water.

And not the good kind of shiver.

"Why don't you go on to bed? I've got a little stuff to do on the computer and don't want to keep you up." I bite my lip. "I can just crash in the guest bedroom so you can sleep."

"Umm… sure?" The hint of kicked puppy dog returns to Thomas' face. I'd likely not have picked up on it, but the unmistakable aroma of Limburger returns in spades. "Everything okay?"

"The bath is wonderful, but I'm still pretty sore all over, not to mention I've got a lot on my mind." I shoot him my best smile. "I don't want to keep you up."

And the lies keep coming.

"Well… okay." Thomas steps into the hallway and disappears. "I'll go turn down the bed."

Ugh. Twist the knife. Normally such a kind gesture would win Thomas big points, but in the moment, it just makes him seem pathetic.

Like he's trying too hard on a first date.

But this isn't our first date. And he's acting the same as he does every night.

Thoughtful. Courteous. Kind. All the things I love about the man.

"Then what the hell is wrong with me?" I mutter as I dip my head below the water.

Water that is suddenly ice cold.

I pop back above the surface, but where before there were bubbles and bath salts, now there is only muck and mud. I inhale to cry out for Thomas, only to realize he'd never hear me. Gone is the palatial bathroom, replaced by Koschei's garden in all its dilapidated grandeur. A glance up reveals the decapitated cherub statue directly above my head, confirming my suspicion.

I'm in the pool from Koschei's garden, where the *bukavacs* rest. Divorcing myself from the panic that threatens to overtake me, I hold my breath, try not to move a muscle, and pray I'm alone.

Reaching from the murky water, I rest a hand on the slick granite and marble at the edge of the pool. When nothing leaps from the muck to attack me, I pull myself from the thankfully shallow slime and stand shivering in the center of the Immortal's dark garden. Silence holds sway, at least for the moment. No music, no menacing voices, no screeching monsters.

I fight a quiver as a slight wind picks up and mutter a complaint about being soaked to the bone. Not surprisingly, a moment later, my clothes are dry.

This is a realm of dream, after all.

I do a full turn, looking for anything that might be itching to kill me. Koschei's palace rests at the periphery of the space, its grinning skull mouth open and pulsing with muted violet light as if daring me to enter. Opposite, the bent apple tree continues to shade the flat sitting rock beneath its branches, a rock that this time lies empty. Half-dead shrubs and trees fill the edges of the place, each covered in hanging moss and the webs of spiders no doubt as big as my car.

Blue mist plays at my feet, hiding who knows what in the grass beneath the black leather boots of Ivanovna. I creep over to the sitting rock to hide beneath the tree and gather my thoughts and have barely rested my backside on the cool stone when the music begins.

Woodwinds and brass fill the air with mystery, while a high-pitched tinkling accompanies a trio of apples that fall from the tree to the ground at my feet. Then, the violins enter the aural landscape as a spark appears in the sky. The crescendoing orchestra sends my heart racing, the music hitting a fever pitch as the glimmer of light assumes a winged form.

The Firebird soars by, a force of nature so quick, I scarcely get a glimpse of its plumage, and yet so powerful, the gust from its wings nearly sends me flying off the rock. The legendary bird lands somewhere behind one of the gnarled trees at the garden's periphery, only to be replaced a moment later by a woman with hair orange like a roaring bonfire and a feathered mask that covers her forehead, eyes, and nose.

In full ballerina regalia, bodice red and tutu fashioned of feathers of every color imaginable, the Firebird's human form flits across the garden. She covers the distance from one end to the other in six bounding leaps, only to disappear again into the dark wood at the clearing's edge. I stand, but remain beneath the tree, awaiting her return.

I don't have long to wait.

Blinded by a flash of brilliance, I can scarcely look on as the Firebird makes a second pass of the garden, the invisible orchestra filling the air with shrill piccolo and bells. I retreat behind the tree and attempt to rub away the blindness. When I again look, she has taken center stage in the Immortal's garden where she dances, like the saying goes, as if no one is watching. From leap to pirouette and back, she dances *en pointe*, all the while artfully flapping her arms as if they were wings, her fingers fluttering like a bird's feathers in the wind. Then, everything stops, and her head jerks to one side.

Though she hasn't spotted me, she has clearly sensed my presence.

I raise my bow, remembering full well the fate of the *bukavac* during my first visit to Koschei's garden, and prepare to defend myself. As the Firebird continues her dance, however, I lower my weapon, entranced in the beauty of her performance. Moving in perfect time with the unseen symphony, she flits this way and that as if she hasn't a care in the world. Lost in the dance and the music, I nearly scream when the bizarre bird-woman rushes the tree and plucks an apple from one of the lower branches.

Returning to the center of the glade with the apple in her teeth, she beats her arms like wings—once, twice, three times—and then she takes the apple and hurls it into the *bukavac* pool. Pleased with herself, she drops to the ground in a graceful crouch as if she's expecting applause for her performance. Then, the strange bird-woman's head jerks again, this time in my direction.

I stand perfectly still, afraid to even breathe.

As if I'm actually breathing in this place.

What is the point of all this? Why am I here?

My mind wanders back to what Anthony said.

"Early on in the story, Prince Ivan captures one of the enchanted creatures, the majestic Firebird, which in turn offers Ivan his allegiance in exchange for its life and freedom."

So, I'm supposed to capture this shapeshifting bird-woman who boasts a wingspan broader than an NBA player's and routinely impales toad monsters on her sword beak.

Yep. This is definitely an Anthony Faircloth production.

As the bird-woman comes to her feet, I rush her from behind and grab her around the waist. Her head darts in my direction, and for the first time, she sees me. Her legs assume an arabesque position before she pulls from my grasp and attempts to flee. Giving chase, I just catch the edge of her feather tutu with my fingertips, only to have her pull away a second time. Together, we proceed through an intricate set of steps as if choreographed and rehearsed. Both like and unlike the forced dance from the Russian fair, I somehow maintain control of my actions in this place, though the compulsion to capture the Firebird is undeniable.

The music undergoes a subtle change, and the bird-woman stretches her arms to the sky. I fear she is about to transform back into her winged form and fly away. I leap at her, grab her arms, and force them to her sides. She pulls away, her arms again stretching wide, and again, I pull them down. Over and over, we repeat the steps of our dance until she finally submits and cranes her neck around to stare at me, her terrified gaze pitiable through the beaked and feathered mask.

A lone violin pierces the chill air. As the full orchestra comes into play, the Firebird and I begin to dance, each movement as natural as if I've performed it a thousand times. The Firebird's pantomimed escapes and my choreographed efforts to recapture her play out again and again as we rush from one end of the garden to the other and back. Though the dance seems to be spiraling out of control, I remember one simple thing with each step, each lift, each leap. This strange creature is destined to help me at some point in what seems an inevitable fight with the Immortal who rules this realm, so I exert what control I have to keep myself from injuring her.

As our routine winds along, her efforts to flee grow less and less insistent, and soon, we are dancing in tandem. The supplication of the Firebird in full sway, I am forced one last time to pull her arms to her sides as she again flirts with escape. The music swells, and as I help her through a series of arabesques, our silent argument finally ends.

For a moment, she rests upon the ground as if deep in thought. Then, without warning, she stands, plucks a feather from her tutu, and places it in my hand. Distracted by its golden glow, I'm too slow to catch the Firebird as she leaps away from me. She shoots me a wicked grin and raises her arms wide. Feathers sprout from her fingertips, and in a blink, the woman is gone, replaced by the majestic bird. She turns her dagger-like beak in my direction, and for a moment, I fear I'm about to be skewered. Then, with a single flap of her mighty wings, the Firebird takes to the sky, and in less time than it takes to breathe, she is gone.

The music shifts again, and I retreat as the purple glow at the palace's mouth goes from subtle luminescence to blinding violet. Shielding my eyes from the brilliance, I trip over the edge of the murky pool where I entered this place. Unable to keep my balance, I fall into the water.

Water that is suddenly warm again.

Wiping the suds from my eyes, I look around Thomas' immaculate bathroom, and a simple realization hits me.

Nowhere is safe.

Just like the last time.

~

"You're awake."

I gasp at the whispered words, the first I've heard in what seems like a year. Thomas stands in the doorway holding the terrycloth robe he got me back at Christmas when I started spending the night on my return visits to Charlotte. My heart fills with gladness and gratitude at his kind gesture, the utter revulsion I felt for him earlier thankfully absent.

"Was I asleep?"

"You dozed off a few minutes ago. After the day you had, I kept an eye on you and just let you sleep."

"How long have I been out?" I study the raisins that used to be my fingertips. "Looks like days."

Thomas laughs. "No more than half an hour."

"Did I... say anything out of the ordinary?"

His expression goes immediately from jovial to worried, the chlorine smell of anxiety filling my senses. "What happened?"

"Take a wild guess." I climb from the bath, wrapping one towel around my body and another around my long dark locks, and sit at the tub's edge. "It was like last year with Goldenberg and Schmuÿle all over again."

Thomas remains silent as I tell the entire story of my encounter with the Firebird. I try to remember every detail, every nuance, so Thomas can help me figure out what it all means.

If only I could do that with the Russian fair. Tell him what I felt. What

I still feel. If anyone could wipe away the cobwebs of doubt, it's this man I've allowed into my life further than anyone in a very long time.

And yet, everything's changed now.

When I look at Thomas, I see the clown.

And dream of the Arabian.

I'm not certain what I'm trying to tell myself, but Archer and Sterling come from my mental toy box, not Anthony's.

"So," Thomas asks. "This Firebird was a woman?"

"Definitely."

Thomas drops into therapist mode. "In that case, let's assume Anthony is somehow involved with this."

"Yes." Hanging at my sides, my hands ball into fists. No matter how much Caroline and Thomas don't want to admit it, this is Anthony. "Let's."

Thomas pauses, no doubt picking up on the irritation in my tone. "If he's following the same rules for creating the settings and characters in his mind as he did last year, then there's one question you haven't asked."

He's right. After everything that happened last fall, I can't believe I didn't think of it.

"The bird-woman. She wore a mask." I cradle my face in my hands. "She's got to be someone Anthony knows, a representation of someone important in his life."

Thomas nods. "When we figure that out, you'll likely have the answer to a lot of questions."

"I'd rather know who Mister Immortal, Koschei the Deathless, is supposed to be. The Firebird is on my side as far as I can tell, while tall, dark, and scary is the one kidnapping little girls."

As if on cue, my phone rings in the next room. Thomas goes scurrying to grab it for me, leaving me alone to think for a moment. At the end of all this, the Firebird is supposed to be an ally. Could she be Caroline? Rachel? Someone I don't know?

All questions for another day. I have a nasty feeling about who's on the line and what they want to talk about. I'm already here with Thomas. It's late, well past Isabella's bedtime, and if it were Mom calling, I'd know. That leaves only one person.

Thomas steps back into the bathroom and hands me the phone. I glance at the screen, and my intuition is proven correct.

"Good evening, Detective Sterling. How can I help you?"

One extremely one-sided five-minute conversation later, I end the call and place the phone on the tub's edge next to the unfortunately empty wine glass.

"What is it?" Thomas asks.

"No rest for the weary tonight." I massage the bridge of my nose. "It's happened again."

7

———

PAS DE DEUX

Sterling shows me under the yellow and black police tape and into the front yard of a duplex just a few blocks from where the Abrams family lives. Police cars litter the street in both directions, their flashing lights and the slight mist falling from the sky giving everything a surreal blue sheen. Families cluster in yards up and down the sidewalk while no less than a dozen officers scout the neighborhood, going door to door and scouring the area for any sign of yet another missing girl.

Not to mention her friend.

Run-of-the-mill Saturday night sleepover. Two eight-year-old girls from Hannah Abrams' school, one class back. Last seen two hours ago watching a movie and giggling uncontrollably. Now, an empty room, an open window, and two sets of footprints in the mud have a good part of CMPD out at the witching hour.

The city went nuts this morning when little Hannah Abrams went missing for all of a few hours by the light of day. I can only imagine the frenzy when the media gets hold of this story.

And what do you know? The whole psychic thing must be firing on all cylinders tonight. There's the first news van pulling around the corner.

"Dammit," Sterling curses under his breath. "Is it too much to ask that just once we get a solid hour or two before the jackals show up?" He steps back under the tape and goes to intercept the far too perky reporter trot-

55

ting in our direction. Set off by a navy suit and pumps, the woman's fair skin and shoulder-length red hair shimmer in the flashing lights of the gathered patrol cars. Conversely, her cameraman's skin is so dark, his face remains all but invisible below his full head of dreadlocks. As the reporter and Sterling meet along the sidewalk, she sidesteps him and heads straight for the house.

No.

Straight for me.

As the cameraman and Sterling pull up on either side of her, the reporter asks a question that never seems to end well for me.

"You're Mira Tejedor, aren't you?" She stops just shy of the police tape. "The psychic from Virginia?"

"Depends." My hands shoot to my hips. "Who's asking?"

"Katie Kaczynski, Channel 3 News." She pauses for all of two seconds as her cameraman gets into position. "So, Ms. Tejedor. Two years ago, you helped the police in northern Virginia find Sarah Goode while just last year, you were the unsung hero that helped crack the Julianna Wagner case. Now the police have clearly called you in on this new series of missing children. What are your thoughts on the case? What is happening to these little girls?"

Sterling steps in. "There's no 'series' of anything, Ms. Kaczynski. The police were called out tonight to investigate a routine missing persons call."

Kaczynski allows her gaze to wander along the army of patrol cars occupying the otherwise empty suburban street. "This doesn't look like any 'routine' call I've ever seen, Detective Sterling." As the cameraman pans to get a full view of the neighborhood, Kaczynski pulls in close. "Not to mention, I know good and well Ms. Tejedor was involved in finding Hannah Abrams this morning in Freedom Park. Three missing girls in the Dilworth neighborhood in twenty-four hours is more than a coincidence, don't you think?"

"Ms. Kaczynski, let me assure you CMPD is launching an investigation into this matter as well as the bizarre circumstances behind the disappearance of Hannah Abrams this morning. More than that, however, I'm not at liberty to say at this point."

"But you've brought Ms. Tejedor in on both cases. If there's no link, does that mean the Police Department now runs all their cases by Charlotte's soon-to-be resident psychic?"

Soon-to-be resident. Wow. Chick's done her homework.

I clear my throat. "Detective Sterling knows all about my unfortunate proclivity for missing persons cases involving young children. I was more than happy to come out this evening to see if there was anything I might add to the investigation."

"Well." Kaczynski pulls herself up tall and straightens her checkered blouse. "All of Charlotte will be waiting with bated breath to hear your thoughts on this case, Ms. Tejedor."

"Come on, Mira." Sterling steps across the police tape. "Let's go talk to the girl's family."

"Mira, huh?" Just above a whisper, Kaczynski's words echo in my mind as we leave her and her cameraman standing on the sidewalk.

I give Sterling a subtle elbow to the ribs. "You and her go way back, I'm guessing," I mutter at his frustrated glare.

"You could say that." Without another word, he rings the doorbell for the left side of the duplex. Barely two seconds pass before the door opens, and a woman a couple years older than me steps out onto the small porch. Her skin pale, a familiar terror is evident in her tired eyes.

"You're the detective from before." Definitely a native, her Charlotte accent is apparent, if not thick. "Sterling, right?"

Sterling offers her a sincere smile. "That's right, ma'am."

The woman searches both our eyes. "Do you have… any news?"

Sterling quickly rests a hand on her shoulder. "No. Nothing like that. Nothing to report at all, in fact. We still have police and some folks from the neighborhood out searching for Elizabeth and Janey. They're going door-to-door, block-by-block. If they're still in the area, we'll find them."

"If…" The woman begins to break down in front of me. "Oh God…"

"Excuse me." I extend a hand. "My name is Mira Tejedor. Detective Sterling asked me to come and see if I could help."

"Millie Baker." She takes my hand and evaluates me with a frank up and down. "Are you with the police?"

"Not exactly." I shoot Sterling a quick glance. "I'm a consultant that specializes in missing persons."

Her brows knit together as she studies me. "And what is it you do, exactly?"

"I can offer quite a bit given the right resources." And here we go again. "I'm what you would likely call a psychic, for lack of a better term."

"Psychic." Her eyes shoot immediately back to Sterling. "Detective, you can't be serious."

"Ms. Baker, please. Hear her out. Ms. Tejedor has a lot of experience, and for someone in her field, a surprisingly high success rate."

I notice he doesn't mention that of the last two girls I found, only one was still alive.

Ms. Baker takes a moment, her gaze flirting between dubious and hopeful, even as the corresponding scents of black pepper and marshmallows vie for dominance in my consciousness. Eventually, however, the acrid smell of onions overpowers the other two, and I see Ms. Baker for what I already knew her to be.

Desperate.

As she shows us inside her home, I chance a glance back and find Katie Kaczynski watching me like the proverbial hawk from her spot at the lawn's edge behind the police line.

The woman wants her story.

Or is that it at all?

~

"So, Ms. Tejedor, what is it you need from me to… do whatever it is you do?"

Funny how the questions are always the same.

I incline my head and offer Ms. Baker the slightest of smiles. "Will you take me to where you last saw Elizabeth and Janey?"

She directs me toward the back of their home where bright overhead lights glare down on the remains of what must have been a pretty impressive pillow and blanket fort. The television is frozen on a scene depicting the newest Disney princess and her sister, a movie I've seen no less than fifty times since it came out on DVD a few months back. Two plates filled with pizza crusts and Jolly Rancher wrappers lie on the carpeted floor. A stuffed tiger, half-buried in the pillows and blankets, stares out at me, its face strangely sad for a child's toy.

"The tiger." I shoot Ms. Baker a sidelong glance. "Elizabeth's?"

"That's Chauncy." She wipes away a tear. "She's had him since she was a year old. Doesn't go anywhere without him."

I kneel by the destroyed pillow fort and stretch out a hand for the tiger. "May I?"

"You need her *toy*?"

"Let her." Sterling's deep bass reverberates in the room. "Trust me."

Ms. Baker's gaze shoots from me to Sterling and back. "If you think it will help."

Anticipation lights up Sterling's features even as helpless submission wafts off Ms. Baker like loaf upon loaf of moldy bread. At her subtle nod, I grasp the stuffed tiger by the neck and bring it to my chest.

"All right, Chauncy." I bring the toy up to my nose and inhale. The various scents of little kid sweat, sugary treats, and popcorn bring a certain girl's face to the forefront of my mind, but not Elizabeth Baker, the girl whose portrait fills every corner of this house.

The features that occupy my mind's eye belong to Isabella. Not an hour goes by that I don't miss that mischievous smile of hers, those innocent yet wise eyes.

And when I'm faced with the reality of another child in danger...

Dammit, Mira. Stay focused. Time to see if Elizabeth has left enough of an impression on her stuffed tiger to clue us in to where she might have gone or even what happened here.

I open my mind and am immediately awash in a lifetime of Elizabeth Baker's memories, emotional pseudo-scents warring with the actual smells coming off the animal's faux fur.

Tears in the darkness of a cold winter night, the stuffed tiger held tight to her chest.

Laughter as she runs through a zoo carrying Chauncy by his back leg.

Wonder at the sight of Old Faithful erupting in all its Yellowstone glory, her favorite toy pulled close by her side.

And then, something raw and definitely more recent.

Fear. Terror. Despair.

Abrupt separation.

Whatever drove Elizabeth from this place must have been horrible for her to leave her Chauncy behind.

Another *bukavac* perhaps?

Or, God help her, something worse?

Though nothing thus far ties this to Anthony or Hannah, the same instinct that has guided me all day tells me to push further.

"All right, Elizabeth," I mutter. "It's clear something scared you to the core. Now, what did you do about it? Where did you go?"

"What are you—" Ms. Baker hushes at Sterling's raised hand.

For almost a minute, I get nothing, and neither the frustration on Ms. Baker's face nor the disappointment on Sterling's does much to help the situation. I'm about to give up and move on to something else when it hits me. Subtle at first, goosebumps roll up my arms as the twin aromas of cocoa and coffee mix in my mind with the dark roast aroma of contentment.

"Hot chocolate." I inhale through my nose. "And coffee." I turn to Ms. Baker. "Does that ring a bell?"

Before she can answer, my senses turn a corner. A multitude of voices erupt in my mind, one trying to talk over the other. The subtle notes of a jazz clarinet play in the background while the frothy hiss of steam heating milk blocks out everything else. Cool air washes over me from above, and I begin to tremble.

"Not here." I clutch the tiger close to my stomach. "A cafe, maybe? A place you might frequent?"

"There's the local Starbucks. We go there most Sunday mornings on the way to church."

"The one on East?" Sterling asks.

Ms. Baker nods. "She always gets the same thing, a hot chocolate and blueberry muffin."

I let the tiger drop. "How far is it from here?"

"A few blocks."

Already headed for the car, Sterling motions for us to follow. "We passed it this morning on the way to the park."

Ms. Baker's eyes bulge in disbelief. "But why would she go there at this time of night? They've been closed for over an hour."

"Any port in a storm, Ms. Baker." I turn for the door. "Now, let's go find your little girl."

Traffic seems surprisingly light for a Saturday night, though admittedly, it is well after midnight. Arriving in just under three minutes, we find the parking lot empty save a rusted out Chevy Impala from the 80's parked next to a fire-engine-red Tesla—the dichotomy of Charlotte, North Carolina spelled out more eloquently than I ever could.

The Starbucks in question, like most of the businesses up and down East, is an old house that's been repurposed for business. This one in particular even has an old garage in the back that attaches to the parking lot. The place is dark, and only the overhead mercury street lamps cast any light on the area.

Sterling flips on one of those footlong flashlights that look like they could double as a club and cautiously moves toward the back ramp. Stepping between the house and the garage, he disappears from view for a moment.

"We're going to find her, aren't we?" Ms. Baker asks. "She's just a little girl."

"Detective Sterling and I will do everything we—"

"They're out front, on the patio," Sterling shouts as he runs up the sidewalk on the opposite side of the building. "Something's wrong with them."

Ms. Baker takes off at a dead sprint across the remaining parking lot. Sterling races after her, leaving me the one bringing up the rear this time. As I round the corner, I see what has Sterling so agitated.

Elizabeth, just as pretty as her pictures, stands arm in arm with her friend Janey, both of their free arms held out in a flourish and their outside legs thrust out forward with only their toes touching the ground. Both of them frozen there as if it's curtain call at the ballet, only the slightest rise and fall of their chests lets me know they're still breathing.

"Elizabeth," Ms. Baker sobs, throwing her arms around her little girl. "What's happened to you?"

"I've got a pretty good idea," I mutter in Sterling's ear.

"What do we do?" Sterling asks.

"Call 9-1-1."

"That's it?" His eyes meet mine. "What about now? Don't you need to —I don't know—do something?"

"No." I take a step back, holding my hands before me, palms out. "I don't dare get too close. You saw what happened this morning when I so much as brushed Hannah Abrams' cheek. Barely made it out in one piece. Not sure I can handle another jaunt this soon."

For many reasons, I avoid mentioning my second trip today into the realm of dream, courtesy of one Anthony Faircloth. I'm nowhere near ready to face the implications of the fair and what I saw there. Plus, though there's no doubt Anthony's involved with everything that's happening to these girls, Caroline would never forgive me if I brought the police down on her son. Not after everything that happened with Jason last year.

Anthony's older brother, all lined up to start at N.C. State this fall, headed out a few weeks back on an American walkabout, or driveabout, I suppose. Last I heard, he was somewhere deep in the heart of Texas and heading west for California. After everything that went down with his girlfriend Julianna's death last year, it's no wonder he wanted to take an extended vacation from Charlotte. Still, with everything that's going on around here, Caroline could certainly use the support of her oldest son right about now.

"EMTs are on the way." Sterling's comment rockets me right back to the present. "Anything else I can do?"

Ms. Baker's sobbing grabs my heart with a fist of thorns, the sulfur and chlorine scents of fear and worry vying for top spot along my mental palate.

"Now, we wait."

Fortunately, the wait is next to nothing. Between Sterling being a cop and the fact that the biggest hospital in the city is literally across the next hill, two ambulances scream up three minutes later. All four of the EMTs work with the girls for several minutes, painstakingly disengaging each from the other's grip without breaking bones. The girls remain immobile like posed mannequins until they're finally separated, at which point they go limp in their respective EMT's arms.

I listen from the periphery as the rescue squads get the pair down to the sidewalk and load them onto stretchers. I'm no doctor, but from what I can gather from all the medical mumbo jumbo, it sounds like both girls are stable with no sign of injury beyond the fact that neither seems able to wake up.

"And you just found them this way?" the lead EMT asks Sterling once the girls are loaded onto the ambulances.

"Just like you saw them."

"Freaky."

A second EMT pops in. "How did you know to even look here?"

Sterling looks back at me, and I answer, "A pretty good hunch."

"Well," the first EMT says, "we'll get these two to the Emergency Room and get them checked out." He turns to Ms. Baker. "Would you like to ride with your daughter, ma'am?"

"Of course." She turns to me. "Thank you, Ms. Tejedor. I owe you everything."

My lips turn up in a sad smile. "It's what I do." Then, under my breath, "Apparently."

As the ambulances pull away, Sterling and I stand beneath one of the green umbrellas on the front patio of the Starbucks.

"So, you going to tell me what's going on?" Sterling, ever to the point, skewers me to the spot with those piercing eyes of his. "Why I've got three catatonic runaways on my docket within twenty-four hours?"

"If I knew, don't you think I'd have already told you?" Great. Now I'm lying to everyone. "I'll sleep on it tonight and get back to you in the morning, all right?"

His gaze drops to the ground for a moment and then returns to mine. "I'm going to the hospital tomorrow to check on all three of the kids. Care to join me?"

"Wouldn't miss it." Unbidden, a vision of the confident Arabian from Anthony's Russian fair flashes through my mind. "Meet you by the main entrance at nine?"

"Sounds good." He smiles. "You must be exhausted. Can I drop you off at your car?"

"Sure." A wave of fatigue rolls over me, and I barely suppress a yawn. "And on second thought, can we make that ten in the morning?"

"Ten it is."

Sterling walks me to his cruiser and opens the door for me. A smile makes a brief appearance on my lips, and there we have it. In one short day, the two of us are right back at square one. My heart races with guilt as Thomas' face flits across my mind's eye, only to be followed by a wave of nausea as his imagined features shift to the half-smile, half-frown of the clown from the fair. As we pull out of the parking lot and head across the hill toward Uptown, I roll down the window, afraid I'm about to lose whatever's left in my stomach.

And that's when I see it.

Parked down a side street, just far enough from the corner, I almost don't notice it, a Channel 3 news van rests, taillights bright and exhaust pouring from the pipe.

Looks like we haven't seen the last of one Katie Kaczynski.

8

______

DANCE OF THE PRINCESSES

"**Y**ou awake?"

Thomas' question yanks me out of a bizarre nightmare where Tunny, the gnome from Anthony's Exhibition, and I are surrounded by carnivorous rabbits with glowing red eyes and horns like the toad-monsters from Koschei's garden. A true dream, I believe, but still terrifying. My heart pounds as blinding Sunday morning light pours through the windows of his guest bedroom. I raise an arm to shield my eyes and roll over to find Thomas standing in the doorway dressed for a run.

"I am now." My voice back to something approaching my normal timbre, I yawn and add, "What time is it, anyway?"

"A little after eight. I was going to go get in a quick couple of miles before it got too hot." He chuckles. "I'm guessing I'll be running alone?"

"Sorry." I keep my eyes firmly on his chest, unable to meet his gaze between my memory of the Russian fair and my moment—if you can call it that—with Sterling last night. "Two trips into dreamland and getting dragged out at midnight have pretty much let the air out of my tires."

"Figured as much." Thomas steps into the room. "You get some rest, okay? I'll be back soon." He turns to leave. "Oh, and coffee's on, in case you feel like getting up."

"You're a lifesaver. See you in a bit." I roll back over and wait for

64

Thomas to leave, kicking myself at the sound of his quiet sigh followed by his heavy steps down to the ground floor.

What the hell's wrong with me? Twenty-four hours ago, I was head over heels for this guy. Now? I can't stand the sight of him and have started throwing smiles at other men. Is it the jitters? After all this time, am I just scared of commitment? In any case, though all of this may have started in the dreamworld of Anthony's mind, now I can't seem to get it out of mine.

I toss and turn for a few more minutes, but between my warring emotions and the delectable aroma of dark roast percolating up from the kitchen, sleep appears to be a lost cause. I sneak down the hall to Thomas' bedroom and grab a pair of his pajama pants before venturing down to the kitchen. In usual Thomas Archer fashion, he's left me out my favorite mug, the sugar bowl, and the hazelnut creamer.

The man knows me well.

One cup of coffee and a shower later, I feel like a new woman, or at least ready to face the day. I head over to the hospital, claim a parking space, and then walk a couple laps of the campus waiting for Sterling to show up. I try to convince myself I left early to be punctual, but deep down, I'm more than aware I'm kidding myself.

I shift my focus instead to the three little girls who all seem to have been struck with a similar illness that sent Anthony Faircloth all but comatose for weeks last year. His malady came from a potent combination of latent psychic talent and the trauma of indirectly experiencing the murder of his first big crush by a person he trusted and loved. Julianna Wagner is long gone and Veronica Sayles, Anthony's teacher, lies in a vegetative state at one of the local nursing homes. The Anthony I know would never subject another human being to the hell he went through, and yet, he's the only common thread. The Firebird, the puppet show, the music. Other than no paintings, it's the Exhibition all over again.

At the moment, I'm not welcome at the Faircloth home, though if I know Caroline, this storm will blow over like others before. She's a passionate mother who guards her children like a lioness, but at her core, she's a reasonable woman who has to see I'm right.

Which leaves me, for now, with these three girls as my only leads.

"Good morning, Mira."

Sterling's rich bass drives my pulse up. I turn and find him coming up the sidewalk from the parking deck. Dressed in a casual shirt and slacks, he looks more like a man who's heading for a coffee date than a cop.

"Good morning, Detective."

"You could always call me Calvin… you know, when it's just us."

Heat rises in my cheeks. "How about Sterling?" I raise an eyebrow. "A good compromise, not to mention it suits you."

He returns my smile. "Sterling it is then."

I follow him into the hospital and through the labyrinth of halls leading to the children's hospital. After a bit of negotiation, the receptionist at the front desk reveals all three girls have been admitted to the same floor and issues us guest badges that will allow us to get around.

On the way up, Sterling turns to me. "I know both the Abrams family and Ms. Baker have met you and understand your role, but let me take the lead on this, okay?"

I offer a noncommittal smile. "Hey, you're the boss."

We step off onto the ninth floor and flash our temporary badges, allowing us back to the patient rooms. The slip of paper the receptionist gave us shows Hannah Abrams in Room 9 while Elizabeth Baker and Janey Campbell are around the corner in Rooms 23 and 24. Sterling leads us to Room 9 first. Beneath the crisp sheets and warm blanket of her hospital bed, Hannah Abrams lies unmoving, her eyes open and staring at the ceiling. Mr. Abrams is piled down on a wall couch at the back of the room snoring peacefully while a woman I suspect is Hannah's mother is asleep sitting up in a chair.

I put a finger to my lips, letting Sterling know to let everyone sleep a moment longer, and step over to the hospital bed. Careful not to touch her, I wave a hand over Hannah's eyes, but her focused gaze doesn't falter.

"Can we help you?"

I look up from the bed and meet Ms. Abrams' gaze. "Sorry. I was just checking on your daughter."

Sterling steps in. "Good morning, Ms. Abrams. I'm Detective Sterling, and this is Mira Tejedor, a consultant we've brought in on the case."

"Don't worry, Helen." Mr. Abrams emerges from his blanket cocoon and shoots me a tired smile. "This is Mira, the woman who helped find Hannah yesterday."

Ms. Abrams' stern expression melts immediately into a beam of gratitude. "Oh." She gets up from her chair and joins me at the bedside. "We owe you so much. Little Hannah here isn't out of the woods yet, but the doctors are confident they'll figure out what is happening soon."

"Good." I shake her hand. "I'm just glad we were able to find her as quickly as we did."

"Are you really a psychic?" She pulls her hand away. "Like the ones on TV?"

Though it's a question I've been asked ten thousand times, I give her a break, seeing as how it's her little girl that's lying comatose in the bed.

"Yes. I'm an honest-to-God psychic, believe it or not." She recoils slightly, clearly afraid she's offended me, but I put her at ease with the warmest smile I can muster. "Any change in Hannah's status?"

Mr. Abrams joins us across the bed. "No change, as far as we know. The doctors say she seems fine medically, but so far, any efforts to wake her or get her to respond have failed. She won't eat or drink, so they're just giving her fluids for the time being. If she doesn't come around soon, though, they said they'd have to put in a feeding tube so she doesn't start losing weight."

"A feeding tube." Ms. Abrams lets out a sob. "Our daughter is going to need a feeding tube."

"Just a temporary one, honey." Mr. Abrams takes his wife's hand from across the bed, the diamond on her left hand sparkling in the lights off the hospital monitor. "She's going to be okay."

They both look to me as if I can tell the future. Can't blame them, I guess. I do introduce myself as psychic.

"If you two will excuse us," Sterling leaps in to save the day, "we need to get going. We just wanted to come by and check on Hannah."

We take care of the not-so-pleasantries of saying goodbye and step out of the room. Sterling leads me around the corner to the other two girls' rooms. I pop my head into Elizabeth's first, but find it empty and her entire bed gone. No doubt they've taken her downstairs to run some more tests that aren't going to tell them anything.

At the end of the hall by the emergency exit, Room 24 awaits. I reach for the doorknob, but some premonition tells me to pull back.

"Sterling, I know it's just a comatose kid on the other side of the door, but would you do me a favor and go in first?"

He gives me a quizzical look and then, with a curt nod, enters. Close on his heels, I step inside. I'm not certain what I was expecting—maybe things flying around the room a la The Exorcist—but Janey Campbell's hospital room is just that. With no family present, she rests beneath a set of perfectly placed sheets in the muted light. Unlike the multitude of emotions and scents that filled the Abrams' room, here there is relative peace. That is, till I take another step forward.

The sulfur scent of rotten eggs assaults my senses. I gag audibly, and

Sterling spins around to check on me. I raise a hand and let him know I'm fine, though "fine" is a bit of a stretch. With my next step, the stench doubles in intensity. Another, and I nearly vomit.

Janey doesn't want me anywhere near her, and therefore, that's exactly where I need to go.

Holding my hand over my mouth, I force myself over to the bedside.

"Get me a chair."

Sterling pulls over the lavender recliner from the corner and deposits it by the bed. "Anything else?"

"A special request." I let down the bed rail, careful not to let my knuckles touch Janey Campbell's bare arm. "If I go down, don't let me hit my head."

I take in a deep breath and take the girl's hand. In an instant, everything goes away. The hospital room evaporates into mist, as does any remaining doubt the three girls on this floor all suffer from precisely the same malady. One beyond any physician's training.

Before I can take another breath, I'm back in Koschei's garden. A cerulean twilight hangs over the place and mingles with the ever-present violet glow emanating from the skull mouth of the Immortal's palace. I whirl around, fully expecting to find an army of *bukavacs* closing in on me from the mud and muck. Instead, I find a little girl in a full-length dress of brightest white asleep at the pool's edge, her long red hair fanned about her freckled face like the sun's corona.

A sound of flapping wings to my rear draws my attention, but there's nothing there. When I turn again, two more girls lie on the ground before me. The three of them form a triangle with each pair of feet at the next child's head. One of these new additions has skin the color of mahogany with a full head of lustrous black curls while the other appears Indian, her shoulder-length hair tied up in pigtails.

The strangest thing? None of them are the girls Sterling and I came to the hospital to see.

Quiet at first, but quickly filling the space, the music begins. A lone oboe plays up and down a scale, the tone ominous as a thick white mist coils about my feet. Then, as the violins come in followed by flute and clarinet and xylophone, the tune turns both mysterious and wistful. One by one, the three girls I came looking for step from the mouth of the palace, each in the same full-length gown as the girls at my feet, and dance toward the garden's center. Meeting there, they each circle the bent apple tree a full three times before peeling off to run at me.

Or so it seems.

Each passes me as if I'm not even standing there and goes to one of the three sleeping girls. Hannah goes for the Indian girl; Elizabeth, the dark-skinned one; and Janey, the pale redhead. At their touch, each still form comes to life, and the three pairs twirl in time with the unseen orchestra. Whirling around me and closer with each pass, the girls' dancing takes me back to the *Tuileries* garden in Anthony's Exhibition.

Even now, the memory of the children's attack in that place still sends a chill up my spine.

These girls can ignore me all day if they like.

Except, how do I get through to them if they won't even register my presence?

Dammit, Anthony. Why are you doing this? And why are you making it so damn hard?

The dancers, all six of them, come together in a circle. First one way then the other, they cavort around the tree and then, as one, step close and pull down one golden apple apiece.

I'm guessing this is straight out of *The Firebird*, but I can't help but recall from Catholic school what happens to girls who take apples from trees in magical gardens.

Especially gardens with snakes.

The girls throw the apples to one another, clearly playing an intricate game with rules I don't understand. Dancing in perfect syncopation with the jolly woodwind tune, the six of them make what is effectively an imprisonment seem almost fun. Several times, I step into their path, trying to catch the attention of any of the girls. My efforts are in vain. With each pass, they skitter around me like river water around a boulder only to rejoin the others as they worship this, the tree from Eden.

Then, a single clap from across my shoulder silences the music and sends all six girls falling to the now even more trampled grass.

I turn, knowing full well what I will see.

There, standing beneath the incisors of his skull palace's grinning mouth, Koschei the Deathless regards me with an amused grin.

"So, Ivanovna." His voice rumbles like distant thunder. "You have returned."

"Let these girls go, you monster."

"Monster?" Koschei laughs, the sound a half-grumbled wheeze. "And the last time we met, did you not think me this Anthony-child you seek?" He spreads his outstretched fingers across his chest and raises his eyebrows in false indignation. "My, how far I've fallen in your estimation."

"I don't know who or what you are, but I do know you're holding these girls against their will." I wave a hand at the Indian child. "I knew only of three. Who are the others?"

"My latest arrivals." Koschei descends from the maw of his monstrous home and glides across the grass toward me, stepping across the girls' motionless forms as if they were merely part of the scenery. "Lovely, are they not?"

"Let them go." I will the bow into my hand and draw an arrow from Ivanovna's quiver. "Or I will strike you down where you stand."

"So dramatic." He waves a hand and the bowstring snaps, sending my arrow flying into the shadows at the garden's edge. "As I told you before, Ivanovna, you have no power here. This is my realm and mine alone." He kneels over Janey Campbell. "As for letting them go, you should be careful what you wish for."

"What is that supposed to mean?"

He looks up at me, his gaze alight with a spark of violet energy. "When I am finished with these and the remaining seven, they will be truly released, from this world and any other."

Fear grips my chest. "You mean to kill them?"

"Sacrifice, I believe, is the more appropriate term."

"To what end, Immortal?"

Koschei shakes his head, his wheezy laugh reverberating in the space. "Not that you have any hope of stopping me, but regarding my ultimate goal, I think I will keep my own counsel for now." He steeples his fingers just below his lips. "And now, I believe I and my young charges will retire to my chambers and prepare accommodations for the others." He snaps his fingers and all six girls rouse as if from sleep. Some yawn while others rub at their eyes, and then, as one, they form a line and head dutifully into the horrible mouth of Koschei's home. With a subtle wink, the Immortal adds, "And since you came seeking monsters..."

He claps his hands together again, the sound like the report of a high-powered rifle. For a moment, nothing happens, and then, the scrub of the forest surrounding Koschei's garden lights up with hundreds of little lights, each giving off a dull red glow. The crimson hue replaces the subtle blue haze that fills the garden.

And then, in the periphery of my vision, one pair of lights... blinks.

"You fared well against the *bukavacs*, brave Ivanovna." Koschei turns and follows the girls across the bridge leading to his foreboding domicile. "Mere luck, however, will not save you from the *skrzaks*." He glances across his shoulder and catches my eye one last time before disappearing into the shadows of his fortress. "Kill her."

9

———

DAYBREAK

From every tree, rock, and shadow, the screaming horde of *skrzaks* descends upon me. Though not one of them stands above two feet high, their stubby legs and club-like feet do nothing to impair their speed. The face of Tunny, the gnome from Anthony's Exhibition, flashes across my mind's eye, though where I always found kindness in his woody gaze, in the *skrzaks'*, I find only blood-red hate.

"Kill her," growls the one in the lead. "As the Master demands." All translucent skin, pointed ears, and fanged grimace, the creature is clearly the product of a child's nightmare.

And I have no doubt as to the identity of that child.

Though how or, more important, why Anthony's mind is doing this continues to elude me.

Holding the stringless bow before me, I backpedal, knowing full well the *bukavac* pool sprawls directly behind me. Unless these things can swim, I can at least keep them all in front of me. As my heels find the stone edge, I brandish the recurve bow, now effectively an ornately carved stick, and wait for the first of the *skrzaks* to come.

The irony of the situation hits me. When the *bukavacs* attacked before, Mr. Abrams brought me out of the garden in the nick of time by dousing my physical body with ice-cold water. His fear and ignorance of what was happening saved me whereas Sterling's relative understanding of the situation may end up being the last nail in my coffin.

As Koschei said, luck isn't going to save me this time.

It's all up to me.

In seconds, I'm surrounded. Four and five deep, the hundred *skrzaks* form a wide half-oval that blocks every avenue of escape but the muck-filled pool one step to my rear. Small though they may be, their sheer number, not to mention their jagged teeth and razor claws, would likely make short work of a lone woman with a quiver full of useless arrows.

And that's the part I don't understand.

Despite my vulnerable state, the *skrzaks* keep their distance, even holding their breath, almost as if they're waiting for something. As if on cue, a sickening squelch from behind me pulls my attention. I spin around and find a lone *bukavac* pulling itself from the muck and inflating its beach-ball-sized throat to bellow at me. With instinct born of desperation, I swallow my fear and step onto the granite and marble edge of the pool. Sprinting along a quarter of its ruined circumference, I stop at one end of the *skrzak* blockade, turn, and jump feet first into the pool. I'm not certain who is most surprised by my leap of faith: the army of *skrzaks*, the *bukavac*, or me.

With the bow held firm in one hand, I force my way through the mud and slime, and in seconds, I'm upon the slime-covered monster. Surprised by my audacity, the horned toad-thing stays perfectly still as if trying to blend in with the muck.

Bad move.

I grab one of the creature's horns and, with a quick scissor kick, pull myself up and onto its back. Before it can react, I straddle it like a horse and dig my heels into its slippery flanks. Reflexively, the thing bellows, releasing the attack it meant for me on the unprepared *skrzaks*. A third of them fall screaming, their clawed fingers far less menacing when covering their ears. Another kick to the *bukavac's* sides sends the monster catapulting from the pool to land amid the *skrzak* horde where it impales two of them on its gnarled horns. Flinging them off with a flick of its enormous head, my steed bucks, trying to shake me from its back as well. Holding on for all I'm worth, I spur the toad-thing's flanks a third time, and it leaps in the direction of the apple tree. The branches are just low enough that I can reach the tree's golden fruit.

Plucking apple after apple from the tree, I hurl them with varying degrees of accuracy into the charging *skrzak* mob. My attack accomplishes little, and soon, we're surrounded again. I manage another kick to the sides of my amphibious steed, and it leaps to another corner of the garden. As the *bukavac* turns to face the mob of angry imps, a cold certainty falls over me. I've been lucky so far, but there are a hundred of the little beasts and only one of me. There's nowhere to hide in the tiny garden and both my monstrous ride and I are already growing fatigued. It's only a matter of time before—

A heart-stopping screech I've heard only once before splits the sky. I, along with the entire mob of *skrzaks*, look skyward. There, I find what I pray is my salvation.

The Firebird, in all her glory, streaks down at our seething melee like a winged meteor. The *bukavac* shudders in its loose skin beneath me. After seeing what the mighty bird did to its cousin during my first visit to Koschei's garden, I can't say that I blame it. The *skrzaks* flee every which way as the Firebird makes a lone pass directly above my head, the back-wash from her massive wings nearly sending me flying from my mount. As my avian savior takes back to the sky, the bow grows warm in my hand. Golden sparks scintillate around the intricately carved wood, and the string is made whole in a flash of fiery brilliance.

The battle joined, I draw an arrow from the quiver and nock it. As I pull the string back to my cheek, the head and shaft of the arrow erupt in orange flame. The sudden heat forces me to release the string prematurely. Regardless, the arrow finds its mark.

Or should I say, marks?

The fiery missile flies straight through the shoulder of a fleeing *skrzak* and imbeds itself in the back of the one in front of him. As the two imps simultaneously burst into flame and fall to the ground, the remainder of the mob sprints into the woods, though a few pairs of glowing red eyes remain, menacing me from the dissipating darkness.

The ascending sun ennobles this imaginary ruin, and the Firebird revels in the glorious sunlight. Once, twice, three times, she swoops over-head before landing directly in front of the lone *bukavac*. The toad-monster trembles beneath me. As I climb from its moist back, the thing's every muscle tenses as if waiting for oblivion at the end of the Firebird's dagger beak. Backing away from the intense staring match, even I nearly jump out of my skin when the mighty bird squawks at the monstrous toad.

The message is clear.

Go.

The *bukavac* leaps back into the muck-filled pond and, in seconds, is hidden from sight, leaving me alone with the majestic Firebird.

"Thank you," I murmur, offering the enormous bird a slight bow.

The Firebird lowers its head in answered deference, keeping at least one golden eye on me at all times. As the mighty creature brings itself back up to its full height, I catch something familiar in its gaze, and a simple question it hadn't as yet occurred to me to ask suddenly springs into my mind.

"Who… are you?"

As impossible as it seems, the Firebird smiles at me before launching back into the sky, leaving me alone in Koschei's garden. Saved a second time from certain death at the hands of the Immortal's legion of monsters, I watch until the majestic guardian of the garden is completely out of sight, and then, without fully understanding why, pull a second arrow from the quiver and fire it skyward. Three breaths pass as I wait for it to fall back to earth. As the arrow strikes the ground at my feet, the entire garden is filled with blinding light.

And then… nothing.

~

"Mira?" Sterling's voice stirs at the edge of my consciousness. "Mira? Are you all right?"

"Sterling." Still seated in the chair, my hand has fallen away from Janey Campbell's. My neck is turned at a strange angle, and my cheek aches from resting on the bed rail. I pull my head up so I can meet his gaze. Sterling does his best to project calm, but both his eyes and the telltale mix of chlorine and sulfur tell a different story. "How long have I been out?" I croak.

Sterling checks his watch. "A solid fifteen minutes."

"Did… anything happen?"

"Other than the both of you moaning like you were sharing the same nightmare."

"What are you two doing in here?" This new voice, female, comes from the door. I peer across my shoulder past Sterling and find a nurse in dark scrubs scowling at me. "Ms. Campbell's parents instructed that no one but family was to be allowed in this room."

"Pardon us, ma'am." Sterling flashes his badge. "Ms. Tejedor and I were the ones who found Janey last night along with the girl in the next room." Putting away his identification, he offers the nurse an outstretched hand. "We just popped by this morning to check on them."

"That's all fine and good." The nurse keeps both hands firmly on her hips. "The family's instructions, however, were quite clear." She pulls the door open wide. "I'm going to have to ask you both to leave."

"That won't be a problem." I pull myself up from the bedside, my legs like jelly. "We were just heading out."

I make it three steps before my knees buckle. Sterling catches me before I collapse into a puddle on the floor.

"Is she all right?" the nurse asks, the expression beneath her raised eyebrow somewhere between concerned and suspicious.

"She's fine." Sterling wraps a strong arm around my waist and helps me exit the room with something approaching dignity. "She's just had a long twenty-four hours."

The nurse touches my shoulder as we pass. "You sure you're okay?"

"Don't worry about me." Keeping my voice to a whisper so the nurse doesn't get wind of my hoarseness, I glance back at Janey Campbell's peaceful form. "These girls need your help way more than I do." I grip Sterling's hand at my waist. "Let's go."

We're almost to the car before any semblance of strength returns to my legs. I take the last few steps without Sterling supporting me, more out of pride than anything, but when I climb into the passenger seat, I fall like a sack of marbles. Beyond spent, it's all I can do to keep my eyes open.

"Drop you off at your car?" he asks with one dubious eyebrow raised.

I let out a quiet chuckle. "I think we both know I'm in no shape to drive."

"What, then?"

"Hmmm..." I cradle my face in my hands. "Can you drop me off at Thomas' place?"

Sterling's forehead crinkles, the faintest hint of rotting apples flitting across my consciousness as he mutters, "Sure."

We're both silent for the next few minutes as Sterling navigates his police cruiser out of the parking deck and onto the main road, the only interruption when I tell him Thomas' address for the GPS. We're about halfway there when he finally breaks the silence.

"So, you and Dr. Archer, huh? You're moving to Charlotte for him?"

I shudder as the clown from the Russian fair grimaces at me from across the void. "That's the plan."

"Funny." Sterling gives me a frank side-eye. "You don't seem overly excited about the prospect."

"Let's just keep our minds on the case, all right?"

"Fine." The fresh-baked bread scent of Sterling's concern cuts off abruptly, leaving only the aroma of moldy cheese. "So, that encounter left you pretty wasted. Did you at least find out something about what's going on?"

I wrestle with what to say or, at least, how much to say about what I know.

"All three of the girls are linked." My entire body shakes, the involuntary convulsion making Sterling jump. "And this thing is far from over."

"There's going to be more?"

"Three more for starters." My eyes slide closed as I picture their faces. "I saw them there." I swallow. "And unless I miss my guess, there will be thirteen before all this is over."

"Thirteen?" Sterling pulls into the nearest parking lot and stops the car. "All right, Mira. What is it you're not telling me?"

I shake my head. Here it comes. "Remember last September…"

"**Y**ou did what?" Thomas' eyes wide in disbelief, he paces the room like a caged animal. "You told Sterling?"

"I had to." Eye-stinging vinegar buffets my senses as I face Thomas' anger. "These girls' lives are at stake. He has to know."

"Has to know *what*? That you hear classical music when you visit their minds? That you fight the monsters you find there? You think he's going to believe any of that?"

"I don't know." My cheeks grow hot. "He seemed pretty on board last fall when I told him about my experiences along the Exhibition."

"Oh, I'll just bet he did." Thomas flops down in the armchair opposite me, his living room suddenly very small. "And what exactly do you think he's going to do with this information? Arrest a boy who spent a month of his life last year in a living hell? Go after his family—a family I might remind you has had multiple run-ins with the police already and is just beginning to heal?"

"Okay, okay." I raise my hands before me in surrender. "What I don't get is why you're so upset. Sterling and I are just trying to help these girls and keep this from happening again."

"And I'm not?"

Thomas' eyes narrow, and my own water from the vinegar filling the room.

Anger.

And something else, something I've never felt from him before.

Deep-seated guilt.

Pungent and nauseating, shame wafts off him like a breeze flowing across a landfill.

"What is it you're not telling me?" I ask, half-afraid of the answer. "Is it bad?"

Thomas pauses. I don't like it one bit.

"Tell me," I whisper.

Thomas lets out a short sigh. "The three girls in question have a lot more in common than monsters and orchestra scores between their ears."

"What are you trying to say?"

"When it was just Hannah, I thought it was merely a coincidence, you know, both her and Anthony falling silent, but now that it's happened to Elizabeth and Janey as well—"

"Wait. How do you know those names?" Katie Kaczynski's knowing smile flashes across my mind's eye. "Have they already made the news?"

"Not yet, but they will."

"Then how?"

Thomas' chin drops to his chest. "I've heard from both their parents this morning."

It takes no more than a second to process. "Wait, are you saying—"

"They're my patients." Thomas rubs at the bridge of his nose. "All of them."

"Oh, Thomas. I'm sorry." Then it hits me. We're not talking about three, but six. With seven more on the way. "In that case, there's more you need to know."

I fill him in on my latest encounter with Koschei, detailing the dream-scape fates of Hannah Abrams, Elizabeth Baker, and Janey Campbell as well as the three new faces. With each description, Thomas' face grows paler. I'm halfway through describing the Indian girl with pigtails, her face emblazoned on my memory, when Thomas' mobile goes off.

"Hello," Thomas answers. "Of course. Put her through."

"Yes."

A pause.

"Oh no."

Thomas sits with the phone on his ear for over a minute, only offering the occasional quick acknowledgement he is still listening, but doesn't say a word until he finally closes the conversation.

"I'm so sorry to hear that. I hope she gets better soon." Thomas glances up at me. "Yes. Of course. I'll be happy to see you this week. Just call the office in the morning."

Thomas returns the phone to the cradle and drops back into his armchair. "That was the Patel family. Their eight-year-old, Sribindu, went missing for a couple hours this morning. They found her balled up in their neighbors' treehouse an hour ago, unresponsive. They're in the ER right now." He looks over at me, defeated. "What do you think of the odds I receive a couple more calls like this today?"

"I'm… so sorry." I rise from the couch and circle to his side of the room. Sitting on the edge of his recliner, I take his hand, my strange revulsion thankfully taking a momentary break. "So, six girls so far, four of whom we know the identity of without a doubt. Any reason someone would be targeting your patients?"

"I've been racking my brain this morning trying to put it all together." He looks up at me, his anger fading into frustration and earnestness. As the cayenne and fresh soap mix in my mind, I squeeze his hand.

"Come up with anything? Any link between the girls? Besides the obvious?"

Thomas sighs. "Some of the specifics are kind of private, if you're okay with that."

"I've already walked around inside two of their minds, Thomas. I think privacy went out the window a long time ago."

"Heh." Thomas' half-laugh breaks the tension in the room or, at least, brings it down a notch. "Good point."

Nothing Thomas tells me is too over-the-top crazy, but I am struck at how different each girl's story ends up being.

He leads with Hannah Abrams, who suffers from garden variety ADHD, though between her meds and Thomas' coaching, she has apparently turned her grades around and is doing rather well.

Elizabeth Baker found out a few months back she's adopted and has been having a hard time processing the information. She's one of Thomas' newer patients, though with his help, she's already learning to accept the news and move on with her life.

Janey Campbell, who met Elizabeth in Thomas' waiting room, has an issue with stuttering and associated anxiety. Thomas and a local speech therapist are working together on this pair of issues, and Janey seems to be turning a corner.

Lastly, Sribindu Patel, the most damaged of the bunch, deals with early onset anorexia nervosa, but even she has managed to put on seven or eight pounds while working with Thomas.

The one thing they all seem to have in common? They sound to me like success stories, which begs one simple question.

Why is Thomas so overcome with guilt at what's happened to these girls, especially since everything indicates all of this has absolutely nothing to do with him?

The doorbell rings, and I don't know who appears more surprised, me or Thomas.

"You expecting someone?"

Thomas' turns his palms up and shrugs. "I figured it was for you." Rising from the couch, he mumbles, "Let's see who it is." Keeping his steps stealthy, he heads for the door and lets out an audible gasp when he peers through the peephole, followed by a few choice words I suspect he doesn't use in front of his patients. Glancing across his shoulder at me, he lets out a defeated sigh. "I'm sorry about this."

"Who is it?"

"Dr. Archer?" comes a woman's voice from the other side of the door. "Are you home?"

Strangely familiar, I can't quite place the voice, though the hair standing at attention on the back of my neck clearly associates it with trouble.

"Please, Dr. Archer. We know you're in there." A few seconds pass before the person beyond the door speaks again. "All right, Thomas. We'll do this your way, but I'm not going anywhere."

"Wait. She called you Thomas." I draw close to the door. "Who is that at the door?"

Thomas glances at me and lets out a long breath, his head dropping. "Look," he groans through the door, "I'll talk, but no cameras."

The thud of something heavy and metal being placed on the porch reverberates through the floor.

Crap. I remember now where I've heard that voice before.

Thomas opens the door. Resplendent in a crimson and silver top that accentuates her shoulder-length red hair, Katie Kaczynski grins from ear to ear.

"And what do you know?" She steps into the foyer, signaling her cameraman to stay on the porch. "Just the two people I've been wanting to talk to all day."

FEU D'ARTIFICE

atie Kaczynski steps between me and Thomas and heads straight for the living room like she owns the place. Thomas follows, his face already well past scarlet as he passes me.

"As if this day hasn't already been bad enough." Thomas circles and goes nose-to-nose with the reporter. "Why are you here? What do you want?"

"What I always want." She slinks down into Thomas' armchair before leaning forward and resting her chin on her interlaced fingers. "The story."

Her faux innocence does nothing but fan the flames of Thomas' anger. "You're not welcome here, and you know it."

I step into the room and clear my throat. "What's going on here, Thomas? When I told you about the reporter from the Bakers' house last night, I noticed you seemed a little put out. Do you... know her?"

"Only in the strictest sense, I suppose." Kaczynski's delighted eyes dart from me to Thomas and back. "Oh no. He didn't tell you?" She splays her fingers across her chest to evince sincerity. "What was it you always said, Thomas? About honesty being the backbone of any good relationship?"

"Katie," Thomas rumbles, the reek of vinegar making an encore appearance. "Not now."

"Thomas." My heart skips a beat. "I don't understand."

"Then allow me to spell it out for you," Kaczynski says. "I, Ms. Tejedor, am the ex-fiancé Thomas apparently never told you about." She swats Thomas' thigh. "Or, may I call you Mira, since we seem to have so many interests in common?"

My fingers ball into fists. "Actually, Ms. Kaczynski, I prefer to keep all dealings with the press strictly professional." My shoulders knot even as a smoldering fire builds in my cheeks. "Ms. Tejedor will be fine."

"Have it your way," Kaczynski answers with a noncommittal shrug. "Professional it is."

Thomas steps between us. "All right, Katie. Everyone's extremely uncomfortable now, and you still haven't told me what the hell you're doing here."

A shadow of Kaczynski's previous grin returns. "Three girls all go missing in the space of twenty-four hours." She glances over at me. "This one leads the cops to all three of them like some kind of psychic bloodhound." Her gaze shifts back to Thomas. "And every last one of them a patient of yours?" She leans back in the chair. "Where else do you think I'd be?"

"How could you know that?" Thomas asks.

Kaczynski smiles. "I *am* an investigative reporter, in case you've forgotten."

"You're actually enjoying this." Thomas' face shifts from a bright scarlet to a dull magenta. "The Katie I knew would never have stooped to this, especially not with someone she used to care about."

"Don't you dare play the sentimental card on me, Thomas." For the first time, something besides glee flows across Kaczynski's face. Something like barely kept rage. "You know how it ended with us. Which of us called it off."

Thomas glances in my direction. "Ancient history, as far as I'm concerned."

"Two years, babe." Kaczynski rockets from the recliner and heads for the kitchen. "To some of us, that's the blink of an eye."

Thomas races after her, both of them fuming, leaving me alone for a moment in the living room. The ceiling fan spinning quietly above my head provides an apt visual for my thoughts.

Thomas has an ex-fiancé? And of all people, her?

How does she know so much about me? About us?

And how in the hell does she know so much about what's going on with the girls? Investigative reporter, my ass.

Drowning out all the rest of the noise, however, is one simple fact that sits in the pit of my stomach like an ice-cold brick.

Thomas lied to me.

A lie of omission, yes, but I'm days from uprooting my entire life to move hundreds of miles to a new town and start building something with him. He knows all about Dominic, Isabella, Mom, Sarah Goode. Meanwhile, I apparently don't even rate so much as a passing reference to the incredibly attractive and successful woman he almost married two years ago. I'm sure Thomas has an explanation, but I'm not in the mood to hear it right now. I march to the door, catching Thomas' gaze across Kaczynski's shoulder from the kitchen, and let myself out before he can try and stop me. Seems he and Katie have a lot to catch up on, and at the moment, I'm not feeling a burning desire to chat with either of them.

I'm halfway to my car when the phone goes off. Thomas, no doubt, begging me not to leave. I slide the phone from my purse. One glance at the screen proves I couldn't have been more wrong.

"Hello?"

"Mira?" Caroline's penitent tone speaks volume. "Do you have a minute to talk?"

I can't help but laugh at the question. "You sure you want to talk to me?"

"We've danced this dance before, haven't we?" Caroline lets out a frustrated sigh. "Would it help if I said I was sorry?"

"Of course. Apology accepted. Now, what's up?" Though I appreciate the sentiment, I know Caroline Faircloth well enough to guess something has come along that scares her even more than I do. "I don't think you called simply to mend fences."

"Hang on. Anthony's coming." For a few seconds, all I hear are Caroline's quick, quiet, breaths in my ear. When she finally answers, her voice is just above a whisper. "We need to talk. It's… about the puppets."

The four words chill me to the core. "I'll be right there."

The cab drops me off at the Faircloth house. Caroline meets me in the front yard, her face pale and her eyes filled with fright.

"Thank you for coming, Mira."

"I'll always come when you need me, Caroline." I pull close. "And you know that." My gaze drops to the ground. "But you've got to trust me and stop freaking out every time life turns the heat up a notch."

"I didn't know what else to do." Caroline buries her face in her hands. "He's my little boy. You know I'd do anything to protect him."

"I do, Caroline. Remember, I'm more than intimately familiar with your devotion to your son." Keeping time with Mussorgsky's pounding melody, The Hut on Fowl's Legs races across my imagination with Baba Yaga cackling from the top eaves. "Still, you don't have to protect him from me. I'm on your side." Black pepper assaults my senses as Caroline's mind goes on the defensive, so I shift the conversation in a different direction. "So, I got here as fast as I could. Tell me. What's the deal with the puppets?"

Caroline's face goes a shade closer to white. "That's why I sent you away before."

"Because I mentioned the puppets in your son's head?"

"Come on." Caroline takes a step for the sidewalk. "Let's take a walk."

We're about halfway down the block when Caroline begins.

"You're not going to like this, but I know what the puppets are and, God help me, where they come from."

I work to keep my anger in check, putting myself in Caroline's shoes even as I imagine Isabella as the one whose fate hangs in the balance.

"Tell me everything."

"I told you before that Anthony has gone off on another classical Russian bender."

"Yeah. Me and Koschei the Deathless? We're on a first-name basis."

"But it's more than just *The Firebird*. He's watched that ballet on YouTube a bazillion times, but there's one he's been even more obsessed with the last few days."

Here it comes. "I'm guessing this is where the puppets come in?"

Caroline nods. "It's called *Petrushka*."

She does her best to tell me a story she's seen only bits of. A Russian traveling show called the Shrove-Tide Fair filled with every sort of folk imaginable. A charlatan magician with a magic cabinet occupied by three dancing puppets. The unrequited love of Petrushka for the beautiful Ballerina and of the Ballerina for the Moor.

At least I know now what to call the clown and the Arabian.

As Caroline soldiers on, her prediction I wouldn't like what I was going to hear proves true. Petrushka, who wears Thomas' face in my imagination as well as Anthony's, pathetically woos the aloof Ballerina while she busies herself trying to dance and trumpet her way into the Moor's heart. Petrushka interrupts their tryst in the Moor's room, enraging the Moor who chases him out into the fair where he slays Petrushka on the spot with a wickedly curved blade. The crowd reports the crime to the local constable, but when he brings the Charlatan to the scene of the murder, they find Petrushka's body is nothing but brightly colored clothing stuffed with straw. The Charlatan leaves the stage carrying the Petrushka puppet only to be haunted by the clown puppet's ghost as the ballet draws to a close.

Creepy wizards bringing puppets to life for the amusement of the paying crowd? Music and murder in equal parts? And all the while, a full Russian orchestra providing the soundtrack?

This Stravinsky guy is right up Anthony Faircloth's alley.

"I know it's scary, Caroline, but one thing is clear. Regardless of how or why, this is Anthony. I know it, and so do you."

Caroline's pale cheeks flush with life. "All I want to do is bury my head and wait for this to blow over."

"Caroline, I—"

"But," she continues, "I know I can't. Not after what happened last year and what he's already had to endure."

I wrap an arm around her shoulders. "What we all had to endure."

Caroline trembles like a baby bird beneath its mother's wing. "So, now what?"

"Now?" I turn us back in the direction of the house. "We go talk to Anthony."

~

Caroline heads to Anthony's room to try to crowbar him away from his video game console. When he hasn't been studying famous Russian ballets with which to torture me, he apparently has been knee deep in a new game called *The Age of Dragons*.

As if the kid needs any help coming up with scenarios and monsters that can kill me.

Funny thing? While it's abundantly clear *The Firebird* is all Anthony, the presence of Sterling and Bolger in this weird *Petrushka* revue is, at the very least, a joint venture. And if the Exhibition was a look deep inside Anthony Faircloth's neuroses, is this tale of three puppets and their not-so-nice master an insight into mine?

"Mira." Anthony steps into the living room. "Didn't think I'd be seeing you again."

"And a resounding hello to you as well, Mister Faircloth."

Anthony's brow furrows. "Mister Faircloth was my father."

Ah, Anthony. Direct as ever. "Your mom and I had a little tête-à-tête just now. Thought we'd bring you in on it." I pat the couch by me, and after a nod of approval from his mother, Anthony joins me.

"I'm guessing you've come back for a reason." Anthony studies my eyes. "What is it you need to know this time?"

Caroline pulls in a breath to discipline Anthony but at my outstretched hand, she holds her tongue and lets me handle the situation.

"*Petrushka*, Anthony. What can you tell me about *Petrushka*?"

"Why…" He looks to his mother. "Why do you ask?"

"There are three girls in trouble now, Anthony, and probably more to come. Every time I come in contact one of them, it's all *Firebird*, but when I touched your mind before, it was all charlatan wizards and dancing puppets. Sound familiar?"

Anthony's hands begin to shake. "It's happening again, isn't it? I'm going to go away." His eyes shoot back and forth like a sentenced criminal looking for a way out of the courtroom. "I don't want to go away again."

I gently grab Anthony by the jaw and pull his gaze to mine. "No one is going anywhere, Anthony."

Without warning, a barrage of hammering snare drums hits me like a million machine guns. My hands fly to my ears, though the action does little to muffle the cacophony that comes from another place entirely. Reality blurs around me. Despite myself, I laugh ruefully as my last words to Anthony replay in my mind.

"No one," I mutter as darkness overtakes me, "except me."

11

PETRUSHKA'S ROOM

I squeeze my eyes shut, trying to block out the fusillade of sound for what seems an eternity. Finally, mercifully, the snare drums halt their relentless pounding. In the imposing quiet, a fanfare of flute, trumpet, and xylophone sounds, followed again by silence. Daring to peek out from my self-imposed shell, my eyes open on a double doorway painted red, each side adorned with a black silhouette of the Egyptian god Anubis stretching the length of each door. Similar to when I appeared behind the blue curtains at the Russian fair, my body stands frozen as if directed by another soul, though this time, thank God, I retain control of my eyes.

A glance down reveals my body is clothed in the red, white, and pink of *Petrushka's* Ballerina while the pain in my toes suggests I stand *en pointe*. My arms held before me in ballet's first position, I can't so much as move a finger as rough hands encircle my waist and force me toward the door. My face stops less than an inch from the crimson and black surface, so close I can trace the grain.

"See." The harsh whisper hisses at my ear even as the speaker's beard tickles my cheek. The Charlatan, as Caroline called the blue-caped wizard from the Shrove-Tide Fair, must be the one who holds me fast. "Through the gap. See what you have chosen. Whom you have chosen."

I peer through the narrow space between the doors, as if I have a choice in the matter. As my vision focuses on the scene beyond, my blood freezes even as my heart breaks. On a floor of black onyx surrounded with icy spikes, Petrushka the clown languishes like a discarded rag doll beneath a cloudless starry sky, a lone mountain in the distance the only feature to the otherwise empty desolation. His pathetic state all but palpable, even the music ridicules him. The occasional short piano run or woodwind tweet give him life for the briefest of moments, only to again go silent, leaving the poor puppet sprawled helpless on the mirror-like stage.

Eventually, the clown pulls himself up from the ground and rushes around as if covered in ants. The music follows his graceless rage, growing wilder and wilder as Petrushka flails his arms in psychic agony. Then, in a moment of utter rebellion, he silently screams at a portrait of his puppet master. Muted trumpets screech out his anger as he leaps and swings impotently at the Charlatan's looming stare, the bottom limit of the frame just out of the puppet's clumsy reach.

Spent, Petrushka returns to the center of the stage and weeps. Wiping the tears from his eyes with a red-mittened hand, he slumps and crosses his arms over his heart. The accompanying duet of flute and piano chokes me with emotion, and as the clown begins to rhythmically strike himself in the head, my heart turns to ice. All in time with a mournful back and forth tune from the unseen orchestra, a kettledrum hit enunciates each pathetic blow, the mittens now serving as boxing gloves.

This bizarre self-abuse eventually stops, and Petrushka rises and meanders across the stage, the haphazard walk of a man sentenced to be always, irrevocably, alone. Then, as a lone piano sounds out the simple yet mournful melody from before, the Charlatan forces me through the door to face this pitiful clown who wears the face of the man I love.

Immediately, both Petrushka and the music shift gears. Frozen to the spot, I can't look away as the clown goes from aimless wandering to dancing, jumping, and cavorting around like a lovesick Looney Toon. The half-frown banished from his overjoyed face, he wastes our precious moments together leaping about the stage while I can do nothing but stand impotently and stare.

Seconds later, the Charlatan returns and pulls me back through the door. "You love this?" comes the same harsh whisper. "A pitiful buffoon?"

My tongue frozen in my mouth, I keep watch through the crack between the doors, helpless. Petrushka lies on the glassy floor, sobbing just beyond the closed portal. Briefly, he beats his head against the door and then falls away from my field of vision. The blaring trumpets sound again, leaving little doubt Petrushka again flails impotently at the portrait of the bearded stranger that holds me in his thrall. Then, with a resounding thud, the white-and-orange-clad clown collapses just beyond the door and doesn't move again.

"He has failed you, and he always will."

The guttural mumble echoes in my mind as the colors swirling around me resolve back into the Faircloth living room. Caroline and Thomas stare down on me from either side. Anthony lies next to me, still and pale. I reach for him, but his eyes flutter open before my fingertips reach his face.

"Mom..." He bursts into tears and launches into Caroline's arms. She stares across his shoulder at me, her gaze filled with the hopeless anger I always found there when we went through this the first time.

But this isn't the first time. That's over. The Exhibition explored the neuroses that made Anthony tick. This new place, whatever it is, seems intent on exploring mine.

∿

Perched in the passenger seat of Thomas' car, I can barely stand to look at him, a man I'm moving hundreds of miles to join without so much as a conversation or a diamond.

No wonder Mom is freaking out. If it were Isabella, I'd be having kittens.

I have no doubt there's some fantastic reason he failed to mention his previous engagement to Little Miss Perky and her perfectly coiffed head of red hair, but that doesn't make it sting any less. Lies of omission are still, after all, lies. Not to mention each glance from him sends chills through me, his every expression transformed in my mind to the twisted half-smile, half-frown of the clown. Still, Caroline didn't think I was in any shape to drive and so... here we are.

"I'm curious," Thomas asks after what seems like several days of silence. "Was it the puppets again?"

Wow. Speaking of lies of omission...

"Just two of them. The Ballerina, again played by yours truly, and... the clown." I pause, afraid speaking the name will make me lose my lunch all over the dash of Thomas' car. "Petrushka."

"Oh. The clown has a name now?"

Fresh-baked bread wafts through my senses, Thomas' concern shining through our little tiff. I review with him what I learned from Caroline about Stravinsky's second ballet, the three puppets, and their respective fates.

"And this time, you didn't recognize anyone?" Thomas glances over at me, and I do my best to repress a shudder as his mouth is twisted into a question mark reminiscent of his dreamworld doppelgänger. "None of the faces remind you of anyone in Anthony's life?"

"Not that I can tell." More lies. I taste bile as the clown stares at me through Thomas' eyes. If I told him that, it would kill him. "All I can say is we seem to be following the plot of Stravinsky's *Petrushka* ballet pretty closely."

"What's next, then?" he asks, returning his attention to the road.

"The third act." Sterling's face flashes across my mind's eye. "Apparently the Ballerina woos the Moor by dancing all fancy for him and showing off her crazy trumpet skills."

"Hm." Thomas chuckles. "So she basically wins him over by tooting her own horn?"

On any other day, his stupid joke would get a laugh out of me. Today is not that day.

"I'm not sure you'd call it winning, exactly. From what I understand, just as the Ballerina and the Moor are getting cozy, the clown, Petrushka, interrupts them. In the last act, the enraged Moor chases him down and kills him with a sword as the Ballerina looks on, helpless. *The Firebird*, at least, has a happy ending. *Petrushka*? Not so much."

Thomas' face darkens with puzzlement. "None of this makes sense. In one story you're cast the hero, in the other a victim, and neither story seems to have anything to do with the other."

"Except they have everything to do with each other, Thomas. Two ballets written by the same composer, set like little traps inside the minds of helpless children, and the main character of each? Me." My stomach does a somersault. "Even Anthony admits he's got to be the common thread here, but unless he's really got me snowed, he's as much in the dark as you and I."

"Don't worry." The cloud across Thomas' face breaks into a smile. "We'll figure all this craziness out."

"I'm sure we will, but what if we're too late?" The hairs on my neck stand on end. "What if one of these girls gets hurt?"

"Hey. I know it's scary, but I have faith in you. You've got this."

"Thanks." Thomas' confidence plucks at my heartstrings, and for a moment, I'm not angry or disgusted or anything but happy with him. One glance in his direction, however, and the clown's twisted face makes a grand reappearance along with a tsunami of confusing emotions.

"Now." Thomas' voice slides almost imperceptibly into psychologist mode. "Are you ready to talk about what's really bothering you?"

"You mean you and Katie 'Ray of Sunshine' from Channel 3 News?" I glance out the window at the passing trees. "We're going to have to talk about that, but I'm not sure if I'm up for that right—"

"It didn't end well with her." Thomas' knuckles go white on the wheel. "Some of it was her fault and some of it was mine, but the whole thing is a chapter of my life I've tried very hard to leave in the rearview mirror."

"But she seemed so nice..."

My sarcasm earns me a withering sidelong glance. "Katie's got her problems just like everybody else, but she's not a bad person. At least not the Katie I knew."

"That's noble, not throwing her under the bus. Good or bad, it usually takes two to tango. One of the toughest pills I had to swallow last year was the fact I was at least as guilty as Dominic for our marriage ending, if not more."

"Your point?"

I work to keep the tremor out of my voice. "No matter how much it sucked, how embarrassing it was to admit my part in the biggest disaster of my life, I still told you about Dominic. Probably way more than you wanted to know."

"And?"

"I guess I don't quite get why the fact you almost married a hot local newscaster a couple years back never came up. I mean, we've been seeing each other almost a year now."

Thomas turns right into his development, catching my gaze as he punches the accelerator. "You really want to know?"

Oh, crap. This is going to be bad. "Sure."

Thomas pulls into his driveway but leaves the motor running so we don't cook in the summer heat. "Katie and I never had any business being together in the first place, but that didn't stop us. It all started three years ago. A friend of mine from the gym invited me to a yoga class to help me 'work on my flexibility' after I pulled a muscle in my back. I ended up near the front of the class and—"

"Let me guess. You ended up asking out the hot yoga instructor."

"Things started out casual, but they got serious pretty fast. Six months in, and she wanted to start shopping for rings. She was thirty-one in Charlotte, North Carolina, and she was ready to settle down."

"And you weren't?"

"I thought I was." Thomas folds his hands across the steering wheel and leans forward as if in prayer. "I did it up right. Nice restaurant downtown. Corner table. Champagne."

I hold up a hand. "Got it." My cheeks, burning like twin suns, feel like they're about to melt my face. "So, how long were you two… engaged?"

"Grand total? Three and a half months. Everything was fine at first, great even, but as Katie went into full bridal mode, I realized with each passing day she was planning a wedding that was never going to happen."

"Cold feet?"

"Even simpler than that." Thomas looks over at me, meeting my gaze for the first time since he parked the car. "I realized she wasn't the one."

"Oh."

"I told her she could keep the ring. Even let her stay a few weeks till she could find a place that suited her needs."

"Wait." I almost keep my voice calm. Almost. "You two lived together?"

Thomas lets out a nervous chuckle. "Did she not hit my house earlier like the proverbial chicken come home to roost?"

Heat rises in my cheeks. "And you never bothered telling me any of this?"

"I'm not proud of how things went with Katie. I could have handled myself a lot better, and ever since then, I've done my best to leave it in the past. I knew we'd eventually have to talk about it, but since you only come down a couple days at a time, the timing just never seemed right." His lower lip trembles, revealing the emotion Dr. Thomas Archer works overtime to keep under wraps. "I wasn't trying to hide anything. I'm sorry, Mira."

Pungent guilt and the clean scent of earnestness. I'll let him off the hook, at least for now. After all, it's not like we don't have bigger fish to fry.

I take his hand. "I'm sorry, too."

He raises a quizzical eyebrow. "About what?"

"About jetting before. Seeing you and her together was a little more than I could handle. I had to get out of there before I said something I'd regret." It's my turn to get emotional. "Did you two get everything all straightened out?"

"For now." Thomas shakes his head. "I don't know how, but she knows all about the first three girls that have gone missing. No doubt she's got feelers out in the community, and as soon as she gets wind of the others, that's only going to fan the flames. If there's one thing about Katie I remember, it's that she knows how to go after a story."

Great. Won't be able to fly under the radar on this one. "She sure as hell knows about me. And Sterling."

Thomas rubs at his brow. "I just want to know how she put together the fact they were all clients of mine so fast."

"I don't know." I bite my lip. "She does sort of have an axe to grind, don't you think?"

"I suppose." Thomas' gaze drops. He's as defeated as I've seen him.

"What about Anthony?" My heart clutches in my chest. "Does she know about him?"

"He didn't come up, thank God. Still, Katie always used to play her cards pretty close to her chest, especially when there was a story involved."

Maybe Katie Kaczynski is just after the latest and greatest story in the greater metropolitan area, but I can't help but think there's more to this than just a journalist's drive.

"So," Thomas asks, "my turn?"

"Shoot."

"What's going on with you?" Thomas asks. "I know everything with Katie has really upset the apple cart, but you've been acting strangely for a couple days now."

"I'm just tired. You know how much these little ventures take out of me."

"You're sure that's all it is?"

"That's the life of Mira Tejedor, psychic extraordinaire." Wow. I really have no business calling Thomas out on the honesty front today. "The lumps just come with the territory."

"All right." Thomas turns off the ignition and steps out of the car. I sit there in silence for another few seconds, shame, anger, and fear all warring for top spot in my mind, before joining him.

"What are you thinking about for dinner?" I ask as we hit the front porch.

"Whatever you want." Thomas unlocks the door, steps inside, and heads straight for his bedroom. "I'm not feeling especially hungry tonight."

Standing alone in the foyer of a house I'd hoped to eventually call home, I curse the ability that allows me to literally smell the war of emotions going on just down the hall. Bad enough having to deal with my own in a fight, but to be buffeted by the other person's is a little much to ask.

Enough. No more feeling sorry for myself. I can't wish away the thing that makes me special any more than I can wish away the sunrise. At least six girls, not to mention Anthony himself, are counting on me and what I can do. Self-pity can wait. It's time get to work.

But first, a little idiot box to deaden the brain. I pour myself a glass of red, flop down on the couch, and flip on the TV just in time to catch a newscast that turns the blood in my veins to ice.

An Indian woman in a white doctor coat is being interviewed by, of all people, Katie Kaczynski. Her name, Vijaya Patel MD, is plastered across the banner at the bottom of the screen.

It takes all of two seconds to put it together.

The call Thomas took earlier. The girl, Sribindu. Her last name was Patel.

God, Charlotte is a small town.

"I can't imagine how it must feel as a medical professional to not be able to help your own child." Kaczynski keeps her game face on, but I recognize the glint in her eye. I have no doubt at some level she's trying to help, but like Thomas said, at the end of the day, this woman is all about getting her story. *"Has there been any change in her condition, Dr. Patel?"*

"Not as yet." Sribindu's mother, strong but clearly upset, considers her words carefully. *"My daughter and several other young girls admitted to this hospital all are suffering from what appears to be the same ailment. Whatever is happening to them has led them to wander from their homes and then left them comatose."*

"And you have no idea what could be causing it?"

"So far, every test we've performed on each of the girls has come back normal. Nothing we've found points to infection or poisoning or any of a hundred other causes, but we're still looking." She wipes away a tear. *"I can assure you of that."*

Kaczynski raises her eyebrows, her piercing gaze dripping concern. *"How many girls are involved thus far, if I may ask?"*

Dr. Patel's gaze drops to the ground. *"To date, six."*

"I suppose, then, the question the viewers would like answered most is what precautions they should take to keep their children safe."

"As best we can tell, my daughter just got up from her bed and walked right

out the front door. I don't know what we or anyone could have done differently." Dr. Patel looks directly into the camera. *"Watch your children. Don't let them out of your sight."*

The camera shifts back to Kaczynski. *"Good advice. Thank you, Dr. Patel."*

"There's going to be a panic if they're not careful."

My body freezes. I was so engrossed by the newscast, I didn't hear Thomas enter the room. "Do you blame them?"

"I suppose not." His voice resigned, Thomas trudges in my direction, the pungent moldy aroma of helplessness running roughshod across my senses. "Did my name come up?"

"Your ex is a reporter. She made a connection. That doesn't mean she thinks you're responsible for all this."

"Six girls from various walks of life with only one common thread between them." He rests his hand on my shoulder. Without hesitation, I take it in mine.

"You didn't do anything to these girls." I crane my neck around to look up at him. No clown. No crooked half-frown. Just Thomas, the man that stole my heart. "You're not to blame."

"Then why do I feel like I've failed them? Like all of this is my fault?"

I squeeze his hand. "We saved Anthony. We'll save them."

"And what about Anthony?" Thomas circles the couch and sits next to me. "We know he's involved in this somehow. What do we do?"

"If he's just another victim of whatever is happening, we save him too."

Thomas lowers his head. "And if that's not the case? If Anthony isn't as innocent in all this as he would lead us to believe?"

"I pray that isn't the case." I rest a hand on Thomas' knee. "I've been thinking about that since the first night the music returned."

"And?"

"I can't imagine why Anthony would be doing this, but if he is responsible and won't stop hurting people, then we're going to have to stop him."

12

PIQUÉ

Two days.

Isabella gets here in two days. The weekend is over, Thomas has to work both days, and my new apartment isn't even close to ready.

Not to mention Caroline isn't answering my calls.

It's every bit a Monday.

Before lunch seems a little early for a glass of wine, so I drown my sorrows in the largest latte my favorite coffee shop can put together. I glance down at the mug in my hand and laugh. When Thomas and I come here, Thomas always asks if I'm going to drink mine or swim in it. I glance over at our favorite table and imagine Thomas' trademark grin, an image that fortunately brings a smile for the first time in a couple of days.

Thomas is taking this so hard. To have one of your clients not doing well must take a toll, but to have several go down at once and know the only thing they all have in common is you? He must be heartbroken.

So far, this thing has hit six girls in total. Three I've met in person—Hannah Abrams, Elizabeth Baker, and Janey Campbell—and three I've only encountered inside a certain fourteen-year-old boy's skull—Sribindu Patel, Quanisha Young, and Colleen Day. The public at large may be oblivious to their identities, but newscasts about "six girls from every part of Charlotte hospitalized catatonic due to mystery illness" has set the city to a low simmer of panic.

96

Last night, Thomas guessed parents all over the city would flee the area with their children in tow, and sure enough, he was right. The second story on the morning news was filled with images of interstate highways crowded in every direction leading out of town.

And I thought the thing with Julianna Wagner caused a stir.

Everyone from doctors to parents to reporters is searching for answers. If Anthony's experience last fall is any indication, however, those answers are going to be a long time coming. I have no doubt the medical powers that be are doing the best they can, but they're not just barking up the wrong tree; they're exploring the wrong forest.

Halfway through my latte, I glance up at the barista who put together my morning jet fuel. She's been keeping a suspicious eye on me since I came in. She let me borrow her pen to sign the credit card receipt and didn't find it at all funny when I accidentally wrote her name at the bottom instead of mine. The fact that I did it in her own handwriting only made it worse.

No doubt about it. I need to get more sleep.

After being up most of the night, I didn't wake up till long after Thomas was gone and didn't get out of the house till almost ten. Still, I feel like I've been run over by a truck. Twice. I'd like to say it was concern over the girls that had me so on edge, or even nerves over Isabella moving down to Charlotte to join me, but truth be told, it was all about Thomas.

Last year, as I walked the Exhibition, the realm of Goldenberg and Schmuÿle was fashioned as much from my own mind as Anthony's. If this Russian fair, again populated with folks Anthony has never met, is the same, then Thomas being cast as Petrushka is all me.

What is it I'm trying to tell myself? What secret or not-so-secret message am I trying to get across? The maddening half-smile, half-frown of Petrushka the clown haunts my every waking moment. Like there's more than one side to this man I love. Does that represent some deep-seated suspicion, or is it merely a bunch of random neurons firing?

No. If last year's experience taught me anything, it's that there is nothing random when it comes to Anthony and me.

From inside my purse, my phone buzzes. Not surprisingly, it's Mom. Other than a few stolen minutes with Isabella, with everything that's been happening the last couple of days, I've barely said two words to her since Friday. She must be going into major withdrawal.

"Mom?"

"Mira, are you okay?"

"Why do you ask?"

"It's all over CNN. About the group of comatose girls in Charlotte. The whole thing sounded way too familiar. I figured you must be in the thick of it."

Great. We've made national news.

"Wait." A horrifying thought crosses my mind. "Did they mention me?"

"No, Mira. I was merely exercising a little Tejedor intuition. But in light of your question…"

Just like I'm sixteen again, I fill her in on everything that's gone down since Friday. Well, almost everything. She's already a bit dubious about me moving almost two states away to be with Thomas when we've been dating for less than a year. The possibility that my subconscious has cast him as a mythical buffoon is the last thing I should share.

"And the worst part? One of the local TV reporters has been all up in our business since pretty much the beginning." I'm halfway through this part when I realize I should have kept my mouth shut. "She even tracked me down at Thomas' place. It's a nightmare."

"She?" Mom is silent for all of two seconds. "What is it you aren't telling me?"

Dammit. Tejedor intuition giveth and Tejedor intuition taketh away.

"Now, Mom. Don't freak."

And then I tell her. Why did I ever think I could keep this from her?

"So." She takes a long breath. "You're moving Isabella hundreds of miles away from everyone and everything she knows so you can 'see what happens' with a man who's already proven he couldn't go the distance?"

"Hey. I just found out myself." I work to come up with something clever to say. As usual, where Mom is concerned, my scintillating wit fails. "And anyway, it's not like that."

"Mira—"

"Mom, you've met Thomas. You know he's a good guy." I attempt to banish Petrushka's twisted grimace from my mind's eye. "One of the best."

"Be that as it may, I've already had to watch you go through the agony of broken promises from a man that didn't deserve you. As your mother, I'd prefer if we could avoid an encore."

"Thomas isn't going to hurt me, Mom."

"We'll see, Mira." I can almost see Mom shaking her head through the phone. "Though I can't help but wonder if you're trying to convince me or yourself."

"Mom—"

"Hold on. Isabella wants to speak with you."

Chastised, I let out a simple "Thanks" and wait for my daughter to come on the line.

"Hi, Mami," comes my favorite voice after a few tense seconds. "I miss you."

"Morning, sweetie. Did you and Grandma have a good weekend?"

Isabella regales me with tales of pizza and ice cream and animated movies, and after a good five minutes of giggles, she asks a question that punches me square in the heart.

"So, Mami, are you ready for me?"

"Almost. The whole thing is kind of a work in progress."

Images of half-painted walls and uncarpeted floors flood my imagination. The contractor my landlord lined up quit halfway through the improvements, I'm guessing because he got a better offer. I got as much done as I could last week, but I was counting on me and Thomas having the entire weekend to get the place in shape.

Seems like someone had other plans.

"Mami?"

Kid's sharp. Can sense when I'm distracted even six hours away. "Sorry, honey. Mami's got a lot on her mind."

"You still want me to come this week, right?"

The faces of six other little girls flash through my mind. "I'm not sure, honey. We'll have to see. There's a lot going on here in Charlotte."

"Don't you miss me?"

Wow. Twist that knife. "Of course I do, honey."

"I love you, Mami." A mischievous pause. "Hey, can we get ice cream at that place we went last time I came to Charlotte?"

I can't help but laugh. "Yes, Isabella. I'll take you back there. Moose Tracks with chocolate sprinkles, right?"

"Yes," she squeals.

A moment later, Mom comes back on the line, her tone measured. Calm.

Always a dangerous sign.

"So, we'll be seeing you Wednesday around lunchtime?"

"If you think you can get Isabella out of bed early enough to pull that off."

Mom chuckles. "She hasn't stopped talking about you for days. I don't think she'll have any trouble waking up."

"Girl definitely knows what she wants."

"Same as her mother."

"Now, Mom…"

"Sorry, Mira. Gotta run. The microwave is burning the popcorn. Call you this week."

"Okay, Mom. Bye."

Unsure if she heard me, I press the End button and return the phone to my purse. Stella the barista continues to eye me like I'm about to pull a gun and hold up the place. I'm gathering my things to leave when my phone buzzes again.

This time, it's not Mom.

"Why, good morning, Detective Sterling. How can I—"

"Mira?" He sounds harried. "Where are you?"

"Down at Mugs on Park Road. What do you—"

"Don't move. I'll be there in five."

He's actually there in three. As he charges through the door, the paranoid barista nearly hits the deck.

"Come on, Mira." His eyes are wild. "We've got to go."

"What is it?"

"I'll explain on the way." Sterling rushes me to his police cruiser, the engine still running, and leaps into the driver's seat. As soon as we hit the road, it's full on lights and siren as we rocket up Park Road toward Uptown.

"What is it, Sterling?"

"It's the girls."

"At the hospital?" My heart clenches up in my chest. "What's happened to them?"

"They're on the roof," Sterling grunts. "All of them."

Driving like we're on the NASCAR track that lies a few miles north of here, Sterling whips through the neighborhood where Hannah Abrams lives, runs the red light at my favorite Starbucks, and somehow gets us to the hospital in under five minutes flat. We pull up right where the ambulances park, leave the car by the curb, and rush through the sliding glass doors that lead to the Emergency Room.

To call the scene controlled chaos would be generous. Security is everywhere, and people in scrubs are running around like it's the end of the world. Pungent sulfur, acrid onion, and sharp chlorine assault my senses as fear, desperation, and anxiety fly at me from every direction.

Sterling flashes his badge at the nearest security guard. "Detective Sterling, CMPD."

The guard raises a finger as he listens to the latest garbled message coming across the walkie-talkie at his hip and then turns to Sterling.

"You here to lend a hand?"

Sterling nods. "The girls you've got wandering around on the roof? I'm the detective in charge of the case." He gestures in my direction. "And this woman is likely the only person in the entire city that may be able to get through to them and get them down safely. Now, how quick can you get us up there?"

The guard hesitates for all of two seconds, his eyes flicking back and forth from Sterling to me, and then rushes for the door, motioning for us to follow with a curt, "Come on."

We weave through a maze of hallways, past the cafeteria on the main floor, and venture into the children's hospital at the other end of the building. The guard flashes his badge to a sensor on the wall, then loads us onto a service elevator and hits the button for the top floor.

"So." The guard gives me a frank up and down. "You some kind of crisis negotiator?"

I give him a thin smile. "Something like that."

Sterling intercedes. "Miss Tejedor is an expert in the type of illness these girls are experiencing. Without her aid, many of them would likely still be missing."

"What? Is she a psychic or something?" The guard gives me a second look, and as the glimmer of recognition hits his features, the elevator door opens and a robotic voice announces we have reached our destination. "Wait, you're that—"

"Yep. That's me." I brush past him and head for a door marked "Stairs" with Sterling close on my heels. "Get us up to the roof before any of the girls jump and maybe I'll read your palm."

The guard wisely shuts his trap and heads for a door at the end of a hallway. As he flips through what looks like a collection of every key in the greater Charlotte area, I can't help but wonder how the hell a bunch of middle-schoolers managed to sneak past all the security and locked doors and get onto the roof. The how can wait, though. For now, the only important is getting them all down in one piece.

One short flight of stairs later, Sterling, the guard, and I end up behind a metal door that clearly leads outside. The temperature in the stairwell is a good twenty degrees higher than inside the hospital and daylight pours in around the door's edges.

"What now?" the guard asks.

Sterling steps forward. "I'll take point." He glances in my direction and positions himself behind the door. "Mira, with me." Opening the door a crack, he peers out, allowing a sliver of blinding sunlight to cut the dim of the stairwell. "Ready?"

Silently, he pushes the door open and steps through with me in tow. The June air is stifling, and the heat coming off the dark surface cooks my feet straight through my flats. Only about a third of the roof is visible from our vantage point, the rest of the view blocked by four large air conditioning units that bisect the top of the building. Each of the two corners I can see is occupied by either hospital security or police. The far pair pores over some sort of blueprint while the near pair is watching something just out of my line of sight and sweating bullets.

Not certain what I expected, but if it was all chaos down below, up here it's eerily quiet with nothing but the croaking of a crow overhead and the steady drone of the fans to break the stillness.

Sterling heads for the nearer pair of guards with me close behind and again flashes his badge. "CMPD. What have we got?"

"Several potential jumpers," the female guard answers as she peers around the corner of the nearest air conditioning unit. "All young girls."

"From at least three different floors of the hospital," the second guard adds. "It's damn weird, Detective. As I understand it, all of them were pretty much comatose. Then, all at once, the whole bunch bolted from their rooms and headed straight for the stairs to the roof. Set off every alarm in the place."

I step in close and keep my voice low. "Are they okay?"

"Well, nobody's jumped." The female guard shoots another glance around the corner and wipes the sweat from her chestnut brow. "At least not yet."

"Where are the parents?" Sterling asks. "They've got to be out of their minds with worry."

"We're gathering all the families together in a waiting room on eleven. Only police, security, a crisis negotiator, and one of the floor nurses are allowed up here. We sent everybody else away when the girls all started edging toward the brink."

"In that case, it's time for me to get to work." I take a single step forward, and the second guard puffs up to his full five-foot-eight, ready to stop me.

The second guard holds up a hand. "Now, hold on there just a—"

"Let her go," Sterling grunts. "She knows what she's doing."

The guards both eye me suspiciously for a moment before separating to let me pass. Cautiously, I step around the end of the wall of air conditioning units and into the sun. My toes curl in my shoes at what I find on the other side.

At the edge of the roof on a narrow ledge, Sribindu Patel stands facing us with her back to oblivion. A nurse in navy scrubs keeps a safe distance, but even from here, the heaving of her shoulders is obvious. She's crying, and I can't say I blame her. Sribindu, her dark, straight hair mussed from lying in a hospital bed, stares blankly, her gaze fixed on nothing in particular. That is until I take another step and fully enter her field of view. Screaming, she takes a half step backward.

"No," the nurse and I shout in unison as I step back around the corner and out of sight.

"The Patel girl is on the edge of the roof just around the corner. Looked like she was in some kind of trance. She got one glimpse of me and almost jumped." I lock gazes with Sterling. "What the hell am I supposed to do if I can't even go to them?"

"I don't know." Sterling's shoulders rise in a frustrated shrug. "The academy didn't cover catatonic girls under the influence of psychic badness. Hell, just the fact that there are six of them makes this all but impossible."

"Six?" the female guard asks, incredulous. "Sorry to burst your bubble, Detective, but at last count, there were ten of them up here."

13

KHOROVOD

"Ten?" I flick my gaze in Sterling's direction. "Dammit. That's four more."

But not thirteen. Not yet.

I scour my scalp with all ten fingernails, trying to banish the headache already brewing at the ends of my neurons. "So, how do we play this?"

"What are you going to do?" the female guard asks. "We've already got one of the nurses and a crisis negotiator trying to talk them down."

"That's not going to work," I groan, shaking my head. "These girls? They're not conscious. It's like trying to talk logic to a sleepwalker."

"Not conscious?" she asks. "I don't understand."

Before I can answer, both of their walkie-talkies go off, and a female voice with a Manhattan accent sounds from both speakers. "Something's changed. The girls have started chanting in unison like—" Her words are cut off by a loud squelch. When the voice returns, the fear in her voice is palpable. "This is the freakiest thing I've ever seen."

"Who is that?" I ask.

"The crisis negotiator," the female guard answers. "Why?"

"Ask her what they're saying." When she hesitates, I add, "Do it."

The guard waits another second and then speaks my question into her walkie-talkie.

"A single word," comes the voice from the speaker. "Over and over."

"What is it?" My hands ball into fists. "What is the word?"

"A name," the negotiator answers. "Here. Listen."

At first, all I hear is static. Then, the quiet voice of one of the girls comes across the radio frequency, just audible above the drone of the fans.

"Ivanovna. Ivanovna. Ivanovna..."

My breath catches as my face breaks out in a cold sweat.

"Mira," Sterling asks. "Are you all right?"

"I'll be fine." It's my turn to wipe the sweat from my brow. "Just need a minute."

He pulls close. "Who or what is... Ivanovna?"

"Believe it or not, I am." I meet his worried gaze. "At least as far as these girls are concerned."

"You?" the male guard asks. "What does that mean? What do you know that we don't?"

I shake my head. "Nowhere nearly enough."

I find a relatively cool spot in the shade of the wall of air conditioning units and hunker down. Sterling stands over me, a dubious look on his face.

"Sterling." I take a breath in an attempt to banish the tremor from my voice. "No matter what happens, don't let me move from this spot. Got it?"

"I don't understand," Sterling rumbles as concern fills my mind, the warm baked bread scent a bit more pumpernickel than I'm used to. "Why would you—"

"I don't know, but think about it. Whatever or whoever is doing this has the power to send ten children to the roof of an eleven-story building to dance on a knife's edge. I may be more older and more experienced than these poor girls, but if the same thing happens to me, I'd like to know I have a backup plan."

"Good point." Sterling considers for a moment. "In fact, I've got an idea." He slips a pair of handcuffs from inside his jacket and shackles me to a sturdy looking pipe. "Can you at least tell me what it is you think you're about to do?"

"The girls are calling for me, but when I so much as showed my face, Sribindu Patel nearly took a header off the side of the building."

"But they're calling out for you, right?" Sterling strokes his strong chin. "What am I missing?"

"Whoever or whatever has brought them up here doesn't want Mira Tejedor." I point to my temple. "They want Ivanovna."

Sterling lets out a quiet harrumph. "And you seriously think giving whoever it is what they want is a good idea?"

"I don't think we have any choice." I pull in a deep breath and begin to clear my mind. "This whole thing is clearly a game to get me to come back to Koschei's garden." I bite my lip till it hurts, getting a good feel of reality before venturing back into the world of dream. "And if I don't get in there soon, I have a bad feeling these girls are going to start jumping."

The female guard rushes over. "Whatever you're going to do, do it. All of the girls just took half a step toward the edge."

"Dammit." I glare into the blue Carolina sky as if staring down my invisible opponent. "Give me a sec." I rest my hands in my lap and let my eyes slide closed.

"So, once you're under, what are you going to do?"

"Unless I miss my guess," I whisper, "some gardening."

It doesn't take long. I've barely taken three breaths of stagnant air before the music washes over me, the melody overpowering the loud hum of the fans.

"Here it comes, Sterling. Here it—"

A blink, and I'm back in Koschei's garden.

And I'm not alone.

Ten girls in flowing white dresses cower en masse at the forest's edge, all of them screaming and pointing in my direction. I raise a hand to let them know they have nothing to fear from me. A moment later, a low growl to my rear makes it clear it's not me they're afraid of. With instinct beyond any I possess in the real world, I dive to the grassy forest floor and roll to one side. A triple jet of flame shoots across my body so close, it singes my clothes, my hair, the skin of my shoulder.

God, everything in this place feels so real.

Monstrous footfalls pound in my direction. I flip onto my back, my heart freezing at the sight of my latest attacker. Three-headed and angry, an honest-to-God dragon the size of a large SUV bears down on me like a freight train. I roll to one side, my elbow striking the edge of the *bukavac* pool, and narrowly avoid the dragon's clawed stomp. As it charges past me, the girls scream as one, each of them frozen in fear.

"Stop," I command the three-headed serpent. "Your master wanted me to return to this place, and now I'm here."

The dragon halts in its tracks, its left head craning around to peer at me with one yellow eye. If I didn't know better, I'd swear the thing was smiling.

"In a place far from here, these girls face true danger, life-threatening peril, but here?" My eyes narrow as the dragon meets my gaze. "Koschei may be one crafty son of a bitch, but in our previous encounters, I believe he let fly one fact too many. He needs these girls, and three more to boot, before he can do whatever it is he's set out to do."

The dragon scrapes at the ground with its front foot, its six-inch claws leaving deep furrows in the earth. It opens one of its three mouths as if to speak and instinct kicks in again as fire erupts from its gaping maw. Chancing another encounter with the horned toad-beasts from before, I roll across the cracked stone edge of the *bukavac* pool and dive beneath the silty water. Facedown, I can't see the fire, but the water across my back goes from tepid to boiling in seconds. Kicking my legs and pushing my hands through the opaque water, I force myself across the decrepit pool, not daring to come up for air. Why I would possibly need air in a dream is beyond my understanding, but as always, I have to obey the laws of physics here, even when my enemies seem able to ignore them at their whim.

I reach the other wall, my fingers blindly brushing the pool's rough stone border. I allow my feet to sink to the bottom and force them through the muck to the stone floor. My lungs burning, I crouch in the shallow water and leap from the pool. Scrambling across the granite and marble edge, narrowly avoiding another triple jet of flame, I fall to the trampled grass of the garden floor.

One thing is clear. Running isn't going to work this time. There's simply nowhere to go.

I summon Ivanovna's bow as the old adage about the best defense being a good offense ricochets through my skull. The quiver suddenly at my back, I clamber to my feet and draw an arrow only to find the dragon gone.

"Ivanovna," one of the girls shouts. "Look out!" One glance at their ten skyward gazes lets me know exactly where it's gone.

Eclipsing the sun, the three-headed dragon dives at me from a crystal blue sky, each of its three enormous mouths open and lined with jagged teeth. I let fly my drawn arrow and dive to one side. Instead of the satisfying *thunk* of arrow sinking into flesh, a resounding clang, like stone impacting metal, fills the air as my arrow shatters against the monster's hide. The dragon hits the spot where I was standing half a second ago and coils like a trio of snakes ready to strike. Backpedaling, I draw a second arrow, aim for one of the thing's six eyes, and let fly.

No such luck. The arrow glances off the monster's chest and flips end over end into the forest edge. Before I can draw a third, the dragon is upon me, rushing me like an enraged bull. I narrowly evade two of its gnashing jaws as it rockets past.

It's getting closer every time, and I won't be able to keep this up forever.

"Save us, Ivanovna," comes a shout from one of the girls I don't recognize. "Save us."

"I'm trying." I take a step back as the creature rounds for another run, knowing that in the long run, I will eventually grow tired, this monster will win, and I will die.

One thing is clear. It's me that Koschei wants to kill, not the children he has so carefully chosen for his enigmatic plans.

And that's when it hits me.

I can't save the girls, but maybe they can save me.

And in doing so, maybe they can save us all.

"All of you." I wave frantically. "Come to me!"

The dragon, poised to charge, halts in its tracks.

"Hurry," I shout. "The dragon won't hurt you."

The girls pause for another moment, and then, led by Hannah Abrams, they rush two-by-two in my direction. Each bearing a golden apple from the bent tree, they surround me, most of them trembling despite the ambient warmth.

"So, Dragon, your master may not care about my fate, but he needs these girls alive, at least for the moment. I can't imagine he'd be too pleased with you if you barbecued one of them."

"There are always more fish in the sea, Ivanovna."

I whip my head to the left to find Koschei the Deathless standing at the mouth to his palace. "Explain yourself, Koschei. You have gone to significant trouble to get me back here, only to sic your pet on me?"

"Ah." Koschei gestures in the direction of the three-headed beast. "You've had the pleasure of meeting my little *zmej*."

"Little?" Maybe a little banter will give me a second to think. "Thing's the size of a small bus."

"She was once small enough to sit in my lap." Koschei crosses the short drawbridge and steps out onto the grass of his garden. I swear the blades of green wilt at his every step. "My, what a healthy diet and a little love can accomplish."

"Love." I gesture to the girls surrounding me like linemen protecting their quarterback. "If you knew the first thing about love, these poor girls wouldn't be separated from their families."

"And yet you are the one that has interposed them between your tender flesh and my little pet with all its hungry mouths. Who is the monster now, Ivanovna?"

"Whatever it is you have planned behind that mask of yours, you can't do it without these girls. They may be my salvation for the moment, but know one thing. No matter what it takes, I will stop you and save them right back."

"Whatever it takes?" Koschei throws his head back and laughs. "You slid a blade between your ribs the last time you faced an impossible dilemma and nearly died as a result. Would you dare risk oblivion a second time?"

"I'm here." The words escape my lips before I can rein them in. "Aren't I?"

"Yes, Ivanovna." Koschei's face grows pensive for a moment. "Yes, you are."

Time for a calculated risk. "Anthony, if you can hear me, listen. Let these girls go. They've done nothing to you, but believe me, they are suffering just like you suffered last year. And their parents? Do you want them to experience what your mother went through when you were gone?"

"Silence." Anger flashes in his eyes. "Do not speak that name here."

Apparently, I've struck a nerve. "Why, Anthony? Because it's the truth? Because beneath this mask of death and destruction is nothing but the same terrified kid I dragged out of his own mind nine months ago?"

I step out from between the girls and move in Koschei's direction. In the distance, the dragon snorts black smoke from three pairs of nostrils, but doesn't move an inch. Koschei, on the other hand, retreats into the mouth of his ghastly abode.

"Don't assume, Ivanovna, that you know the heart that beats in this breast or that these girls are nearly as safe as you might believe." He gestures behind me. "They may have nothing to fear from the *zmej* at the moment, but from themselves…"

I spin around, Koschei and his three-headed guard dog for the moment forgotten, and find exactly what I feared. The ten girls now stand atop the cool granite and marble of the pool's edge like numbers along the face of a clock. Each of them faces outward, arms stretched out to their sides, eyes closed. A wild wind whips through flowing white dresses and hair, a wind no doubt echoed on a hospital rooftop far away. Behind each of them, a *bukavac* rests in the brown muck. With mouths closed and horns directed at the small of each girls back, they wait.

"At my slightest whisper, my merest whim, these children will gladly fall upon the raised horns of destiny. Would you have their deaths on your conscience, Ivanovna? Their pain." He mimes wiping away a tear. "The agony of their families?"

"Stop this, Anthony."

The eyes of the Deathless narrow almost imperceptibly. "I am Koschei." He claps his hands together and each of the girls take a single step back toward the pool. "Say it."

A quick scan reveals most of the girls stand with one heel over the water. Not one of them can afford another step toward the muck and monsters, and unless I miss my guess, there are ten girls atop an eleven-story hospital flirting with the abyss as well. "Very well. Stop this... Koschei."

"Better." His hands go to his sides with a flourish, and the girls all inch back onto the grass. The grand gesture is clearly a distraction. I shift my head to the right and find the *zmej* creeping along the forest edge in my direction.

"Call off your pet, Koschei. You worked very hard to get me here, and I suspect if you truly wanted me dead, the *bukavacs* or *skrzaks* or whatever else you have hidden in your little garden of insanity would have struck by now." I walk to the golden apple tree and take a seat on the flat rock that rests beneath its outstretched branches. "I'm guessing you wanted to talk, so let's talk."

"I believe each of us has already said what we came to say, would you not agree?"

"And yet, here I am, still alive, sitting in a garden of your imagining. Meanwhile, you stand there holding every card, and yet, you continue the conversation." I cross my arms and tilt my head to one side. "Some people, it seems, never tire of hearing their own voice."

"I would not be so flippant, Ivanovna. Do not forget where you are."

"And where would that be?"

For the first time, Koschei remains silent. No quick retort. No subtle menace. Just thoughtful silence.

"If you will not release these girls," I whisper, "at least let me lead them back to their beds so they can rest."

"They are mine." Koschei's hands ball into fists at his sides. "Forget that at your peril."

"Emblazoned on my memory." I turn in the direction of the pool and find the girl who shares a face with Hannah Abrams. "Time to go back to sleep."

"Sleep," she mutters, and the other nine all follow suit. The back-and-forth murmuring fills the air and even my eyes begin to grow heavy at the hypnotic chanting. At the forest edge, the *zmej* lowers itself to the ground and lets out a trio of blazing yawns. As if sleepwalking, the ten girls march single-file back into the mouth of Koschei's palace. The Deathless surveys each as they meander past and as the last passes into darkness, he shoots me one last look, his previous air of malice making a brief reappearance.

"And then, there were three." With that, he vanishes into the purple incandescence and shadow. As always, the drawbridge remains arrogantly open, as if he dares me to follow.

But I've already brought ten girls back from the edge of oblivion, indirectly defeated an invincible dragon, and somehow managed to verbally outmaneuver the mastermind behind the whole thing.

Time to wake up and find out what's happening back in the real world.

Not to mention, I'm in desperate need of a drink.

BRISÉ

"Mira?" I've never been so glad to hear Sterling's baritone in my entire life. "Are you all right?"

"The girls." My voice sounds like a half-strangled *bukavac.* "Are they..."

"They're fine." My clearing vision attempts to focus on the broad-shouldered shadow standing over me. "In fact, they're all here."

My eyes shift to Hannah Abrams lying unconscious with her back to the metal side of the air conditioning unit. Past her, a girl I don't recognize rests on her side, pale, her breathing shallow. My vision won't focus any farther than that, but the jumble of blurry figures all in a line must be the remaining eight.

"What happened?" I ask. "How did you get them down?"

Sterling rests a warm hand on my shoulder. "It was looking pretty bad for a minute there. All ten girls stood there like statues for the longest time. Then, as if they all heard the same silent command, all of them took a step forward. I was certain we were going to lose them. There they waited on the edge of the building for almost an hour, and then, just like the first time, all ten stepped backward and sat down on the roof as if nothing had happened."

"They all came down." I breathe a sigh of relief and inhale sharply. "Wait. They're safe now, but did they... wake up?"

"If only." Sterling reaches across me, releases my wrist from the handcuffs, and helps me sit up. "For a bunch of escape artists that were fast enough to evade hospital security and make it to the roof of this place, they ended up tottering around like a bunch of sleepwalkers. It was like herding cats, but we somehow managed to get them all to settle down here in the shade while we wait for reinforcements to arrive."

My vision continues to clear. Down the line and working with Janey Campbell, the female guard from before shoots me a puzzled smile before returning her attention to the hyperventilating girl at her side. The other guard sits at the end of the line, apparently poised to tackle any girl who so much as moves. Blue-clad medics rush from patient to patient, while at the stairwell leading back down into the hospital, a woman who is no doubt the crisis negotiator talks on her cell phone. Even through my blurred vision, the tremor in her hands is obvious.

Emotions waft over me as my mind awakens from its latest sojourn in the world of dream. Chlorine anxiety. Freshly baked concern. An undercurrent of sea mist connoting relief. Weird thing? The storm of feelings is completely centered around the adults. But the girls?

"Something strange is going on, Sterling. The girls, it's like they're not here."

"What?"

"Everybody walking on this planet gives off a psychic fingerprint." I glance at the guard. "She hits me like the chlorine off a swimming pool."

Sterling raises an eyebrow. "And me?"

"You really want to know?" My single chuckle flares the headache brewing above my left eye. "You're all cherry pie and soap." I try to maintain my smile. "Nice to know you still care."

The color rises in the dark skin of Sterling's cheeks. "So, what do you get from the girls?"

"That's just it. Even with my eyes closed, I can always at least feel when another person is around. These girls? They're invisible to me." I reach out for Hannah Abrams' hand, wanting to test a theory, but pull up short at the last second. I barely made it out of Koschei's garden alive this last time and don't have anywhere near the energy required to withstand another walk on the wild side.

"Any idea what that means?" Sterling asks.

"An idea, yes, though it's a stretch." A groan escapes me as I stretch my aching back. "Both this year and last, every time I've ventured to wherever it is all the insanity happens, the only abilities I've possessed are those afforded me by my role there."

Sterling raises an eyebrow. "A role that was always dictated by young Mr. Faircloth?"

"More or less, though my own understanding of the character I'm portraying has always been a factor as well. The first time, along the Exhibition, I took the role of storyteller; in Koschei's realm, the Princess Ivanovna; at the Shrove-Tide Fair, the Ballerina. Whether speaking, fighting, or dancing my way into and out of each challenge, there's been one commonality no matter the setting."

"And that would be?"

"My natural sense of others' emotions doesn't work there. The other five senses work, so to speak, but in the realm of the mind, I become another."

"Another?"

"Mira Tejedor and all she can do takes a back seat, and I think I've figured out why."

"Hit me. It can't be any weirder than everything else that's happened this week."

"I always figured when I walked the Exhibition, that Anthony was dampening my senses or something, but now I think it's actually that when I'm on the other side, I'm no longer physically in my own head-space. What if the girls are the same?"

Understanding blossoms in Sterling's eyes. "You don't think they've just been put under. You think they've been… taken."

"No different than if someone broke into their house and carried them out the front door." I peer down the line at the girls' glazed over faces. My fingers curl into fists. "Their own legs may have done the walking, but in every way that counts, these children have been abducted."

"So, if this is truly a kidnapping case, who's the kidnapper? You can't really think it's the boy."

"At the very least, Anthony is somehow involved. I mean, ten comatose children tortured in their minds by demons and creatures from a Russian ballet? It's practically a smoking gun covered in fingerprints." A tear courses down Hannah Abrams' otherwise placid face, and my heart grows cold. "The only question now is why."

Over the next half hour, an army of medics hits the roof and descends upon the ten unconscious victims. Five receive IV fluids, and all ten get their feet bandaged for burns sustained from walking barefoot across the scorching roof. The sun is directly overhead by the time the last stretcher disappears down the stairs, leaving Sterling and me roasting with the crisis negotiator.

"That was the strangest thing I've ever seen." The negotiator kneels next to me. Looking like she's been through the wringer, she's sweated right through her navy pantsuit, and her curly brown hair lies drenched against her scalp. I have no doubt I look even worse. "How in the world did you get those girls to come down from the ledge?"

"A little something I learned way back in grad school." I scramble to my feet, finally clearheaded enough to stand without falling over. "I met them where they were."

"Oh." I see her next question coming a mile away. "Is it true, then? Are you really a psychic?" She stares at me like a twelve-year-old looks at a mall Santa Claus—told by everyone not to believe and yet desperate to do just that. "Is that even possible?"

I reach out for her nametag and flip it around. "Melinda Frank. Tell me. Where'd you go to school?"

"Columbia University."

"And no doubt you earned some kind of advanced degree and have a ton of experience to land a job like the one you have, right?"

"I have a Masters in Psychology." Her brow furrows. "And ten years on the force."

"And with all of that school and time in service under your belt, can you come up with any other logical explanation for what you just saw?"

Her gaze drops. "I suppose not."

I offer what is at best a weary smile. "Welcome to my world."

It takes almost four hours, but by the time the dinner carts start appearing for the kids on the ward who are still conscious, the hospital has managed to sequester all the girls involved on one end of one floor. Hospital security is posted at either end of the ten adjacent rooms, and a call from Sterling even has one of Charlotte's finest on site. Fortunately, the windows don't open and the rooms have been stripped down as much as possible to ensure the girls can't hurt themselves. Each of them is required to have a family member present at all times until the hospital can call in enough sitters.

I have no doubt these measures are as extreme as anything the hospital has ever done.

Still, it's not enough. Not by a mile.

Fortunately, my theory that Anthony's abilities can kill has never been proven, but I've felt firsthand what the power of his young mind can do. A little push from that brain of his sent his sister to the hospital last year, and on more than one occasion, it's reached me all the way across town. Hell, Veronica Sayles still sits on a ventilator in a nursing home on the south end of Charlotte after crossing him on his own turf. I can't imagine he is capable of killing anyone, at least not on purpose. That being said, the evidence of his involvement in this is undeniable, and the fact that all the girls are physically all right for the moment means one thing and one thing only: Anthony and whatever is making him do these things don't want to play right now.

Collectively back to their near-comatose state but otherwise deemed medically stable, the girls all rest comfortably in their beds, basically sleeping if the doctors are on target with their assessment. Thanks to Sterling, I've been able to interview each of the families. I started with the Abrams and Baker families since we'd already met and then progressed through the rest, most of whom had never heard of me before. Though some of the girls disappeared from their homes while others were found in their beds too terrified to move, there is one common factor in all of the cases.

Fear.

And now, one last interview.

Sribindu's mother, who strikes me as whip smart, has a few theories. As an accomplished nephrologist, psychiatry isn't her forte, but without knowing all I know about the real cause of the girls' shared state, her ideas are pretty sound. We discuss collective hysteria, mass psychogenic illness, and dissociative fugue states, all logical theories if you haven't walked the minds of the girls involved and already had to deal with immortal demons, horned monsters, and three-headed dragons, all choreographed to a Stravinsky soundtrack.

"Anything else you'd like to add?" Sterling asks Dr. Patel. "Anything that might shed some light on the subject?"

"Not that I can think of." She grabs a tissue and wipes away a tear. "Sribindu was doing so well after losing her father last year. She was gaining weight, making friends again, even seemed happy." She chokes back a sob. "And now this. All the work she and Dr. Archer have done. Now she's gone, and nobody can tell me why."

"Dr. Thomas Archer?" Sterling shoots me a questioning glance.

"You know him?" Dr. Patel asks.

Sterling's eyes narrow almost imperceptibly. "I'm familiar with his work."

"He's been so good to Sribindu. And so heartbroken when I spoke to him yesterday."

Sterling purses his lips. "I'm certain he was." He offers her his card, as he did for all the other family members. "If you think of anything else that might help, please give me a call."

"Thank you for speaking with us." I give Dr. Patel's hand a firm shake and follow Sterling to the door and out into the hallway. Sterling speaks briefly with the police officer on the scene, then shows me to the elevator and presses the down button.

"So, when were you going to tell me?" he asks as the doors slide shut.

My gaze doesn't budge from a long scratch on the elevator's faux wood floor. "Tell you what?"

"That most of the victims have undergone therapy with your boyfriend."

My cheeks grow warm. "Thomas didn't do anything to these girls."

Sterling shakes his head. "You told me all about the whole *Firebird* thing and your suspicions about Anthony, but couldn't be bothered to let me in on a little fact like that?"

"I didn't want you to draw the wrong conclusions. Thomas is just as worried as we are about these children."

"Archer is the only real-world link between a bunch of kids in the hospital all suffering from the same—what did Dr. Patel call it—'dissociative fugue' state? Pretty big coincidence, don't you think, especially considering who else is among his clientele?"

The doors open on the first floor. Sterling and I each hold our silence until we're back to his police cruiser, though the anger wafting off him hits me harder with his every step. A thunderstorm is brewing in his mind, and I have a feeling I'm about to get soaked.

"Just so I've got this straight." Sterling barely has us out of the parking deck before he starts the third degree. "You've known this whole time these girls were Archer's clients?"

"He told me yesterday, after the count went from three to six. As you can imagine, most of the parents called to check in." As we pull to a stop at a red light, Sterling and I lock gazes. "You have to believe me. He's crushed by all of this."

"Wait." A connection forms in Sterling's eyes. "Have you two already visited the Faircloth house in reference to this matter?"

My teeth clench involuntarily. "Yes."

"Another little fact that you conveniently left out?"

"Look. Anthony has said he's innocent of all this from the very beginning. Nothing Thomas has seen in Anthony gives us a clue as to any change in his behavior."

"But you yourself said you were sure the kid was involved and even more sure that he likely wasn't acting on his own."

Angry tears sting the corner of my eyes. "You think Thomas Archer, who's been helping the troubled children of the greater Charlotte area for over a decade, would have anything to do with something like this?"

"Sorry, Mira. My job is to examine facts and draw connections. You tell me the fact that most of the ten girls we just pulled off that roof having the same psychologist doesn't make you bat an eyelash, and I won't mention it again."

"It's not Thomas." I look away. "It can't be."

"You're awfully quick to jump to his defense, Mira. Look, I know you two are tight, but you've been seeing him less than a year. How well do you really know him?"

"With what I do for a living, getting to know someone pretty quickly just comes with the territory." I do everything in my power not to cringe as the clown's crooked half-smile, half-frown encroaches on my thoughts. "Do you think I'd leave Georgetown and uproot my daughter's life if I wasn't sure I was doing the right thing?"

"You sounded none too sure the last time we discussed the subject." Sterling clears his throat and turns his eyes back to the road. "Not to mention, love can cloud anyone's judgment."

The fire in my cheeks goes white hot. "This isn't Thomas. I'd bet my life on it."

And yet, I'd be lying if I said the possibility Thomas is somehow involved, even unwittingly, hadn't crossed my mind. While it's possible Anthony may have run into each of these girls in Thomas' waiting room, that still doesn't answer the question of why he would do something like this. That being said, one fact has been on my mind since my latest trip to Koschei's garden.

These girls' minds all seem to be trapped in a nightmare version of Stravinsky's *The Firebird*, and whoever Koschei represents controls their strings with an iron grip. Inside Anthony's head, however, another ballet is playing, and in *Petrushka*, Thomas is anything but in control.

There, he's just another puppet.

As am I.

And Sterling.

Anthony is a smart kid. Even if his conscious mind can't reconcile his involvement in all of this, at least a part of him is trying to let me know that Thomas, Sterling, and I are all victims here.

And that leads to the big question.

Who is the true puppet master behind all of this?

Sterling seems worried that Thomas is manipulating Anthony, while I'm worried about the opposite problem. Disguised beneath the turban and magician's robe, this aged Mussorgsky clone with the enchanted flute no doubt holds the answer to a multitude of questions. Since he wears the face of Anthony's father, I'd pegged the Charlatan as yet another character sprung from the mind of my favorite psychic fourteen-year-old.

But what if I'm wrong?

And if the kid isn't the one calling the shots, then who the hell is?

15

THE MOOR'S ROOM

"**I** can't believe you've brought that man, of all people, to my home." Caroline eyes me with something just this side of fury. "In case you've forgotten, he and that skeleton he calls a partner are the ones that kept raking Jason over the coals last year."

"I haven't forgotten." Caroline and I stand in her kitchen on opposite sides of the granite-topped island where just a week ago we made mimosas. I crane my neck and peer back through the doorway to check on Sterling. On his best behavior, he stands impassive with his hands in his pockets, just inside the foyer, waiting for us to return. "Truth is," I mutter, turning back to Caroline, "he was coming whether I was with him or not."

"What does he want here, anyway?" Caroline glances past me at the man standing framed by her front doorway. "Julianna's case has been closed for months."

"Actually... he's here to talk to Anthony."

Caroline's already pink cheeks go full crimson, the vinegar of her anger so strong, it almost makes me cough. "You think I'm going to let that man anywhere near my son?"

"Caroline, like Detective Sterling mentioned before, he is in charge of the investigation into the disappearances of all the young girls you're hearing about on the news."

"And you went and told him Anthony is involved?"

"Anthony is not a suspect." My hand slaps the granite countertop in frustration, and I'm not sure which of us jumps higher at the sound. "Look, I know I must sound like a broken record, but when an acid trip version of Stravinsky's first ballet is playing itself out in a bunch of comatose girls' heads, and the second one is running on continuous loop between your son's ears, that cannot be a coincidence."

"Of course not, but—"

"Nine months ago, it was your child who was lying there in a coma. If Detective Sterling had been looking into Anthony's condition back then, wouldn't you have wanted him to turn over every stone till he found something?"

"I suppose." Caroline's gaze drops to the floor. "The six girls. Are they doing all right?"

"Six?" I perk up my ears. The Faircloth home is silent. No TV. No radio. Nothing but the A/C's quiet hum. "Have you not seen the news today?"

Caroline's gaze returns to mine, her eyes wide with fear. "What's happened now?"

"A lot." I circle the island and put an arm around her. "First, it's not six anymore. It's ten."

"Ten?"

I fill Caroline in on the events of the day, my story culminating on the near forced suicides of ten girls roughly the age of her son. Her entire body shakes, her maternal instinct warring with itself as the plight these girls face truly hits home.

"Fine," she says eventually, "I'll allow Detective Sterling to speak with Anthony, but he's going to have a long talk with me first."

"I'd expect nothing less."

Caroline and I rejoin Sterling in the next room where he does his best to feign patience.

Surprise, surprise, the emotion sniffer inside my brain knows different.

"So, Detective Sterling, you've decided you want to interrogate my other son?"

Sterling's mouth turns up in that long-suffering smile I've already seen half a dozen times today. "Ms. Faircloth, I'm not here to interrogate anyone. I'm just gathering facts."

"Pardon me, but last time you were 'gathering facts,' my oldest almost spent a few decades behind bars."

"Caroline…"

"Don't worry, Mira." She shoots me a sidelong glance. "I plan to cooperate fully with this fine representative of the Charlotte Mecklenburg Police Department. A lot of young lives are at stake." Her eyes shoot back to Sterling. "I didn't say I was going to be friendly."

Caroline and I sit on the couch with Sterling perched across from us on the edge of their old recliner. The tension in the room is thick, filling my senses with an aroma like salsa a day or two past its prime. As sickeningly sweet waves of frustration roil through me, I wait for either Caroline or Sterling to budge an inch, hoping I won't throw up first.

Finally, it's Sterling that capitulates.

"Ms. Faircloth, I owe you and your family an apology. Last year, as you well know, the circumstances of the Julianna Wagner case led us down a lot of wrong paths, and I'm more than aware of how much that cost you and your family."

"Thank you, Detective." Caroline actually allows a smile to break through her stony facade. A very small one. "Believe it or not, I appreciate that."

Sterling leans in. "How is Jason, anyway?"

"Still recovering, but better. He decided to travel the U.S. for a few weeks while waiting for college to start in the fall. He's headed back this way. He called last night from somewhere between Amarillo and Oklahoma City."

"Glad to hear it." Sterling clears his throat. "Everything that went down in September couldn't have been easy on him. I'm—"

"With all due respect," Caroline interjects, "let's dispense with the pleasantries and get on with the real reason all of us are here." Her eyes slip closed as she pulls a deep breath through her nose. "If you want to talk to Anthony, we're going to have to set some ground rules."

Sterling does well not to roll his eyes as the concept of "ground rules" is thrown at him a second time this week. Instead, he listens intently as Caroline reviews the parameters of what she'll allow.

"First, all interviews will be carried out here in our home where Anthony feels safe."

"That won't be a problem." Sterling's long-suffering smile doesn't budge an inch.

"Second, we will have a lawyer present during any and all interviews."

Sterling shifts in his seat. "Not trying to be difficult, Ms. Faircloth, but do you already have representation? Time is of the essence, and if it's going to take more than a few hours…"

"Understood, Detective. We need to get moving on this. Still, if there's any question I don't wish Anthony to answer, you have to let it drop, deal?"

"For now." Sterling glances in my direction, utter frustration seeping from his every pore. "What else?"

"Only one thing." Caroline crosses her arms. "In this house, what I say goes."

With no doubt her comment is directed as much at me as at Sterling, I join him in a respectful nod.

"Fine, then." Caroline puffs out a resigned breath. "Anthony, can you come out here, please?" Her question met with silence, she raises the volume a few decibels. "Anthony?"

I raise an eyebrow. "Maybe he's taking a nap?"

"My son? Boy hasn't napped since he was two." She stands and rushes for the bedrooms, leaving Sterling and me alone. A few seconds pass before a sound hits me, a sound I truly can't tell if I'm hearing with my ears or my mind.

Sobbing. Quiet sobbing.

"Come on, Sterling." I jump up from the couch and follow Caroline down the hall. "Something's off."

Sterling wastes no time. In seconds, we're down the hall in the open doorway leading to one of the bedrooms.

But this isn't Anthony's room.

It's Rachel's.

The sobbing, however, is all Anthony.

"She won't wake up, Mom." Distraught, he hovers over Rachel's trembling form. "What's wrong with her?"

The girl is drenched in sweat despite the air conditioning leaving me with goosebumps. Though unresponsive to Caroline shaking her shoulders, the girl's eyes are wide open and filled with fear, a fear I've seen on far too many faces lately.

"Mira." Caroline glares back at me, anger and terror and desperation all pouring out of her till my stomach threatens to burst from my body. "This is what you've been talking about, isn't it? What's been happening to all those poor girls?"

I rest a hand on her shoulder. "I'm afraid that's exactly what it is."

Her eyes shoot to her son. "Did you do this, Anthony? Is this you?"

Anthony meets his mother's gaze, and his sobbing breaks down into a full-on cry.

"We don't have time for that, Anthony." Caroline lets go of Rachel's shoulders and grabs Anthony by his. "Now, tell me. What happened?"

Anthony swallows back his tears and looks up at his mother. "We were playing a game on the Xbox." He gestures to the fantasy scene frozen on the TV screen and the pair of discarded controllers on the carpet. "Then, she just stopped."

"Stopped what?" Caroline asks.

"Everything." Anthony's gaze shifts to me, his voice cracking. "Mira, help her, please."

"I'll try, Anthony." I open my mind, hoping against hope I can peek into Rachel's without being drawn into the realm of dream a second time today. "I'm doing everything I can here."

"Please, Mira." He pulls himself up from the floor and rushes me. "I'll do anything."

"Anthony." I backpedal out of the room and into the hall, away from his grasping hands. "Wait."

But it's too late. As the kid's arms wrap around my knees, the music swells, the air fills with perfume, and though already exhausted from my walk through Koschei's garden, I am immediately somewhere else.

Trapped behind yet another doorway, I peer through the crack upon a *mise en scène* that is neither Koschei's garden nor the Russian fair. It's similar to Petrushka's room from my last tour of Anthony's mind, though while the clown's living space was at best austere, this place is opulent to the point of outlandish.

Orange hues cover the walls, walls painted with lush flowers and crystal springs, a true oasis in this desert of the mind. Music fills the air as strings, brass, and woodwind assault my ears again and again like hammer strikes. At one end, at the edge of what I can see, rests a bed covered in the skin of an enormous Bengal tiger situated between two palm trees laden with fruit. Atop the bed, flipping around a coconut like a cat playing with a ball of yarn, lies the Moor.

Despite the ridiculous blackface, there's no doubt the Moor is an avatar for the man I just left in the Faircloth house. He has Sterling's piercing eyes, the strong set of his jaw, the detective's wide shoulders.

I try to go to him, but a rough pair of hands at my waist holds me in place. I have no doubt if I could turn, I would find the Charlatan at the other end of those arms, but as with every visit to this insane ballet of puppets and puppet master, I am paralyzed. An unknown weight drags at my right hand, something smooth, round, cool. I try to glance down at the trumpet I know all too well rests in my grasp, but my eyes are locked on the blue-and-green-clad Arabian just beyond the door.

From his lavish bed, the Moor shakes the coconut like a child checking a present beneath the Christmas tree, then explores every crevice of the husk with his eyes, tongue, hands, feet. After scooting across the floor with the coconut in a strange seated dance, the Moor leaps from the ground in a rage and hurls the fruit to the ground, striking at it several times with his scimitar before sneaking away as if the brown husk hides a bomb on the cusp of exploding. Then, in another reversal, he falls to his knees and bows before the coconut twice, almost as if in worship. All the while, the unseen orchestra continues to play. I've barely begun to process the bizarre dance when a trumpet fanfare sounds and the hands at my waist push me through the door.

Shocked by my sudden appearance, the Moor leaps onto the coconut as if I plan to steal it. Instead, I dance past him *en pointe*, my right arm bringing the trumpet to my lips. A triumphant tune pours from the bell of the horn as I dance around my suspicious host, and then, when the song reaches its climax, I hurl the trumpet to the far corner of the room. In answer, this living puppet that wears Sterling's face kicks the coconut to the opposite end and rushes at me, a lustful set to his eyes.

We dance.

The Moor whirls past me and the two of us end up at opposite ends of the room. Though I could likely escape, the music and the intoxicating aroma of the room mix with his intent gaze, and my inhibitions fall away. The song transitions to a different melody, one composed of trumpet and flute, and we meet in the center of the room. My leg goes to the sky as his hands find my hips. As the Moor spins me around and around with his muscular arms and hands, I can't stop smiling, as if I've finally arrived at exactly the one place I've always, desperately, wanted to be.

Our dance takes a peculiar turn as the Moor breaks from me and sits in the middle of the floor, clapping in time with the music as I continue to dance, as if he's one of those toy monkeys with cymbals. Still, despite the ludicrous nature of our one-sided dance, I feel ever more drawn to Sterling's dream doppelgänger, though with his frequent belly-shaking laughs, it's clear I'm more amusement to him than anything.

An eternity later, I fall into his arms. For a moment, it's as if my every dream has come true. Held by the lover of my dreams, every other man seems but a distant memory. I thrill as he runs a line of kisses up my side, my mind exploding with desire, my body with lust.

Then, in an instant, both he and the music change.

Glaring at me, he leaps to his feet and waves his fists in the air. For a moment, I fear he will strike me, and then, just as suddenly as before, both the Moor and the music return to sultry bliss. His outburst already forgiven, I allow the Moor to take me by the waist and lead me to his bed. Drawing me close, he cups my breast in his hand, and every nerve in my body screams out in rapture.

The Moor leans in to kiss my neck when a muted trumpet from another realm accompanies a rapid-fire banging at the door. I know what's about to happen, yet remain helpless to stop it.

Petrushka, his half-smile, half-frown firmly in place, pushes halfway through the door and waves his arms wildly, looking for all the world like an actual hand puppet. His red-gloved hands beat on his chest, pantomiming his heart breaking at my betrayal. Then, without warning, the Charlatan forces him through the door as he no doubt forced me before. Petrushka runs at me, as if to show me that despite everything, he still loves me. I barely have time to suffer the revulsion the pathetic twisted version of Thomas' face always brings on before the Moor leaps from the bed and shoulders between us. Unable to get to me, Petrushka runs for the door only to have it slammed shut in his face by a gleeful Charlatan.

He's trapped in here with the Moor.

And me.

The Moor chases Petrushka about the room while I in turn chase the Moor, fearing for the clown's pitiful life. Like a rag doll given legs, Petrushka sprints the periphery of the room with the Moor close behind, a clumsy dove pursued by a brutal hawk. Cornering the white-and-orange-clad clown, the Moor trips Petrushka as he tries to escape, then does his best to crush his skull beneath his heel, all in time with a comical orchestral score.

Then, the last humiliation.

The Moor grabs Petrushka by the back of his shirt and picks him up like a proverbial sack of potatoes. Spinning him around till he's punch drunk, the Moor kicks the clown in the rear, sending him flying through the door in defeat to face his master.

Full of himself, the Moor struts back to his bed, clearly eager to prove himself every bit the tiger whose skin covers the luxurious collection of pillows and cushions. Though the part of me that is Mira recognizes how wrong every bit of this is, the Ballerina remains more than ready to consummate this relationship. As if controlled by another, I sit next to the Moor and lean in for a kiss. His eager hand again finds my breast, and in that moment, the agony and ecstasy warring inside me find their voice.

A scream wells up from the bottom of my soul, bringing down the entire room in a conflagration of quite literally shattered dreams. The last thing I see before everything fades to gray is the Moor's crooked black-face mouth, his disappointment made flesh.

Not that different from Petrushka's.

Not that different at all.

I awake, as I have so many times before, flat on the floor staring at a blurred ceiling. Grateful for the pillow beneath my head, I blink a few times and try to clear my vision.

Caroline, an unconscious but somewhat more peaceful Rachel draped across her lap, looks down on me with worry etched in her features. Sterling, whose previous frustration has melted into full-on fret, holds a damp rag to my forehead.

"You okay?" he asks. "You were moaning and kicking so much, you broke a sweat."

"About as well as can be expected." I try to sit up, but failing that, just let out a quiet groan. "God, that was intense."

"How so?" Caroline asks. "What did you... find this time?"

"Nothing that's going to help Rachel," I croak. "At least not as far as I can see." I reach out for the girl's still form, but thinking better of it, allow my arm to fall to the floor. "Is she okay?"

Caroline's eyes drop to her daughter. "She seems to have stabilized, whatever that means. She looked like she was having the mother of all nightmares before, but now she's just sleeping. You're sure you didn't do anything while you were away?"

"Not that I know of." My entire body trembles. "Rachel... wasn't there."

"So, where did you go this time?" Sterling grasps my arm to help me sit up. I pull away as if I'm being attacked. Regret washes over me as he tries to hide the hurt in his gaze.

Whatever I just saw in Anthony's head, it's not his fault.

"I was dragged back to the other ballet," I mutter, trying to cover up recoiling from Sterling's touch. "The one running in Anthony's head." Knowing full well what I'm going to be forced to watch the next time I enter Anthony's thoughts, I can barely find the strength to say the name. "*Petrushka.*"

"And what did you see?" he asks.

"I'm so sorry, Mira." Anthony's plaintive sob from the door saves me from having to answer the damning question. "I didn't mean—"

"I thought I told you to go to your room, young man." Caroline fixes Anthony with a no-nonsense glare.

"But, Mom…"

"No buts." She points past his shoulder and toward the hall. "Back to your room right now. The grown-ups need to talk."

"Caroline." I manage to sit up. "It's all right. He's just—"

"Remember what I said before, Mira?" Her eyes flick to Sterling and then back to me. "My house. My rules." She raises an eyebrow at Anthony. "Now, go to your room."

"Yes, ma'am."

As Anthony sulks down the hallway, Caroline directs her attention fully back to me. "So, nothing you saw can help my daughter. Can it help Anthony?"

"Caroline, please, it's not like that."

"Not like what?" She crosses her arms. "Are you keeping something from us?"

"What?" I search Caroline's face, and find only anger. "Why would you ask that?"

Caroline's gaze drops to her shoes. "Detective Sterling told me all about Thomas' little secret. That all these girls, not to mention Anthony, are his patients."

If looks could kill, Sterling would no doubt burst into flames at my glare.

"Caroline, please." I raise my hands before me, trying to defuse the situation. "We're all just trying to figure this thing out."

"So, I'm supposed to open up my home, let the police talk to my child, but you get to keep your cards close to your chest and protect your man? Is that how this is going to work?"

I swallow away the anger. "That information wasn't mine to tell."

Caroline jabs a thumb in Sterling's direction. "And yet spilling the beans about my son was?"

Dammit. She's got me there. "Look, Caroline. I'm sorry. I'm doing the best I can here. I mean, it's not like any of my grad school professors gave a seminar on what to do when a client is... well... Anthony."

"I get that. Really, I do." She shakes her head in frustration, hot cayenne wafting off her like smoke from a bonfire. "But from here on out, there can't be any more secrets. Agreed?"

"Agreed." The lie is barely off my lips before Sterling's gaze meets mine. I shake my head in disgust as first the Moor's, then Petrushka's disapproving gazes flit across my mind's eye. "So, Caroline, what are you going to tell Thomas?"

"Funny you should ask. Before Detective Sterling spilled the beans, I called Thomas to let him know what was going on with Anthony and Rachel."

My heart freezes in my chest. "What did you tell him?"

"That you had gone under after Anthony grabbed you. That we needed his help." Caroline looks away. "Seems we're all going to have a lot to talk about when he gets here."

A rap from the front foyer echoes through the house.

"Speak of the devil," Caroline mutters as she rises to answer the door.

16

GARGOUILLADE

"Hello, Thomas." Caroline's voice lacks the usual warmth present when she addresses the man who has been counseling her son for the better part of his life. "You got here quickly."

"Mira." The concern in Thomas' voice is all but palpable, even from down the hall. "Where is she?"

"She's in Rachel's room," comes Caroline's sarcastic voice, "and unlike my daughter, she's conscious."

Rushing feet head my way, and in a moment, Thomas is by my side. If I recoiled from Sterling's touch, I nearly leap out of my skin when Thomas rests his hand on my leg.

"Mira, are you okay?"

A groan escapes my lips. "Well, I've done back to back trips into the ether with nothing but half a plate of reheated hospital food to sustain me. I can't seem to make my legs work. And to top it all off, there's a white-hot ice pick doing its best to jab its way out of my skull. Other than that? I'm just peachy."

Thomas reaches for my hand, but sensing my aversion, he turns his attention to Sterling.

"Detective."

"Doctor."

Thomas searches Sterling's face, and a realization hits his own.

"You know." His gaze shifts to Caroline. "You all know." His eyes

130

return to me, though where I expect to find anger, there is only sadness. "Thank God."

Sterling doesn't waste a second. "So, all these girls are indeed patients of yours?"

"Most of them." Thomas rises from my side and sits on the bed next to Rachel. "The first six at least. Mira told me the names of the four latest victims from the hospital. To my knowledge, I don't see any of those girls or their families." He rests a hand on Rachel's calf. "I've seen plenty of this little girl, though."

"So, now there are eleven." I shake my head slowly from side to side. Even that small movement brings a fresh wave of nausea. "From what I've gleaned from Koschei's taunts, there are just two to go."

"Two to go? Till what?" Caroline asks. "Thomas, what's going on? Mira and I have been beating our heads against a wall trying to figure all this out. While it's clear Anthony must somehow be involved in all this, none of the rest of it makes any sense. According to you, he's recovered from last year's events and doing better with each passing month. He's back at school and going through life almost like nothing ever happened. What possible reason would he have to hurt these girls? More than that, other than possibly running into them in your waiting room, he doesn't even know any of the victims but his sister."

Thomas raises his hands before him in a defeated shrug. "I wish I knew what to tell you."

No one says a word for a few seconds, and in that silence, a sequence of curious facts intrudes upon my thoughts.

Despite everything that went down last year, this afternoon marks the first time the four adults in our circle have all been in the same room at once. Me, Caroline, Thomas, Sterling. Marry that factoid with the list of stars of the *Petrushka* revue going on in Anthony's head and a glaring difference between my experiences in the Exhibition and what is happening now comes to light.

In my role as Scheherazade, I was the star of Anthony's art gallery of the insane. Sterling had a big part as well as the better half of the perennial odd couple, Samuel Goldenberg and Schmuÿle, despite the fact Anthony had never met Detective Sterling or his ever-so-pleasant partner. Though only mentioned in passing, even Thomas' existence was recognized in his capacity as the ever-predictable Kalendar Prince.

Of us all, however, no one's presence along the Exhibition was more quintessential than Caroline's mantle as the all-powerful witch who lived at the end of the hall.

I still shudder at the name.

Baba Yaga.

And yet, in both the new environs, Caroline's absence is glaring. Present from the very beginning in the Exhibition, this time she is either missing for a reason I can't fathom, or, as with Yaga, disguised beyond my ability to pierce her veil.

Another simple fact. Other than Anthony, Thomas, and Rachel, Caroline is the only other person who could possibly have encountered each of the first six victims.

Though it pains me to consider such a betrayal, I can't rule out the possibility I'm not the only one here still keeping secrets.

Between that and the fate that might await Petrushka the next time my eyes remain shut for more than a second, I need a moment.

"Caroline, can you help me up? I think the strength in my legs is coming back." I reach out a hand and she helps me to my feet. "Mind if I go freshen up?"

Her look of consternation fades into the genteel southern smile I'm more familiar with. "Of course, Mira. Do you need—"

"I'll be fine." I step past her.

"Mira?" Thomas asks. "May I—"

"Look, everyone." I raise a hand. "Back to back trips through other people's heads may do a number on me, but I think I can make it to the bathroom by myself."

I pass through the doorway just across the hall and lock the door behind me. A glance in the mirror reveals a mug I barely recognize as my own. I turn on the faucet and get the water as hot as I can before splashing my face time and again, trying to wash away the horrible, inexplicable loathing.

Thomas, his kind features twisted in my mind into the lopsided grimace of Petrushka the clown, gazes at me with equal parts longing and regret.

Sterling, his handsome face covered in sinister blackface and his lustful eyes raking my every curve, devours me from the void.

And Caroline, swathed in Yaga's wrinkles and rags, cackles at me through her clanging iron teeth, as terrifying in her absence this time around as she was in her inescapable presence last year.

Unable to face the three of them, I stand before the mirror and stare into my own pained eyes. My emotions run the gamut. Anger. Sadness. Revulsion. Even a few moments for self-pity. As the seconds stretch into minutes, I try to decide which of the three people discussing me in the next room is ultimately going to come for me.

Ultimately, it's Thomas' voice that comes through the door a few minutes later.

"Mira? Everything all right in there?"

I don't say a word.

"Mira?"

"Just putting myself back together." I choke back a sob. "I'll be out in a minute."

"Okay." Even without my built-in emotion sniffer, Thomas' disappointment comes through loud and clear. "We're all in the living room when you're ready." Slow footsteps lead away from the door, and I am alone again.

For all of two seconds.

A knock stirs the anger brewing at my core like a flaming stick shoved in a hornet's nest.

"What?" The venom in my voice more than I intended, I dial it back a bit. "I said I'd be out in a minute."

"Mira?"

Crap. Not Thomas.

"What is it, Anthony?"

"I'm sorry, Mira." I can barely hear his choked up voice through the wood. "For all of this. For everything."

I go to the door but can't bring myself to open it. "It's okay, Anthony. It's not your fault."

"Not my fault?" A low thud, his forehead no doubt hitting the wall. "All these girls. Rachel. You. It's just like last time, but a hundred times worse."

"We'll figure it out, kiddo." I hope my words sound more convincing to Anthony than they do to me. "I promise."

"Don't give up on me, Mira." The tremor in his voice breaks my heart. "Please."

I pull in a deep breath, turn the lock, and open the door. My heart breaks as I come eye to eye with this young man in whose mind I have seen both wonders and horrors.

"Never." Steeling myself for… whatever, I open my arms wide and despite himself, Anthony falls into my tight embrace.

No swell of music this time. No heady perfume. No gusts of wind. Just a frightened child and the only person on the face of the earth who can banish the monsters beneath his bed. We share a moment that seems to last days.

I'm not sure how much time passes, but the sound of someone clearing their throat brings us back to the present. Behind Anthony, Caroline's eyes brim with tears. I almost expect her to banish Anthony to his room again, but instead, she drops to one knee and joins our embrace.

"Mira," she whispers. "We've been talking, Detective Sterling, Thomas, and I."

Wow. That doesn't sound good.

"And?" I manage to get out, as Anthony and Caroline together squeeze me so tight, I can barely breathe. "What do you think?"

Caroline pulls away and peels her son off me before joining us in a triangle on the floor. "As frustrating and maddening as all of this is, we're in it together. It's going to take all of us to see this through to the end, and it seems all the cards are finally on the table."

For a moment, it is Baba Yaga's ancient visage and not Caroline's that peers back from her kind eyes. Despite my best efforts, my hands tremble. "God, I hope so."

"That being said," she continues, "we're still in the dark. One thing, however, remains clear. Just like last time, Anthony may be the door to the answers we seek, but you, Mira, are the key. Rachel and the other girls are counting on us. On you." She forces a smile onto her pained face. "I'd be lying if I said I wasn't terrified by all of this, but if you're still willing to help, I'm in."

"Thank you, Caroline." Despite the hint of suspicion still gnawing at my gut, I return an exhausted grin. "Try and keep me away."

"So, what now?" Thomas asks as he helps me into his car. "Where do we go from here?"

"I don't know, Thomas. I just don't know."

I never thought it would be this awkward with Thomas again, and yet, here we are, alone for the first time today, and neither of us knows what to say.

Mere seconds have passed since Caroline and Anthony left to take Rachel to the hospital, for all the good that's going to do. Unless I'm way off on this one, there's nothing for her there. Sterling decided to join, though to mend bridges with Caroline or because he knew how odd it would be between me and Thomas, I'm not certain.

Regardless, that leaves just the two of us here. I was ready to talk marriage with the man a week ago. Now? I can barely stomach looking at him. Whether these are my true feelings coming through or I'm just a puppet getting my strings pulled, it doesn't change one simple fact.

Nothing is the same.

"I'm surprised Caroline didn't ask you to check Rachel before they left," Thomas says.

"I had planned to, at least before the whole thing with Anthony went down earlier." A chuckle escapes my lips. "She knows as well as I do that a third trip into La La Land today would probably not have ended well." I let out a yawn and buckle my seatbelt. "Tomorrow, though, a visit is in order."

"What time do you think you'll go?" Thomas pulls out of the driveway and drops the car into drive. "If you want, I can reschedule a couple of my patients and come with you."

"No," I answer far too quickly. "That won't be necessary."

"Oh." For the next couple of minutes, Thomas is quiet, focusing solely on the road. The way he hits the gas and brakes and the squalling of tires around a tight corner, it's clear there's a lot going on upstairs. "So, are you staying at my place tonight?"

My cheeks go hot, and I pray Thomas doesn't look my way. "Isabella and Mom are due in two days. I think I'm going to crash at the new apartment tonight after I get as much done as I can." I shoot a furtive glance his way. "I hope that's okay."

"Of course." The short response speaks volumes. "Makes sense."

"It's just... there's so much to—"

"Come off it, Mira. Remember who you're talking to. You may be able to read minds, but I've been a psychologist for the better part of a decade." He lets out a quiet laugh and shakes his head. "Your mom isn't the only one who can smell bullshit a mile away."

"I'm sorry, Thomas." I bite my lip so hard I taste copper. "What is it you want me to say?"

"I don't know." He pulls into a left turn lane and waits for the light to turn green. "Tell me what's really going on. Tell me you still love me. Tell me the woman who talked me into walking every inch of Greenway in Charlotte hasn't gone away forever." The light green, he makes the turn and accelerates onto the tree-lined lane. "Just tell me... something."

"Fine, but it's not anything you want to hear."

"Try me."

The beginning of a headache erupts above my left eye. As if this wasn't painful enough.

"Have you researched this other ballet at all? Not *The Firebird…* but *Petrushka?*"

Thomas' lips draw into a fine line. "Not quite what I wanted to talk about, Mira."

"It's relevant." The throbbing above my eye doubles. "I swear."

"Fine." He hits the accelerator. "I looked into it a bit yesterday. Read the Wikipedia article and watched a bit of the ballet online." He glances over at me. "You're right. Those puppets are creepy."

"Imagine if you were one of them." Not that I have to. Glancing down into my lap, I picture the Ballerina's costume cascading down my form. The petite red vest, the lace pantaloons, the white frock. The weight of the trumpet in my hand anything but a distant memory, I interlace my fingers before I continue. "When I go there, I'm the Ballerina, just as I was Scheherazade in the Exhibition or Ivanovna in Koschei's garden."

"You already told me all this." Thomas glances over at me. "There's more, isn't there?"

"I hate to say it, but… I'm not the only familiar face there."

"Yeah, you told me that the Charlatan/Magician guy was Mussorgsky from the Exhibition. That's why this whole thing has to somehow involve Anthony." One eyebrow shoots up in question. "Is that what's got you so freaked out?"

"You're not listening. It's not mine or Mussorgsky's presence there that worries me." My head drops. "It's yours."

"Mine?"

"You're there, and this time, you got way more than just an honorable mention."

"So… who am I ?" Less than a second passes before it hits him. "Wait. I'm the clown, aren't I?" His entire body shakes as he mutters the word. "Petrushka."

"And that's not the worst of it." The street of two-story brick mansions just outside the car window shifts to a row of restaurants and shops, one of mine and Thomas' favorite areas to spend our weekend nights. "Sterling is there, too."

"Of course he is." Thomas shakes his head slowly. "The Arabian, or whatever he's called."

"The Moor," I mutter.

Thomas' voice goes dead. "So, in this dreamworld you've been visiting, he's the one you want and I'm the sad sack clown who dies at his blade?"

"I'm sorry, Thomas. I didn't—"

"Last year, when you walked the Exhibition, you told me all about Samuel Goldenberg and Schmuÿle. Back then, I couldn't figure out why these two cops you said you couldn't stand ended up being such an intrinsic part of the experience, and yet here Sterling is again. First, the rich Jew in his opulent mansion, and now the Moor with his royal clothes. Meanwhile, I'm some pathetic creature the Ballerina barely tolerates, much less loves." His eyes narrow. "And that's not even what bothers me the most."

Here it comes. God, the man's insight is something to behold.

"Anthony had never met Detective Sterling until today, and therefore everything before that pertaining to him is colored by your perceptions, Mira."

My intestines tie themselves in knots. "It doesn't make sense to me either." My gaze drops, unable to meet Thomas'. "A week ago, everything was so clear, but after all that's happened the last few day, everything feels different."

"Bad different?" Thomas asks, a new trepidation in his voice.

"I don't know." I pull my arms tight around my torso. "I'm all screwed up inside, and I don't know how to fix it."

Thomas turns onto the street leading to my new apartment and drives the last three blocks in silence. As he pulls into the driveway, he glances over at me and as our eyes meet, the hurt pouring off him doubles in intensity.

"In that case, take all the time you need, Mira." He slides the car into park. "I'm no psychic and don't have the first clue about any of that, but if you're having doubts that are coming out in your walks through these kids' minds—"

"Thomas—"

"No, let me finish." Thomas massages the bridge of his nose, his eyes sliding closed. "If you're having doubts, then maybe you should take some time and give it some thought. When you're ready, we'll talk."

"But, Thomas—"

"Stop." As he again meets my gaze, the cold clinician's eyes I encountered on our very first meeting make an encore appearance. A musty smell, not unlike moldy bread, invades my senses. "For the moment, eleven little girls and their families are counting on us." His gaze focused straight ahead, he lets out a sigh. "Till all this is over, maybe it's better if we just keep our focus on the problem at hand."

My heart breaks at his words, but at my core I know he's right.

"See you tomorrow?" I ask as I step out of his car.

He doesn't even look my way. "We'll see."

17

GLISSADE

A good night's sleep would have been nice.

Hell, I'd have been happy to get in even an hour or two.

Instead, I tossed and turned for half the night after Thomas dropped me off, unable to erase his disappointment from my mind. Miraculously, the unexplainable revulsion that has of late accompanied my every thought of him let up for a few hours, allowing his true smile to fill my mind, untouched by Petrushka's grotesque masque of greasepaint and wretchedness.

Once I finally nodded off, the rest of the wee hours were spent waking from one nightmare after another. First, a score of horned toad-monsters dined on my still beating heart while Rachel and the other ten girls looked on helplessly, their white dresses like ghostly shrouds in the dim light of the garden. Next, a vile version of Koschei the Deathless wearing the face of my ex-husband immolated me with black flames pouring from the orb of dark glass at the end of his staff. Most terrifying of all, the last ended with the Moor and Petrushka embroiled in a violent tug of war with none other than yours truly in full Ballerina garb serving as the rope.

I awoke screaming from that last one, drenched in a puddle of ice-cold sweat.

My every instinct tells me these nightmares are in fact what they seem and not another attack from the mysterious entity manipulating me and everyone I love like so many puppets. That being said, one thing became quite clear as I rocketed out of the bed shrieking at the top of my lungs just after five this morning.

No more sleep for Mira.

As a result, my apartment is basically spotless. Amazing what four hours of pre-dawn elbow grease can accomplish. Nothing left to do but vacuum and do the laundry and dishes.

Good thing, I guess, since Mom and Isabella arrive tomorrow afternoon.

"Tomorrow," I mutter, rubbing at my eyes and trying to suppress a yawn. "Fantastic."

No way this mess with the girls and Anthony and Caroline will be sorted out by then. One more person to juggle. Two, if Mom decides to stay a few days.

But on second thought, if I can convince Mom to stick around and take care of Isabella while I finish working this case, that would be a huge load off my shoulders.

Wouldn't be the first time. That's what she'll say.

As I cut and place the last piece of shelf paper in the master bath, my stomach rumbles, the unexpected sound startling in the relative silence.

Guess that means it's time for breakfast.

There's nothing in the fridge, and I don't really feel like eating out alone, but Thomas is already with his first client for the day, Caroline is no doubt busy with Rachel and Anthony, and I'm not calling Sterling. Not after he and Thomas, or at least their dream doppelgängers, tore me in two last night.

Looks like I'll be keeping my own company for the next few hours.

A quick shower and blow out later, I feel a little more human. I slide into a pair of comfortable jeans, a well-worn t-shirt, and some sandals and hop in the car. One of my favorite breakfast spots sits a stone's throw from the best Starbucks in town, though my enjoyment of the front patio is a bit spoiled by the memory of Elizabeth Baker and Janey Campbell frozen there like living statues.

Still, a hash brown cup and a double shot of espresso are in order if I'm going to make it past noon today. I promised Caroline I'd come to the hospital and check on Rachel this morning, and I'll be damned if a little thing like sleep deprivation is going to keep me away.

Oh boy. As if lured in by my renewed determination, here comes the headache again. Same spot, different day. Like a railroad spike straight through the forehead.

If only it wasn't too early for a glass of Cabernet.

I try to get in touch with Mom en route, but the call goes straight to voicemail. My mother, the Luddite. No matter how many times I remind her, she never remembers to charge the smartphone I bought her. Guess I'll try again later.

I park next to some construction tape in the parking lot across from my two destinations and hike down the hill to The Mayobird to pick up some breakfast. Halfway there, my phone chimes.

"Mom," I whisper. "Finally."

I whip out my phone and put it to my ear. "Hello?"

"Good morning, Mira."

Not Mom.

Sterling.

"So, I have the honor of the first call of the day."

A tired laugh comes across the line. "If only that were the case."

"Oh, really?" I cross the street. "What's going on?"

"In case you've forgotten, just yesterday, ten little girls almost took a group header off the roof of the largest hospital in Charlotte. You think I got to sleep a wink last night?"

I try unsuccessfully to suppress a yawn. "Well, that makes two of us."

I grab a seat in one of the metal outdoor chairs, my stomach lurching as my nose detects more than a hint of bacon from the next table.

Sterling regales me with tales of being debriefed and dressed down no less than three times through the night by higher and higher echelons of local government. He did his best to keep me out of the discussion, but apparently, my name is sitting on the desk of the chief of police. Maybe even the mayor's.

Guess my low profile isn't quite so low anymore.

"So, what now?"

"I don't know." Sterling sighs into the phone. "Fortunately, none of the girls did anything last night but lie there and sleep, but their parents have been calling nonstop."

"I'm about to grab breakfast and coffee, but I'll be there sometime in the next half hour."

A distinctive click on Sterling's end of the line intrudes on our conversation. "And what do you know? Another call." He clears his throat. "See you in a few, Mira."

He's gone before I can even say goodbye. I step into the refrigerated air of the restaurant and grab something quick I can eat on the way. Up the block and in and out of Starbucks in five, I head back to my car. Bonnie Tyler wails from the speakers in the few seconds between there and the hospital. As I enter the main entrance of Carolinas Medical Center, I down the last swallow of my latte and toss the cup in the trash.

Ready.

"Ms. Tejedor?"

Crap.

Loitering by the bank of elevators that lead to the children's hospital, Katie Kaczynski tracks me with her cunning gaze. She is without her dreadlocked cameraman, but that does nothing to lessen the unease her smarmy stare leaves at the pit of my stomach.

"Ms. Kaczynski. What a… pleasant surprise."

She stands, not quite blocking my passage, and raises a hand. "Just a moment, please."

Wow. That sounded almost polite.

"I saw your interview with Dr. Patel. She looked heartbroken."

"What do you expect?" She runs her fingers through her fiery red mane. "Her daughter is in no better shape than Anthony Faircloth was nine short months ago, yes?"

"What?" I rein in my emotions, as if Kaczynski is the one who can sniff out what someone is feeling. "How do you know about that?"

"Charlotte may be the biggest city between D.C. and Atlanta, Ms. Tejedor, but it's still a shockingly small town. Didn't take much digging to find out the reason for your initial visit nine months ago."

"Regardless, I have nothing to say to the press at this time. I'm here to help, and I'd just like to leave it at that if it's all the same to you."

"Of course." She steps back. "The truth is, I think we both want the same thing here."

I raise an eyebrow. "Ratings?"

"No." She deflates a bit. Is it possible I actually struck a nerve? "At the root of it all, don't we both just want to help these children?"

I step past her. "If that's the case, then stay out of my way and let me do my job."

She bristles for a moment and then forces her shoulders to unbunch. "Wait."

I stop and glance back at her. "Yes?"

She swallows her pride, almost visibly. The pepper emanating off her shifts to a minty aroma. "Look, I'm sure I come off as the stereotypical jealous ex, but I'm just doing my job here, just like you. You'll notice I haven't dragged Thomas' name through the mud."

"I have noticed and appreciate it more than you know. Thomas and I have more than enough problems already."

"And I want nothing more than these girls to be returned to their families whole and healthy." She offers me a smile that at least on the surface seems genuine. "I think we can both agree on that, can't we?"

I retract my claws. Halfway, at least.

"Good to hear." I hand her a business card. "You find out anything you think can help, give me a call."

When I walk onto the floor this time, it's quite different. The usual spate of rolled eyes and snickers is replaced with furtive glances and whispers. To the man, Sterling's guard detail knows exactly who I am, and more than one addresses me as "Ms. Tejedor" when I walk past. The twenty-four rooms of this floor are divided into two parallel corridors and the eleven girls and their families take up almost an entire hallway.

Not surprisingly, the twelfth room on that side remains empty.

I'm almost to Room 8 where Rachel is being put up when Sterling's voice catches me from the other end of the hall.

"Mira."

"Good morning, Sterling."

As tired as I've seen him, the man still manages to slide into his trademark smile. "A word before you visit the Faircloths?"

"Sure."

As he peers at me, Sterling's "all business" veneer falls away, and concern touches his eyes. A faint hint of fresh-baked pumpernickel drifts across my senses. "You okay?"

"Fit as a fiddle." I pour every bit of energy I have into my best megawatt smile. "Why do you ask?"

Sterling pulls in close. "Between you and me, you're looking a little rough."

I raise an eyebrow. "You're one to talk."

"Sorry." Sterling raises both hands in mock surrender. "Just appears I'm not the only one running on fumes today."

"I'll sleep when I'm dead." I turn back in the direction of Room 8. "Something you need to tell me besides pointing out the obvious?"

Sterling rubs at his neck the way he does when he's getting exasperated. "Actually, I just wanted to know what you had planned."

I cock my head to one side and let out a sarcastic laugh. "I had planned to get some sleep last night so I could do this with a clear head. Instead, I'm exhausted. The only thing keeping me from curling into a ball and sleeping for a week right here in the middle of this hallway is the twenty ounces of caffeinated goodness I poured down my throat on the way over."

"So." Sterling pulls even closer, his voice dropping to a low mutter. "What's the play?"

"What I intended to do yesterday before Anthony's desperation changed my itinerary."

"You're going in there like this?"

"What choice do I have? You think I'm going to walk in the room and tell Caroline, 'Sorry, chica, but I'm tired' or something?" My eyes well up. Damn sleep deprivation. Always leaves me an emotional wreck. "Rachel is counting on me."

"They're all counting on you." Sterling motions up and down the hallway. "Eleven girls, their families, and every cop, doctor, nurse up here." Sterling's hand returns to his neck. "I just don't want you to go in there unless you're ready."

The pumpernickel aroma kicks into overdrive. He's really worried, and it's beyond anything with his job.

"I appreciate your concern, Detective Sterling, but I'm a professional."

"A professional walker of other people's minds?" Sterling crosses his arms. "As I recall, you'd never done that before nine months ago and never again until this week."

"And that puts me about ten light years ahead of anyone else you can bring to bear."

His gaze drops. "I just don't want to see you get hurt, Mira."

"Me neither." I step in the direction of Room 8. "Keep an eye on me?"

Sterling shakes his head. "You're really going back in there."

I rest a hand on the door. "Just need a few more frequent flyer miles to get that ticket to Tahiti." I step into the room, my eyes taking a moment to adjust to the dim light. The curtain drawn, Caroline's shadowy form hovers over Rachel, who lies in the bed, hooked to a series of monitors. And there, sitting beneath the television hanging on the wall, Anthony plays a video game, oblivious to my presence.

"Mira." Caroline steps around the bed and meets me halfway. "So glad you're here."

"That makes one of us." I try unsuccessfully to stifle the latest in a series of yawns. "Any change in Rachel's condition overnight?"

Caroline shakes her head. "She just lies there perfectly still, not making a sound, but any time I start to nod off, I hear her whimper, and I'm up again."

"Funny how one little girl who won't wake up is keeping the rest of us from getting any sleep."

Caroline takes a closer look at me. "You sure you're up for this?"

Sterling, who has stood respectfully to one side this entire time, clears his throat. "That's what I said."

"Stop it, both of you." I sidestep around Caroline and go to Rachel's bed. "We all know Rachel's only in this shape because whoever is behind all this wants me back in there."

"And so your first instinct is to give them exactly what they want?" Sterling peers out the window. "You know, there's a reason our government doesn't negotiate with terrorists."

I lower the bed rail, a frustrated grunt escaping my lips as I perch on the arm of the chair by Rachel's bed. "I swear, Sterling. You're talking like I'm not the only stinking break you've had on this case."

Caroline rests a hand on my shoulder. "I think we're both just concerned about you."

"I'll be fine, and even if that's not the case, what does it matter? We have to do something today, or tomorrow it's twelve girls, and the next thirteen, assuming, of course, that everything Koschei has told me even remotely resembles the truth."

"All right, Mira." Sterling plants himself next to the bed. "Tell us. What do you need?"

"Just believe in me." My hand trembles as I reach for Rachel's brow. "Because ready or not, here I go."

There's no music this time, the utter silence shattered only by the screeching roars of the *bukavacs.* From every corner of Koschei's garden they stare at me, their slitted yellow eyes harboring a rage fueled by hate and hunger. A thought, and the bow is back in my hand, arrow nocked and string drawn. One of the *bukavacs* advances a step, and I bury an arrow in its glistening neck. A dozen or so remaining monsters narrow their eyes further, but not one of them dares move an inch.

Before I can take another breath, the forest all around the garden's periphery lights up with a hundred pairs of glowing scarlet eyes, signaling the return of the *skrzaks*. Though none of them step from the dark edge of the wood, their every eye is trained on me.

Waiting. Patiently. For what, I don't know.

In the distance, the *zmej* roars, its trio of throats achieving a strange three-part harmony of brass and fire. In fear, I visually sweep the sky, but find nothing. No three-headed dragon, no bird with plumage the hue of open flame, no masked ballerina with feathered wings sprouting from her arms. Breathless, I reach into a fold of my green and gold tunic and confirm the Firebird's feather is still in my possession.

Thank God. It's still there.

If all goes according to the original work—and with Anthony running the show, I have no doubt of that—a moment of desperation is coming soon where I will be forced to call upon the indebted Firebird to save me from my fate. In Stravinsky's ballet, the Firebird's dance enslaves the monsters, frees the princesses, and destroys Koschei forever. For a moment, I consider bringing out the feather now and letting the chips fall where they may, but in the end, think better of it. All things with Anthony are about the story, the timing, the moment. Only eleven girls have been taken to this point, not the thirteen of which Koschei himself spoke. To play my trump card now would almost certainly mean disaster when the moment actually arrives. Like Scheherazade's dagger from the Exhibition, the time and place will reveal itself in due time.

Besides, for once, I stand at the center of Koschei's garden and nothing is actively trying to kill me.

"You dare enter my garden again, brave Ivanovna?" His lips turned up in an exasperated snarl, Koschei steps from the violet incandescence of his palace. "Or perhaps 'foolish' is the more appropriate word?"

"Cruel Koschei, you've abducted ten innocent children and now an eleventh that is dear to my heart, brought all of them to a place of darkness, death, and despair, and you have the gall to question my return." I level the bow at the Immortal, aiming the drawn arrow at his skeletal chest. "Your actions are all but an engraved invitation."

"What you speak is true, Ivanovna. And in fact, I am strangely glad you have returned. I would have words with you." He gestures about the garden. "As you can see, I have assembled my various pets and set them where you can see each one so you need not fear attack during our parley."

"Parley? You seek to surrender?"

"No, Ivanovna." Koschei chuckles, the wheezy sound as menacing as the countless glares boring into me from every direction. "There will be no surrender, I suspect, from either of our camps. I do, however, wish to discuss terms."

"Terms?" I lower the arrow an inch. "Terms of what?"

His lips spread in a malevolent grin. "Why, of your inevitable defeat, of course."

18

KOSCHEI'S PALACE

"Defeat?" I fight to keep the tremor from my voice. "You stand in the mouth of your very own fortified palace with an army of monsters awaiting your every command, and yet, you still take the time to parley with a lone woman armed with nothing but a bow and some arrows?" I lower my weapon and return the arrow to my quiver. "I get the distinct feeling there's something you're not telling me."

"A courtesy," Koschei mutters half a second too late. "Nothing but a simple courtesy."

"Of course." I peer around at the myriad stares from Koschei's menagerie of monsters. "So, I have to admit I'm a little disappointed. Nothing else to throw at me but your collection of horny toads, a few goblins, and a three-headed lizard?"

Koschei throws his head back and laughs. No hesitation this time. "You know as well as I, Ivanovna, that the denizens of this place are limited only by imagination. Bluster all you want, but trust that you have but scratched the surface of the forces I can bring to bear against you."

"I have no doubt of your ability to summon the worst of the worst to your defense, Koschei, but one simple truth remains."

His pale eyes narrow at me. "And what might that be?"

Steepling my hands together as if in prayer, I bring my fingertips to my lips. "If you were planning on setting another terror on me, I suspect you'd have already done it." I allow myself a faint grin. "I've managed to defeat everything you've thrown at me thus far, Immortal. As for 'discussing terms' or whatever you're calling our little heart-to-heart, know that I recognize this conversation for what it truly is." My smile grows wide. "You're stalling."

"Silence, Ivanovna." Exasperation returns to Koschei's gaze. "You speak out of turn."

"I speak the truth." I stride in his direction. "Regardless, I didn't come here to speak with you." One of the *bukavacs* raises its front leg, but returns it to the ground at my glare. "I came to see the girls, and in particular, the one called Rachel."

"And what makes you think you will ever see their innocent faces again?"

I take another step. "The simple fact that we're still talking."

Koschei fixes me with an angry glare, a glare that fades over the following seconds into a self-satisfied smirk. "Very well. We have spoken long enough." He walks down the tongue-like bridge of his palace's skeletal entrance and meets me at its forked tip. Before I can say a word, he gives me a subtle bow and gestures for me to enter his abode. "My home, Ivanovna, is yours."

More terrified by his sudden hospitality than anything else he's said or done, I stride past Koschei and onto the bridge. Glancing back, I fully expect to find the scores of creatures from the garden converging on me, but they've all disappeared into the ether, leaving me alone with the master of the house. He hasn't moved an inch, his wasted features all but obsequious as he offers me a humble bow and silently waves me inside.

A step inside Koschei's palace, and it's like I'm back in the Exhibition or, at least, *The Old Castle* where a certain blue-clad troubadour used to hang his saxophone. While Modesto's stone home was strangely cozy with its many carpets and tapestries, Koschei's palace is every bit as austere as the Immortal himself.

As I wander the halls alone, I almost expect Baba Yaga's taunts to ring down from the vaulted ceiling. In fact, I'd welcome the clang of her metal teeth if, for even a moment, the terrible sound would break the godforsaken silence.

"Hello?" My shout echoes back at me like a chorus. "Rachel?"

A door at the far end of the hall opens a crack, the aged wood and rusted hinges making not a sound. With every step I take, the door opens further. Beyond and just visible in the dim light of a sputtering torch, the bottom of a spiral stone staircase awaits. Perfectly aware I'm walking into a trap, I pass the open doorway and begin my ascent. In my experience, when Anthony Faircloth leads you down the cherry path, you follow. No matter the obstacles he puts in your way, whatever lies just off the path is invariably worse.

In my life, I've only hoofed it to the top of the Washington Monument twice, once as a child and once last summer with Isabella as we toured the Mall in D.C. Both times, I swore I'd never do it again.

Compared to Koschei's tower, the Monument barely qualifies as a stepladder.

A spiral eternity of granite and flickering candlelight later, I come to a small landing beneath a low ceiling. Lit only by a lone torch hanging from the wall, a door fashioned of oak and iron blocks my path. I press my palm to the wood, fully expecting to find it barred from within. Instead, the door opens with ease as if the hinges are freshly oiled. My heart hammering in my chest, I step through and push the door shut behind me.

The room opens up onto a long hall with beds lined along either side like a hospital ward.

Or, strangely, a nursery.

Six beds fall on each side of the room while a barely visible thirteenth rests at the far end of the rectangular hall. Above each bed, a solitary candle flickers, revealing slumbering forms in each of the twelve beds along the walls. The thirteenth, however, remains empty.

I'm not sure which turns my blood to ice faster, knowing Koschei has already claimed his twelfth victim, or the thirteenth bed with its turned down bedclothes and fluffed pillow. So inviting. So deadly.

I yawn, a wave of drowsiness washing over me like a warm ocean wave.

"Shake it off, Mira." I slap myself and am amazed anew at how real the sting feels in this realm of dream. "You've got work to do."

Silently, I creep down the hall. With each passing bed, I recognize the girl within. Hannah Abrams. Elizabeth Baker. Janey Campbell. Each pale and breathing shallowly, their hands rest crossed over their chests, as if they're dead rather than merely sleeping. Little Sribindu Patel lies on her side, curled into a ball, trembling. My heart insists I go to her and do whatever I can to ease her suffering, but then, I remember why I'm here.

Slipping past the remaining captives, I find Rachel's bed at the far end on the right. Kneeling by her side, I brush a few loose strands of red hair from her face. Adorned in white gossamer like the others, her sleep, like Sribindu's, is troubled. She tosses from side to side, the worry on her brow making her appear an old woman.

"Rachel? Can you hear me?" When I get no answer, I take a chance. "Trilby?"

"She can't hear you." Koschei's low rumble echoes through the room. "None of them can."

I shoot up from the floor and turn to face Koschei. The Immortal stands just inside the door, every aspect bristling with confidence. "Why have you taken these girls?" I step out into the narrow space between the eleventh and twelfth beds. "I demand an answer."

"You will have your answer soon enough, Ivanovna, but despite the fact that your quest is hopeless, I will again hold my tongue regarding my plans for these lovely young ladies." My stomach turns as he licks his lips, his tongue like an undulating slug across the ruin of his face. "Their fate is, after all, so delicious."

"You plan to kill them. I may not know how or why, but I do know where I am and the power behind this place. What possible purpose could their deaths serve? For God's sake, they're just little girls, not pawns in a game."

"But that's exactly what these children are. Pawns. Expendable pieces in a deadly game of chess. Now that the twelfth has been taken, I trust you finally comprehend how this was never going to end with you as victor, fair Ivanovna."

"The twelfth?" I dash to the bedside, knowing full well whose face I will find when I arrive. Nausea hits me like a tidal wave as her face comes into view. Dark hair splayed across the silk pillowcase like the corona of a dark star. Skin so pale, she appears dead already. Closed eyes I've looked upon almost every night since the day of her birth.

"Isabella."

I spin around, the bow appearing in my hand with a razor-sharp shaft nocked and drawn. Without a word, I let the arrow fly, only to shudder as the bolt shatters in midair an inch from Koschei's chest. I fire another pair of arrows only to have them meet a similar fate.

"You are strong, Ivanovna." Koschei's smile reminds me of a serpent's. "But you cannot hurt me in my own realm." He takes a step in my direction. "Here in this place, my will reigns supreme."

My entire body shakes with anger. "What have you done to my daughter?"

"The same as I have with the others." Koschei stops by Hannah's bed and strokes her cheek with his corpse-like hand. "Their bodies may rest in another world, but their souls lie here with me, and here they will remain."

"Let her go, you bastard."

"But that would be foolish." He steps into the center aisle and heads in my direction. "As I said before, I need thirteen young women, and your lovely daughter is but the twelfth. If I released her as you ask, I would simply be doubling my remaining work, don't you see?"

"Take me if you must…" I lower the bow, hands trembling in frustration. "But let her go. Please. Just let her go."

"No, fair Ivanovna, young Isabella will remain here." He draws close enough that the fetid odor of his breath burns my nostrils. "As for your brave offering to take your daughter's place, for whom do you think the thirteenth bed awaits?"

Without warning, cold iron manacles clamp down on my wrists and ankles. Lengths of metal chain clink as I'm jerked to the floor and dragged from Isabella's side. Every attempt to reach the Firebird's feather tucked inside my tunic fails, the shackles at my wrists nearly wrenching my arms from their sockets as I'm hauled across the rough stone floor. As I'm dragged onto the empty thirteenth bed, I strain with all my might against the unyielding bonds, but to no avail.

I'm caught, like a fly in a spider's web.

Effectively mounted to a medieval rack with the chains holding my limbs growing tighter by the second, I hold in the inevitable screaming for as long as I can. I fight with everything I have, but my best isn't enough. With each passing moment, the sweet oblivion of surrender becomes more tempting. Then, without warning, an eye-watering miasma assaults my nostrils. Pungent and breathtaking, the powerful odor somehow invigorates me. I pull on the chains again, and for the first time they give.

I suck in a deep breath, hoping for another hit of my strongly scented second wind, and yank at the chains with every ounce of my strength. Abject pain erupts through my entire body, though the focus of this pain isn't my arms and legs, but my ears.

Frigid agony assaults my head from either side, first from the left and then from the right. I cast a glance in Koschei's direction only to find the

Immortal as surprised at the turn of events as I am. I inhale to scream, only to feel the weight of the manacles disappear from my wrists. The bed vanishes from beneath me, then the other beds, then the room itself, until all that remains is my ravaged form floating in the impenetrable ether.

"Next time, Ivanovna." A glance to my left reveals the fading silhouette of the Immortal. "And trust me," he whispers with a menacing laugh, "there will be a next time."

~

"She's coming around." An unfamiliar voice. "Cancel the Code Blue." My eyes open on a multitude of men and women in scrubs and white coats peering down at me from all sides. Somehow, I've made it onto a gurney and a couple of the medical professionals hold restraints in their hands as if ready to strap me down. A quick glance down my body reveals a rivulet of blood at the inside of my right elbow where they've placed an IV.

"What's happening?" I croak.

No one answers me, but no less than three of the doctors and nurses surrounding me let out sighs of relief. As if choreographed, all but one step away and head for the door. The last, a medical student in a short white coat who looks like she just graduated from high school, doesn't seem able to let go of my wrist. Her trembling fingers tight over my radial pulse, I look around the room with aching eyes until I find Sterling's blurred silhouette.

"Welcome back, Mira." Visibly shaken, he looks down on me with concern, but also with guilt I've never noticed in his eyes before. "How are you feeling?"

"Like I've gone ten rounds with a grizzly bear." Even the thought of trying to sit up makes my head spin. "Did something happen?"

"You had a seizure, Ms. Tejedor." The student looks down on me through rectangular spectacles. "Or at least a set of convulsions we can't quite explain. We hit you with smelling salts, sternal rub, finally had to resort to ice water in the ears to get you to come around. To be honest, I'm kind of surprised you're able to talk right now."

Smelling salts and ice water in the ears, huh? Well, that makes a lot of sense.

I pull my other hand across to grasp hers, grateful for the show of compassion, but before I can say so much as a word of thanks, the remainder of the events that transpired in Koschei's palace comes rushing back like a tsunami.

"Isabella." My eyes shoot to Sterling. "He's got Isabella."

"No." Caroline joins Sterling by the gurney, her face pale.

Sterling's eyes narrow in confusion. "How?"

As if on cue, my phone rings in my purse. I don't need to be psychic to know exactly who is calling.

"Mira?" Sterling asks.

"Bring me the phone." When he hesitates, I add, "Now."

Sterling digs in my bag and brings out the still-chirping phone. As he glances at the screen, his eyes go cold. "Mira, I'm sorry." He hands me the phone. "It's your mother."

I will my left arm up and over the gurney's side railing and pull myself to a seated position. My stomach threatens to rebel, but somehow, I keep my breakfast down as I answer the phone.

"Hello? Mom?"

"Mira?" The hint of panic in her voice, though not unexpected, chills me to my core. "Thank God you picked up. Something's wrong with Isabella. I don't know what to do."

"Where are you?" My hand trembles so badly, I nearly clock myself in the head with the phone.

"We just pulled into Charlotte a few minutes ago." A pause. "I stopped at a gas station to fill up and grab us some drinks."

"What are you doing here?" My cheeks go hot. "You weren't supposed to arrive till tomorrow afternoon."

"It was Isabella's idea." I can almost see my mother burying her face in her hands. "She… wanted to surprise you."

Of course. "What's wrong with her, Mom?" As if I don't know. "Is she… okay?"

"We left before sun up this morning. Isabella slept most of the way here. We stopped for lunch a couple hours back, and she was fine. Now she won't wake up." Mom's breath catches in her throat. "Wait. This thing you're investigating with all the comatose girls. Is that what this is?"

The blood freezes in my veins. "Don't ask me how, Mom, but I'm pretty sure that's it."

Mom starts to hyperventilate. "And I brought her here. Into the thick of it. Oh God, Mira, I'm sorry. I'm so sorry."

"It's okay, Mom." I swallow down the anger and frustration and keep my voice as calm as possible. "You didn't know." I lock eyes with Caroline. "None of us knew."

"Oh God, Mira. This is all my fault—"

"All right, Mom. Stay with me. You can't freak out on me right now. I need you."

"Okay." She takes a deep breath. "What do you need me to do?"

"First, tell me exactly where you are."

They're stopped at a gas station just a few miles from the hospital. I give Mom directions on how to get here and tell her to take Isabella straight to the ER when they arrive.

"We'll meet you down there, okay?"

"We?" Mom asks. "Is Thomas with you?"

"Not at the moment." My heart sinks. "I'm here at the hospital with Detective Sterling. He's investigating the case."

"Oh." I can hear the wheels turning in Mom's head even through the phone line. "Everything okay between you and Thomas?"

Sterling's features shift in my mind to the grotesque blackface of the Moor even as the memory of Petrushka's pathetic dance cavorts across my memory. The pair of images brings a hint of bile to my tongue. "A topic for another time. Just get Isabella to the hospital as quick as you can."

I end the call and hand my phone back to Sterling. "It's just as I feared."

I fight to hold back the tears, but that battle's over before it's begun. I bury my face in my hands, sobbing uncontrollably. Caroline comes up on one side and Sterling on the other. Their hands on my shoulders provide little comfort.

"Mira?" Anthony steps up and joins his mother beside me, his words as choked as mine. I forgot he was even here. "Is this really my fault?"

"No, kiddo. It's not." I reach out and muss his hair. There's no doubt Anthony is somehow at the center of this, but one look in his sorrow-filled eyes and my heart clenches. Even at my most cynical, I can't believe he'd do this to me, to Isabella, to his own sister. That being said, there's no other mind on the planet that could create this specific brand of madness, which leaves me as well as the others in quite a soup.

At Caroline's nod, I take Anthony's hand. "Listen, kid. I know this all looks bad, but you have to believe we all recognize you're as much a victim here as Isabella, Rachel, and the rest of the girls. No matter what, I'm on your side. Understand?"

"Thanks, Mira." He swallows back the fear and anguish wafting off him like rotten eggs. "Thanks for believing in me."

"So, Mira." Sterling squeezes my shoulder. "What now?"

"Before, I was just doing the right thing. Helping the helpless. Now that Rachel and Isabella are involved, it's personal." I climb down from the gurney, my hands balling into fists at my sides. "I'm bringing our girls home. All of them." I lock gazes with Sterling. "And God help anyone who gets in my way."

19

—————

EN AVANT

"How is she?" I ask the ER doctor.

"Just like the others." He leans in close with his penlight and checks her pupils a second time. "She appears neurologically intact. Her heart and lungs are fine. EKG and vitals are all normal. We haven't done the EEG yet, but I suspect it will be like with the other girls." He slips the light into the front pocket of his white coat and turns to face me. "If I didn't know better, I'd swear they were all just sleeping."

"And dreaming." I rub the bridge of my nose. "Don't forget about the dreaming."

"And there's nothing that will awaken her?" Mom asks as puzzlement at my comment crosses the doctor's face. "A shot? Maybe some medicine?"

"I'm sorry, Ms. Tejedor." The doctor addresses my mother. "We've tried all the standard methods to awaken your granddaughter, even resorted to some pretty noxious stimuli. She withdraws from pain, but that's about it. We can't even get her to open her eyes, much less come awake."

"Oh, God." Tears form at the corners of her eyes. "This is all my fault. All my fault."

"Mom, come on." I wipe a tear from her cheek. "If it weren't today, it would've been tomorrow afternoon when you arrived."

The doctor shoots me a concerned glance. "Tomorrow afternoon?"

"Excuse my mother…" I check his name tag. "Dr. Haydn. She didn't do anything but drive my daughter down from the D.C. area this morning to see me." I give Mom a stern "keep your mouth shut" glare. "She's just upset and blaming herself for Isabella getting sick."

Haydn rests a hand on my mother's arm. "You can't blame yourself, Ms. Tejedor. Sometimes children just get sick." He pulls in a deep breath through his nose. "And if this is, in fact, the same illness that's affected the eleven other girls we have in the hospital right now, understand that some of the best medical minds in the state are working around the clock trying to come up with some kind of answer."

Mom locks gazes with me. She doesn't know the whole story yet, but she understands one thing as well as I do. The answer to the strange malady affecting these poor girls is beyond any test this hospital can run or treatment the doctors can provide.

It's all up to me.

And now, my own daughter is under the gun.

As if I wasn't under enough pressure.

"Can you make sure she gets put on the same floor with the other girls?" I ask.

Haydn nods. "Actually, we've made that our standing protocol, but those rooms are filling up fast. Twelve girls. That's half the rooms on that floor." He signs a paper handed him by a nurse and then returns his attention to us. "None of us know exactly what is happening with these girls, but God willing, there won't be any more."

"God willing, indeed." I don't let on that I know for a fact there won't be any more. Twelve of the thirteen beds in Koschei's palace have already been filled, and I have it on good authority the thirteenth is meant for someone who wouldn't be admitted to a children's floor. "Thanks for all your help with my daughter, Dr. Haydn. Anything more we can do?"

"Can one of you two agree to stay with Isabella around the clock for the next couple of days?" Haydn offers a frustrated smile. "We've already tapped most of our sitters and after the thing that happened on the roof, we're not leaving any of the girls without direct supervision."

"I will stay with her." Mom silences me with a glance. "For as long as it takes."

We make arrangements for Isabella to be moved to the room next door to Rachel Faircloth's and as the doctor heads on to check on another patient, Mom pulls me to one side.

"I must say." Those three words, and I'm sixteen years old again. "I'm surprised Thomas hasn't shown his face around here. Is everything okay with you two?"

"We're fine, Mom. He's just busy and—"

I stop midsentence as Mom levels her patented "don't bullshit me" gaze at me. Having a mother who's effectively a walking, breathing lie detector has its ups and downs for sure. Definitely made navigating high school a bit on the difficult side.

"Mira?" she asks. "What aren't you telling me?"

"Fine." I let out a heavy sigh. "We had a fight."

The two of us alone for the first time since we each arrived at the ER hours ago, I quickly fill Mom in all the sordid details. The missing girls. Koschei. His garden and palace. The Firebird. The Russian fair. The Moor.

Petrushka.

"You should have seen Thomas, Mom. When I told him he was cast as the clown in the Russian fair, it was like I let the air out of his balloon. I'm not sure what bothers him more, the possibility I might see him that way or that Anthony might. In any case, he dropped me off at the apartment last night in a huff and hasn't called all day."

Mom raises an eyebrow. "Have you called him?"

I shake my head, abashed. "He has clients today."

Mom's mouth turns down at the corners. "I'm not telling you how to live your life, but you can't really complain about Thomas giving you the cold shoulder when you—"

"Stop." My brows knit together. "I didn't want to bother him."

"Mira, Mira, Mira. You can lie to yourself all day long if you like, but you can't lie to me. Now, tell me the real reason why you haven't called this man you're moving hundreds of miles for."

Skewered again. "Look, Mom. I'm embarrassed. Is that what you want to hear? Against my better judgment, I told Thomas the truth about Petrushka and the Moor, and now, like it or not, I'm having to deal with the repercussions."

"That's part of it, honey." She rests an index finger on her cheek, her eyelids sliding half-closed. "Now, out with the rest."

"The rest?" I search myself, and then, it hits me. "I guess the truth is I really don't know how I feel right now. About him. About Sterling. I'm… confused."

"Ah. That's better. So, two men, one Mira, and you're trying to figure it out?"

My cheeks go hot. "Something like that."

"Might I suggest you figure out how you feel by talking to each of these men and not a pair of shadows that only live between a boy's ears?"

Wow. Trust Mom not to mince words.

"It's almost three," I mutter as I slip my phone back inside my purse. "Thomas' last client is scheduled for the next hour. I'll call him after that, all right?"

"Good. The surest way to kill a flower is to not water it." She steps over to Isabella's bed and takes her hand. "And what about the other corner of this little triangle?"

As if summoned, Sterling rounds the corner. "Good afternoon, Mira." His gaze drifts to Mom. "Those eyes. You must be Mira's mother."

"Rosa Tejedor." She gives Sterling a quick up and down as she shakes his hand before returning her attention to Isabella. "Mira has caught me up on most of what's been happening the last few days, Detective Sterling. Thank you for all you're doing for Isabella and the others."

He looks down on my unconscious daughter. "Any change in her condition?"

"None as yet." I squeeze Isabella's hand. "How are the other girls?"

Sterling shakes his head. "I went around to each family as you asked. Other than some fretful sleep in a few of them during the last time you were under, no real change."

"Good." I massage my temple. "At least, I hope that's good."

"What next?" Sterling asks. "Any thoughts?"

"I need a night to rest up before I venture back to Koschei's garden to confront tall, dark, and scary, but there's no doubt that's exactly where this is leading."

"And you're sure going back is the best idea? It's a trap set just for you."

"And yet, Koschei or whoever is behind all this madness can't just take me when he wants like he can the girls. If I go back there, it's my choice. That has to mean something." My hand goes to my side where in another world the Firebird's feather lies tucked inside Princess Ivanovna's tunic. "Not to mention, I still have at least one trump card up my sleeve."

~

"Hello, Thomas."

"Hi, Mira." Even across the phone line, the fatigue that colors Thomas' words is unmistakable. And it's only a little after seven. He must have had one hell of a day. "Any news?"

"He has Isabella."

I tell him everything. About the nightmares, running into Katie Kaczynski at the hospital, my latest walk through Koschei's garden via Rachel Faircloth. No more secrets.

"Twelve beds, twelve girls, and only one empty bed remaining."

"Why do I have the feeling I know exactly who the thirteenth bed is meant for?"

"As always, you're right on target." I squeeze my eyes shut as a flash of memory hits me like a freight train. The manacles about my wrists. The chains pulling me to the bed. Koschei's wheezy laugh. "He tried to take me this time, Thomas."

"Koschei?"

I let out a trembling breath. "Whoever he is, he's getting stronger. He put me in that bed at the end of the hall, and I couldn't escape no matter how hard I fought. If the doctors hadn't shoved smelling salts up my nose and sprayed ice water in my ears, I'd never have made it out."

"And Isabella?"

"Just like the others."

"What is she even doing here?" Thomas asks. "It's only Tuesday."

"Mom brought her a day early." I pinch at the bridge of my nose. "Isabella wanted to surprise me." I glance over at my daughter's still form, her chest rising and falling beneath the starched hospital sheets. "We've got her here with all the other victims. I couldn't risk her being separated from the others now that all of them are bound to Koschei's realm."

Thomas takes a breath. "He was just waiting for her to arrive, wasn't he?"

"More than that." My free hand balls into a fist. "Whoever is behind Koschei clearly had this planned all along."

"What do you mean?"

"Think about it. A few days before Isabella is due to arrive in town, a little girl goes missing and draws me back into the world of dream."

"You want Mira Tejedor," Thomas interrupts, "you put a child in danger."

"First one. Then two more are taken. Then three. Then, on the off chance he didn't have my attention, Koschei turns up the volume by having ten girls threaten to leap off a building. And that's where it gets personal. Rachel." My eyes slip closed. "Isabella."

"He springs the trap." Thomas pauses on the line. "Oh Mira, I'm so sorry."

I choke back tears. "I'm guessing the asshole couldn't get to Isabella when she was still up north, but once she was within range of—God help us—Anthony, it was all over but the crying."

"Anthony." I can almost hear the gears turning in Thomas' head. "This has to be him, but I can't fathom why he'd do something that would hurt you so profoundly after everything you two have been through."

Isabella shifts in the bed. I rush to her side, praying her eyes will flutter open and she'll look up at me with a whispered, "Mami?" Instead, her breathing resumes its metronome-like rhythm.

"Dammit." I fists clench at my side. "Dammit. Dammit. Dammit."

"Mira?" Thomas' voice leaves my jackhammer heart racing even faster. "What are you thinking?"

"If Isabella's arrival in Charlotte was all part of the plan, then one thing is clear. Whoever's face is hidden behind the Koschei mask knows far more about me than is healthy for any of us."

"About both of us." Thomas sighs. "You're talking to the treating therapist of half a dozen girls who may never wake up again. As far as I've been able to put together, I'm the only common link between any of them. How do you think it's going to look when that comes out?"

"I spoke to Katie. She said she wasn't going to—"

"Katie isn't the only reporter in Charlotte, Mira. At this point, it's not if it comes out, but when. Don't you see?"

"Of course I do." I hang my head. "God, Thomas, this thing is tearing us apart. How are we going to make it through?"

"Stay strong, Mira. Somehow, we'll figure this out."

"Okay." I take a moment to collect my thoughts. "So, what now?"

"Honestly?" Thomas asks. "As I see it, the next step is figuring out which one of us this 'Koschei' is trying to destroy."

"Which one of us?" I pull the phone away from my face as if slapped. "What are you talking about?"

"Consider this, Mira. You're drawn back into the world of dream, danger at every turn, your friends attacked, your daughter comatose. Clearly an attack on you, but..."

"Also an attack on you." I've been so busy rolling with the astral punches, it had never occurred to me I might not be the ultimate target of Koschei's attacks. "It's like we were saying before. Want to hurt Mira Tejedor? Hurt her daughter. Want to hurt Thomas Archer?"

Thomas' voice goes dead. "Hurt the woman he loves."

My heart freezes in my chest. "God, Thomas. I'm so sorry. About everything."

"Stop, Mira. We'll figure all of that out when this is done. For now, we have twelve little girls and you to worry about."

"But, Thomas—"

"Not now, Mira." A sharp intake of air comes across the phone line. "Look. No matter what, my feelings for you haven't faltered, not even a bit. Right now, however, I need to be objective if we're to puzzle this out." He pauses. "For the moment, I think it's best if we put all the personal issues between us on the back burner. You know, so we can focus."

"Agreed." His words leave me simultaneously comforted and cold. "For the moment."

"Good." Thomas drops into full-on therapist mode. "So, let's get started. Anyone you can think of in either of our pasts who might have an axe to grind?"

Before I can answer, a chime comes across the phone line. Thomas' doorbell.

"You expecting someone?" I ask as Katie Kaczynski's far too innocent smile flits across my mind.

"No," Thomas answers. "Actually been looking forward to a quiet evening all day."

The phone goes dead for a few seconds as Thomas heads to answer the door. Then, the sound of a turning lock hits my ear along with seven words that stop me dead in my tracks.

"Detective Sterling," Thomas' voice suddenly goes even more monotone. "What are you doing here?"

20

MASQUERADE

I'm at the police station in twenty minutes flat. Would've gotten there faster, but as usual, every third road in Charlotte is under some form of construction. How long does it take to put in a stupid trolley, anyway?

Sterling's cruiser is parked in its usual spot. The dark blue sedan may look just like all the others, but after the last several days, I know the license plate as well as my own. I head inside and am nearly past the front desk when an officer stops me.

"I'm sorry, Ms. Tejedor, but you're going to have to wait out here."

"You're kidding, right?" Unfamiliar with this particular cop, I walk over to the desk and check his nameplate. "Officer Martinez."

"Not kidding, ma'am. Just following orders."

My hands shoot to my hips. "Whose orders?"

His eyes flicker up and to the right. "Detective Sterling's."

"Really?" Heat rises in my cheeks as I lean in. "I assume you know I'm an official consultant working with Detective Sterling on the very case he's investigating."

He draws back as if I have leprosy. "I know exactly who you are, Ms. Tejedor, and why you're here. I'm still not allowed to let you back."

I reach out a hand to rest it on the cool wood, and Martinez pushes his chair back from the desk as if I've pulled a gun on him.

"Please," he whispers. "I'm just following orders."

Wow. He's actually scared. I pull my hands up before me, palms out in surrender. "Whoa, whoa, whoa. We're just talking here."

"Sorry," he says. "People like you give me the creeps."

The heat radiating from my face doubles in intensity. "People like me?"

"You know." His gaze drops to the floor. "Psychics." He chances a cautious look up into my eyes. "At least the ones who can actually do what they say they can do."

I don't know whether to be pissed the guy's treating me like I've got Ebola or impressed that he's actually open-minded enough to respect someone with my abilities. "Look," I check his nameplate again, "Rick." I cross my arms and keep a safe distance. "I don't know what you've heard, but I'm not going to hurt you, or anybody, for that matter." I shoot him my winningest smile. "Not that I could even if I wanted to."

"Is that why the Sayles woman is still lying in a hospital bed nine months later?"

I pull in close. "How do you know about that?"

"The whole force knows." He shrugs. "At least pieces of it." Warily, he leans forward as his voice drops to barely audible. "Last year, it was made pretty clear that anyone who leaked the full extent of your involvement in the Julianna Wagner case would be suspended without pay, but cops talk, especially about the weird stuff." His lips pull tight in a straight line. "We all know exactly what you're capable of."

I raise an eyebrow. "Between you and me, Officer Martinez? Despite the fact that Veronica Sayles got exactly what was coming to her, what happened to her was beyond anything I can do alone, and as far as I know, that was a once in a lifetime event."

"Once in a lifetime, huh? From what I hear, you've had several 'once in a lifetimes' in just the past week."

"Do tell."

"Well…" He draws up and squints at me. "You've been sniffing out these missing kids like a bloodhound with basically a hundred percent success rate, and just yesterday, you kept all those girls from taking a group header off the hospital rooftop."

"Wow, you're certainly… well informed."

"Like I said," Martinez whispers conspiratorially, "cops talk." He bites his lip. "Not everyone believes the stories, but I do."

"And why is that, exactly?"

"My mother. She ran afoul of a *bruja* back in our village in Mexico when I was eight. She was never the same. Always nervous, looking over her shoulder, worried about the least thing." He pales a shade. "And her stutter. She never had it before that day. Followed her till the day she died."

Though my hands ball into fists, I keep my voice calm. "I'm very sorry to hear about your mother, Officer Martinez, though I'd be careful who I was calling witch." I force my mouth into the slightest of smiles. "I'd hate to have to turn you into a frog."

"Wait here, Ms. Tejedor." Martinez quickly excuses himself. "I'll let Detective Sterling know you're here."

I'm not kept waiting long. Martinez doesn't make a reappearance, but Sterling is at the desk scant seconds later.

"Hello, Mira." Sterling massages his neck. "Can't say I'm surprised to see you here."

"I'm guessing not, since you left word I wasn't to be allowed back to see Thomas."

Sterling inhales through his nose at the mention of Thomas' name. "I'm sorry about having to bring him in, Mira. As far as I'm concerned, Dr. Archer is no more a suspect than you are, despite his connection to eight of the twelve victims." He glances across his shoulder in the direction of the door he just came through. "My bosses didn't exactly see it that way."

"And the thought of humiliating Thomas by dragging him down to the station didn't have anything to do with it?"

Sterling pulls back as if struck, the cayenne of his frustration hitting me like a tidal wave. "Watch it, Mira. You and I may have had a disagreement or two in the past, but don't question my integrity."

My cheeks grow warm again, though this time out of embarrassment rather than anger. "Sorry. My mouth got ahead of me." I rack my brains, looking for an olive branch. "So, how is Thomas?"

"He's fine." Sterling's eyes go wide as he fights back his exasperation. "Just so you know, I made sure it was me that brought him in. I wanted to make sure he received the appropriate amount of… respect."

"Oh." My heart sinks another couple of inches in my chest. "Is he under arrest?"

"Not at this time. His relationship with his six patients, Rachel, and Isabella is circumstantial evidence at best, but more importantly, regardless of his utter lack of any kind of motive, there's simply no crime to even charge him with."

"No crime?" I gape. "Those girls are being kidnapped, plain and simple."

"Mira," Sterling says. "You know I believe in you and what you can do. I've seen it with my own eyes. But the rest of the force? And especially the deputy chief? Not so much."

"But—"

"Look, I go telling them about fantasy dreamscapes and psychic kidnappings, and I'll be out of a job." Sterling scans the station. "Those girls have been worked up by some of the best doctors in all of North Carolina with no clear diagnosis. No infection. No poisoning. No nothing. Beyond what you've seen on your mental forays, there's not even a shred of evidence of foul play. As far as CMPD is concerned, something weird is happening to the girls of Charlotte, and we're trying to figure it out to keep it from happening again, but we're not looking for a suspect." He again glances back at the door. "At least not at the moment."

"So, Thomas is free to go?"

"When we get done taking his statement? Of course." Sterling disengages and rests his hand on the doorknob. "Don't worry, Mira. I can't make any guarantees, but as best I can, I won't let anything happen to your man, all right?"

"All right." My cheeks burn hotter, with embarrassment or another emotion, I'm not quite sure. "Thank you, Sterling."

Without another word, Sterling disappears behind the door. A minute or so later, a replacement for Martinez comes out and takes his seat at the desk. This new officer is a black female, maybe five years younger than me. She greets me with a smile and a bottle of water.

"Courtesy of Detective Sterling." She motions to the collection of chairs along the wall. "He wanted me to let you know he and Dr. Archer should be another half hour or so, if you'd like to wait."

"I'll be right here." I grab one of the chairs in the far corner, tucking my purse tight beneath my arm in case any of the three delinquents sitting across from me get any ideas.

As I get settled in, one simple fact becomes apparent. I've misjudged Sterling. The Moor may hate the poor clown's guts, but out here in the real world, Sterling actually seems to be looking out for Thomas.

The world of dream is, after all, just that.

On the other hand, I know twelve little girls who would argue that point if they could only open their eyes.

Quick inventory. Thomas is with Sterling. Caroline is with Rachel. Mom is with Isabella.

No one to call. No one to talk to.

I guess I sit and wait.

I mindlessly browse social media on my phone, the news, the stock market, but Isabella's pale face continually intrudes on my thoughts regardless of how hard I try to distract myself. I catch myself nodding off more than once, but force myself to stay awake no matter how tempted I am to give in to the sweet release of sleep. The station's coffee goes down like battery acid, but at least it helps keep my eyes open.

After what seems like hours, I glance up at the female officer who gave me the water. I motion to my watch, and she shakes her head and signals three-zero with her fingers.

Thirty minutes. That's what she said forty minutes ago.

Another few minutes pass, and my head again starts to bob. I pinch myself, desperate to stay awake. I refuse to fall out of my chair here in front of God and everybody.

I am Mira Tejedor. I've fought my way out of insane art galleries, tower prisons, and creepy puppet shows. Surely I can stay awake another thirty minutes.

~

My eyes open on a Russian cathedral in the distance, the gray-skied backdrop of *Petrushka* filling my vision from horizon to horizon. Dammit. I guess everybody has to sleep sometime.

The ear-splitting snare drum assaulting my ears fades into a pleasant melody as stall by stall and person by person, the Shrove-Tide Fair returns to existence. This time, at least, I am spared the terror of being trapped in a body that won't obey my commands, though I do find myself again disembodied, a passive observer of the events of the fair, a wraith among a throng of villagers who only exist in a world of imagination.

I recognize many faces from my first walk through the fair. Beneath the constable's silver helmet, the face of Sterling's partner, Mitch Bolger, surveys the crowd, waiting for the first person to step out of line. The Russian girl that in some strange way is Hannah Abrams walks arm in arm with this world's version of her father, her vibrant yellow dress and gold coat setting off a face still pallid from the Charlatan's enchantment.

But at least her smile has returned.

Even the cloaked man with his bunch of colored balloons puts in an appearance. I catch a glimpse of his face this time, and I'll be damned if he's not the spitting image of the Janitor from Anthony's Exhibition. Previously known as the Sage and I suspect far wiser than he lets on, the wall-eyed Janitor has now been reduced to distributing balloons to frolicking children.

I contemplate how so many of the mighty among the Exhibition have fallen, and no one more so than me, all-powerful storyteller reduced in this place first to a Ballerina puppet and now a mere specter who can do nothing but watch.

The earnest merchants man their stations, pitching their wares to anyone who might pause for half a second. Peasants and noblemen alike circle the various musicians and dancers, as the carousel spins on, the boys and girls atop its army of mermaids and dragons squealing with delight.

Throughout the crowd, young maidens in full-length dresses of light pink or sky blue both flirt with and spurn the advances of a group of coachmen in long coats and black top hats. One coachman in particular, his royal blue coat in stark contrast with his reddish-brown beard, takes the rejection from the Hannah Abrams lookalike quite hard before chasing her into the crowd, his hands dramatically crossed over his heart.

Lovers kiss. Drunkards fight. Women gossip.

The second-floor balcony of the theater now abandoned, the ancient Master of Ceremonies with his knee-length beard, midnight blue robe, and lute has joined the revelry. At his subtle nod, the theater's frontage erupts in sparklers and fireworks, the yellow lace at his wrists flashing with each strum of his instrument even as the orange feather tucked in his fur cap bursts into flame.

Before I can fully process what I'm seeing, the crowd parts and two lines of the maidens from before rush out from beneath an arch at the far end of the square. Faceless no longer, these maidens now wear the features of the girls taken by Koschei. Older than their real world counterparts, each set of eyes retains a semblance of innocence. Fortunately, I don't count Rachel and Isabella among their number.

At least, not yet.

The music swells, a lively tune, and soon each pair in pink and blue is twirling arm in arm in an intricate folk dance as the yellow-clad Hannah Abrams looks on beatifically, all to the grand enjoyment of the merry mob.

In line and spinning in time with the song, each of the maidens sheds her outer coat as their leader in gold and yellow steps to the center and leads the eight girls in a *khorovod* not that different from the Dance of the Princesses from the world of *The Firebird*. Soon, the yearning coachmen return and pair off with the maidens, their frustrated flirtation brought to life in dance. From the crowd, the coachman in blue returns and pulls the Hannah Abrams doppelgänger in yellow to the center of the square. For a moment, they dance in perfect step, arms about each other's waist as if they were lovers reunited after years apart.

For a moment, happiness fills the festival and the fact that I'm trapped in a nightmare doesn't seem all that important.

The music shifts, a dark prelude to a high-pitched oboe solo that returns fear to my heart. A bearded peasant I haven't seen before steps to the center of the square, the offending instrument at his lips. Not alone, he quickly becomes the fair's new focus as the rubberneckers oscillate between laughs and screams at the sight of the fully grown brown bear he leads by a chain. The peasant playfully wrestles with his muzzled costar before pushing the animal away and looking directly in my disembodied direction. Only then do I realize I have, in fact, seen this man before.

Nine months ago. Along the Exhibition.

Hartmann the Cart Man, albeit in need of a serious shave, peers at me in confusion for half a second before returning his attention to his ursine companion and forcing it to the ground in a playful takedown. As the triumphant peasant takes his bows and stomps back into the mob, a man in a long gray coat and top hat appears, his bearded face unmistakably that of Jason Faircloth, Anthony's older brother.

Drunkenly dancing with the two Gypsy women that earlier accompanied the Master of Ceremonies, it's clear this character has designs on each of them that go far beyond getting his palm read. As the music shifts into a lively jig played on violin and woodwind, the carnival comes alive, and no more so than when the man begins to throw money into the air. Seeing even a semblance of Jason behaving in such a way burns at my soul, but nothing like the searing fire that hits my core when the features of the two Gypsy women morph into grownup versions of Rachel Faircloth and my daughter, Isabella.

Whoever is behind this, they know how to play my emotions like a master violinist.

God help them when I finally discover the face behind their mask.

Soon, the music shifts again into a heavy tune, the beginning of a new routine. Tympani drum and brass accompany nine coachmen as they caper in traditional Russian style, but the men aren't left dancing alone for long. Thank God, the coachmen remain mere ciphers on the stage of wherever my mind is trapped.

Small blessings, as my mother always says.

As a light snow begins to fall, Hannah Abrams in her yellow frock leads the collection of girls in pink and blue dresses in a line to join the coachmen, the tune that accompanied the maidens' previous dance making a resurgence. Paired off, the coachmen and maidens commence a traditional folk dance, the music going faster and faster until the beat and their movements hit a fever pitch. The peasant and his bear, the merchant, and the gypsies all return, and the entire gathering falls into the mother of all dances as the sun finally sets on the bizarre extravaganza.

Snow continues to accumulate as the sky falls to twilight.

Only then do things get truly weird.

A collection of masqueraders wearing enormous animal heads run, dance, and even crawl to the center of the square from every corner. Pig, goat, and fish are all represented as the triumphant mixture of trumpet and drum shifts into a frenetic tune of woodwind and brass that reminds me of the *William Tell* Overture on acid. From nowhere, a man dressed as a black devil, complete with horns and tail, sprints from the shadows of the theater and terrorizes the crowd with leaps, kicks, and pirouettes. Eventually fought off by the coachmen, the fair resumes its revelry and all appears well until a muted trumpet playing in minor key signifies another shift. A cry in the distance brings everyone's attention back to the Charlatan's booth.

In a blink, I find myself disembodied no longer. Back in the red, pink, and white form of the Ballerina, I stand staring at the inside of the booth's blue curtain.

My heart freezes.

Since Caroline first explained to me the events of *Petrushka*, I've read every article on Stravinsky's ballet, studied every synopsis, even watched a video of the entire performance.

I know how this ends.

I've known for days.

God help us all.

21

DEATH OF PETRUSHKA

A tear courses down my cheek.

I can't so much as raise a hand to brush it away.

The muted trumpet transitions to the whine of a distant oboe, bringing my limbs to life. In the dim light of the Charlatan's booth, the Moor grabs for Petrushka, his flailing arms striking both me and the curtain, if not the clown. Petrushka, his face identical to Thomas' right down to his sideways smirk, bolts from the curtain. The Moor follows close behind, a golden scimitar held above his head in a fury. Suddenly able to move, I leap *en pointe* after the dark Arabian that wears Sterling's face and strive in vain to stop the inevitable.

The three of us—Petrushka, Moor, and Ballerina—make one more pass behind the blue curtain. Then, it's out into the square. The crowd parts like the Red Sea as Petrushka flees for his life. His body limp and uncoordinated like the hand puppet he represents, the clown is no match for the unstoppable Arabian. Petrushka catches my hand as he rushes past, and I squeeze his fingers half a second before the Moor catches him by the waist of his pants. Spinning the white-and-orange-clad clown around twice, the Arabian brings his flashing blade across Petrushka's back, the attack a strange mirror of the clown's cudgel ambush from the beginning of the play, but far more deadly. Raising his arms in triumph, the Moor doesn't even give poor Petrushka the benefit of a backward glance as he slumps to the snow-covered cobblestone.

The clown's porcelain face shatters on impact with the street as a pair of tambourine strikes sound in the distance.

"No!" I scream, the first and only word I've been able to say in this horrible place.

In a blink, the Moor vanishes, and a moment later, I disappear as well. Again a disembodied wraith, I am forced to watch as the events of *Petrushka* play out in the only way they can.

For a moment, the clown lies there still as death. The music drops to a quiet tremolo of violin punctuated only by a high-pitched tone of a piccolo as his limp body twitches once, twice, three times. Then, the right side of his face demolished, Petrushka pulls himself up from the ground. A clarinet solo fills the air as the clown slips and his head falls again to the cobblestone. Forcing his broken face once more from the street, Petrushka peers around at the crowd. Tears flowing from his remaining eye, he accepts a kerchief from the girl wearing Hannah Abrams' features before finally falling to the ground, never to move again.

Petrushka the clown leaves this plane not with a fanfare of brass or the boom of a kettledrum but with the hushed tones of a mournful flute.

～

"Thomas."

I'm up and moving before I've come fully awake. I head straight for the door leading to the room where Sterling is questioning Thomas. The officer at the desk goes wide-eyed as she instinctively reaches for her pistol.

"No need for firearms." I whip past her. "Just get me to Detective Sterling. Now."

She rushes after me. "But he said you were to wait out here."

I turn on her like a snake coiled to strike. "You people are supposed to 'serve and protect,' right?" I grab the door handle and give it a yank. Locked. "Then get me to Sterling before something horrible happens."

Sterling explodes through the door, nearly knocking both of us over. "Mira. Thank God you're still here." He grabs my hand and yanks me through the door. "Come on."

Sterling and I sprint down the short hallway, stopping at a door at the end of the hall. A table sits at the center of a standard interrogation room with one of its three chairs, the one opposite the no doubt two-way mirror, resting on its side. In the far corner, a cop that looks like he just started shaving hovers over Thomas' slumped form, a pair of fingers at Thomas' neck.

"His pulse is going a mile-a-minute." The young cop glances up at Sterling and me. "He's still breathing, but he doesn't look good."

"Mira." Sterling grabs my hand and locks gazes with me. "We've already called 9-1-1 and paramedics are on the way." He squeezes my fingers gently. "You have to know, we… I… didn't do this."

"I know." I let go of his hand. "God help me, I know."

Sterling did not, in fact, just impale poor Thomas with a wickedly curved blade of gold.

Just someone wearing Sterling's face.

With God as my witness, that someone is going to pay.

"What happened?" I rush over to kneel by Thomas' side. "Tell me everything."

The young cop retreats to give me some space. "I wasn't here when it happened. Detective Sterling had me watch him while he went to get you."

I crane my neck around and catch the usually unflappable Calvin Sterling about as flapped as I've ever seen him. "Tell me."

Sterling swallows. "We were just talking, Mira. Reviewing the facts. Trying to establish some link between the various girls involved. He had just taken a sip of water when…"

"When what?"

"Look. At first, I thought he was choking, but before I could even stand up to help him, he began to… race around the room." He wipes the sweat from his forehead. "I've never seen anything like it."

My heart sinks. "Anything else?"

Sterling crosses his arms. If I didn't know better, I'd swear he was on the edge of tears. "He ran three laps around the table, panicked as if the Devil himself was hot on his heels, and then screamed as if he'd been struck. His arms shot to the sky and he fell face first onto the concrete." He kneels by my side. "Would've split his head open if I hadn't caught him."

But he did hit his head. Hit it hard. Shattered his porcelain skull.

Just not in this place.

Dammit. How could I have not seen this coming?

At least Thomas' question about which of us is the target has been answered.

Missing girls. Anthony's involvement. Rachel. Isabella. Now Thomas himself.

Whoever this is, they're gunning for me and want me to suffer at every step.

A moment later, the paramedics arrive. As they descend upon Thomas, Sterling and I retreat to a corner of the room.

"Why do I have a feeling you know exactly what's happening here, Mira?" Sterling studies me through squinted eyes. "It's the same as the girls, isn't it?"

I massage the area above my right eye in a vain attempt to stave off the inevitable headache. "I wish I knew."

Sterling strokes his chin. "There's something you're not telling me, isn't there?"

Fantastic. This talk didn't go well with Thomas. Can't imagine it's going to go any better with Sterling.

"Look, I've told you everything regarding *The Firebird*, right?"

His lips curl into a rueful grimace. "In gory detail."

"Well, there's something else going on besides fiery birds, monsters, and immortal sorcerers." I look away, unable to meet his gaze. "Another place entirely."

Sterling shakes his head. "Of course there is."

"That place and the events there are without a doubt responsible for what just happened to Thomas."

"And yet it's not related to everything happening with the girls?"

"It is and it isn't." I swallow back tears and more pride than I'd like to admit. "*The Firebird* was the first of Stravinsky's *Ballets Russes*. His second was a work called…" I can barely say the word. "*Petrushka.*"

I tell Sterling everything. My role in the performance. Petrushka's face. The identity of the Moor. The unrequited love of the clown for the Ballerina and of the Ballerina for the Moor.

Petrushka's final fate.

"The Moor. This Arabian who wears my face. He killed the clown?"

"Struck him down like he was nothing." I wring my hands. "And there wasn't a damn thing I could do about it."

Sterling's hand goes to his neck the way it does when he's feeling stressed. Or guilty. "Then, this is my fault."

I grab his chin and turn his gaze to mine. "You didn't do a thing. Someone with a particularly nasty axe to grind is systematically pitting everything and everyone I love against each other, but that person isn't you, Sterling."

"Everyone you love?"

God. This is getting complex. "Everyone I care about. Let's not get carried away."

"Sorry. This is neither the time nor the place for—"

"Understatement of the year." I step over to the nearest paramedic. "So, how is he?"

"He seems to have stabilized." She looks up at me. "His pulse is back below a hundred and his breathing has normalized." One eyebrow rises quizzically. "Other than the fact we can't seem to rouse him, he basically looks like someone who's sleeping."

"Hmm." I glance in Sterling's direction. "Where have we heard that before?"

"What now?" Sterling asks.

I kneel at Thomas' side. "We let these fine professionals do their job and take Thomas to the hospital." I take Thomas' cool fingers in my hand and give them a tight squeeze. "Then you and I get back to work figuring out exactly who it is I have to put out of our misery."

Sterling and I follow the ambulance to the hospital, siren wailing and blue lights flashing. Once inside, Sterling leaves to interface with the contingent of cops keeping watch over the girls in the children's hospital while I stay with Thomas in the ER to help get him checked in. After I'm confident everything with Thomas is settled, I step out to get some water and cross gazes with one of the doctors that worked with me nine months ago when it was me lying unconscious on a hospital gurney.

"Ms. Tejedor, right?" he asks with a sheepish half-grin.

"Impressive memory, doc."

"A story like yours?" he says. "Not easy to forget."

I try like crazy to recall his name, and failing that, allow my eyes to drift down to the name badge hanging off his white coat.

Ah. That's right. How could I forget?

Holst.

Anthony would be so jealous.

I glance past him to where a newspaper with my face plastered across the cover rests askew at the nurses' station. "And the fact that my name and picture is all over the front page didn't help to jog your memory?"

His cheeks pink up a bit. "I'd be lying if I said 'Mira Tejedor, psychic' hasn't been a topic of discussion around the ER the last few days." He raises an eyebrow. "I'm not the only one around here who remembers you and everything that went down last year. Not to mention, it's common knowledge you're working with the cops on the weird case with all the comatose girls upstairs."

"Famous or infamous, doesn't matter. Never wanted to be either." I chuckle, though it comes out more like a sigh. "What's that ancient Chinese curse? 'May your life be interesting' or something along those lines?"

"If that's the case, then you are definitely among the cursed, Ms. Tejedor." Holst draws close, as if afraid someone might hear us. "If you don't mind me asking, what the hell is going on with all these kids? It's like nothing I've ever seen."

"I wish I knew." Before I can expound on my explanation, a familiar voice sounds from the opposite end of the ER.

"I was his fiancé for over a year. Now, let me see him." The practiced non-accent covering just a hint of native Charlottean can only be one person.

Katie Kaczynski rounds the corner and immediately locks gazes with me.

"Tejedor," she grumbles as she stalks in my direction, dressed in a t-shirt and yoga pants, her flaming red hair pulled back in a ponytail.

Nice to know she doesn't spring out of bed looking like a model off the cover of *Vogue.*

An alarm sounds and Dr. Holst scoots to another room as Kaczynski stalks closer.

"Where's Thomas, Mira?" she asks. "What the hell is going on?"

"I could ask you the same question." I pull close and drop my voice a few decibels. "We just got here a few minutes ago. How did you even know he was here?"

She shoots me a withering look. "I wouldn't be much of a reporter if I didn't keep my ear to the train tracks, now would I?" When it's clear I haven't the first idea what she's talking about, she rolls her eyes and adds, "I was listening to the police scanner, if you have to know." She glances around the ER, clearly upset. "We may have broken up months ago, but it doesn't mean I don't give a shit when a 9-1-1 call for a Dr. Thomas Archer goes out."

"Sorry." Can't believe I'm saying the word, much less meaning it. "Come on."

I lead Katie to the room where a nurse in mauve scrubs and matching clogs is adjusting one of the machines pumping fluids into Thomas' arm. Though Thomas appears pale and his breathing shallow, he still looks a ton better than he did crumpled on the interrogation room floor. Katie Kaczynski, unfortunately, doesn't have that image as a frame of reference.

"My God," she stammers as she rushes to his side. "Thomas. Wake up." She grabs his hand and mutters "Thomas" once more before breaking down in a fit of sobs.

Call me crazy, but all of a sudden I feel like the outsider here.

Kaczynski glances back in my direction as she wipes her tears away with her bare arm.

"What the hell happened?" She turns back to the bed. No hint of artifice colors her words, the anxiety and grief more than backed up by the nauseating mix of chlorine and vinegar pouring off her as if from an open fire hydrant. "Why won't he wake up?"

I shake my head in frustration. "That is the question of the hour, I'm afraid."

"I don't understand. There's not a mark on him." Her eyes find mine a second time. "Wait." She rises from the bedside, fists clenching and unclenching at her sides. "This is the same thing as all the girls." She begins to pace. "Isn't it?"

"Seems that way." No sense in hiding the truth, or at least this part of it. "Now—"

"Seems that way?" The chlorine and vinegar wafting off her shift toward cayenne, leaving my eyes stinging. "Seems that way?" She marches over and stabs a finger in my chest. "I don't want to hear that from you. Not when it's *your* fault."

I recoil as if she's slapped me across the face. "My fault?"

"That's what I said." Her arms cross, and the pepper coming off her doubles in intensity. "I have no doubt you think I'm just another pretty head of hair they stick in front of the camera to regurgitate the news, but I've been doing this gig for almost a decade now. I can put two and two together."

"Oh, really?" My arms cross, mirroring Kaczynski's. "Do tell."

"Well, let's see." Not quite a smile, her lips spread maniacally even as her gaze takes on a zealot's fire. "You shoot into town nine months ago at the request of a comatose boy's mother and over the course of a single week, do something entire teams of doctors couldn't do. You bring him back from the edge, put him back the way he was before, maybe even better. Mira Tejedor, the big psychic superhero, saves the day."

She's lucky Mira Tejedor, the big psychic superhero, isn't flattening her nose right now.

"Nine months later, everything hits the fan again. But this time, it's not one child. It's twelve. And now, their therapist has been caught in the crossfire."

"You think I'm responsible for this?"

She studies me for a moment. "Not intentionally."

I raise an eyebrow. "Then what are you suggesting?"

"That you spread it. The madness." She pulls back from me, almost imperceptibly, and the slightest bit of sulfurous fear invades my senses. "Like an infection."

A laugh escapes my lips at the ludicrousness of her accusation. "You have no idea what you're talking about."

"Don't I?" Her lips pull back in a snarl. "You touch Anthony's mind, spend nine months getting close to Thomas, and now he and several of his clients are all in the same state as the kid who brought you to Charlotte in the first place." She turns back to Thomas. "Maybe you meant to do it, maybe you didn't. Either way, the evidence is lying unconscious in a bed right in front of us."

I suck in a breath to argue with her, my hands balling into fists as the adrenaline already coursing through my veins shoots through the roof, but a part of me knows that in some way, she's right. I pull up beside Katie Kaczynski, and the two of us look down on Thomas together for almost a minute without either of us saying a word.

Kaczynski eventually breaks the silence.

"You saved the Faircloth kid. I have no doubt of that." She stares at me sidelong. "Now, save Thomas. He and I may have missed our window, but I still love him." She brings the heel of her hand to her cheek in a vain attempt to stop the tears. "I can't stand to see him this way."

"I'll fix this." Not sure whom I'm trying to convince with the muttered three words, Kaczynski or myself. "I swear."

"You'd better, Mira Tejedor." Her hand drops to her side. "You'd better."

22

CHAÎNÉ

"I hate to tell you this, Ms. Tejedor, but as you can see," Dr. Sands, the neurologist working on Thomas' case, points to a collection of squiggly green lines marching across his computer screen, "Dr. Archer is exhibiting a significantly disordered sleep architecture."

"Disordered..." My gaze wanders from the screen and over to Thomas' still form. Covered with adhesive electric leads, his freshly shorn scalp looks like something out of a science fiction movie. "What exactly does that mean?"

Dr. Sands gestures to the screen. "A waking EEG usually shows fast low-voltage waves that aren't particularly synchronized. As we fall asleep, everything slows down and synchronizes into stage I sleep. As we hit stage II, we start see sleep spindles and K complexes." He points to a large disturbance in the eighteen parallel squiggles. "Like those."

"So, he's asleep?"

"Wait, there's more." He points to the screen where the relatively tame collection of squiggles goes nuts. "Now, these are delta waves, signifying deep sleep, stage III or IV." He looks at me expectantly. "Don't you get it?"

"Sorry." I'm sure I learned all this stuff a million years ago in my botched attempt at grad school, but the neurons where I kept all the info on sleep physiology no doubt got repurposed years ago. "Help me."

He lets out a disappointed sigh. "Well, you see, we normally go

180

through four or five sleep cycles each night, each one lasting around ninety minutes, with more and more time in REM as the night goes on."

"That's where we dream." I cross my arms defensively. "I do remember that much."

"Exactly." He turns back to the monitor. "Dr. Archer. He's not cycling every ninety minutes but every ninety seconds or so." At my dumbfounded gaze, he lets out another sigh. "How can I put this? His brain is all over the place. Light sleep. Deep sleep. Dreaming. Not dreaming. Awake. Not awake. It's like nothing I've ever seen." He bites his lip. "That is, till this week."

My scalp tingles as I anticipate the answer to my next question. "I'm guessing all the girls have exhibited similar findings on their EEGs."

"All I've examined." He meets my gaze. "Just three girls to go. I believe we're doing the Faircloth girl at 12:30 and your daughter around 2:00. Would you like to be present her exam?"

"I wouldn't be anywhere else." I look back at Thomas. "The rapid cycling. Is it hurting him? The others?"

"Honestly, we really don't know. Nothing here appears consistent with seizure activity or else we'd be doing a lot more. We believe the most prudent approach at the moment is to simply continue providing supportive care and wait for them to wake up."

"Wait." I let out a frustrated chuckle. "Pardon me, Dr. Sands, if your plan doesn't inspire a ton of confidence."

He rests a hand lightly on my shoulder. "I'm sorry, Ms. Tejedor. We're all doing the best we can here."

I manage a smile. "You can say that again." I lean in and kiss Thomas' cheek. "See you upstairs, sweetie."

I step out of the room and into the hospital hallway where Sterling is waiting for me. Leaning against the wall in his usual dark suit, he regards me with patience and compassion. Still, a part of me cringes as an unbidden image of the Moor bringing his golden scimitar across Petrushka's back filters across my imagination.

"How's Dr. Archer?" he asks.

"About the same."

"Thanks for answering my text this morning." He heads down the hall and motions for me to follow. "Wasn't sure if you'd be up."

"They booted me out of here around midnight. Told me to go home and get some sleep."

"And could you?"

"The right combo of alcohol and antihistamines apparently can work miracles." At Sterling's worried glance, I raise my hands in mock surrender. "Don't worry, Detective. All I had in the fridge was a leftover half bottle of wine. That and a couple of Benadryl did the trick."

"Not too well, I hope." Sterling takes my chin and pulls my gaze up to his, the concern in his eyes not diminished in the slightest. "We need you clear of mind today, in case you've forgotten."

After I finally managed to convince—I can't believe we're on a first name basis now—Katie to go home last night, Sterling and I had a moment to chat. Much of the conversation is lost to me between my concern over Thomas, Isabella, and the others. Not to mention what may have been closer to a full bottle of wine and closer to half a dozen of the little pink insomnia killers.

One point of our conversation remains crystal clear. This has to end today.

Koschei and his menagerie of monsters, the dark garden surrounded by even darker forest, the palace where he holds the souls of twelve girls and, possibly, the man I love.

All of it.

"What do we do now?" Sterling asks.

"Let's check in with Caroline." I let out a sigh. "Then, we'll go see Isabella."

Sterling escorts me to the elevator bay at the other end of the hospital, neither of us saying another word until the elevator stops on the floor holding Isabella, Rachel, and the rest of the girls.

"Archer's going to be okay," Sterling offers quietly. "Isabella and the others too."

"You don't know that, but thanks." I trudge down the hallway, not wanting to see either my daughter or Caroline's in such a way. Stopping outside the door of the Faircloths' room, I shoot a look back at Sterling. "And now, the person that really needs your brave face."

We step into the room together. Caroline is seated on the bed next to Rachel's pale form. Stroking Rachel's wavy red hair, Caroline sings her daughter a lullaby while Anthony sits in the opposite corner curled up with a tablet computer. Though his earbuds are firmly in place, I can hear the music blasting from the door.

And it's awful.

"Good morning, Caroline."

Caroline looks up at me and manages half a smile. "Good morning, Mira. Detective."

Sterling gives her a quick nod as I ask, "Apologies, but what in God's name is Anthony listening to?" I raise an eyebrow. "And is he trying to go deaf?"

Caroline shakes her head. "I keep telling him to turn it down, but five minutes later, it's right back at max volume." She gestures at Rachel's placid face. "I've got bigger fish to fry this morning, wouldn't you agree?"

Sterling steps forward. "How is your daughter this morning, Ms. Faircloth?"

"About the same." Caroline answers wearily. "Thank you for asking."

Somewhere along the last twenty-four hours, Caroline and Sterling managed to come to a truce, which is a good thing, because I'm going to need them both to be strong and of one mind for what I have planned.

"And…" Caroline hesitates. "How is Thomas?"

"No change." I sit on the bed next to Caroline and pat Rachel's leg. "He's downstairs getting the same test Rachel has scheduled for this afternoon."

"Did they find out anything?" Caroline asks, her voice somehow hopeful. "You know, that might help him or… the others?"

"Just that whatever is going on with him is basically identical to whatever has happened to all the girls."

"Oh, God." She wraps her arms around me and squeezes me tight. "Mira, I'm so sorry."

"It's all right." I gently push her away and meet her gaze. "We're all in this together now."

Fear fills her face. "You're planning on going back in there, aren't you?"

"I have to, Caroline." I glance back at Sterling before returning my attention to Caroline. "It's like last year with Anthony all over again. The doctors are doing their best—I have no doubt of that—but at the end of the day, the answer to what's going on isn't going to be found in a blood test or a brain scan."

Caroline shivers. "But the last time you traveled the land of *The Firebird*, that monster nearly took you."

"Agreed." Sterling pulls close behind. "What do you think is going to be different this time, Mira?"

I cast my mind back to my Ivanovna persona's encounter with the

Firebird. My capture and release left Princess Ivanovna with a trump card tucked in her tunic.

The Firebird's feather.

Anthony gave me the answer, an answer I've confirmed with far too many hours of online research over the last few days.

The Firebird's feather. The Danse Infernale. The destruction of the egg containing Koschei's soul. Everybody lives happily ever after.

My only hope now is that the boy's legendary attention to detail is as on target with Stravinsky's works as it was with Mussorgsky's.

I explain my plan to Sterling and Caroline. They both stare at me like I've got three eyes, but when all is said and done, they agree.

And now, for the hardest part.

The fact that my adversary, witting or otherwise, sits just a few feet away, no doubt absorbed in yet another piece of classical music that's likely going to do its best to leave me dead.

"Hey, kiddo." When Anthony doesn't respond, I slide over to him and gently pull out one of his earbuds. "What are you listening to?"

He keeps his eyes firmly on the screen. "You don't want to know."

My stomach ties in knots. "And why is that?"

He doesn't answer.

"Anthony, sweetheart." Caroline appears at my side. "Mira asked you a question. What are you listening to?"

Anthony looks up at his mother, still avoiding my eyes. His face turned up like he just took a sip of spoiled milk, the rank smell of embarrassment mixes with sulfurous fear as he struggles to come up with an answer.

"It's important I know, Anthony." I kneel by his side. "And somewhere deep down, you know exactly why I'm asking."

He hesitates another second, then turns the tablet around. On the screen, another ballet plays out before my eyes, one I've never seen.

On a stage designed to appear like a wooded glade, three circles of what I can only describe as aborigines leap, stomp, and cavort about in the most ungainly dancing I've ever seen. Unlike the stylized beauty that pervades *The Firebird* and *Petrushka*, this ballet is ugly. Primal. Not to mention, the miniscule sound audible from Anthony's earbuds is a far cry from anything I would call music.

"What is that?" Sterling asks.

"Stravinsky," Anthony mutters. "His third major ballet, *The Rite of Spring.*"

"More Stravinsky?" My heart sinks. "And what's the gist of this one, Anthony? More monsters? More death?"

"No." His chin falls to his chest. "At least, no more… monsters."

"The Rite of Spring?" Caroline asks. "But I thought you hated that one."

"I do." Anthony refuses to meet my gaze. "It's not pretty like the others."

I rest a hand on Anthony's knee. "Then why are you listening to it, Anthony?"

For the first time since I entered the room, Anthony looks me straight in the eye. "Because it's important."

I catch Caroline's wary eye. "What do you mean by that?"

"It's just important." Panic fills his gaze even as tears well at the corners of his eyes. "Now, leave me alone. I need to watch this."

"Anthony Faircloth!" Caroline reaches for the tablet, but I grab her arm.

"It's okay," I murmur. "Just let him be."

Caroline's eyes flash. "I'm going to jerk a knot in his tail if he talks back like that again." She nudges his foot with her knee. "You hear me, Anthony?"

Anthony ignores his mother, and Sterling and I excuse ourselves so she can have a "discussion" with her son on proper manners. Once we're out in the hall and the door clicks closed, Sterling turns toward me and takes my shoulders.

"Are you sure you know what you're doing?"

"As sure as I've been of anything since this all started back up…" I walk over to Isabella's room, adding a muttered, "which is not at all."

I let myself in, leaving Sterling outside so I can talk with Mom for a minute. She hasn't moved an inch from where I left her the previous night. Collapsed in a chair between Isabella's bed and the door, the true matriarch of my family glances up at me, her probing gaze only slightly diminished by fatigue.

"Thomas?" she asks.

My head drops. "Same as the girls. Same advice, too." My eyes slip closed. "Wait, wait, wait."

"They don't know you very well, then." Mom gives me a tired smile. "You, Mira Tejedor, have never been particularly good at waiting."

"Thanks, Mom." I walk over to the bed and sit by my daughter. "How is she? Any change?"

"She hasn't moved, but her breathing has stayed nice and regular, so that's something."

"I'm going to go in there and bring her out, Mom." I fight to keep my voice from breaking. "I swear I'll get her out of there."

"Or get yourself killed trying."

"Mom—"

"No, Mira. Listen. This thing's already got your daughter and your man. I don't want to see it take you as well."

"If I don't do something, we might never get Isabella back. Is that what you want?"

"You know it isn't. I'm just afraid of what might happen if you go off all half-cocked. You said yourself that monster had you dead to rights last time."

My cheeks grow warm. "I have a plan, you know."

I tell Mom what I have in mind, and to her credit, she holds her tongue till I'm finished.

"So, let me get this straight." Mom fixes me with a look that terrified me when I was six. "Your strategy to defeat this Koschei the Deathless and his army of monsters is to go in basically unarmed and alone and call down this Firebird creature to save your tail? Are you insane?"

"Insane enough to try." I take Isabella's hand in mine and gently squeeze her cool fingers. "I've got to do something, Mom. I'm the only one who can."

"I know." She stretches her arms above her head and pops her back before leveling her patented no-nonsense gaze at me. "Tell me what you need me to do."

We invite Sterling in and set up the room for what I know is going to be the roughest mental sojourn yet. Twelve of the thirteen victims lie in beds along this same hallway, much like the beds in a certain immortal sorcerer's tower prison. Anthony, the mind no doubt powering this insanity, is just on the other side of the wall, actively filling his head with more and more musical ammunition by the second. This world's version of Petrushka lies comatose several floors away while the man who wears his attacker's face will be standing guard over my unconscious body.

And worst of all, the mastermind behind all of this madness remains a mystery, as any puppeteer worth their salt would be.

Still, if Anthony's mind truly is the sandbox where my mysterious enemy has been building castles, they're in for a rude awakening.

Anthony is, if nothing else, a boy who plays by the rules inside his own head.

Mom helps me sit Isabella up, and I climb into bed behind her.

"Whatever happens, don't let them take me from her." I shoot Sterling as stern a look as I can manage. "Understand?"

"You won't be separated, Mira, and unless it all goes to shit, I'll make sure neither of you leaves this room."

"Good." I turn to my mother. "Mom, stay with Isabella. Keep her comfortable. Soothe her if she needs it."

"How will I know?"

My mind flashes back to Anthony from nine months ago, his face racked with pain as he fought to warn us of the danger coming from someone we trusted.

"You'll know." Then, with one last look into Sterling's eyes, I add, "Don't let me down, Detective."

A hint of fear plays across his face. "Be careful, Mira."

I rest my fingers on Isabella's temples. "I think we left careful in the rearview mirror about five exits back."

23

CARILLON

Upon my previous arrival at Koschei's garden, I found myself surrounded, the horde of *bukavac*, *skrzak*, and *zmej* all waiting for me, the entire spectacle nothing but a big show to lure me into the Immortal's trap. An echo of the cold iron of the manacles at my wrists and ankles hits me, burning my limbs and taking my breath.

This time, the trampled grass stands empty, the abandoned pool of silty water remains still, and the forked drawbridge leading to Koschei's palace for the first time stands closed.

No music fills the space. In fact, not a single sound intrudes upon the perfect silence.

"Hello?" I whisper.

A flutter, like wings, sounds from somewhere above.

The Firebird? The *zmej*? Something far worse?

I creep over to the bent tree heavy with golden apples and flop down on the flat stone beneath its branches where I found Hannah Abrams what seems like a century ago.

I'm here to face Koschei, to bring him and the Firebird into opposition, and finish this thing. So, of course he's chosen this particular visit to close up shop and fly south for the winter.

Winter.

Funny. With every visit to Koschei's garden before this one, the air has been warm, even muggy, but this time, the skies are gray, the surrounding trees bare, and the temperature just shy of frigid. A gentle snow begins to fall, much like the snow from the Russian fair, the flakes stinging my face as they melt on my skin.

God, everything here feels so real.

"Hello?" This time, I shout. "Koschei the Deathless. Come out and face me."

My words echo among the trees, the crackling rustle of snow on dead grass my only answer.

Unbelievable. Last time, I walked directly into Koschei's trap without a second thought. The least he could do is show up for mine.

My hand steals inside my tunic where the Firebird's feather rests. My fingers grip the warm quill and for a moment, I consider pulling it forth and bringing my ace in the hole into play.

"Not yet," I mutter. "Not until the moment is right."

I stretch out my hand and summon the bow before taking my first fateful step toward Koschei's palace. Last time I was invited in, but gaining entrance today may prove a bit more challenging.

I draw close, the brackish water filling the moat bringing memories of *The Old Castle* from the Exhibition. As I stare up at the horrible skull facade, I am careful not to disturb any of the stones at the water's edge for fear of waking whatever might rest in its murky depths.

"Mami."

The single word hits my ears as both shout and whisper. I gaze up through the falling snow and haze at the tower where the girls are being held and find Isabella's terrified eyes staring back. A blast of wind sends a million little ice splinters into my eyes, and when I look again, she is gone.

At my feet, however, lies something that wasn't there a moment before.

A coil of rope.

Is this mysterious boon a gift from Isabella or simply another invitation into Koschei's mousetrap? I'd prefer to believe the former, though I have little doubt the Immortal would like nothing more than to watch me struggle to scale his fortifications and then bind me with the very cord I just climbed.

As Thomas would no doubt say, however, sometimes a rope is just a rope.

I pull the strongest arrow from my quiver and tie the tightly braided cord to the shaft. The palace is fashioned of stone, but the drawbridge is wooden.

What I wouldn't do for Baba Yaga's mortar and pestle right about now.

Peering through the ever-increasing snow, I focus, level the bow at the center of the drawn bridge, and let the arrow fly. With an echoing *thunk*, the shaft embeds itself in the ebony wood. Before I can talk myself out of what may be the worst idea in the history of ideas, I tie my end of the rope to the decapitated statue that guards the *bukavac* pool and return to the moat. The rope as taut as I can manage, I take the braided cord and walk myself out hand over hand until my body dangles above the turgid water. Then, I kick my legs up over the rope, cross my feet, and begin the long process of shimmying across.

The dark leather boots protect my ankles, though the rope quickly begins to dig into the skin of my hands and fingers. I'm halfway across before my backside dips beneath the moat's surface. The frigid liquid leaves me shivering so badly, I nearly let go of the rope. Somehow I hold on for the last few feet, and after what seems an eternity, I finally make it across. There's no landing beneath the drawn bridge to speak of, but the thick soles of my boots find purchase along a small outcropping of rock just above the skin of the water. My raw fingertips dig into a crevice in the bridge's ancient wood, and despite the agony, I pull myself up.

Inch by inch and fingertip by fingertip, I scale the massive rectangle of ancient oak, my faltering grip on the metal studs in the wood the only thing keeping me from falling. With each trembling grasp, I expect the bridge to lower and force me beneath the icy floe, but as I reach the top and my fingers find purchase on one of the skull's incisors, I allow a single ray of hope to invade my consciousness.

"Outstanding effort, brave Ivanovna." Koschei's voice booms down from above. "Your courage has exceeded my expectations." The Immortal's petulant sigh fills me with equal parts rage and fear. "But the time for such foolishness is over."

A loud clunk sounds from within the palace, and soon, the din of chains clanking on a spool reverberates through the stone and wood, no doubt the bridge's windlass. The topmost reach of the bridge, now at my waist, pushes out and nearly dislodges me. I work my legs until my feet find the top of the door. Without wasting a moment, I kick both legs out and force myself up the wet vertical stone of the palace wall. My numb fingers are just able to reach the bottom of the skull's nasal cavity. The rough stone tears into my flesh, but somehow, I hold on.

"So tenacious, Ivanovna." Sarcasm drips from Koschei's voice like wet mold. "Would that we were allies, but alas we are fated, as ever, to be on opposite sides."

I struggle to pull myself up, but my spent arms have nothing left. As I hang there from the skull's bare face, I know it's just a matter of time until my raw fingers give up the ghost.

"Yes, Ivanovna. You have failed, and eventually, you will fall. But fear not, for you will not be alone as your lungs fill with water and mud." The cracking of ice echoes up from below followed by a bellow ripped from the heart of the sea. "Allow me to introduce the *vodyanoi*."

I chance a glance down and find the half-frozen moat churning like a pot of gray soup. Then, despite the dim light, I see him.

Half-man, half-fish, the *vodyanoi* pulls himself above the ice, his webbed fingers clinging to wet stone. Covered in blue and white scales from the crown of his enormous head to the fin at the end of his tail, the merman looks up at me not with hunger but with lust.

"A handsome devil, isn't he, Ivanovna? And unlike my other servants, the 'one in the water' does not wish to kill you." Koschei laughs, the sound almost as chilling as the wind whipping the now heavy snow past my face. "He merely awaits his latest bride."

Another glance down, and the *vodyanoi* meets my gaze with a knowing smile, his lips spreading wide amidst a goatee made up of whiskers like that of a catfish. In his bulging eyes, I find new strength and pull my torso up into the gap.

Koschei must be loving this. Trapped between certain death at his immortal hands and an even worse fate below, my only refuge is inside the left nostril of his palatial home.

Somehow, I don't think Wonder Woman has to put up with this shit.

"Mami." Isabella's voice, just above a whisper. "Look."

"Look?" I keep my voice low. "Look at what?"

"Take the rope, Miss Mira." This time, it's Rachel's voice that hits my eardrums. "We'll pull you up."

I crane my neck around to peer out from my stony cell and find a miracle.

Fashioned from bed sheets tied together end to end, a makeshift rope hangs just out of reach. I stretch out my arm until my muscles scream, but to no avail. Barely visible in the now heavy snow, salvation rests so close and yet so far away.

"Take the rope, Mami," Isabella insists. "We'll save you."

"All of us." Rachel again, accompanied by a chorus of voices I've never heard before. "We won't let you fall."

My first thought: It's a trick. These girls are all under Koschei's control. He's made that more than plain. How difficult would it really be for him to force them to tempt me into doing something foolish?

My second thought: As of five minutes ago, I'm fresh out of options.

With nary a look down at what awaits me if this is merely a cruel ploy, I bring my legs beneath me, kick out from the side of the palace, and grab for the rope. My hands slick from melted snow and blood, I slide several feet until my fingers find the knot connecting the next bed sheet.

I climb. Hand over hand, I pull myself up the rope, walking the wall as I was taught in a middle school gym class a lifetime ago. A frustrated growl echoes up from the moat, no doubt the *vodyanoi* as he realizes he's spending the evening alone.

Or is he?

My hands slip, and I slide down the makeshift rope almost to where I started. The howl from below devolves into a throaty chortle.

Not happening.

I start again, hand over hand regardless of the pain, my feet somehow finding purchase along the slick stone. I make significant headway—mental note to groan at that pun if I survive—but as I arrive at the top of the skull and the wall goes flat and straight vertical, I find I have nothing left.

Hanging there like a forgotten yo-yo, all the frustration and fear and fatigue flow out of me, and I break down in tears. It's no longer a matter of if I'm going to fall, only a matter of when.

I'm in the middle of calculating whether I can leap from the wall, summon the bow, and land a lethal blow to the lecherous merman while somehow managing to survive a fall from such a height when a second miracle occurs.

The rope pulls me up an inch. Then another. Then a foot. I chance a look up and find Hannah Abrams' smiling down at me through the driving snow.

"Hold on, Miss Mira," comes her almost chipper voice. "We're pulling you up."

And somehow, I do. For the interminable few minutes it takes the girls to haul me all the way to the top of Koschei's palace, I hang on for dear life. I half-expect to find the Immortal sorcerer waiting for me at the end of my ignominious ascent, but as I pull myself across the short wall, I find only twelve smiling girls in white dresses, all of them dry despite the raging snowstorm.

"Thank you," I get out between pants, "but… how did you do it? How did you free yourself from Koschei?"

"I asked them to help me." The gaggle parts, and my daughter strides toward me wearing an ivory nightgown, as grown-up as I've ever seen her. "And they did."

"Isabella."

I drop to one knee and stretch my arms wide and without a moment's hesitation, the otherworldly version of my daughter rushes to my side and nearly crushes me with a bear hug.

"Mami, I'm so scared."

Rachel steps out of the crowd and joins in the hug. "We're all scared, Miss Mira."

Something's not clicking. I squeeze Rachel and Isabella tight and then stand to address the dozen gathered girls. "One thing I don't understand. All of you know my true name. How is that even possible in this place?"

Hannah steps forward. "The Master may call you Ivanovna, but we know the truth." She gestures in Isabella's direction. "Your daughter taught us."

Isabella.

Just like she said, she is her mother's daughter.

For better or worse.

"What now?" I ask.

"What now, indeed?"

I spin around at the guttural voice to find an amused Koschei watching the entire proceeding from a safe distance down the parapet. The bow is in my hand in an instant, the arrow pointed directly at his dark heart.

"Now, now, Ivanovna." His patronizing tone fills my exhausted body with new strength. "You already know too well the futility of such an attack." He turns from me, offering a clear shot at his back, as if daring me to fire. "Put away your weapon. We have things to discuss."

I consider his words and then return the arrow to my quiver. "Fine. Talk."

He turns to his right so that I see him in silhouette. Truly a skeleton of a man, he picks at his sparse beard before facing me anew. "It would seem, Ivanovna, that we have reached an impasse."

Isabella steps in front of me. "My mother's name is Mira."

I pull her behind me and out of the Immortal's line of vision. "Ignore her, Koschei. Your feud is with me."

"But, as you have no doubt ascertained by now, the fates of these girls, much like the fate of your lover in yet another world of imagination, are all inseparably intertwined with yours." Koschei's face turns up in a knowing grin. "Your victories are theirs, as are your defeats." His head drops. "I hadn't considered that the opposite might also be true."

My hands ball into fists at my side. "What are you talking about, Immortal?"

"Our several encounters have each ended, if not in your victory, at least with my plans temporarily thwarted. Some of your victories have been your own while in others you have been rescued from certain death. These girls. Your friends on the other side. The fiery creature whose feather you keep clutched close to your breast."

Shit. There goes my trump card.

"So, we've reached—what did you call it?—an impasse." My arms cross before me. "What now, oh wise and powerful Koschei?"

"Ah, Ivanovna, if only the flattery had started earlier." Any hint of joviality leaves his features. "You cannot defeat me, at least not here in my own palace, and regardless of my best laid plans, you somehow always seem to find a way to persevere."

My thoughts go to Baba Yaga, who kept sending me away from the Exhibition time and time again until I eventually learned to make that sojourn under my own power.

"Send me away all you want, Koschei. I will return again and again, stronger each time, until I finally find a way to destroy you."

"You boast unnecessarily, Ivanovna." Koschei's eyes narrow. "I know good and well of your victory against the witch at the end of the hall and the teacher from *Tuileries*."

A gasp escapes my lips. "You know of the Exhibition?"

Koschei's smile returns. "I know many things, Ivanovna."

"If that's the case, then you know I will eventually prevail."

"Perhaps." Koschei hawks a wad of spittle onto the stone at his feet in a move reminiscent of Yaga herself. "To fight you here seems a repetitive waste of time, and yet sending you away, as you say, only allows you to grow stronger and wiser." He brings his hands together, his fingers writhing like a quartet of emaciated serpents. "There is, fortunately for me, a third option."

The blood in my veins freezes. I struggle to keep the fear from my eyes.

Koschei raises his hands to the sky, and music returns to the world of dream.

Bells. The ringing of a great carillon.

A magic carillon.

In my studies of *The Firebird*, this is the moment where Koschei's horde overpowers Prince Ivan and drags him to the wall of petrified knights to share in their fate. The arrow is in my hand before I can think, and yet no target presents itself.

"Where are your monstrous servants now, Koschei? Your *bukavacs*? Your *skrzaks*?" My eyes sweep the sky. "Your *zmej*?"

Koschei laughs. "In one way or another, you've defeated each of my minions, despite overwhelming odds, and to send you again to your place of origin is only to risk you coming back more powerful than before." He begins to spin a finger in the air. "Perhaps it is best to send you to a place where you can do no more harm."

Before I can say a word, the stones beneath my feet vanish, replace by a scintillating hole. The girls scream as I drop through the coruscating mass of light. Instinctively, my arms shoot out to my sides, my raw fingers catching the edge of the stone.

"You monster!" Isabella screams. "Where are you sending her?"

His eyes meet mine. "Your mother once fared well in a world fashioned by Mussorgsky." A wave of the Immortal's hand, and I'm sucked through the hole, his last words hitting my ears like a pair of iron fists. "I'm curious to see if she's up for a repeat performance."

24

NIGHT ON BALD MOUNTAIN

Phantom hands draw unseen bows across the strings of a thousand invisible violins, weaving a warbling tone not unlike a swarm of locusts. Darkness envelops me as the unnerving trill echoes from every direction, bringing new terror to my heart. The violin is soon joined by cello and contrabass, the martial underpinning quickly punctuated by soaring woodwinds as if something ancient and evil is catching its breath to speak. The violins shift into a frenetic melody as the brass section comes to life. Blaring tuba, trombone, and trumpet hit me with physical force, each note building and building until the ominous tune becomes a living thing. The opening run ends in a pair of tympani drum strikes, the dark heartbeat of this musical monstrosity.

As the violins begin anew for a second run through the menacing melody, the darkness recedes. The scene that unfolds around me chills me to the core.

Above me, threatening sky.

Below me, cold, unforgiving earth.

And I am naked.

Sitting up, I cast a bleary glance down my body. Neither Ivanovna nor the Ballerina, nor even the Lady Scheherazade, I recline atop a lone mountain as Mira Tejedor, bare as the day I was born, defenseless against the elements in this hell to which Koschei has banished me.

Wait.

196

Bare.

Mussorgsky.

God help me, I know this tune and, more importantly, exactly where I am.

As the brass and strings launch into their third pass, I utter the name of this piece. Each word falls from my lips like thunder.

"Night on Bald Mountain."

As if to punctuate my proclamation, a bolt of lightning streaks down from the darkened sky and strikes the ground mere inches from my feet. The rocky surface explodes, the shower of stone and earth throwing me to the edge of the precipice. I peer down through the ephemeral clouds and shudder. If the chasm below even has a bottom, I can't see it.

I stand, the jagged stone digging into my feet like dragon's teeth. Backing away from the edge of the rock face, I seek shelter upon the bare mountain face.

May as well look for a glass of water in the middle of the Sahara.

Another thunderbolt strikes the mountaintop as the brass continues its assault on my senses, the concussive blast nearly sending me over the edge. I pull myself to my feet, my hands and knees stinging from scrapes left by the unforgiving ground. The taste of copper fills the air, mixing with the ozone stench left by the lightning strike.

Every tour I've taken of a certain boy's imagination has felt genuine, intimate, real, but nothing I've encountered along the Exhibition, Koschei's garden, or the Shrove-Tide Fair has prepared me for such desolation.

A blast of arctic wind hits me like a prizefighter's uppercut, hurling me into a sharp outcrop at the opposite edge of the craggy mountaintop. In short order, an icy rain begins to fall, the rushing sleet scouring my skin like sandpaper even as the gale threatens to steal the very air from my lungs.

I tell myself for the thousandth time there's no need to breathe in this place, and yet, within seconds, my chest burns for oxygen all the same.

"Anthony..." I groan, hoping against hope uttering the name will gain me some small reprieve. "Please."

Answered only with blaring symphony and howling gale, I try again.

"Anthony..." I fall to one knee, the effort of speaking his name a second time leaving me wasted and useless. "Don't let it end this way," I get out with the last dregs of air in my lungs.

"Mira." A quiet voice hits my ears even as the blasting wind lets up long enough for me to take a quick breath.

"Hello?" My heart swells with hope, even as my mind flirts with unconsciousness.

"Mira." A second voice, this one louder than the first.

"I'm here." I peer around the desolate mountaintop, and find myself still alone. "Help me."

"Mira." This third voice sounds in my right ear. For the first time, I detect the accent. French, but not the smooth flowing French I grew accustomed to nine months ago along the Exhibition. This guttural speech reminds me far more of the witch who once resided at the end of the great hall.

My head swimming, I force myself up from the ground and crane my neck around to find three crones in decrepit rags looking down on me with maniacal smiles. Their gnarled canes held in even more gnarled hands, the trio scuttles around me atop naked feet hardened by serrated stone.

The nearest licks her lips, and I wonder if I have suddenly become tonight's main course.

"Mira Tejedor," says the one eyeing me like a rare steak.

"Come to join our dark Sabbath, have you?" asks the second.

"And be our fourth?" adds the third.

"Pardon?" Despite the wind, I stand and cover my breasts and nethers. "For what purpose do you three need a fourth?"

"The three of us are strong," whispers the first, "but without a fourth, we are incomplete."

"Have you come to join us?" The second draws close, her face strangely familiar.

"We have but this night to complete our black Sabbath and bring new life to this desolate place." The third remains distant, her face cloaked in shadow, though her voice strikes a chord.

"Who are you?" I ask. "And what is this Sabbath of which you speak?"

As one, they laugh, though there is no mirth in the sound.

"Driven from our home, we now reside in this torment." The first spits on the cold ground as the unseen orchestra continues to play.

"Our paradise truly lost..." the second mutters, barely audible over the thundering percussion.

"We have decided it truly is better to reign in hell." The third crosses her arms and shoots me a questioning glare. "Well, Mira? What say you?"

"Your paradise?" I look into each of their eyes, trying desperately to piece things together. "Where is that? Who are you?" I draw in a breath. "How do you know my true name in this place?"

"Ah, Mira Tejedor," says the first.

"Do you not recognize us?" pouts the second.

"After all," the third murmurs, "you yourself were responsible for the ousting of the last to complete our circle."

Still in a fog, my brain scrambles to make sense of their words.

Then it hits me.

Three women. French accents. And they know my name.

The women of *The Marketplace at Limoges*, but far from the elegant young ladies I remember from the Exhibition. Once attired in the finest silks, satins, and lace, their wardrobe now consists of threadbare rags. And young is no longer a description anyone would use to describe this trio.

"Brigitte?" I ask the first.

She answers with a subtle curtsy out of sync with her raggedy dress.

"Sophie?" I seek her eyes, but the second witch refuses to meet my gaze.

I turn to the third, the one that matters most. "Antoinette?"

She draws close and faces me nose-to-nose like the iron-toothed hag who fought against me every step of the way as I struggled to bring Anthony Faircloth back into the light. "The same."

Somehow, a smile finds its way onto my face. It would appear Anthony heard me after all.

And just like last time, as strange as it seems, the cavalry takes a decidedly witchy form.

"You require a fourth, you say?"

"Since the Charlatan came and took from us our home at *The Marketplace at Limoges*, we have been consigned to this place." Antoinette peers around, sadness and anger warring on features distorted yet not that dissimilar from those of a young boy in a hospital room a million miles away.

"The Charlatan?" I ask. "From the Russian fair?"

"Evicted, we were," Sophie says, "sent from the warmth and hospitality of our temperate home to spend the rest of our days on this wretched mountain."

"Reduced to rags, our bodies ravaged, our faces ruined." Brigitte clutches her cane in her knotted hand and points it at me. "But look at you, Mira Tejedor. Unblemished, flawless, as beautiful as ever."

My eyes narrow at the witch. "And yet, just as banished as the three of you."

"Did you fall afoul of the Charlatan, even as we did?" Sophie asks.

"No." My addled mind fights to put it all together. "My argument is with the Immortal, Koschei the Deathless." I tremble in the cold. "His home lies in a completely different place."

"Hmmph," Brigitte rolls her eyes. "Not as different as you'd like to think."

I grab Brigitte by the fragile scraps of cloth that cover her torso. "And what is that supposed to mean?"

Antoinette steps forward and separates us. "Mira, I see in your mind many names. The Ballerina. Princess Ivanovna. The Lady Scheherazade. Are not each of these women in essence a distorted version of you?"

"Perhaps." I debate whether to call out the simple fact that the three women standing before me are all nothing but shadows of the same boy, but decide I will learn more if I keep up this charade of a conversation. "What of it?"

"If those three women are all just different extensions of you, is it not possible that the same could be said of the three places they reside?"

"But the world of *The Firebird* exists in the minds of twelve girls while the Russian fair of *Petrushka* rests in the mind of... a young man."

"And the third place?" Antoinette searches my face, her expression amused. "What of the Exhibition the others and I once called home?"

"Destroyed." I shudder, and not from the cold. "The Exhibition is no more."

Antoinette's subtle smile spreads into a wicked grin. "Is it, now?"

"Time is wasting," Brigitte interrupts. "Will you join us at the altar? Or do you plan to stand there disrobed and continue this pointless conversation until we all shrivel away?"

"It would appear I have little choice." I step out of the circle of witches. "Lead on."

The crones hobble away single file, their faltering steps still more facile than mine on the uneven terrain, and I find myself wishing I too had a cane. Brigitte in the lead takes us to a narrow, zigzagging path that leads down from the summit. The music continues, the tune shifting from bombastic to soothing before starting again at the beginning. The temperature remains frigid, but the wind dies off once we are down the mountain a bit and despite my nakedness, my shivering lessens a degree.

"Put this on." Sophie drapes part of her torn dress across my form, the makeshift poncho covering me even as it leaves her half-naked. "At least you can maintain some semblance of modesty when we are in the presence of our other guest."

"Someone else is here?" I run before the three witches and scan their horrid faces. "Who is it? Where are they?"

Brigitte laughs, the wheezy cackle not unlike Yaga's. "So eager, Mira Tejedor."

I grab Sophie by the shoulders. "Whoever it is, take me to them."

Again, Antoinette pulls me off one of her sisters. "Fear not, Mira. We're almost there."

The trail ceases to veer back and forth and instead proceeds down the mountain like the thread of a screw.

A very narrow thread.

The distant moon disappears behind a bank of clouds, plunging the trail into darkness and revealing a flicker of flame straight ahead. My curiosity getting the better of me, I rush from the three women, racing down the widening trail until I come to an enormous bonfire burning by an empty rectangular slab of stone, all situated atop a landing carved into the mountainside. A circle of small stones that appears to have been placed there centuries ago surrounds the fire and altar. Atop the slab of stone lie cut ropes that no doubt once bound a sacrifice to whatever god or goddess these witches worship.

I stand on holy ground.

Or, considering my company, unholy ground.

I warm myself by the roaring fire until the trio of ancient enchantresses catches up to me.

Brigitte enters the circle first. "Where is he?" She rushes to my side, her anger palpable. "What have you done with him?"

I take a step back and nearly fall into the fire. "Done with who?"

Sophie toddles over to the altar as fast as her bent legs will carry her and fumbles with one of the severed section of rope. "His bonds have been cut." She peers at me, furious. "She must still carry the Sultan's dagger from the Exhibition, but where can she have hidden it?"

"Where, indeed?" Brigitte adds.

Antoinette, the last to enter the circle, steps over to my side and raises an eyebrow. "In a previous existence, you were Scheherazade, the storyteller. Perhaps you willed the dagger to your side, or maybe even spoke our guest out of his predicament."

"Guest," I ask, "or prisoner?"

"How very astute," Antoinette murmurs, "though I must wonder for whom you ask such a question, the Prince or yourself?"

"Prince?"

Brigitte eyes me for a moment before turning to Antoinette. "The three of us are strong enough to leave this place without her. If she won't tell us where the Prince is or what she's done with him, perhaps she can take his place on the altar." She draws close, sniffing at me like a dog at raw meat. "One way or another, Mira Tejedor, you are going to help us escape this hellhole."

"Leave her alone." Sophie hobbles over from the altar and interposes herself between Brigitte and me. "Do you not remember when she stood for us in the Exhibition? Gathered us together? Sent us through the Gates? None of this is her fault."

"And yet see where we stand now." Brigitte turns her anger on Sophie. "Exiled, crippled, humbled." Her attention returns to me. "And now, the only suitable sacrifice for the ritual that can free us from this place has been allowed to escape."

"Not the *only* suitable sacrifice." Antoinette eyes me like a vulture studies a carcass on the highway. "Take her, Brigitte."

"Wait," I stammer. "This prince of whom you speak. I haven't seen him, and I certainly didn't free anyone. I can't even free myself."

"Regardless," Antoinette whispers as she motions for Sophie to help Brigitte, "you will now take his place upon the altar."

Painfully aware of my nakedness, I raise my fists before me. "Like hell I will."

I back away from the trio of witches as quickly as my bare feet will take me, for all the good it does me. In a blink, Brigitte and Sophie have my arms and are dragging me backward around the fire toward the altar.

"Why are you doing this?" I scream until my lungs give out. "There must be another way."

"An eternity or a day," Antoinette mutters. "Impossible though it is to know with any certainty how long you've been in a place where time has no meaning, let me assure you of one simple fact." At her raised hand, Brigitte and Sophie stop their inexorable march. "My sisters and I will not be spending one instant longer here than we must." She claps her hands together in a gesture reminiscent of Baba Yaga atop her hut. "Bind her."

Brigitte and Sophie, their grip as unbreakable as steel, force me onto the altar and pull each arm toward the iron rings driven into the granite. My body barely covered by Sophie's rag, my naked back, bottom, and legs run roughshod across the jagged stone.

"Stop," I beg. "Please. I can help you."

As Brigitte and Sophie bind my arms, Antoinette leans over me, her face upside down. "My apologies, Mira, but doors don't open without keys, and you, in the absence of our previous sacrifice, are that key." She makes a poor effort at a conciliatory smile. "Trust that we will make this as painless as possible."

I open my mouth to fire back a sharp remark, but the whole thing is pointless. Twice now, I've been lured into a trap, dragged one flat surface or another, and bound.

I'll be damned if I'm going to die this way.

I struggle against the coarse cords that tear at my wrists and ankles. To no avail. I plead with the witches to think this through, but my words fall on deaf ears.

I am naked. Bound. Helpless.

A part of me waits for a rescue from the real world, another miracle in a long succession of all but divine interventions. Nothing happens.

Perhaps I am finally so deep that I cannot be reached, this imaginary world within an imaginary world too far removed from reality.

Koschei has built his most recent trap quite well.

This time, my fate is up to me and me alone.

The three witches take their positions: Brigitte at my left hand, Sophie at my right, and Antoinette at my head. A low chant fills the space, the syllables and words leaving their shriveled lips as so much garbled nonsense.

The tune, however? That, I recognize.

The song Brigitte, Antoinette, and Sophie sing is "The Marketplace at Limoges" from *Pictures at an Exhibition*, but where Mussorgsky's composition was fast and light, this version is a dirge, the witches' voices deep and resonant like the recordings of those Tibetan monks that were so popular a few years ago. Nothing about the song, however, provides any solace, as Antoinette, inverted above my head, draws a long, black blade from within the folds of her ramshackle robes.

"And now, Mira Tejedor, seer of dreams, you die so that we may live."

"Not if I have anything to say about it." This new voice quickens my heart, the crisp British accent the only change from a timbre I know as well as my own. "Now, release the woman or I will put you down like the mongrels you are."

My gaze shoots in the direction of whoever dares speak with such boldness. There, at the far end of the altar, resplendent in spotless orange and white, stands the witches' missing prisoner. Though his blue boots, checkered pants, and floppy orange hat mark him as Petrushka, the man that towers over us is no clown, but a prince.

A prince I've never met in person on this side of dream, though his name was legendary along the Exhibition where even the sharpest of tongue spoke of him with respect.

More importantly, though, the man in orange and white looks down on me with the steely eyes of Dr. Thomas Archer.

This, ladies and gentlemen, isn't just any prince.

He is *my* prince.

25

THE KALENDAR PRINCE

"**M**ove that dagger one inch—" The Kalendar Prince points a curved blade not dissimilar from the Moor's at the instrument of death clutched in Antoinette's knotted hand. "—and your sisters will be pulling it from your cold, dead heart."

"Good Prince," Antoinette purrs. "Allow us this simple ritual of blood, and we will bring you with us as we escape this godforsaken land."

The Prince takes a single step forward, his nimble foot coming to rest by my naked hip, and redirects his scimitar at Antoinette's throat, stopping the tip just shy of her windpipe. "Step away from her, witch, or it will be your blood upon this altar."

"But, Good Prince—"

He lets out a laugh. "Do you think I've somehow forgotten that before you captured this unfortunate soul, I was the one bound to this stone?" With a flick of his wrist, the Prince knocks the dagger from Antoinette's hand and sends it clattering across the uneven rock. "Now, let her go before I lose my patience with the lot of you."

"Very well." Antoinette looks left and right at her coven, her voice dropping to a low groan. "If that is the way it is to be." She clears her throat. "Take him."

The flurry of motion following Antoinette's command brings home the fact that my three captors are anything but the arthritic old hags they appear to be. I strain at my bonds anew, desperate to help the Kalendar Prince, and fail.

Fortunately, he needs little in the way of assistance.

Brigitte and Sophie dive at the Prince's ankles, their movements a blur, though their gnarled hands close on empty air. The Prince, already in midair, flips over Antoinette and out of my field of vision, though I hear him land a moment later on the stone to the witch's rear. Brigitte and Sophie scurry after him, as does Antoinette, leaving me alone on the unforgiving rock. Soon, the unmistakable sounds of a scuffle hit my ears. The melee lasts but a minute, with nothing but garbled shouts and the thud of fist impacting flesh to mark the passage of time. Once, twice, three times I hear what sounds like bags of potatoes being dropped to the ground. Then, the swish of a blade followed by the clang of steel on stone and my right arm is free.

I roll off the slab, trusting the rope knotted at my left wrist has enough slack that my arm won't rip out of its socket. Landing in a low crouch, I take in the scene. At the head of the enormous stone table, the Kalendar Prince stands over the three fallen witches. Using scraps of rope from about the rocky landing, he ties each of their hands behind their backs, waiting until all three are bound before chancing a glance up at me.

"Well?" he asks. "What are you waiting for? I already severed one of your bonds. If you had any sense, you'd already have undone the other knot and fled."

I stifle a gasp at the Prince's words. Though kinder than any man I've ever met, Thomas makes no bones about calling me out when my brain just isn't firing on all cylinders. The brutal honesty, though frustrating more often than not, is one of the man's more attractive features.

"Thank you," I mutter through a forced smile. "I'll get right on that."

It's strange. Other than the absence of the white makeup covering his face, the differences in the creature I know as Petrushka and this dashing Kalendar Prince are negligible. The clumsy red mittens now sleek leather gloves, the Prince's garb is otherwise identical to the clown's.

And yet, everything is different.

Whereas the clown's every movement evokes pity bordering on revulsion, the Prince exudes confidence, masculinity, power. At the Shrove-Tide Fair, the graceless steps of the form in white and orange brought derision and scorn, but the deftness now evident in those same feet and hands commands nothing but the utmost respect.

To put it simply, if Petrushka is the personification of "can't," then the Kalendar Prince is the epitome of not only "can" but "will."

How could I have been so fooled?

I've nearly freed myself from the knotted cord about my left wrist when the first of the witches stirs.

"Free us," cries Sophie, tears running down her cheeks as she looks up at the Prince. "We meant you no harm."

"Liar." He rests the heel of his boot on Sophie's collarbone. "Tell me why I shouldn't break your crooked neck this instant."

"Because we all want the same thing." Brigitte, who apparently has been playing possum, glares up at the Prince through one swollen eye. "To leave this place and forget we were ever here."

"If you let us live, we will show you the way." Antoinette, also not nearly as unconscious as she appeared, raises her head, keeping one eye on me and the other on the Prince. "Does that arrangement sound equitable to the both of you?"

"Show us the way?" I gesture back to the stone slab where I nearly met my end moments before. "I thought the only way out of here involved plunging a dagger through someone's heart. A 'ritual of blood,' I believe you called it?"

Brigitte bows her head, her dingy mop of hair falling across her twisted face. "The ritual of summoning would have brought the help we need and made our escape from this hell a far easier endeavor." If I expect to find even a hint of contrition on the witch's face, I am sorely disappointed. "All magic comes with a price, but as we were exiled here, so may we return from whence we came. The path back to sanity, however, is long and filled with dangers beyond your imagining."

"Sanity? You mean the Exhibition? Koschei's garden? Good God, the Russian fair?" My eyes shoot to the Prince and back to Antoinette. "You call any of that sanity?"

"Perhaps 'order' is the more appropriate term." Antoinette, her hands still bound behind her, rises from the ground far more gracefully than I would have thought possible. "Before the Exhibition, there was naught but chaos. The Exhibition brought order to all our lives. We knew the rules. We knew our place. After you sent us through the Bogatyr Gates, we were indeed free, but without the edicts and constraints of the Exhibition, chaos returned."

"Returned indeed," Brigitte adds, "and far worse than before."

"It wasn't all bad." Sophie comes to her feet and strides in my direction. "For a while, all of us were free to come and go as we pleased. That is, until the new order came."

"The new order?" I ask.

"Quiet, Sophie." Brigitte leaps up, her hands still bound behind her. "Does not our current fate pain you enough that you attempt to bring more hell down upon our heads?"

Sophie pulls herself up straight, and with no more than a fleck of fear in her gaze, looks Brigitte square in the face. "It is the truth." Her gaze shoots in my direction. "The truth freed us before. Perhaps it can again."

I stride over to Brigitte, doing my best to keep from trembling. Despite her being bound and apparently helpless, the power of the last witch I met in the world of dream remains permanently etched in my memory.

Power like that deserves respect.

"How interesting that Sophie is now the spiller of secrets, Brigitte. As I recall, you were the one among the women of the *Marketplace* with the loosest tongue."

Brigitte's eyes narrow at me. "And see what that has gotten us? Me, Sophie, Antoinette banished to a desolate mountain. The Kalendar Prince, never before even seen in this realm, sent to join us in exile. Even you, the omnipotent storyteller, appear trapped right along with the rest of us with little hope of escape."

"Funny." I let me lips curve into a sardonic smile "I'm not feeling particularly omnipotent at the moment."

"Storyteller?" The Kalendar Prince, who has stood back and observed the entire exchange, chooses this moment to reenter the conversation. "But they called you Mira. Is it possible you're—"

I raise a hand. "You speak true, good Prince. In this realm, I have many names. Some call me Mira, others Ivanovna or the Ballerina, but you may know me as Scheherazade."

"The Lady Scheherazade." The Prince doffs his white silk hat and bows low before me. "I am Toma, known in this realm as the Kalendar Prince, and I am at your service."

"Oh, don't worry, your highness." I cover my mouth in an effort to hide my smile. "I know exactly who you are."

Toma brings himself back up straight and again dons his hat. "Then, fair lady, you clearly have me at a disadvantage."

"All of us are trapped atop the same mountain prison." I let out a rueful laugh. "I would argue none of us have any particular advantage at the moment."

"Perhaps." Toma answers my sarcastic laugh with one of his own. "A Prince without subjects, a storyteller cut off from her story, and a trio of witches denied their ritual. Can there be any hope for such a crew?"

"While you two are nothing short of adorable," Antoinette hawks a wad of spittle onto the stone, "might I suggest you halt your courtship until all five of us are out of mortal danger?"

As if her very words remind the mountain of our presence, a mighty wind gusts from below, the blast of cold air extinguishing the fire and dropping the temperature to nothing. In seconds, my teeth begin to chatter as yet again, the authenticity of Anthony's world of dream is proven in spades. As my entire body shakes uncontrollably, I peer around at the witches who all seem perfectly comfortable despite the chill. Toma, on the other hand, trembles in the cold, though he does his best to hide it.

"Lady Scheherazade," he says. "That scrap of cloth can't possibly be providing you with any warmth." Before I can argue, the Prince slides the white silk shirt over his head and offers it to me. "Here. Take this."

"Th-thank you."

I accept the gift, even as I do my best to avert my eyes from Toma's bare chest. Though his body mirrors Thomas', this entity called the Kalendar Prince doesn't know me, doesn't know what I am to the person he embodies, doesn't look at me the way Thomas does.

To look upon the Prince's half-naked form when his eyes are those of a stranger...

"Well..." Antoinette's eyes pass from Toma to me and back. "Now that everyone is incredibly uncomfortable, shall we begin?"

Toma releases the three witches from their bonds, and we take off single file. Sophie takes the lead at Antoinette's insistence, no doubt because of her earlier insubordination. Antoinette follows her, with Brigitte close behind. I have no doubt placing a body between herself and the Prince's blade had something to do with her decision. Toma walks before me, all to keep an eye on the witches, while I bring up the rear. Neither of us are crazy about leaving me last in marching order, but he and I agree it seems preferable to having one of the witches who just tried to ritually sacrifice us to some elder god in a position to stab me in the back.

Especially considering the path that lies before us.

The serpentine trail leading down the mountain makes the path from the summit to the altar look like a four-lane highway. The ground wet from the storm with loose stone everywhere, making our way down proves far slower than I imagined. As the moon sets below the mountain range in the distance, the descending darkness makes the path even more difficult.

"So glad we decided to walk," Brigitte moans as she slips on a hunk of wet rock. "At least with the ritual, only one poor soul had to die." She shoots a hateful glance across her shoulder. "Now we all get to share in Death's cold embrace."

"Quiet," the Prince commands. "And keep moving."

"As you wish, Good Prince," Brigitte mutters. "As you wish."

As we continue down the mountain, I touch Toma's arm and hold him back as the trio of witches forges ahead.

"Can we trust them?" I whisper in the Prince's ear. "For all we know, they could be leading us into another trap."

"They could, indeed." He takes my hand. "Though I don't believe that to be the case."

I narrow my eyes. "And why would you think that, oh great Kalendar Prince?"

"First, they have as much a vested interest in getting off this mountain as we do. Second, there is strength in numbers, and if we encounter trouble, they might need our help as much as we need theirs. Third, and most importantly, there is only one way off this mountain, and that way is down." He points his sword off the edge of the path. "Do your eyes see what mine see?"

I follow his blade. At first, I can't make it out, but as I strain against the darkness, what has Toma so excited becomes apparent.

One thing about a night on a barren mountain—there are no trees to block the view.

"They do." As tiny as a star in the night sky and twinkling just enough to complete the illusion, a solitary light below beckons us. "What or who is that?"

"That, Lady Scheherazade, is a question we'd both like the answer to." Toma's eyes return to the path before us, which for the first time in what feels like hours stands empty.

"No." Toma rushes down the slippery stone to the next bend. "No, no, no."

"What is it?" I call out, feeling my way after him as quickly as my bare feet will carry me. "What's wrong?"

"The witches," he shouts. "They're gone."

"But that's impossible. They're so—" I halt mid-sentence, remembering the breathtaking speed Brigitte and Sophie exhibited when I was tied to the stone altar. "Old…"

"Old and wise, Lady Scheherazade," he mutters as I catch up to him. "And more than a little crafty."

"So much for your 'safety in numbers' theory." I bury my face in my hands. "I suppose they figured they'd be better off without a trained swordsman in their midst."

Toma's mouth draws down in a pensive pout I've seen more than once the times I've bested Thomas in an argument. "I suppose so."

"What now, then?" Another blast of cold cuts through my borrowed silk shirt. "Do we forge ahead, knowing they could be lying in ambush and waiting to slit our throats?"

"I suppose so." Grim resignation washes over Toma's just visible features. "Unless you can think of another option."

"In that case…" I step around the Kalendar Prince. "I will take the lead, and you watch our backs, agreed?"

Toma puffs up, offended for all of half a second before deflating with a resigned sigh. "Agreed. Lead on, Lady Scheherazade."

26

PETRUSHKA'S GHOST

Minutes, hours, days pass as Toma and I inch our way down the spiraling path. A literal descent into darkness, over half of each ever-longer circumference of the mountain passes in utter shadow. The stars blotted out by storm clouds from horizon to horizon, even seeing my fingers before my face proves a challenge, much less the dark, wet stone beneath my feet. With each circling of the peak, however, the distant twinkle in the valley Toma spotted before makes a reappearance, growing with each cycle. Ephemeral in the distance, eventually I make out the beginnings of a shape.

Hanging in midair like the frames of the paintings from the Exhibition, a veiled rectangle taller than it is wide awaits us below, dim light pouring around its edges as if we stand in a darkened room viewing a door left ajar. As we trudge closer, something about our surroundings triggers a memory, though I can't quite put my finger on it.

"What troubles you, Lady Scheherazade?" Toma asks. "I must admit, I was rather enjoying our conversation, but I fear you find my contribution to our exchange tedious at best."

"My apologies." I grit my teeth. "I have a lot on my mind."

The truth is, talking to Toma is one of the most surreal experiences of my life. The British accent aside, every word that comes out of his mouth channels Thomas. He and I have spent so much time together of late, we're to the point where we finish each other's sentences, and yet, Toma speaks to me as if we've never met.

As if we haven't shared our thoughts.

Our dreams.

Our bodies.

Throw in the fact the Kalendar Prince speaks of the Exhibition with an encyclopedic knowledge of Mussorgsky's magnum opus that can only come from Anthony Faircloth, and it's all I can do to walk in a straight line.

"Toma." I break the silence. "I can't shake the feeling I've been here before." The light pouring around the door in space has just come into view for the hundredth time, triggering yet again the buried memory. "Does any of this seem familiar to you?"

"I may know the Exhibition, good lady," the Prince says, "but this place of desolation is unknown to me."

"Then why are you crying?" Peering across my shoulder, I can't help but note the glint of tears streaming down his cheeks. "This place means something to you, doesn't it?"

"No," he says a little too quickly, "I've never seen this place." He clears his throat. "Never."

Methinks the Prince doth protest too much.

"Toma, come here."

I wait for him along the path. As he strides forward to join me, the previously sure-footed Prince trips over a loose stone and stumbles forward, falling flat on his face at my feet.

And that's when it hits me.

All new and improved this go around, Toma may be the Kalendar Prince, but he wears the form and clothing of Petrushka the clown. An image of the lone mountain in the distance I saw from the crack in the door leading to Petrushka's room floods my mind, as does the realization of where we are and why everything looks so familiar.

"I have it."

Toma rises from the ground and brushes himself off, his bare chest just visible in the dim light. "Have what?" he asks, obviously irritated.

I keep my eyes on his as best I can. "What this place is. Where we are." I draw close and whisper, "Who you are."

"I am the Kalendar Prince," he proclaims. "I have no idea what you're talking about."

"You are indeed the Kalendar Prince, just as I am Scheherazade, but here in this realm, I have many names." I rest my chin on my interlaced fingers. "I may indeed be the famed storyteller of *Arabian Nights*, but to others, I am known as Princess Ivanovna, and to others still, I am simply the Ballerina." His shudder at the name confirms my suspicions. "Beyond those three faces, however, the truth is even stranger."

The Prince's eyes, still welling with tears, narrow at me. "And what truth might that be, storyteller?"

"That all three of those faces are lies, or at least permutations of the truth."

"I don't understand." Toma begins to shake. "What do you mean?"

"What I mean is that all the faces I wear in this realm are false."

"But you are Lady Scheherazade of the Exhibition, victor over both the witch and the traitorous teacher from *Tuileries*."

I shake my head sadly, my heart breaking as the Prince trembles with fear, his proud outer shell crumbling beneath the weight of the truth. "That may be true, Toma, but what did the witches call me as I lay helpless on their stone altar?"

"I don't remember." He looks away. "Another name. A strange name, as if from somewhere far away."

"You do remember, Toma, or at least some part of you does." I take his hand. "It's okay. We have all the time we need. Now, tell me. What did the witches call me?"

Toma's lip quivers, his mouth momentarily curling into the half-smile, half-frown that is the clown's permanent face. "They called you Mira."

"All of it." I incline my head to one side and offer a faint smile. "Say all of it."

"They... they called you Mira Tejedor."

"Good." I take his other hand. "Now, what I say next may come as a bit of a shock, but I am not the only one here who goes by many names."

"I am Toma, the Kalendar Prince." He brings a bare arm across his face to wipe away the tears. "I need no other name."

"Regardless," I keep my tone even and true, "you have others." The corners of my own eyes well with unbidden pools of stinging salt. "In a place far from here, Mira Tejedor knows a man. A great man. A scholar and a helper of others. His name is Thomas Archer."

"Archer?" Toma says. "An expert with a bow, no doubt."

"Oh, he's a straight shooter, all right, but his weapons are words." I perform a quick bow. "Much like mine."

"And this Thomas Archer? He is your... friend?"

"We are..." My heart breaks as the hopeless love of Petrushka the clown emanates from the shaken eyes of the Kalendar Prince. "...more than simply friends."

Toma looks away. "I see."

"Not entirely." I pull his eyes back to mine. "You see, just as I have many names, so do you." I squeeze his fingers gently. "In this place, you are Toma, the Kalendar Prince, and back home, you are Thomas Archer, a psychologist and my lover, but there," I point to the light in the distance, "you are known as Petrushka."

"Petrushka?" His lips wrap around the syllables as if they've never formed the word, though his eyes fall, despondent.

"Yes," I murmur. "Petrushka... the clown."

Rage fills the Prince's face. "I am no clown."

"And I am no ballerina. That doesn't change the fact I've shared this grand stage with you more than once."

"Stage?" he asks.

"Somehow, our mountain spirit has left us free to speak our minds, but I swear to you that every time we've encountered each other before, we were but puppets, dancing on the strings of a Charlatan magician." I point a trembling finger at the rectangular eclipse in the distance. "A magician that no doubt waits for us on the other side of that door."

Toma's body shakes, but it's not with the chill but unmitigated rage. "I am no clown, Lady Scheherazade, and I am no man's puppet."

I rest a hand on his bare shoulder. "And yet, here you are, half-naked on an imaginary mountain envisioned by a man who died over a century ago, a Kalendar Prince."

"What of it?" he asks, his eyes defensive.

"A question, then." I guard my tone carefully, as I don't want to make the situation worse. "What, may I ask, is a Kalendar Prince?"

"What sort of question is that?"

"A simple one." I step carefully. "Who are the Kalendars?"

"We are a religious order, much like the monks of the Christian or Buddhist faiths."

Fantastic. Now I get to hear Professor Faircloth speak. "And you are their prince, a prince of monks. Does that make any sense to you?"

He gives a derisive snort. "It is simply a title."

Perhaps a different tack.

"Another question, then. The numbers embroidered in gold thread in each of the squares along your checkered pants. What do they mean?"

"Numbers?"

I kneel before him and take the cuff of his pant leg. Barely visible in the dim light, I run my fingers along the fabric until I come to one of the numbers, the rich thread embroidering easily identifiable as a five. "Your checkered pants. They form a calendar."

"And your point is?"

"That you are the Kalendar Prince because you met with and helped a boy the same day every week for years, and his brain made a funny connection between two words." I pull in a breath as I prepare to lay out the truth. "In his mind, you are a prince, though someone else has painted you a clown. All the while, in reality, you are a psychologist who barely believes the conversation we are having is possible."

"You're saying this isn't real? The mountain? The witches? You?" His head drops, despondent. "Me?"

"Oh, the both of us are very real, and in very real danger to boot, but our true bodies and selves exist far from here." I wipe away a tear. "A million miles from here, you lie comatose in a hospital bed at the hands of an unknown adversary. Your only crime? The fact that you know me."

Toma digests all of this for a moment. "Why exactly are you here, Lady Scheherazade? Or should I say, Mira?"

"Whoever it is that's after me, they've set out to destroy my life. They took ten innocent girls, then a friend's daughter, then my own child, and lastly..." I meet his gaze. "My love."

Toma takes a step back. "You came here to this hellish place to save me?"

"To save you all," I mutter, "but things didn't go as planned."

I start at the beginning, telling Toma first about my experiences in Anthony's Exhibition and then the world of *The Firebird*. I lead with its basis in a popular ballet by the composer Stravinsky, then move into Koschei's garden and the monsters who live there, the Princesses in captivity, the events that occurred in the Immortal's palace, and end with my one trump card, the gifted feather from the Firebird, the only hope I have of stopping all of this and bringing thirteen innocents back from the edge of death.

"I returned to the garden with the intent of facing off against Koschei and completing the cycle by summoning the Firebird, but he banished me to Mussorgsky's Bald Mountain before I had the chance."

"So, Mira, if I am to believe what you say, then you and I possess the forms of a pair of characters from a century-old piece envisioned by some random composer."

"Yes. Rimsky-Korsakov." Anthony would be so proud. "That's exactly what I'm saying."

"And we are currently banished to a hell imagined by his contemporary, Mussorgsky, from which you hope to escape so you can continue to wage a two-front war in realms imagined by their successor, this man called Stravinsky."

I exhale, my eyes sliding closed in exhaustion. "As convoluted as it sounds, that's the truth as I understand it."

"Can I assume my counterpart in what you deem the 'real' world, this… 'psychologist' as you call him, thinks all of this is utter insanity?"

"He might." I smile as a hint of Thomas peeks out through Toma's eyes. "He just might."

"Then I suspect he and I would have much to discuss." Toma steps around me and moves down the trail. "Shall we?"

~

Our journey ends at the edge of the mirrored floor of Petrushka's room, the walls around the stark place where the man standing beside me performed the heartbreaking dance of Stravinsky's famous clown now gone. I chance a look back at the foothills that surround the colossal mass of rock that haunted Mussorgsky's dreams, trying to calculate how long Toma and I have been walking. When I again turn to face the all too familiar door that stands just ajar in the room's far corner, I find that the Kalendar Prince and I are no longer alone.

By the door, Sophie, Brigitte, and Antoinette, wait for us like snarling dogs. Their attention initially all on me, as one, they each shift their gaze to Toma.

That's when everything changes.

Toma—or should I say, Petrushka—abandons any semblance of decorum and rushes from one end of the space to the other, twisted into one frantic contortion of terror after another. Gone instantly is the sense of calm majesty that was the trademark of this man who calls himself the Kalendar Prince, replaced irrevocably with the pitiable lamentations of a buffoon.

"What have you done to him?" I motion to Petrushka's flailing form as he beats his body against the wall beneath the portrait of the Charlatan. "What's wrong with Toma?"

"We have done nothing, dear Mira." Brigitte steps forward, grinning with assumed victory as she allows my true name to roll off her tongue. "The high and mighty Kalendar Prince has merely reverted to form."

"Lies." I take another step in the witches' direction. "The three of you have enchanted him." My eyes shoot to Petrushka, the poor clown banging his head into the wall in time with an even more frenetic version of the music that directed his movements during my last visit to this hell. "Now, free him, and let us be on our way."

"Do not try to blame us for your ignorance." Sophie watches me from the corner of her eye. "We may have begun with a disagreement back on the Bare Mountain, but my sisters and I are not the ones who returned the clown to his cage."

"Disagreement?" I seethe. "You were planning to kill me."

"Semantics." Antoinette steps in front of Brigitte and Sophie, hushing them with a simple finger to her lips. "Along the Exhibition, we each had a role, did we not? We the gossips, you the liberator, even the Clown Prince of Kalendars spoke some order into the place."

"And now he's beating his skull against a wall while the four of us stand and talk. Am I the only one who sees something wrong with this picture?"

At the last word, Sophie's eyes grow wide and the demure woman of the *Marketplace* at Limoges peeks through her witchy facade.

"What?" I stride in her direction. "What did I say?"

Antoinette steps into my path. "As I was saying, each of us once served our various roles along the Exhibition."

"Granted." No longer cold, I tremble now with fury. "What does that have to do with this place?"

"Everything, I'm afraid." Antoinette gestures around the space. "A room." She points to the door. "A portal." She extends a finger toward Petrushka who now sits on the floor rocking like Anthony used to on a bad day. "A man."

"Riddles." My hands ball into fists. "This place is nothing but riddles within riddles within riddles."

"Precisely." Antoinette's smile widens even as the venom seems to leave her stare. "You have finally discerned what it is you came here to learn."

"What?" My eyes dance between the three witches. "What are you talking about?"

The trio gather themselves together and leave through the door the Charlatan pushed me through an eternity ago. First Sophie, then Brigitte, leaving Antoinette hovering in the open doorway, her part in this drama not yet complete.

"Go to him," she whispers. "He may be the Kalendar Prince, but he is also Petrushka the clown. If you are to win this day, you will need the both of them."

I rush to Petrushka's side and cradle his head in my arms. "I don't understand," I shout, as his rocking grows more violent. "What am I supposed to do?"

Antoinette rests her hands on her hips. "A puppet with cut strings may indeed be free, but without another's guiding hand, he is nothing but a discarded toy."

"He needs me." Fear grips my chest. "But I don't know how to help him."

"Don't you?" Antoinette purrs. "You've seen how this ends. The last act of this travesty. The moment before the curtain falls." At my blank expression, she adds. "Think, Mira."

"Dammit, I don't—"

Wait.

Petrushka. I've watched the whole stupid thing on the internet one too many times to forget the ending now. The climax may indeed be the moment the Moor cuts Petrushka down with his golden scimitar, but that's far from the end.

The Charlatan is pulled to the center of the fair to answer for Petrushka's death only to emerge victorious yet again as he grasps the straw-filled corpse and holds it above his head, revealing that the clown in orange and white has only ever been a puppet. The crowd disperses, the constable releases him, and the Charlatan smiles, victorious. The magician's triumph is short-lived, however, as the spirit of Petrushka returns from the great beyond in the ballet's final disturbing scene. From atop the Charlatan's Booth, Petrushka's ghost thumbs his nose at his former master. The Charlatan, in turn, scurries off into the night, terrified at the sight of the flailing, screaming specter.

"Petrushka, in his own way, gets the last laugh."

Antoinette tilts her head to one side. "Not if you don't hurry." And with that, she disappears, the door clicking closed behind her with the finality of a revolver being cocked.

I rush after her only to find the double doors without handles or knobs or even a crevice to try my nails. The jet-black silhouettes of the god Anubis carved into each crimson leaf mock me with their mouthless faces. I race back to Petrushka's side where he has gone from simply rocking to pounding his head on the mirror floor. The shattered glass slashes his face with each new strike.

"Stop it," I scream, pulling his bleeding head into my lap. "Stop it, now."

Nothing I do or say accomplishes a thing. I scan the room for anything I can put between the clown's bleeding head and the jagged floor. Neither his silk hat nor the shirt he lent me seems up to the task. Then, I look up, and find my answer.

Hanging slightly askew on the wall, the portrait of the Charlatan stares down at us, its eyes following me wherever I move my head.

"Hold on," I struggle with what to call the pathetic shell of a man bashing his own brains in as I look on helplessly. "I'll be right back."

I run at the wall and leap as high as my legs will take me, but the painting sits so high on the wall, I come nowhere close to its bottom edge.

"Come on, Mira." I back up for a second run at the wall. "You can do this. You used to do the high jump in school, for God's sake."

In another world, in another body, in a universe ungoverned by someone else's imagination.

My second run meets with no more success than the first, as does my third, fourth, tenth.

"It's hopeless." My back slides down the wall as I crumple in the corner. "I can't do it." With bitter tears coursing down my face, I consciously decide to finally, mercifully, give up, when a voice from another time and place echoes in my mind.

"*As Mira Tejedor,*" rolls Mussorgsky's deep Russian baritone, "*you are powerless to save the boy, but as the Lady Scheherazade, your potential is limitless.*"

I pull myself up straight, stare up at the Charlatan's mocking portrait, and for the first time in what feels like several lifetimes, speak what I wish to happen.

"The Ballerina, suddenly clothed in her red vest, pink skirt, and fine pointe shoes, leaped higher than even she dreamed possible and grabbed the Charlatan's portrait from the wall."

Color swirls around me, and in seconds, the witch's rags and Toma's shirt disappear from my body only to be replaced by the garb of the Ballerina. Before I can even take inventory, I find myself skirting the wall to a near corner of the room. Then, by instinct, I run parallel to the wall full tilt and perform a grand jeté the likes of which has never been seen in the real world. At the height of the jump, I snatch the frame from the wall and then stick the landing as if I was born for the role.

Not wasting another moment, I rush to the clown's side, force the painting beneath his face, and issue an order as fiercely as I've ever spoken. "Stop it, Petrushka, or Toma, or Thomas, or whatever name you'll answer to. Stop it, and listen."

Petrushka stops mid-thrash and inclines his ear in my direction, though he refuses to look me in the eye. Instead, he stares down at the smug image of his tormentor, his scarlet blood dripping onto the canvas.

Even now, faced with the architect of all his suffering, poor Petrushka can't speak, the muted trumpet blaring his lamentations as the pathetic clown flails his arms in an impotent rage.

"Petrushka." My volume grows with each syllable. "Toma. Thomas Archer. Hear me and hear me well."

For the second time in as many minutes, I somehow get through to him. This time he looks up at me, his half-smile, half-frown struggling to form a word.

"Say it," I shout. "Whatever it is, let it out."

His entire body shaking, Petrushka raises his hands to the cloud-laden sky/ceiling and screams out a single word, a word of defiance, one of the simplest words in the English language.

"No!" The pained howl shakes the mirror floor beneath us.

Stravinsky imagined muted trumpets as the voice of Petrushka.

His voice is muted no longer.

With purpose and agency unimaginable moments before, Petrushka sweeps the portrait up from the floor and runs at the nearest wall. Hanging the frame at just above waist height, he forces his upper body through the suddenly ephemeral canvas—an experience I know all too well—and the music resumes.

I rush to his side and peer out through the frame, now a window that looks out upon a Shrove-Tide fair covered by the blanket of night.

It plays out just as I remember from my many viewings of the ballet. Unaware he's being watched, the Charlatan walks the streets with the straw man form of Petrushka held beneath his arm. Music begins to build, and with a vengeance, the muted trumpets of Petrushka's vocifera-tion blare one last time. Startled by the taunting melody, the Charlatan cranes his head around until he sees my Petrushka, his arms flailing, a puppet with no master.

Terrified at the sight of Petrushka's "ghost," the Charlatan sprints from the scene, leaving the street empty as the falling snow doubles in inten-sity. Petrushka hangs on as long as he can and then falls forward, his entire body limp.

"Petrushka," I cry. "What's happened?" I drag his body back through the frame and lay him out on the mirrored floor. "Tell me what to do."

"You've already done all you were supposed to." He coughs a mouthful of crimson onto the reflective floor and then looks up at me with a blood-tinged smile. "Thank you... Mira."

27

EMBOÎTÉ

A cascade of sensations hits me all at once.

The prismatic darkness of eyelids that won't open.

The pungent aroma of ammonia, not in my mind but actually searing my nostrils.

The rasp of starched sheets weighted down with hospital issue blankets.

And above all, the burning in my chest as my body refuses to breathe.

Seconds pass, then minutes, and despite the panic that threatens to explode out of me like an out-of-control nuclear reactor, my body still refuses to move. Somewhere above my head, a machine beeps rhythmically, the tempo going faster and faster with each passing second, no doubt in time with my racing heart.

I will my mouth open, but my teeth remain clenched, my lips pressed tight as if held together by undertaker's glue. A shriek builds inside me, my entire body tensing as I struggle against the strange paralysis that's overtaken me.

Faces flit across my mind. Thomas, his features cycling between Petrushka's pathetic simper and Toma's proud smile. The three witches, the abundant wickedness in their eyes tempered with a deeper wisdom. Sterling, his stern expression colored with disapproval. And last of all, Isabella, looking down on me from atop Koschei's palace, her mercurial features shifting back and forth between hope and despair.

"Mami." Her silent lips form the word that's woken me from a dead sleep a thousand times. "Don't leave me here all alone." Her eyes plead with me as she disappears behind the palace's stone parapet. "Mami!"

"Isabella!"

The scream erupts from the depths of my soul.

I sit bolt upright from my cocoon of blankets and starched sheets. My aching eyes sweep a room that is dim, but not dark. To my left, a hospital bedrail keeps me from spilling out of my bed and onto the floor. A pinch at my left forearm reveals an IV line connecting me to a bag of fluids hanging above my head. The machine monitoring my heart begins to slow, and as I settle back into the covers, I notice warmth at my right hip. There, sharing the narrow hospital bed, lies Isabella, as pale as I've ever seen her and seemingly oblivious to my ear-splitting wail.

The rest of the hospital, however? Not quite so oblivious.

"Ms. Tejedor," says the first nurse into the room. "You're awake." She turns to a second nurse, a tall blonde, who's about three steps behind her. "Mandy, go get Detective Sterling and page the doctor, stat."

The second nurse gives a curt nod and steps back into the hall while the first, on the shorter side with shoulder-length dark hair and eyes that suggest southeast Asia, turns and offers me a warm smile. "Welcome back."

"Thanks." My voice comes out like wet velcro. "What happened?"

"We've all been really worried about you." She comes around to my side of the bed. "Are you in any pain?"

"Nothing you can fix with a pill." At her confused glance, I add, "I'm fine."

She nods, wasting not a second as she checks my pulse with agile fingers even as she unkinks my IV with her other hand. Once she's sure I'm all right physically, she launches into the litany of questions I learned back in grad school that are used to check and see if someone is coherent and oriented. After a solid minute or so of the good-natured badgering, I get my metaphorical feet beneath me and raise a hand.

"Look, I remember my name, the date, who the president is. I'm fine. What I need to know is—" A glance out the window reveals only darkness. "Wait a minute. When I got here, it was still morning. What time is it?"

The nurse checks her watch, but refuses to look back up.

"All right. Now you're scaring me." I take a deep breath, my heart pounding. Funny. After nearly suffocating a few minutes ago, even the stale hospital air tastes as sweet as molasses. "Tell me, please. How long have I been out?"

"It's 1 a.m.," she whispers as she fiddles with my IV line.

"I've been out thirteen hours?"

"Not exactly." She meets my gaze. "Friday morning shift arrives in around six hours."

"Friday?" I gulp. "But I got here Wednesday morning. I've been out almost two days?"

Before she can answer, both our eyes shoot to the door in answer to the brisk footsteps echoing in the hallway beyond.

"Mira." Sterling hits the room at a dead run. "You're awake."

"More or less." I let out a groan. "My nurse here says I've been out over thirty-six hours."

Sterling catches the nurse's gaze. "She doesn't know?"

"Doesn't know what?" I try to climb out of bed, pulling myself halfway across the rail before collapsing back onto the stiff mattress. "Look, no matter what happened out here, it's nothing compared to what I just went through on the other side. Spill."

Sterling's gaze drops to the floor while the nurse busies herself adjusting the volume on the machine monitoring my heart.

"All right, you two, I may not have my strength back yet, but if someone doesn't start talking, there's going to be hell to pay." Even with that, neither of them says a word. "Dammit, Sterling, what happened to me?"

"Okay." Sterling's eyes lock with mine. "Look. This is going to be hard to hear, Mira, but we almost lost you."

"What?"

"Detective." The nurse shoots Sterling a sidelong glance. "Are you sure you don't want to wait for the doctor?"

I clear my throat. "Excuse me, but what do you mean you 'almost' lost me?"

Sterling pulls himself up to his full height. "I mean, as far as we can tell, you almost died." He pauses. "Isabella too."

"Detective Sterling." The nurse's previously amiable expression evaporates as she attempts to burn a hole through Sterling's forehead with a laser-like glare. "We talked about this."

"Isabella?" My heart freezes. "Tell me everything." As the nurse inhales to speak again, I answer her death stare with one of my own. "*Everything.*"

Sterling raises an eyebrow in the nurse's direction. "Well?"

Frustrated, she shrugs and heads for the door. "Cat's out of the bag now." She shoots Sterling one last irritated glance before stepping out into the hall. "The doctor will be up in a few minutes. Try not to scare my patient any more than you already have."

As the door clicks closed, Sterling sits at the foot of the bed just below where Isabella's feet make a small ridge out of the sheets and blankets. "You sure you want to hear all of this right now?"

I wipe the sleep from my eyes. "Start at the beginning."

Sterling nods. "You'd been… gone a couple of hours." He rests a hand on Isabella's leg beneath the covers. "Everything was going just like all the other times. Isabella was resting in her bed, and we had you over here on the recliner. You seemed troubled, but nothing too out of control." His smile evaporates. "I had just put a pillow behind your head and put up your feet when the shit hit the fan."

"What did you see?"

"This wasn't my first rodeo, you know. I've seen you in trouble before, but nothing like this. You usually get worked up when bad stuff is happening on the other side. You start breathing fast, break a sweat, maybe even kick around a bit. This was totally different."

Sulfur fear and fresh-baked concern war in my head, the first emotions I've sensed since waking up next to Isabella. "Different how?"

Sterling's shoulder rises in a half-shrug. "Everything just stopped. You went pale. Your pulse went to nothing. Hell, you all but stopped breathing."

"And Isabella?"

"A minute later, the same thing happened to her. Scared the shit out of me. I almost broke the call button when I hit it. And you should have seen your mom. She started screaming bloody murder and ran out into the hall for help. They had half the hospital in here before you could say Stravinsky."

"It's a little early for jokes, Detective," I whisper weakly. "What happened next?"

Sterling glances at the door. "One of the doctors said they weren't equipped to take care of adults up here and—"

"Wait." My breath catches. "They didn't separate me from Isabella, did they?"

Sterling shakes his head. "The doctors were not happy with me, but I made them keep you up here, just like I promised." A half-smile reappears on Sterling's face. "Fortunately, whatever spell came over you two only lasted for a couple of minutes."

"So, Isabella's okay?"

"She's fine, Ms. Tejedor." A doctor I haven't met before steps into the room. "Physically, at any rate. We're not sure what happened that had you both so... ill, but we followed your express wishes to not be separated from your daughter." The doctor, roughly my age and sporting a good day's worth of stubble, shoots Sterling an irritated look. "Your cop boyfriend made certain of that."

"He's not my—" I begin, but stop at Sterling's hand on my leg.

"How many times do I need to explain this, Doctor Flynn?" Sterling fixes him with an equally perturbed gaze. "When Mira is doing her thing, she is not to be separated from the person with whom she's working. Period."

Flynn raises a hand in surrender. "Please. No more talk about all the psychic mumbo jumbo. Ms. Tejedor may be back among the conscious, but we still have twelve comatose little girls on this floor. We're no closer than we were yesterday to figuring out what the hell is going on, and all these fairy tales aren't helping us get any closer to the truth."

"Fairy tales?" Heat rises in my cheeks. "With all due respect, Dr. Flynn, I almost died at the hands of one of those 'fairy tales' you're so quick to dismiss."

"Listen, Ms. Tejedor—"

"No, Dr. Flynn. You listen. This 'psychic mumbo jumbo' is as real as anything you learned about in whatever medical school handed you a diploma. Just because you don't understand it doesn't mean it can't kill me and every one of the girls you say you're trying to save."

"Ms. Tejedor—"

"I'm not finished." I pull in another deep breath, my lungs still hungry for air. "My daughter and I, across the room from each other, apparently both stopped breathing within seconds of each other, only to miraculously recover minutes later. You can read all your textbooks cover to cover trying to figure out why that happened, but unless you allow for something outside your limited understanding, you'll never find the answer you're looking for."

Flynn puffs up like a cornered cat. "Frankly, Ms. Tejedor, we went along with your wishes only at Detective Sterling's insistence, but if you want the truth, we were about two seconds from intubating the both of you and wheeling you off to the ICU when you finally stabilized. Last I checked, tarot cards aren't particularly effective when treating cardiopulmonary arrest, so trust that if anything even remotely like that happens again, all bets are off."

"I understand." Black pepper floods my senses, wafting from Flynn like stinging smoke off a dumpster fire, as I lock gazes with Sterling. "Now, if you'll excuse us, the Detective and I have a few things to discuss."

"Very well, Ms. Tejedor." He turns to leave. "Now, please try to get some rest. I'll be back around to check on both you and Isabella in a few hours."

I wait for Flynn to step outside and then grab Sterling's hand. "Okay, I've got to tell you something, and you're not going to like it."

He locks gazes with me, his eyes narrowing. "You're going back in there, aren't you?"

"Exactly." My eyes drop. "How did you know?"

"First things first, I'm not stupid." Sterling squeezes my fingers. "Second, you went in there to bring out your daughter, and unless I'm missing something, she's still stuck wherever it is you go when you go away."

My eyes well with tears. "I've got to save her, Sterling. I'm the only one who can."

"You didn't let me finish." Sterling brings his forehead to mine, his breath quick. "No matter what's gone down between us, Mira, you've got to know you're the bravest woman I've ever met. I don't know how you do whatever it is you do, but I do know one thing. If whomever you're facing on the other side has your daughter, then they are in for a world of hurt."

"But what if I can't do it? Can't stop him?" I choke back my fear. "Whoever is behind the guise of Koschei the Immortal has defeated me at every turn. Baba Yaga was tough, God knows, but all she ever did was send me away from the Exhibition until I grew strong enough to dig in my heels. With Koschei, it's different. It's like he knows what I'm doing, what I'm thinking. No matter what I try, he always seems to have the upper hand."

"But you hold the trump card, right?" Sterling asks. "The Firebird's feather."

"That's the thing." I take a pained breath. "He even knows about that."

"He what?"

"He said as much when we faced off atop his palace." I deflate, like someone let the air out of me. "Koschei all but spelled out my own plan for me, and what's worse, he didn't seem too worried by the proposition."

Sterling locks gazes with me, incredulous. "And yet, you still plan on going back."

"What choice do I have? That monster has my child."

"I understand. I don't like it, but I understand." He lets out a quiet sigh. "So, when are you planning this last ditch assault?"

"At first light." I stretch my free arm above my head and let out a yawn. "Seems only fitting to face Koschei at daybreak. That's the way Stravinsky wrote it."

"You going to sleep till then?" Sterling asks.

"If I can. It's just… wait." My gaze flits around the room. "Where's Mom?"

"That one's on me." Sterling shoots me a sheepish grin. "She'd been up for over thirty hours keeping an eye on you and Isabella. I sent her to the hotel after dinner last night. Told her to get some sleep and that I'd call her if there were any developments."

"But you haven't, right?"

"Not yet."

"Don't wake her, then. She needs her rest."

Sterling gives my hand a gentle squeeze. "So does her daughter."

"Five hours of sleep and I'll be ready." I pause, choosing my words carefully. "You'll stay with me, won't you?"

"Of course." Sterling's head drops. "But what about Archer?"

"Thomas." My eyes slide shut as the events of my last sojourn through the world of dream breaks over me like an ocean wave. I nearly break and tell Sterling about my night on the Bald Mountain: my encounter with the witches, my journey with the Kalendar Prince, the moral victory over the Charlatan, but at the last second, I hold my tongue. In some strange way, discussing Toma/Petrushka with Sterling feels like the deepest betrayal.

Three men, a proud prince, a pathetic clown, and a skilled psychologist, all jockey for the spotlight in my mind's eye. Each, however, peers at me with the same steely blue eyes that make my heart race each time they meet mine, eyes shut by the same vile entity that has my daughter.

No matter what it costs, I'm bringing them out of there.

Thomas. Isabella. Rachel. The girls.

All of them.

"Promise you'll keep an eye on him for me," I answer eventually. "And if I don't make it out of there…"

"Don't talk like that. You've always pulled through before. This time will be no different."

"We don't know that." I pull my hand from Sterling's and turn to face the window across the room, my emotions as obscure to me as the darkness just beyond the glass. "If I don't make it back, tell Thomas I love him, all right?"

Sterling pulls away as if I've slapped him. "You think he wants to hear that from me?"

"As long as he hears it." I turn back to face the man and wrap my arms around his muscular chest. "Thank you, Sterling."

A sharp intake of air, and he returns my embrace. "I've got to admit, Mira, I'm way confused right now."

"That makes two of us." I squeeze him even tighter. "Now, shut up and hold me."

28

DIALOGUE

The first light of day drags me from whatever twilight state my addled brain has been trying to pass off as sleep. Sterling snores in the recliner across the room while Isabella lies next to me, her body in exactly the same position it was hours before. Meanwhile, my every muscle aches as if I've gone ten rounds.

I sit up and pull Isabella's head into my lap, stroking her thick hair as her chest rises and falls in the dim light of morning. As terrified as I am of what's to come, simply looking into her innocent face steels my resolve.

One way or another, this thing with Koschei ends today.

"Mira," comes a whispered voice.

My eyes shoot to Sterling, but he's still dead asleep. Isabella as well.

"Over here," the voice beckons. "May I come in?"

My gaze shoots to the door where Anthony Faircloth peers at me through his predictably skewed glasses.

"Anthony?" Instinct kicks in, and I pull Isabella to me, a mother bird sheltering her chick from an invading snake. "It's barely light out. What are you doing up?"

"I couldn't sleep." He tiptoes over to the bed. "Looks like I'm not the only one."

My pulse roars in my ears. "How did you even know I was awake?"

"I know a lot of things, Mira." Anthony sighs. "Most of which I wish I didn't."

"Like what's coming next?" I search Anthony's eyes for even a glimmer of malevolence, but as always, all I find is sad innocence, if not a bit of hurt at my words. "You know what's about to happen, don't you?"

"I don't." Tears well at the corners of his eyes. "I swear."

The icy wall around my heart begins to melt. "Don't cry, kiddo. I believe you." I pat the bed in the spot Sterling occupied just hours before. "Come and sit with me. Let's talk."

It's Anthony's turn to hesitate. "What are you going to do to me?"

"No agenda, Anthony. Just come and sit." At his fear-filled eyes, I offer my most innocuous smile. "Please."

Another moment's hesitation, and Anthony takes the last couple of steps and pulls himself up onto the corner of the bed. "Okay," he mutters as if he's just laid his head on the proverbial chopping block. "Here I am."

"Yep. Here you are."

My skin crawls. This is the first time the two of us have been alone together since that horrible day nine months ago when Veronica Sayles nearly killed us both. I've seen him at least a dozen times since and we've never had to fight to find something to talk about.

Now, I barely know what to say.

"So, Anthony Faircloth," I ask eventually, keeping my voice low. "I have a question for you."

"Yes, Mira?"

I lean across Isabella's unconscious form, but not close enough to touch him.

I've learned my lesson on that front one too many times of late.

"You've told me time and again that Stravinsky has your ear these days. *The Firebird. Petrushka.* That *Rite of Spring* thing you were watching on your tablet the other day." A memory of the cacophony of the last piece pounds at my mind like the stomping aboriginal dancers of Stravinsky's masterpiece. "What is it about these works that speak to you? Why those ballets? Why now?"

Anthony's eyes glaze over, a look I've seen more than once when the boy is in full on concentration-mode. His fingers begin to play an invisible instrument, though piano or violin or trumpet, I have no idea. Regardless, this silent music captures him and holds his mind as surely as the pair of Stravinsky's works has held mine for the last few days. He remains in this otherworldly state for the better part of a minute before his eyes focus again on mine.

"You've seen my room," he begins. "All the books and comics. I've read them all. I know every story by heart, every note of a hundred symphonies, the dialogue of a thousand movies. You know what they all have in common?" His entire body trembles. "A beginning, a middle, and an end."

"Endings, huh?" I barely manage to keep my voice low. "That's kind of… final."

"I am no threat to you, Mira." Anthony shakes his head sadly. "At least not on purpose."

"Anthony, I—"

"Let me finish." His head drops. "In the last week, you've faced Koschei and the monsters from *The Firebird* half a dozen times. Been trapped in the world of *Petrushka*, unable to so much as control your own limbs. Had your life turned inside out by music and images you've never heard or seen." His eyes return to mine. "And it's not the first time something like that has happened."

"You don't have to do this."

"But I do." His tears, welling before, begin to fall in earnest. "I've caused you nothing but pain, Mira. Forced you to endure the Exhibition. Pushed you into the role of Scheherazade. Left you near death more times than you've probably ever told me."

"Anthony—"

"We both know that everything that's happened the last few days has my name written all over it. Now ten innocent girls, my sister, your daughter, even Dr. Archer are in horrible danger."

"Wait." My hand absently goes to my left eyebrow to massage the twinge of pain blossoming there. "How do you know about Thomas?"

Anthony shoots me a withering look. "Even with my earbuds in, I can still hear."

Touché. "So, we're agreed that whatever went down between us nine months ago is somehow back with a vengeance."

Anthony turns away and stares out the window. "Sure seems that way."

"So, what do we do now?"

"That's why I came to talk to you." His eyes again return to mine. "This story has gone on long enough. It has to end."

"Agreed." My eyes narrow. Like so many times before, both in person and by proxy in the Exhibition, I have no idea where this child, wise beyond his years, is going next. "What do you suggest?"

"To bring this travesty to a close, I fear similar tactics to what you employed nine months ago may be necessary."

"Nine months..." My stomach knots. "And what tactics might you be referring to?"

Anthony sits up straight, his hands resting loosely in his lap. "In the Exhibition, there at the end, you sacrificed yourself to bring an end to the madness. Slid Scheherazade's dagger between your ribs and straight through the storyteller's heart."

"But..." The blood drains from my face even as my heart skips a beat. "How can you possibly know that?"

"I was there, Mira, remember? The Exhibition was me, us, whatever. Whether I was a dirty gnome or a snotty troubadour or a frightened boy, I was a part of everything that happened there."

"But, you said you didn't remember any of that." I fight the instinct to reach for his hand. "Your mother and I had to explain it all to you weeks later."

"I didn't." Anthony bites his lip. "At least not at first. When I first woke up, those few weeks of my life while I was away were like a blank slate. But over the days and months that followed, my time in the Exhibition filtered its way back, piece by piece. A stray image here. A daydream there." He shivers. "And then, there are the nightmares."

"Nightmares?"

"The witch coming for me with her mortar and pestle. The monster from *The Old Castle* climbing from the moat and chasing me down the stone hallways." His fingers tap away anxiously at the plastic bedrail. "The fire that destroyed the Gnome's forest burning me alive."

"Oh, Anthony..."

"The dreams haven't all been bad. I've dreamed of *The Bogatyr Gates* so many times in the last nine months, I'd swear I walked that snowy landscape myself, dodged the taloned claws of Baba Yaga's hut, stepped through the scintillating Gate of Heroes. On other nights, I've danced with my sister on the *Ballet's* stage, sought counsel with the composer, argued with the schoolteacher..."

"But you've never told me or your mother any of this. You said you didn't remember."

Anthony's eyes slide shut. "I lied."

"And you're telling me this now?" I can barely breathe. "Why?"

"When I was in trouble last year, you came from almost two states away to help me. You risked your life time and time again for a child you'd never met, and against impossible odds, you saved me."

"And I'd do it again."

"That's the thing. This time, it's not just me. Thirteen lives are in danger. Your daughter. My sister. You risked everything for me. Would you expect me to do any less?"

"Of course not." Again, I will my hand not to reach out and brush the earnest tears from Anthony's cheek. "I'm glad you told me all of this, Anthony, but I still don't understand what it is you expect me to do?"

"Simple." Anthony's eyes shoot open, his bloodshot glare sober and resigned. "I want you to kill me."

"What?" I recoil from his earnest stare. "That's insane."

"Not here, Mira." He peers at me through his skewed glasses like a professor explaining basic addition to a college student. "In the dreamworld."

I let out a sigh of relief. "Sorry, kiddo, but no one's killing anyone, understand?"

"Wait," Anthony says. "Hear me out."

Like I'm going anywhere. "All right. Shoot."

"Koschei the Deathless, your nemesis on the other side?" Anthony regards me from beneath raised eyebrows. "That's me, without a doubt."

"How can you possibly know that?" My heart goes cold. "Unless you've been holding out on me about the last week as well."

Anthony shakes his head. "I may be able to recall the events of the Exhibition, but as to the recent stuff? Nothing but what you've told me." Anthony raises a shoulder in a subtle shrug. "Doesn't change the simple fact that if Mira Tejedor is getting sucked into fantasy worlds based on Russian ballets, Suspect Number One is sitting right across the bed from her."

My lips curl up in a rueful half-smile. "Truer words were never said."

"You asked about Stravinsky. Why I've been listening to him so much."

"Your new obsession?"

"Not exactly." Anthony eyes shift left and right. "Since the nightmares about the Exhibition picked up, I tried to push my brain in a different direction. You know, kind of like... drowning out one earworm with another."

I shudder, my encounter with the witches atop Mussorgsky's Bald Mountain rushing across my thoughts like a flash flood. "And how's that working out for you?"

"I'm not sure, but I can't help but notice where that has led us." Anthony rests a hand on Isabella's leg. "It's scary to admit, Mira, but I'm the center of all this. You know it. I know it."

I let out an exasperated sigh. "That doesn't mean you have to die."

Anthony's cheeks pink up. "You can argue with me all you want, but Stravinsky's first three ballets have one thing in common. *The Firebird* resolves with the death of an immortal, *Petrushka* ends with the death of a puppet, and *The Rite of Spring* terminates as the maiden chosen for the sacrifice literally dances herself to death to bring an end to the cold." He fixes me with as dark a stare as a fourteen-year-old boy can manage. "No matter what either of us do, before this is all over, someone is going to die."

For the thousandth time this week, my heart breaks. "You really don't know what's going to happen next, do you?"

"All I know is that when you go in there this time, you can't hesitate or worry about what happens to me. If it comes down to it, and you need to destroy Koschei to save Rachel, Isabella, Dr. Archer, and the others, I want you to do it without a second thought."

"Anthony…"

"No. We both know how *The Firebird* ends. If things on the other side are proceeding at the pace they did in the Exhibition, you've got to be pretty far along in the story by now." He narrows his eyes, studying me. "I assume you already have the Firebird's feather."

He knows.

Just like Koschei did.

"I do."

Anthony's hands ball into fists. "Then use it. Summon the Firebird, send Koschei and all his monsters into the Infernal Dance, and destroy him once and for all."

"But Anthony, what if Koschei really *is* you? You know better than anyone what happens to a person who is killed when a part of them is engaged in the dreamworld." The image of Trilby's form crushed beneath the taloned foot of Baba Yaga's hut floats before my mind's eye and chills me to my core. "Your sister almost died last year."

Anthony crosses his arms. "She survived."

"The trauma sent her into seizures. She was in the hospital for days."

He lets out a quiet harrumph, his eyes shooting to the door leading to the hallway. "I'd argue she's not doing much better at the moment."

Damn. Skewered to the wall twice in fifteen minutes by a fourteen-year-old.

"Anthony, I can't—"

"Just do it, Mira. Save my sister, your daughter, yourself. It's the only way."

"What's the only way?" Sterling rises from his slumber and saunters over to the bed. "Mr. Faircloth. What are you doing in here, young man?"

"Our room is next door. Mom's asleep and Rachel, well…" Anthony's gaze traces Isabella's sleeping form.

"Mira?" Sterling shoots me a raised eyebrow. "Everything okay?"

"Not even close, but don't worry. Anthony and I are just talking."

Sterling comes around to my side of the bed. "You still going through with this?"

"Sun's up." I put on the most confident smile I can manage. "Time to make the donuts."

"This isn't funny, Mira."

"I'm not laughing." I again meet Anthony's expectant gaze, and one simple fact becomes crystal clear. "Wait. You didn't come here just to talk, did you?"

Sterling's gaze passes from me to Anthony. "Do you know something about all of this?"

The boy's eyes close in concentration. "For days now, when Mira touches any of the girls, she is pulled into *The Firebird* to face an immortal enemy. However, when she touches me, she is pulled into *Petrushka* and faces a completely different set of challenges." His eyes open on Sterling. "History has proven time and again the difficulty of winning a two-front war, has it not?"

A baffled look crosses Sterling's face even as Anthony's plan begins to crystallize in my mind.

"You want me to touch you and Isabella at the same time, don't you?"

Anthony nods. "Whoever is putting you through your paces, they've kept you off balance from day one, making you jump from one story to the other and back again, never allowing you to find your feet." He offers me his hand. "But if you walk my mind and the girls' together…"

"Over my dead body." Caroline's irritated twang comes from the door. "Anthony William Faircloth, you get off that bed and come here right now."

Anthony looks to his mother, frantic. "But Mom, we've got to—"

"The only we in this room is me and you, and we're about to have a little talk."

"Caroline." I keep my voice low and even. "Everything's okay. Anthony just wanted to—"

Her head tilts to one side. "Oh, I know good and well what he came in here to do."

"Ms. Faircloth," Sterling says, "your son is just trying to help."

"With all due respect, Detective, my son spent the better part of a month in a coma last year. With Rachel all but catatonic next door, excuse me if I'm not excited at the prospect of anyone 'walking Anthony's mind' at the moment."

"Mom," Anthony half-grunts, "if we want Rachel back, this is the only way."

Caroline's eyes slide shut. "And you were going to do this without even asking me."

My cheeks get hot. "I didn't ask for him to come, Caroline. He—"

"I wasn't talking to you, Mira." Caroline comes to the bed and strokes Anthony's hair. "My brave boy, how could I possibly risk losing you again?"

"Mom, Mira has spent the last week fighting for her life in worlds that can only have sprung from my mind. Regardless of whether I want to be, I'm already involved." He reaches a hand up and takes his mother's. "Please, let me do the right thing."

Caroline squeezes her son's hand even as her gaze passes to mine. "All right, Mira. You're the expert here. If it were Isabella, would you let her do this?"

I shake my head wearily. "Though we had no other choice at the time, your son and I started something nine months ago that's come back to bite all of us." I swallow back the tremor in my voice. "Like it or not, he's a part of this. And more than old enough to decide for himself."

"I suppose he is." Caroline lets out a resigned sigh as she sits by Anthony on the bed. "In that case, I'm staying too."

"Okay…" I study Caroline's face, the set of her jaw, the tension in her shoulders. She's not going anywhere. "I appreciate the support, but what about Rachel? Doesn't she need you?"

"Jason is with her. He just got back into town. Woke me up when he came in the room. That's when I realized Anthony was missing." She breathes an exhausted laugh. "Took me exactly one guess to figure out where he'd gone." Doing her best to maintain her composure, Caroline reaches out and touches my shoulder. "So, do we do this like we did before?"

"Hold onto Anthony's hand and don't let go." I open my mind wide and am instantly flooded with the worry and fear emanating from Caroline and Anthony as well as dozens of emotions from the surrounding patients and families and medical personnel. Wrapping my fingers around Isabella's, I reach out for Anthony's free hand.

"Sterling?" I ask. "Can you stay?"

"I'm not going anywhere, Mira."

"Thank you."

I interlace my fingers with Anthony's and immediately am filled with music and darkness and foreboding. I meet his gaze and offer him a weak grin.

"No backing out now, kiddo."

He looks back, not even a glimmer of a smile on his face. "Remember what I said, Mira. If that's what it takes to finish this, I want you to do it without a second thought."

"Wait," Caroline asks. "Do what, exactly?"

The words are the last I hear before a veil of inky blackness falls only to rise again on Koschei's garden where I find myself alone. The previously decrepit place now covered in a blanket of white snow, only a few distinguishing features remain.

The surrounding forest naked of leaves.

The lone apple tree arching over the flat stone now as bare as its brethren.

A slight disturbance in the snow, beneath which rests the *bukavac* pool.

And Koschei's skull palace, grinning at me from the far end of the clearing. Its drawbridge down, the faint purple glow coming from the mouth entices me closer. As if the open invitation isn't enough, a blast of cold wind reminiscent of my time on the Bald Mountain hits me from behind and nearly knocks me to my knees.

In the distance, the sun rises on this place for the second time in my many visits, and I take the first snow-laden step on the path to whatever fate awaits me.

All right, Koschei the Deathless.

Bring it.

Let's find out how immortal you really are.

29

DANSE INFERNALE

In a way, returning here feels like a homecoming.

After my time on the Bald Mountain, its desolate rocky face devoid of anything appealing to the eye, Koschei's garden under a foot of snow is actually quite striking in its beauty, its stillness, and—dare I say—its purity. Still, it's strange. Anthony is a stickler for detail, and in every version of *The Firebird* I've been able to find online, perpetual summer seems to be the order of the day.

As snow begins to fall anew, my mind wanders to another place. Another time.

Another battle.

The snowswept landscape surrounding the Bogatyr Gates, the only escape from Anthony's Exhibition. Baba Yaga's hut atop its pair of giant chicken legs continuing its lumbering march to freedom with all the disparate facets of Anthony Faircloth within. Madame Versailles and I fighting quite literally to the death.

My death.

Nine months ago, and yet as fresh and terrifying as if it happened yesterday.

As I approach the toothed arch leading into Koschei's abode for what will no doubt be our final confrontation, the snow seems fitting. I trudge through the knee-deep drift, Princess Ivanovna's tunic, bracers, and knee-high boots serving to protect my feet and legs from the wet chill. Still, the slick surface of the palace's stone tongue nearly sends me into the frozen moat more than once. Another few careful strides lead me inside, and though I've prepared myself as best I can, I barely stifle my gasp as I step beneath the doorway's great incisors.

Where an enclosed stone hallway once wound away from the entrance, a spacious courtyard now awaits, its upper reaches open to the leaden sky above. An enormous seven-sided enclosure, the toothed doorway I've just passed appears the only way in or out. Two per wall, the twelve princesses hang in their ivory nightgowns, their wrists chained to the stone and their toes dangling well beyond my reach. Shivering as the falling snow accumulates on their heads and shoulders, all twelve turn toward me as one and stare silently, agape with terror.

Wait. It's not me they're staring at, but the wall behind me.

I crane my neck around and find a thirteenth set of manacles hanging empty above the palace's jagged entrance.

Koschei.

Not a creature of subtlety.

Much like the boy who I fear unwittingly hides behind the sorcerer's mask.

"My dear Ivanovna." The rough voice hits me like an iron fist to the gut. "I must say I was quite surprised to sense your return to my garden. Some people, it would seem, never learn."

"I've heard those words before." I return my eyes to the center of the courtyard where Koschei the Deathless stands, his shoulders shaking with laughter. "Know one thing, Immortal. With God as my witness, this will be our last meeting."

"Then we are in agreement." His wrinkled features shift from amused to deadly serious. "This ends today."

The clink of chains above my head draws my attention. Turning slowly and never letting Koschei out of my sight, I study the faces of each of the Immortal's captives. Each set of eyes appears more terrified than the one before, and none more so than Isabella's.

"The girls. They cannot speak. What have you done to them?"

"During your last trip to my abode, I allowed a moment of lenience. Gave the whole lot of them the run of the palace." His eyes narrow. "You saw how that turned out."

"Afraid of twelve little girls, Immortal?"

"Not even remotely. They are, at worst, an inconvenience." A perplexed cast invades his expression. "I must ask. However did you escape the Bare Mountain?"

"You've spoken twice to me about the wisdom of keeping one's own counsel, Koschei." I fight the instinct to summon Ivanovna's bow. Even the sharpest arrow in that quiver will not win this day. "You have your secrets, it would seem, and I have mine."

"Very well." Koschei takes a step in my direction. "So, our impasse continues."

"Impasse?" My hand sneaks inside my tunic, grasping for the Firebird's feather. "I think not."

My fingertips have just brushed the soft down at the feather's base when cruel hands erupt from the snow and seize my legs, pulling me down to the snow-covered ground. Clawed fingers tear my hand from my tunic, my bleeding arm leaving an arc of crimson across the pristine snow.

Snow that remains pristine for just a moment longer.

From beneath the obscuring drift of white, a horde of *skrzaks* rises like demons from an icebound hell. The host of two-foot monsters swarms at me like ants, and within seconds, I'm completely at their mercy. As its tribe chortles the same wheezy laugh, the *skrzak* chief stands silent above my head, studying me like a middle-schooler studies a frog on dissection day.

"What are you waiting for?" I struggle in vain against the multitude of rough hands.

The *skrzak* chief leans over me. "You wish to die?"

"I wish for this to be over, once and for all." The thirteenth set of chains just visible above the throng, I scramble for anything I can say or do to rob Koschei of his victory. "Now, finish this."

"But... that's not how this ends." In the *skrzak* chief's inverted countenance, the rage and bloodthirst I found seconds before is joined by a third emotion.

Sadness.

Again I'm taken back to the Exhibition where just months ago, I faced a similar scenario. In *Tuileries*, I was overrun by a multitude of dwarfish adversaries while one among them stood alone and forlorn.

The connection forming in my mind is shattered as a crushing pressure at my throat cuts off my air. My gaze shoots down my body where the now divided *skrzak* mob has allowed their dark master to pass. Standing just below my feet with the tip of his staff buried in the flesh below my chin, the immortal sorcerer stares down at me with unbridled malevolence.

"And so it ends, Ivanovna." The wood of his staff digs deeper in to my windpipe. "This victory shall be sweet."

"You haven't won yet." My voice barely a whispered grunt, it's still loud enough to be heard. "With my dying breath, I will still defy you."

Koschei throws back his head and laughs. "Still, Ivanovna, you preen and bluster, even in the moment of your defeat?"

"I have in my possession the one thing that can bring you down, Koschei." I smile, despite the pain. "You know of what I speak."

The Immortal strokes his scraggly beard. "I can only assume you refer to the gift bestowed upon you by the Firebird." He looks to the *skrzak* chief. "Within her tunic, you will find a feather. Retrieve the creature's foul plumage." His smile grows wide. "And destroy it."

My gaze shoots upward in time to catch the moment of hesitation in the *skrzak's* eyes.

"Do it now," Koschei demands, "stupid gnome."

Gnome.

That's it. That's why this is so familiar.

All of this. The Immortal. His palace. His monstrous servants.

They're all Anthony.

And though they look nothing like they did in the Exhibition, I've met these two sides of Anthony before.

The gnome who lives in the woods and the lone boy surrounded by marauding children.

And we stand in a garden, no less.

How could I have been so blind?

"Anthony," I whisper. "It's not too late. Just listen to me."

"If you will not be silent, Ivanovna…" Koschei pulls his staff from my throat and raises its full length above his head.

"Anthony." Emotion cracks my voice. "Please."

"Enough." Koschei swings the staff at my head, and my eyes instinctively clamp shut.

The whistling of wood through air ends in a sickening crack.

And yet, I feel no pain.

My eyes open on a miracle. Above my head where the *skrzak* chief had stared down at me with an inverted snarl stands Tunny, the gnome from Anthony's Exhibition.

My friend.

"Nice to see you, Scheherazade," he grunts, his voice like a falling tree. "Been a while."

His oaken hand, held above his head, now sports two splintered fingers, but in the remaining three, he grips the business end of Koschei's staff.

Yet again, the little gnome with the big heart has saved me.

Looks like whomever or whatever is in control of Anthony is slipping a bit.

Koschei yanks his staff from Tunny's fractured hand. "You dare?"

Tunny, as confident as I've seen him, shoots Koschei a wicked grin. "As a matter of fact, we do."

A horrendous cracking echoes from outside as the *vodyanoi* erupts from the frozen moat in a shower of jagged ice and lands just inside the entrance. A literal fish out of water, the previously terrifying merman shoots me a knowing smirk as he pulls a familiar silver saxophone to his lips.

Hope swells my heart. "Modesto?"

The *vodyanoi*, covered head to toe in scintillating blue and white scales, gives me a subtle nod as he launches into a haunting melody both foreign and familiar. What pours from the bell of his instrument isn't quite the tune I remember from the Exhibition, but a twisted variation, somber and dark, as different from "The Old Castle" as Koschei's palace is from Modesto's home.

"Hold her," Koschei grunts to his *skrzaks*, "and rid my home of this filthy gnome." He steps across me and stalks in the direction of the troubadour turned merman. "Meanwhile, I must deal with this insubordination."

The dozen or so *skrzaks* keeping me out of commission don't move an inch, but the rest of the horde descends upon Tunny like a swarm of bees. For a moment, I fear for the little guy's life.

I needn't have worried.

A wooden mace appears in Tunny's uninjured hand, and with each swing of his oaken arm, a trio of *skrzaks* goes flying. He's dispatched a good dozen of them before the horde decide as a whole that discretion may indeed be the better part of valor. Tunny wastes little time descending on the monsters holding me to the ground, and in seconds, I'm free. He yanks me to my feet, no small feat for someone who is two feet tall on a good day, and then leaps past me to resume his attack.

I summon Ivanovna's weapon of choice to my hand and launch myself at the throng of *skrzaks* rushing at me, the recurve bow acting as a battering ram. In the real world, I may not be particularly imposing, but against a horde of creatures that, however vicious they may be, don't quite come to my knees, I do all right. As Tunny and I deal with what seems an endless mob of pint-sized savages, Modesto and Koschei grapple beneath the toothed arch leading back to the garden, the battle witnessed by twelve terrified girls in chains, the ability to so much as scream stolen from them.

Forced to the center of the courtyard, Tunny and I end up back to back as the *skrzaks* surround us. The crimson glow from their hate-filled eyes glisten off the jagged teeth of a hundred hungry mouths.

"Tunny," I shout across my shoulder. "What now?"

"You guard my back," he grunts as he clocks another *skrzak* with his club, "and I'll guard yours."

"My, Tunny." Despite the dire situation, I let out a laugh. "Whatever happened to the sweet little gnome I met a year ago?"

"Only nine months have passed, Scheherazade." He groans as he tears a *skrzak* from his head, losing his two-pronged hat in the process. "And everybody has to grow up some time."

I swing the bow and knock the nearest four *skrzaks* onto their backs, though half a dozen fill the gap in their line before I can so much as take a breath. I chance a glance back at the door to find a dozen *bukavacs* pouring past the battling *vodyanoi* and Koschei. A moment later, a terrible roar in strangely beautiful three-part harmony pierces the sky as the *zmej* reenters the fray.

"They're trying to keep me off balance, Tunny," I shout. "Doing whatever they must to keep me from bringing out the feather." I glance in his direction, and we share a desperate look. "If I can get a moment, I can end this."

"Then," Tunny shouts, "a moment you shall have." The gnome pulls in a deep breath and dives his hand into the snow at his feet.

"What are you doing, Tunny?" I cry out as a *skrzak* clamps its teeth down on my ankle. "They're going to kill us."

"These monsters are Koschei's servants," he huffs. "The trees of the forest are mine."

From the already disturbed snow erupt a score of gnarled roots that strike out at the surrounding *skrzaks*. Pummeled, strangled, and crushed by the flailing tendrils, the inner circle of red-eyed creatures falls. Less than a second passes before the next rank of monsters climb over their fallen compatriots to resume the attack, but in that second, I steal a hand inside my garment and grasp my ace in the hole.

"And now, Koschei," I shout as I pull the scintillating orange feather from the fold of my tunic, "we end this."

"No!" Koschei runs at me, the embattled *vodyanoi* already a distant memory. "You'll destroy everything."

"Another sentiment I've heard before." I hold the feather above my head and pull in a deep breath. "Hear me, Firebird. I call upon you to repay your debt."

As if in answer to my request, an enormous winged shadow falls across the snow-covered courtyard. A glance up, however, reveals not the Firebird but Koschei's *zmej* swooping down, its terrible roar exploding out of its three mouths in balls of blue flame. With nowhere to go and no way to retaliate without dropping the Firebird's shimmering plume, I stand defiant and try to ignore the fact I've pinned the hopes of thirteen families on one boy's hopeless obsession with the imagination of a long-dead composer.

As I steel myself for an excruciating death, an ear-splitting shriek pierces the air. The Firebird falls from the sky like a flaming meteor and collides with the *zmej*, sending the dragon hurtling into one of the court-yard's inner walls. The three-headed monstrosity narrowly misses crushing Isabella as it slides down the wall to the snowy ground. I reas-sure my daughter with a subtle nod, and the fear in her eyes shifts to tempered steel.

That's my girl.

"No." Koschei's eyes widen in fear as the Firebird lights before him. "To me, my minions," he shouts. "Immortality to the one who brings me the Firebird's head."

The mob of *skrzaks* surrounding Tunny and me dissipates only to charge the Firebird. All the *bukavacs* remaining join the attack and even the wounded *zmej* attempts to rise from the ground for a chance to even the score. I freeze, terrified the Firebird may be overpowered and slain.

As before with Tunny, my fears are woefully ill-founded.

A particularly aggressive *bukavac* is the first to fall, impaled on the Firebird's sword-like beak and tossed aside like a discarded toy. A solitary beat of the mighty creature's wings sends a dozen *skrzaks* to their knees and gives the remainder of the mob of dwarfish monsters pause. Even the newly emboldened *zmej* stops its charge when faced with the Firebird's steady gaze. In a shimmer of light, the enormous bird shifts into the masked ballerina, dressed as before in her scarlet bodice and feathered tutu. The fanciful melody that accompanied the Firebird's last appearance resumes in earnest, and from her first step, the masked ballerina commands the attention of everyone present.

And then, with an ear-shattering orchestral hit, everything changes.

The *skrzaks, bukavacs, zmej,* and even the *vodyanoi* all join in with the ballerina in red, her every movement and gesture sending the gathered monsters into a strange delirium of dance and decadence. The Firebird takes her turn with each faction of Koschei's army, inciting a frenzy in each of their clans.

At her command, the bonds of the Immortal's twelve captives spring open, releasing the princesses and allowing them to slide down the walls to join the insane dance. Even Tunny spins around in time with the accelerating music. Only Koschei and I seem immune to the enchantment, the Immortal ranting and raving at the masked ballerina as his control over the situation slips further from his grasp.

At once frantic and graceful, the entire assemblage, my feathered ally at its heart, cavorts this way and that, the tightly choreographed movements growing faster and faster as the intermingled strings, brass, and woodwinds fill the air and the percussion pounds at us with near-physical force. For what seems an eternity, the bizarre juxtaposition of the scene holds true: the horrible and the beautiful, the grotesque and the elegant, the dreamily fantastic and the painfully real.

As the music hits its climax, the Firebird raises her arms high above her head and then brings them forcefully to her sides as the orchestral accompaniment concludes with a sonic boom. In answer to her silent command, every living thing in the courtyard other than the masked ballerina and me falls to the ground, the twelve girls all collapsing in a circle like a dozen dominoes.

For the moment, at least, Isabella seems safe.

A new song fills the space, a gentle lullaby, and the Firebird launches into a different routine. She visits each of the fallen one by one, sending both monsters and maidens into a deep sleep. *Skrzaks, bukavacs, zmej, vodyanoi,* Tunny, and even Koschei himself are all putty in her graceful hands.

Then, it's my turn. I steel myself against falling under her enchantment, but instead of attempting to render me unconscious, she merely motions for me to follow her.

She leads me out of Koschei's palace and back to his garden, where the snow has risen to just below my knees. In a blink, she disappears from my side and reappears by the ancient apple tree at the garden's center.

"What is it?" I ask. "What do you want me to do?"

Without a word, the masked ballerina motions to the base of the naked tree.

"I don't understand. Is there something here you wish me to find?"

At her simple nod, I step to one side and my knee impacts something hard. I glance down and find Tunny, moving as if half-asleep, pushing through the snow. He must have followed us from the palace, despite the Firebird's spell.

Or because of it.

I turn on the masked ballerina. "What have you done to him?"

With a dismissive frown, The Firebird shakes her head and again points to the ground. Tunny, his brown scalp and eyes just visible above the white, forces his way through the snow and joins the Firebird. Like a mother bird with a chick beneath its wing, the two of them stand there silent by the stone where I found Hannah Abrams on my first visit to Koschei's garden.

A moment that seems an eternity ago.

At the Firebird's direction, Tunny dives his hand into the snow as he did before. This time, it's the roots of the apple tree that obey his command. The countless woody tendrils lift the enormous flat stone from the ground and reveal what rests beneath. Glowing a sickly green, a translucent egg the size of my head lies in a hollow beneath the spot where the stone rested moments before.

Only then do I remember.

It would seem I have one last task to complete.

I crunch through the snow and join the feathered ballerina and ensorcelled gnome beneath the naked tree.

"My turn, I suppose."

The Firebird nods solemnly.

"I face Koschei one last time, destroy the egg before his eyes, and this is over."

Again, she nods.

I kneel beneath branches once laden with golden apples and pull the glowing egg from its resting place. My heart races in the moment, though my elation as I grasp the warm shell in my fingers is tempered by the inescapable feeling I'm still missing something.

I leave the Firebird and Tunny by the apple tree and return to Koschei's palace. As I step beneath the toothed doorway, no ambush awaits me, no attack. Instead, the various enchanted monsters all stir from their slumber. *Bukavacs, skrzaks,* and *zmej* alike stretch as if they've been dozing for years. The *vodyanoi*, half-conscious at best, flops around like a beached mackerel in the midst of a nightmare. The girls all remain blissfully asleep.

And there, at the center of it all, the architect of this madness.

Pulling against his staff in a solitary struggle to regain his feet, Koschei is nearly upright when he spies me and, more importantly, the artifact resting in my hands.

"Stop this now, Ivanovna." His eyes narrow as he takes a cautious step in my direction. "You toy with forces far beyond your ken."

"I understand far more than you give me credit for." I hold the egg above my head, it's putrescent glow spoiling the purity of the snowy courtyard. "For instance, I know all too well what lies within this fragile shell, and what happens if it breaks."

"Do you?" His eyes spit hate, though my threat stops him in his tracks. "Do you truly?" For the first time, a hint of sadness invades the sorcerer's voice. "If you did, I suspect you wouldn't be so cavalier with something so precious."

"More precious than your immortal soul?" Shocked by both the shift in tone and Koschei's pitiful stare, I cradle the egg close to my chest. "Tell me. What is this thing?"

"Ah, dear Ivanovna." A feminine voice from somewhere behind me. Like so many things in the realm of dream, the intonation is in equal parts familiar and foreign. "After all this time, we have finally arrived at the moment of truth."

Keeping one eye on Koschei, I turn to receive this new player.

Or, in this case, not so new.

From the toothed doorway, the Firebird in the guise of the masked ballerina flounces into the courtyard with an enchanted Tunny in tow. Her smile, just visible beneath her mask, appears far more cat than bird.

"So you can speak." With trembling fingers, I hold aloft the feather. "If that's the case, then, Firebird, complete your debt to me and reveal to me what lies within this egg."

The Firebird laughs. "Oh, I'll tell you what's inside, Mira Tejedor, though I owe you no debt." Her head tilts to one side. "At least, none you'd care to collect."

The utterance of my true name chills my heart and steals the strength from my limbs. "How do you know that name? Who are you?"

"A familiar face." Her fingers go to the edge of the feathered mask. "Though likely the last you expected to see in this place." She pulls the mask away and shakes out her headful of long red locks. When again we lock gazes, Katie Kaczynski's are the eyes that stare back.

"But how? Why?" I tuck the egg beneath one arm and point an accusing finger at the unmasked Firebird. "You may be Thomas' ex, and you probably hate my guts, but you have nothing to do with any of this." My eyes narrow. "Sorry. Not buying it."

"Of course not, Mira. Though she may be jealous of your relationship with her ex-fiancé, the newswoman wishes you no harm." The cruel smile on her face blossoms into a full, wicked grin. "In a strange way, in fact, she actually admires you." The smile disappears. "Just as I once did."

"But… if you're not Katie, then who the hell are you?"

"Someone you never expected to see again." Her voice drops into an all too familiar French accent. "I merely wore the reporter's face to see that look on your own."

My blood turns to ice. "No."

"Yes, Mira Tejedor. I am the Firebird, what the Russians call *Zharptitsa* and the French *L'oiseau de feu*, but you know me by a different name." She regards me with a self-satisfied smirk. "Like an unborn child, I've waited for nine long months, and now, my moment has finally arrived. Look now, Mira Tejedor, upon the true face of your persecutor."

Poised *en pointe* on one muscular leg, the ballerina spins once, twice, three times. With each spin, her hair lightens, and as she comes to a stop, her ginger tresses have shifted to blonde, framing a likeness that has haunted my dreams for nearly a year.

"Something still doesn't smell right here." I study the unmasked ballerina, watching for the slightest twitch. "Veronica Sayles lies comatose in a hospital bed a million miles from here."

"Speak not that name," the Firebird spits. "You will address me correctly, Mira Tejedor, or you and all who remain here will suffer the consequences."

"Very well," I murmur as a full understanding of who and what I face dawns on me. "It would appear the play is to you, Madame Versailles."

30

APPARITION

"Music to my ears." Versailles, still arrayed in the Firebird's garb, spins a slender finger in the air. Responding to her silent command, two dozen *skrzaks* scurry to gather behind her. Climbing over each other like ants upon a dead rodent, the swarm of dwarfish monsters contorts their freakish bodies until their intertwined forms assume the shape of a chair. No sooner has the throne of flesh and bone formed than Versailles takes her seat and regards me with a triumphant grin. "You have no idea how long I've waited for this moment, Mira Tejedor. How many nights I've plotted exactly what I would say when I finally had you at my mercy."

Versailles gazes at me from atop her gruesome seat of power. Still, confident as she is, the once teacher from *Tuileries* doesn't take her eyes off me for a second.

Words from an eternity ago echo in my mind. *"Overconfidence leads only to failure."*

It would seem the woman has decided to heed her own words.

The sickly green light of the orb in my hands pulsates slower and slower with each passing minute. Recent revelations aside, now is not the time to lose sight of the endgame.

"Looks like this time you're the one with all the answers." I cradle the egg tightly to my chest. "So tell me, Madame Versailles. What is it that rests inside this shell?"

Her smile diminishes ever so slightly. "Not going to give me the pleasure, I see." She adjusts her position, leaning forward on her monstrous throne. "If you must know, the egg contains precisely what you think it does."

"Koschei's immortal soul."

"Precisely," Versailles hisses. "Unfortunately for you, that is not the pertinent question."

"Very well." Exasperation leaks into my purposefully cool tone. "What should I be asking?"

She lets out a long-suffering sigh, the frustrated teacher in her coming to the fore. "The question, Mira, isn't the contents of a magical egg from a ballet that's been around for over a century. Any music historian could tell you that." She lounges across her throne of flesh, arms crossed. "But who Koschei is and what he represents in this place? That, you may wish to consider."

Versailles snaps her fingers, and Koschei trudges over to her *skrzak* throne, kneels before her, and kisses her hand.

"What would you have me do, Mistress?" he intones.

"Simple," she purrs. "Tear off your face."

Koschei recoils. "My face?"

"Yes, you mewling child, your face." Her eyes narrow. "Or at least the face of Koschei the Deathless." Her gaze wanders to me. "Let the interloper see you for who you truly are."

"But, Mistress..."

"Your face," Versailles snaps, "now."

Without another word, Koschei drops his staff to the snowswept ground and claws at the skin just above his left eye. The ripping sound as he pulls the wrinkled skin from his scalp and cheeks turns my stomach, yet I can't look away. Beneath the Immortal's decaying flesh lies a bearded face with devious eyes that know only wickedness.

When they belonged to the Exhibition's composer, these eyes contained warmth and wisdom, but now serve only as windows into the cruel soul of the Charlatan.

"Not that one, imbecile." Versailles rolls her eyes in melodramatic fashion, I assume for my benefit. "Show us your true face."

The Charlatan works at his face anew, his thick beard tearing away to reveal smooth adolescent skin, his dark mane resolving into a similarly full head of unkempt hair, his merciless glare replaced by a pair of sad eyes peering out through glasses resting slightly askew on a likeness I've gazed upon a hundred times.

Anthony Faircloth's, in all its innocence and vulnerability, is the face that stares back at me from behind the Immortal's double mask. I've seen the boy's trembling lower lip enough in the last few weeks, though I'm relatively certain this particular version of Anthony is the one I met nine months ago in the garden from *Tuileries*.

"Antoine?"

"Forgive me." His eyes shoot from me to Versailles and back. "She is so strong."

"Fight her, Antoine. Don't give in to her darkness."

"As if the boy could so much as lift a finger against me." Versailles spins her own finger again, and Antoine/Koschei answers with a clumsy pirouette. "In this world of *The Firebird*," she gloats, running her hands down the bright plumage of her garb, "my will reigns supreme."

"But how did you create such a place?" I ask. "You were defeated. Dying."

Versailles laughs. "That, Mira Tejedor, is the best part." She stands from her throne of bone and sinew and twirls around, arms out in exultation. "I created none of this, but rather, stole it. All of this, all that you've seen since your first visit to Koschei's garden now belongs to me." She strides over to the nearest wall, stepping across the helpless form of one of the girls whose name I can't recall, and runs her fingers along the granite. "Formed from the imagination of a child, taken from the mighty Baba Yaga, and then abandoned by you." She narrows her eyes at me, her lips pulling into a thin smile. "The Exhibition and all its wonder is now mine."

"So... this is the Exhibition."

Versailles eyes dart in my direction. "What else would it be?" At my dumbfounded gaze, she adds, "Think about it, Mira. Where did you first encounter me?"

"Along the Exhibition," I answer after a moment. "In *Tuileries*."

"A garden, much like the one outside this palace, no?" She shoots me a beatific smile. "And the second time?"

"*The Marketplace at Limoges*." Understanding dawns on me. "Wait. The Shrove-Tide Fair. You were there?"

Versailles offers a solemn nod. "I doubt you recognized me among the many revelers, though I did maintain one small aspect of my dress from *Tuileries*—just to see if you were paying attention."

A flash of memory. A wizened old man playing a lute, his knee-length beard coursing like the tail of a gray comet across a robe the color of twilight, the trim on his sleeves fashioned from decidedly out-of-place yellow lace.

Not to mention the feather in his cap, scintillating with orange light as if afire.

God, I've been such a fool.

"You were the Master of Ceremonies." The man's subtle wink from my first visit to the Russian fair finally makes sense. "You're responsible for everything, *The Firebird*, *Petrushka*, all of it."

"And you couldn't have played your role better if I'd handed you a script." Versailles shakes her head in mock sadness. "How does it feel knowing that despite all your bluster, you've been nothing but another puppet on my stage?"

The truth unfolds before me. If Koschei's garden is in fact a warped *Tuileries*, and the Shrove-Tide Fair represents a twist on *The Marketplace at Limoges*, then the forest surrounding the garden is Tunny's home from *Gnomus*, and we currently stand within *The Old Castle*, the blue-and-white clad troubadour now the whiskered merman that swims its moat.

"So, you did all of this..." I motion to the huddle of girls in white dresses at her feet, half trembling in fear while the others still sleep. "Took all these children from their families, hurt Anthony and Rachel and Isabella, put Thomas into a coma, all just to get back at me?"

"At first." Her eyelids slide closed. "In the moment you left me to die as the Exhibition crumbled around us, my one thought, my lone desire, was that you die with me. And then... a wondrous thing happened." Her eyes snap open. "I didn't die."

Thunder cracks in the distance, ripping through the gray sky like cannon fire.

"In taking the others from the Exhibition, you may have freed the boy, but in a way, you freed me as well."

A chill pierces me to the core. "You were supposed to die that day."

"And yet, here I am." She strides over to me. "In your last ditch effort to be rid of me, you forgot one simple fact." Her eyes flash with orange fire. "The others and I didn't merely live along the Exhibition. We *were* the Exhibition."

Icy fingers squeeze my heart. "And when I took everyone else away..."

"I became the Exhibition, and the Exhibition became me. It would appear a boy's fervent imagination isn't quite so easy to snuff out."

"But why all this? *The Firebird*? *Petrushka*? None of this was here before."

Versailles reaches out a confident hand and strokes my hair almost affectionately. "If there is one thing I learned from you, Mira Tejedor, it's that in this place, victory goes to the one who holds the most power." Casting a glance around the courtyard, she snaps her fingers. In answer, Tunny, Modesto, and her entire retinue of monstrous servants leap to their feet. "After the boy's ordeal, he understandably retreated from the framework of Mussorgsky and found a different muse. That doesn't mean, however, that the well-worn pathways left in his mind simply ceased to exist."

Another snap, and the girls rise from the ground and form a tight wedge with Isabella at the point. Twelve sets of otherwise innocent eyes stare at me, devoid of even a hint of emotion. With all of them completely in her thrall, there won't be any help coming from that corner.

I run my weary eyes over the drowsy gnome and the half-fish troubadour, the mismatched pair positioned at Versailles' sides, and a rush of faces I first met in the Exhibition floods my memory. Rachel/Trilby, defiant in the face of her previous mistress, now a slave to Versailles' Firebird and staring at me from the corner of the courtyard in abject terror. Hartmann the Cart Man, once the man whose life was literally turned upside down, now the bear-wrestling peasant from *Petrushka*. Likewise, Samuel Goldenberg and Schmuÿle, now the Moor and constable from the Russian fair. Even Mussorgsky, the composer of the Exhibition, has fallen under the sway of Versailles, the Charlatan puppeteer ironically just another of her marionettes. And I can't forget the women of Limoges, transformed into a trio of crones and banished to an isolated peak Mussorgsky imagined over a century ago.

Gnome, Troubadour, Teacher, Farmer, Ballerina, Gossips, Composer.

They're all here somewhere. Just like before.

All, that is, save one.

"If this is truly the Exhibition, then where is its mistress?"

Versailles' nose crinkles in disgust. "As the boy's obsession shifted from Mussorgsky to Stravinsky, the various aspects of his presence among his mental construct became rather nebulous, and I, the only entity left intact from its original conception, was left the task of designing the new world. Though the boy's imagination alone fuels the imagery of this wondrous place, I was intimately involved with shaping every facet, every locale, every character to my whim." Her lips spread wide in a victorious smile. "There is only room in this new Exhibition for one Mistress."

"And that would be you," I mutter between clenched teeth.

Versailles stretches her arms wide, her delicate flesh and bone transforming into full-fledged wings of scarlet, orange, and gold. "A caterpillar trapped inside its chrysalis, I grew and grew until I emerged, the butterfly of this story and more powerful than I could have ever dreamed."

"You grew, all right." My hands ball into fists at my sides. "Like a cancer in poor Anthony's mind."

Versailles raises her shoulders in a dismissive shrug. "You speak your metaphors, and I will speak mine."

"So, you now have me, my daughter, my friends, and ten innocent girls in your power." I study her eyes for any hint of emotion. "What now?"

Versailles steeples her fingers before her chin. "Now, Mira Tejedor, you have a choice." She motions to the glowing egg in my arms. "You hold in your hands the very essence of Anthony Faircloth. Cast it to the ground and end this, freeing yourself, your daughter, your lover, and all the innocents that languish in pain in this place, but know this—you will be sending the boy back to hell, a winter from which his mind will never recover, with only I, his teacher, to accompany him till the day he dies."

My blood turns to ice. "And my other option?"

Versailles' smile widens. "Take my place."

"What?"

"Exchange roles with me. Free me from the prison of the boy's mind and allow me to walk the world again."

I struggle to pull in air. "You want… my body?"

"I've proven my power beyond any shadow of a doubt. Thirteen minds lie catatonic merely because I will it. I sent those ten girls running to leap to their deaths with little more than a suggestion. Even you, the mighty Mira Tejedor, have performed perfectly the dance I choreographed for you." She returns to her throne to survey the abomination she has created in her own image. "My final hurdle? To assume your body, your mind, your existence. To live again."

"You're insane." My entire body trembles with fear and rage. "What you suggest is impossible."

"Strong words from a woman who walks the minds of others as if she were strolling the halls of her own home."

"How do I know you're not lying?" I hold the egg above my head. "Don't forget, I understand how Anthony Faircloth's mind works better than anyone. As the avatar of Prince Ivan, I'm supposed to win this fight, destroy Koschei, and return the world to order. What if destroying this egg and ending this right now is exactly what he needs me to do?"

Versailles laughs. "You still don't see." She gestures to the thirteenth set of manacles hanging above the palace's toothed doorway. "Thirteen bindings for thirteen princesses and not a Prince Ivan in sight."

"I am Ivanovna."

"You fool." Versailles laughs. "There is no Ivanovna."

"But Koschei said—"

"Just another puppet telling you exactly what I wanted you to hear. In the story I have chosen to tell, you're just another victim, Mira, and, alas, there is no hero coming to save the day."

"You're lying."

"Perhaps. However, consider this. When last we fought, you risked everything and in the end, won at best a temporary reprieve." Versailles gestures to the stone walls surrounding us. "I survived your first try at destroying me. Who's to say I wouldn't survive again?"

"Do you know what else survives when everything else is destroyed?"

"Please," she answers through clenched teeth. "Enlighten me."

"The cockroaches."

"Enough." The smile evaporates from Versailles' face. "Make your choice."

Two doors lie before me, no doubt a tiger waiting behind each. With no idea how much of what she's told me is fact and how much fiction, one thing is exceptionally clear.

No matter which door I choose, she wins.

"Very well, Versailles. You know all too well destroying the egg isn't an option. If I do as you require, everyone goes free?"

"I need only one body, Mira," she purrs. "The girls were merely practice, and I only took the Faircloth girl and your daughter to ensure I had your undivided attention."

"And Thomas?"

Versailles chuckles. "The good doctor, as you like to call him?" Her self-satisfied smirk returns. "While the world of *The Firebird* exists to serve my unique needs, I engineered the whole of *Petrushka* just to watch you squirm." Her eyes, already cold, turn to ice. "You must know, watching you suffer these last few days has made my own nine months of torture almost bearable." Her eyelids close, giving me a brief respite from her stony glare. "Almost."

"I'd gathered as much." I fight to keep the fear from my voice. "Still, you haven't answered my question."

She inclines her head in a subtle bow. "Only you must remain, trapped here among the world of Anthony Faircloth's imagination as you left me all those months ago. The rest, including the boy himself, will go free." She shoots me a wink. "You have my word."

"Your words are poison."

A quiet sigh escapes her lips. "Still, it would seem you have little choice in the matter."

A recurring motif in Anthony's various worlds of dream.

"Very well. How do we begin?"

She motions to the section of wall above the toothed arch leading out to Koschei's garden. "Twice now you've evaded my chains. Unless you desire your daughter to languish in a hospital bed for the rest of her days, you will place your hands in the shackles of your own free will and accept your fate."

I pull the egg tight to my chest. "And this? Anthony's essence?"

Versailles motions to Antoine/Koschei. "Go, child. Take the egg from her before she decides to do something heroic." She cocks her head to the side and shoots me a disparaging look. "Or stupid."

The strange being that wears Koschei's body and Anthony Faircloth's face creeps silently to my side, the awkward sidling somewhere between threatening and pathetic. With trembling hands, the decrepit wizard takes the egg from me and returns to his mistress' side, his fourteen-year-old cheeks awash with tears.

"Now, Mira Tejedor," Versailles whispers. "To the wall."

And here we are. The point of no return. No more stalling. No more resistance.

She's won.

Without a word, I march to the wall and turn to face Versailles, my hands high above my head beneath the toothed arch. "Do it."

"Liberation comes for many this day, Mira Tejedor." Versailles raises her arms high and brings them back to her lap. In answer, the heavy iron manacles descend from the wall and clamp down on my wrists. "And now," she says with a deliberate pause, "to prepare the sacrifice."

"Sacrifice?" Despair floods my mind. "But—"

My captor's eyes take on a disappointed cast. "Oh, Mira. Still so naïve."

My entire body shakes in hot anger as the chains retract and pull me upward. "You gave your word."

"You said it yourself, my dear. My words are poison." She waggles her finger in the air again. "An exchange of essences requires a lot of energy and, more importantly, a ritual." The wicked grin from before returns to her face. "As with all things created by this boy's imagination, nothing matters but the story, and as my plan depends solely on his abilities, I have to play this his way."

Antoine/Koschei's head drops in shame. "I'm so sorry."

"It's not your fault, Anthony." Barely audible, the words pass my lips. "Not even a bit."

Black lightning crackles across the sky as Versailles stands barking orders at her minions.

"*Skrzaks*, secure the princesses."

The throne of *skrzaks* breaks apart, the creatures joining the throng of their grotesque brethren. The mob of monsters breaks into twelve clusters, each surrounding a kidnapped girl.

"*Zmej*, guard the door."

The three-headed dragon stomps a path through the snow and curls itself beneath the gruesome doorway leading out to the garden.

"*Bukavacs*, to the periphery. Prepare for the sacrifice."

The twelve horned toad-monsters assume positions beneath each of the empty shackles around the courtyard, their hungry maws turned upward.

My stomach threatens to rebel as the outcome of this sacrifice crystallizes in my mind.

"As for you two," Versailles motions to Tunny and Modesto, "my feet are dirty."

The gnome and the half-fish troubadour fall prone at her feet and lick at her pointe shoes like a pair of starving mongrels while Antoine/Koschei sobs uncontrollably, his shoulders heaving in time with the anemic green light cast by the egg in his hands.

"Leave them alone," I scream. "They have nothing to do with this."

"Ah, Mira, so much emotion you have for what are nothing but figments of a young boy's fancy."

"These three are way more than that." My gaze flicks from Tunny to Modesto to Antoine/Koschei. "They represent everything in Anthony Faircloth that is good and whole."

"And in their humiliation is your final defeat. Your lover slain before your eyes, your daughter lost to you forever, innocents damned to spend the rest of their lives in tortured suffering because of your failure, and now, the boy, your paragon of goodness and light, licking at my toes." Her eyes dance with cruel joy. "And the best part? You are powerless to stop me. Chained as you are, even the modicum of power granted you in this place cannot help you. You are alone this time, Mira Tejedor." Versailles saunters in my direction, stopping directly beneath my dangling feet. "No army musters across the next hill to help you fight this battle. No magic word sits on the tip of your tongue to help you escape your chains. No prince waits in the wings to save you from your fate."

"Excuse me." This new voice, accompanied by a fanfare of muted trumpets, sounds from the opposite end of the courtyard. Versailles spins, and as one, our eyes shoot to the uppermost reach of the far wall to discover a familiar figure in a silky white shirt, red-and-orange checkered pants, and boots the color of midnight. Staring down at us, he lets a devil-may-care grin spread across his face. "Did someone say Prince?"

31

PROFONDES TÉNÈBRES

My heart swells with hope even as a river of profanity spews from Versailles' mouth.

"Impossible," she screams. "I watched you die."

"You watched Petrushka die." Though a British accent again colors his words, I'd know the voice anywhere. "You, Madame Versailles, are not the only one to find liberty in death. As the clown breathed his last, so was I freed."

"Freed, you say?" Versailles studies the figure in white and orange. "And with whom, dare I ask, do I have the dubious pleasure of conversing now?"

"I am Toma, the Kalendar Prince." He leaps from atop the courtyard wall, slides down an impossibly long silk scarf, and lands between two of the gathered clusters of *skrzaks*. "Definitely not at your service."

"Call yourself what you will, you still represent all that is pathetic in a man." Versailles shoots me a sidelong glance. "You could do so much better."

Undaunted, Toma closes on Versailles. "Your lies, Queen of Deception, are no longer any of our concern."

"I see." Versailles waggles a finger at her side. "A different tack, perhaps."

"Toma," I scream. "Look out behind you!"

In a flash, Toma's scimitar appears in his hand and with one fluid motion, the Kalendar Prince guts midair a pair of leaping *skrzaks*.

"Call off your dogs, Versailles," he commands. "I may wear the clothes of a clown, but you will find my steel sharp and my skills anything but laughable."

"Very well." Versailles pulls her winged arms tight across her chest. "Humor me for a moment, though. However did you escape the Shrove-Tide Fair? Even if you survived the Moor's blade, that story is over."

"We may have had something to do with that." The words, uttered in a guttural French accent, echo up from below my feet. Chained to the wall, I see nothing when I glance downward but my own hanging body and the snow-covered ground. Still, I have little doubt as to who stands beneath the toothed arch.

The *zmej* backs into the courtyard, the three witches from the Bald Mountain driving it back like a trio of lion tamers. Each looks up at me in turn and then glides toward one of three different spots along the granite wall. The other creatures previously under Koschei's command and even the Firebird herself wisely give these latest arrivals a wide berth.

Brigitte heads east, Sophie west, and Antoinette south. As the witches assume their positions around the periphery of the snowswept circle of stone, Versailles looks on with calculating eyes, apprehensive though not visibly shaken.

"You may have slain our original fourth," Brigitte begins.

"But in the end, we stand with Mira," Sophie adds.

"With all we have and all we are," Antoinette concludes.

"As do I." Toma holds his scimitar high above his head, the curved blade still dripping with *skrzak* blood. "Prepare to meet whatever awaits you beyond the veil."

As I attempt to decipher what has led to the witches sudden change of heart, they, Toma, and even Tunny and Modesto all converge on our common enemy.

"No army, Versailles?" I glare down at the surrounded Firebird. "No Prince?"

"Silence." Versailles stretches her wings wide. "Have all of you forgotten where we are? What I represent in this place?" She again dons her feathered mask. "I am the Firebird, you pathetic wretches, and in this world, my will is law."

Her winged arms drop to her sides and the orchestral hit sounds anew, freezing the entire assemblage in place. Without another word, the Firebird launches again into her dance and my heart sinks as all present, including the witches and even Toma, join in the frenetic spectacle. Prince, witches, gnome, merman troubadour, *skrzaks*, *bukavacs*, *zmej*, and princesses all fall in step with the feathered ballerina in red. Only Antoine/Koschei and I seem immune. Just as before, friend and foe alike cavort about the space in utter synchrony, each set of steps more brazen than the one before, and none more pained than those of the Kalendar Prince.

As Toma's crazed contortions lead him near Antoine/Koschei, both shoot a terrified glance in my direction, a helpless boy trapped in a hell of his own creation and the man I love yet again a puppet, his strings controlled by the cruelest of masters.

In a blink, my mind flashes back to our fateful first meeting.

A stormy autumn afternoon in Charlotte, NC at the office of one Dr. Thomas Archer. A skeptical psychologist and a desperate mother look on as two strangers, a comatose boy and an out-of-her-depth psychic struggle to make that crucial first connection.

We've all come so far since that day.

Strange that only three of those faces are represented here.

If only Caroline were…

My God. That's it.

"Antoine."

He ignores me.

"Antoine, listen to me."

Though he remains silent, his eyes find their way to mine.

"Are you in control of your own actions?"

He turns his head one way, then the other, and gives me a subtle nod.

"I'm chained, and the others are helpless under the Firebird's enchantment." Aching with desperation, it's all I can do to keep my voice from cracking. "But I have an idea, and I'm going to need your help."

His eyes drop. "Whatever you're planning, it won't work." With a pained grunt, he raises the egg above his head. "She's too powerful."

"Antoine," I scream. "What the hell are you doing?"

"The only thing I can." The emerald egg, so fragile, rests precariously in his trembling hands. "I have to end this before anyone else gets hurt."

"Don't do it." I strain at the chains that hold me to the wall to no avail. "There's another way. I swear it."

"I know you're trying to save me," Antoine says. "Your every instinct is to leap into the breach and protect me from myself. It's what you always do."

"You can't destroy that egg." The irate tone I inherited from my mother comes out in spades. "You'll die."

"And take Versailles and all of this with me." His lip quivering, the boy's terrified gaze shoots from me to the Firebird as she flits past in the midst of her second pass through the Infernal Dance. "I appreciate your concern." He purses his lips, his voice dead. "But as long as this egg exists, this world where the Firebird reigns supreme exists as well."

"But according to the story, the egg contains Koschei's immortal soul, and you, like it or not, are Koschei."

"You once held your life in your own hands." Antoine/Koschei narrows his bespectacled gaze at me. "The last time we faced Versailles, you sacrificed everything to bring her evil to an end. Why would you think I'd do any less?"

"Listen to me. Things are not the same." I again struggle in vain against the chains at my wrists. "The Exhibition was our creation, born from the meeting of our two minds." Spent, I let out an exhausted sigh. "This place and the rules governing it belong to Versailles."

"But I am here, as are Tunny, Modesto, Trilby, the women of the *Marketplace*." Antoine's voice drops to a whisper, and he waits until the Firebird again passes between us before speaking again. "Versailles said it herself. This is the Exhibition."

"Exhibition or not, it doesn't matter."

Or... does it?

I've been so stupid. He and I are situated inside a reimagined version of *The Old Castle* and surrounded in turn by nightmare versions of the garden at *Tuileries* and Tunny's forest from *Gnomus*.

This is the Exhibition, indeed.

And if this is the Exhibition...

"Antoine," I shout as he prepares to hurl the egg into the courtyard wall. "Whatever you do, don't drop that egg."

"And what might you two be talking about?" Versailles lands beneath me, her eyes full of venom. "Ah, Mira. You've already played your last card. The gnome, the troubadour, the women of the *Marketplace*. They're all powerless to help you. Even your much vaunted Prince is again nothing but another puppet under my command." She points an outstretched finger in the direction of Toma, and he silently answers with a clumsy dance reminiscent of the crude steps of Petrushka the clown. "What possible hope have you now?"

"Just one." My eyes narrow. "You chained me to this wall, Versailles.

Forced me to watch as you've beaten, subjugated, and humiliated everyone I love."

"What is it they say?" She smiles like a snake that's just eaten a baby bird. "Simple pleasures are the best."

"The irony though? In doing so, you've given me the one weapon I need to defeat you and win this day."

"Oh, really?" With a single sweep of her winged arms, all assembled save Versailles, me, and Antoine, fall to the ground as if a bomb has exploded at the Firebird's feet. "And what weapon might that be, Mira Tejedor?"

"Time." I narrow my eyes at her. "Time to process the string of lies you've been cultivating. Time to decipher your endgame." I answer her wicked grin with one of my own. "Time to recognize the one simple fact you've been so desperate to keep from me since this all began."

"*Bukavacs, skrzaks, zmej,*" she spouts angrily. "Rip this woman from the wall and dine upon her entrails."

"On second thought, creatures of Koschei's garden," I murmur as the vile horde rises and aligns on my dangling form, "hold fast." As one, Versailles' retinue freezes midstep. A hundred pairs of eyes look up at me, each monstrous expression shifting from ravenous to reverent.

"What have you done?" Versailles screams. "This is *my* world. My will is law."

"I hate to be the one that breaks this to you, but this was never your world. You may have shaped it to your will, turned friend into foe, perverted respect into disdain, but in the end, this is the Exhibition and only one person's rules matter here." I shift my gaze to meet the hopeful stare of Antoine/Koschei. "Isn't that right, Antoine?"

In an instant, the boy sheds the Immortal's body and stands before me whole and smiling for the first time since we last met at the Bogatyr Gates. "Indeed it is, Lady Scheherazade."

"No." Versailles' hands ball into fists in frustration.

"Yes." I peer at the shackle holding my left wrist and then the one clamped around my right. "Just when all seemed lost," my voice adopts the volume of distant thunder, "the manacles holding the storyteller lowered her to the ground."

Before I can take another breath, the iron chains binding me extend downward, extra links appearing as if from air. In moments, my feet are again on the ground and I am buoyed by a rush of power I haven't felt in a very long time.

"So." My adversary glares at me, the anger in her eyes all but palpable, but behind the fury hides no small amount of fear. "It has come to this."

"Indeed it has, Versailles. You created the worlds of *The Firebird* and *Petrushka* to ensure your every advantage. You've given me new names, new roles, new abilities. But as you so kindly reminded me before, this is a world of story." I snap my fingers, and the manacles holding my arms disappear. "And I, you vindictive little bitch, am the storyteller."

"Then it would seem, storyteller, that our tale has come full circle." The rage and fear in Versailles' eyes evaporate as cool contempt overtakes her features. "Though your will trumps all else this place, your words have no power over me." In a shimmer, the Firebird costume vanishes and Versailles stands again garbed in her yellow lace dress, the teacher from *Tuileries* I first met months ago. "You cannot stop me without sentencing the boy to an eternity of suffering, and you and I both know such ruthlessness is beyond you." As confident as ever, her triumphant smirk from before returns for an encore appearance.

"Though you may have won this day, I swear to you this. Should you find another way to escape this place, you will never know a day's rest. Your every spare thought will be spent wondering when I am coming for you and yours again, always questioning if your latest nightmare was merely a bad dream or a visit from one who hates you with the passion of a thousand suns." All mirth leaves her face as she steps into my space, so close, the heat of her breath singes my skin. "You've seen what I can do. What I can take from you. In the end, I may not have the power to defeat you, but neither can you destroy me."

"That may be true, but I know someone who can."

Her eyes narrow. "And who might that be, Mira Tejedor?"

Courage springs anew in my chest. "In this place, you will call me Scheherazade." I cross my arms, defiant. "But that, Madame Versailles, isn't the name you should fear."

"What do you mean?" She retreats a step. "Of whom do you speak?"

"Though I care deeply for the boy, my compassion for him pales in comparison to a mother's love."

"Don't." Versailles takes another step back, tripping over one of the *skrzaks* and landing hard on her backside. "You can't bring her here."

"Oh, but I can." My hands fold together at my waist. "Did you think I hadn't noticed?"

"Please," she pleads. "Not her."

"Every character I met along the Exhibition has made an appearance in one or both of the nightmare worlds you wrought to trap me."

I swing both arms above my head and clap my hands together twice, the sound echoed in a couplet of strings and tympani that nine months ago would have filled me with terror.

"Every character, that is, except the one you'd never be able to control."

The orchestra blares again, a triplet.

"The one more powerful than you could ever dream of being."

A third triplet rips the sky, followed by a run of six notes, each rumbling tone more deafening than the one before.

"The one who can and will end you."

"No," Versailles screams. "You can't do this."

Her words are drowned out as the ubiquitous orchestra launches into the main body of "The Hut on Fowl's Legs," Mussorgsky's musical ode to the most fearsome character in all of Russian folklore. The powerful melody booms down from the gray sky, the dramatic strain soon accompanied by the distant sound of pounding feet and splintering trees. The crushing gait louder with every unseen footfall, Versailles and I each steel ourselves for what is to come.

Neither of us is kept waiting for long.

Exploding through the toothed gate of Koschei's palace like an enormous wrecking ball on chicken feet, the Hut on Fowl's Legs leaves a gaping hole in the granite wall where I hung moments before. Filling a window at the hut's uppermost reaches, a single bloodshot eye glares down as the sound of rushing feet tromping down two flights of stairs echoes from within.

Nine months ago, if you'd told me a day would come when I'd view the creature that lives in this bizarre house as the cavalry, I'd have laughed in your face.

God, how times have changed.

The door to the hut springs open, filling the air with smoke laden with the aroma of freshly cooked meat. Though I'm more than aware I stand in a world of dream, I still shudder to guess which unfortunate soul it was that knocked at the witch's door.

The orchestra fades into the background as Baba Yaga, crouched atop her stone mortar with pestle in one hand and ever-sweeping broom in the other, glides out of her home and comes to rest before me and Versailles.

"Greetings, storyteller." A voice that could curdle milk.

I offer a subtle curtsy. "Baba Yaga."

Yaga's attention shifts to Versailles. "And one I'd hoped erased forever."

"Sorry to disappoint you, witch." Versailles pulls herself up to her full height, one hand over the other at her waist to keep her fingers from trembling. "Neither your destruction of *Tuileries* nor this one's pathetic attempt at—"

Yaga cuts off Versailles' rant with a clang of her iron teeth. "Insolent creature. Even the Lady Scheherazade who bested me during our last encounter deigned to offer an old woman the proper courtesy." The witch raises the pestle high above her head, her eyes narrowing into dark slits. "Address me with less than a respectful tongue again, and I will crush you into pulp and feast upon your marrow."

Versailles pulls in a quick breath, her furious gaze shooting to me. A sharp retort no doubt rests on the tip of her tongue, but in the end, all that comes out is a quiet, "Yes, Mistress."

"Better." Yaga's eyes return to me. "You summoned me, storyteller?"

"My apologies, mighty Yaga, but the situation was dire."

"A moment." Yaga climbs down from her mortar and leaves us. Walking the periphery of the courtyard, she stops to whisper with each of her witch sisters in turn, all the while Versailles looking on as if watching an executioner sharpen their axe.

As Yaga's impromptu conference with the former gossips of *The Marketplace at Limoges* ends, she returns to our side via a circuitous route, taking time to examine in turn the various sights.

The menagerie of monsters that lies sprawled from one end of the courtyard to the other.

The dozen young girls in their dresses of white, freed from their chains and huddled together in one corner, as afraid of the witch as they were of Koschei.

The clown-prince shaking uncontrollably at the far end of the space.

The half-fish troubadour gasping for air as he wallows on the snowy ground.

The gnome she nearly immolated nine months ago lying in a stupor, a flask of firewater pressed to his lips as he hums the tune from "Promenade."

And last but not least, the bespectacled adolescent holding his own soul before his chest in the most fragile of vessels.

"Madame Versailles." Yaga peers down her bent nose at once-teacher from *Tuileries*. "Am I to understand you are responsible for this sad state of affairs?"

"Have mercy, Mistress. I've clawed my way back from the edge of oblivion to stand here among you again."

"Among us?" Yaga directs the handle of her broom at Versailles' nose. "You stand against us, just as you did before." She waves an arm at the entire assemblage. "You've left the gnome half-dead, turned the troubadour into a fish, and ripped the boy's soul from his body." Yaga shakes her head in mock sadness. "What happened to you, Versailles?"

"The storyteller." Versailles levels an accusing finger at me. "She ruined everything."

Yaga licks her dry lips, choosing her words carefully as she takes my measure. "Painful though it may have been, the Lady Scheherazade's arrival at the Exhibition brought necessary change." Yaga surveys the carnage once more. "All of this, Madame Versailles, is a perversion."

"A necessary one." Versailles' eyes drop. "I wished an audience with Lady Scheherazade."

"An audience?" The words almost catch in my throat. "This entire place, the garden, the palace, the fair, is nothing but an elaborate trap, you deceitful harpy. With God as my witness—"

At Yaga's raised hand, I hold my tongue.

"No need to go on, storyteller. I've already seen and heard more than enough." Yaga raises the pestle above her head, and the floating mortar flips itself nearly upside down to accept her naked feet. Once the enormous stone bowl stands righted again, Yaga stares down her pointed nose at us. "Only one question remains, Lady Scheherazade." Neither smile nor frown twists her terrifying mien. "What would you have me do now?"

"Yes, Mira." Versailles growls my name. "What would you have her do?"

I lock gazes with Versailles. "You know exactly why I brought her here." I look up into the horrible face that has haunted my every night for months. "Among those who once walked the Exhibition, Madame Versailles is an outsider, an anomaly."

Yaga's head tilts to one side. "As were you once, storyteller."

"True." Even now, despite all that's changed, the witch's voice still leaves me weak in the knees. "I, however, have sought only to help whereas Versailles has nearly brought ruin to the Exhibition, not once, but twice. Though she stands again defeated, I have no doubt her continued existence only guarantees that we will all gather here again in the future, and who knows what destruction will follow in her wake the next time."

"So, Scheherazade, you have appointed yourself judge and jury but balk at the role of executioner?"

"I've done more than my part to rid this world of her madness." The recalled pain of the Sultan's dagger sliding between my ribs takes my breath. "I can do no more."

"And you, Versailles?" Yaga asks. "What have you to say for yourself?"

"As if I anything I might say at this point would change the outcome one iota."

Yaga regards Versailles with something approaching a smile. "I would hear your side, teacher of *Tuileries*."

"I'm certain you would." Versailles' fearful countenance shifts to one of scorn. "I wouldn't give you or the damned storyteller the satisfaction." Her gaze shoots to me. "This whole thing is a farce."

"A farce, you say?" Yaga's eyes narrow at Versailles. "You consider me unjust?"

"The two of you may pretend all you want. That my fate is undecided. That my impassioned defense might sway the opinion of the mighty Baba Yaga." Versailles' eyes go cold. "But I know all too well whose eyes look out from behind the witch's mask."

"Very well." Yaga rests her pestle against the upright mortar and takes her broom in both hands. "If you will not defend yourself, Madame Versailles, then I will render my judgment now."

Versailles lets out a sarcastic snort. "I reject your so-called judgment, witch." In a shimmer, Ivanovna's bow appears in Versailles' hand. "I choose to decide my own fate."

Before either of us can move, Versailles spins and levels an arrow at the egg held before Antoine's chest.

"If I am to die today, I'm taking all of you with me."

Yaga and I scream in unison as she lets the arrow fly. The staccato crack followed by the dull thud of steel meeting flesh sends ice through my veins. A dark shaft protruding from his chest, Antoine drops to his knees, the shattered egg crumbling to scintillating dust in his trembling hands.

"Anthony." The name catches in my throat. "No…"

Yaga shrieks.

Versailles cackles.

And darkness falls.

32

THE RITE OF SPRING

Murky shadow.

Oppressive silence.

Utter nothingness that seems to last an eternity.

And then, violins.

First one, then two, then a full section, the mood of the music somber and mysterious. Soon woodwinds and tympani join in. And then, a French horn, as a single point of light appears in the distant sky.

The scene has changed completely, the dark forest, decaying garden, and ancient palace all wiped away in favor of a fantastical cityscape that stretches in both directions as far as the eye can see. In some ways reminiscent of the Bogatyr Gates from the Exhibition, the architecture appears ancient and Russian.

Dear God, we're going on to the next scene. Despite everything that's happened, this world Versailles helped create is playing straight on to the end of *The Firebird*.

In the original ballet, the death of Koschei breaks all of his various enchantments and returns the world to normal. The horde of monsters, the garden, the palace—they all return to the hell from whence they came. The freed princesses line up opposite the dozen princes that previously fell to Koschei's sorcery, each couple more in love than the one before. Then, as the music swells, the triumphant Prince Ivan and the most beautiful of the thirteen princesses arrive on the scene in all their royal splendor and literally lead the paired princes and princesses off into the sunset.

In true fairy tale fashion, everyone lives happily ever after.

The scene that unfolds before me now, despite the trumpet fanfare blaring from everywhere and nowhere at once, is anything but happy.

First, as Versailles was careful to ensure, no princes arrive to claim their princesses. Even Toma, my Kalendar Prince, appears shell-shocked to the point he can barely stand.

The princesses all cower beneath the apple tree, the only element other than the still-falling snow remaining from Koschei's garden. The trauma of their ordeal shows in each pair of exhausted eyes.

The trio of witches minister to Tunny and Modesto, the gnome and troubadour each returned to their original forms and lying unconscious on the cold ground.

And then, a sight I never dreamed.

Crouched with Antoine's still form draped across her lap, Baba Yaga wailing.

In college, I had the privilege of visiting St. Peter's Basilica in the Vatican and have seen the Pieta with my own eyes.

Michelangelo didn't capture a tenth of the emotion of this moment.

"No, no, no," she blubbers between heaving sobs, her voice not Yaga's but Caroline Faircloth's. "Not my Anthony."

"Caroline?" I ask. "Is that you?"

"Speak not that name here, Scheherazade." Yaga's screech returns with a vengeance. "You may have won my respect, storyteller, but we are far from friends."

"My, my, you two." Versailles looks down on us from atop the wall of the city of white and gold. "Trouble in Paradise?"

Yaga glares up at the teacher from *Tuileries*, her tears doing little to quench the fire in her eyes. "Enjoy your next few breaths, Versailles. They will be your last."

"Empty threats, witch." She sweeps a lithe arm before her, gesturing around to the walled city before us and the surrounding countryside. "Though things may not have gone exactly as I planned, forget not that all you see, touch, hear, and feel in this place was shaped to my exact specifications. Now that the boy has been dispatched, all of this is mine. In fact, you only see me at this moment because I wish it to be so." She vanishes from one parapet along the high wall only to reappear behind another. "I can be anywhere at any time and wear any face I choose. Walk my realm at your peril."

"What now, then?" Refusing to wear the costume of Princess Ivanovna another second, I will my garb to transform into Scheherazade's sarong. "Anthony lies dying in his mother's arms, Tunny and Modesto will never awake, and the rest of us are trapped here in the world of *The Firebird*. You've won, Versailles. What more could you possibly want?"

"Only what I've wanted every moment of every day since you left me there on that snowswept hill by the Bogatyr Gates." In a flash, Ivanovna's bow reappears in Versailles' hand. "To see you suffer."

I draw the Sultan's dagger from the green folds at my waist. "You dare attack me with my own weapon?"

"Don't be silly, Mira," Versailles hisses. "This arrow isn't meant for you."

As Versailles shifts her aim up and to the right, I have no doubt as to her intended target.

"Isabella," I scream. "Down."

"Too late, Mira Tejedor." Her voice drips with acid. "Should you ever find your way home again, you and Caroline Faircloth can mourn togeth—"

A curved blade erupts from Versailles' midsection, severing the bowstring even as it steals the gleam from her eyes. The arrow nocked to slay my daughter goes flying end over end into the distance while Versailles, shock still etched in her features, plummets from the wall and hits the ground, a golden scimitar protruding from her back. Yaga and I both stare up at the place where she stood, the teacher from *Tuileries* replaced by a regal figure dressed in green and blue.

No longer slathered in mocking greasepaint, the Moor looks down on us from atop the high wall. His face impassive, jaw set, and eyes devoid of emotion, he studies each of us one by one, his gaze finally coming to rest on me. The fluffy blue feather that previously adorned his silk turban has been replaced, the plumage of the new feather orange and shimmering with an inner fire.

There, above the dispassionate gaze belonging to one Detective Calvin Sterling, rests…

"The Firebird's feather." Toma shoots me a sidelong glance. "Did you summon the Moor?"

"Of course she did, you fool." Yaga casts a hateful glare in the Kalendar

Prince's direction. "Despite all your talk, you weren't proving particularly useful, now were you?"

"Quiet, Yaga." For reasons I will likely never understand, the witch obeys my barked command. "And no, Toma, I didn't summon the Moor."

At least... I don't think I did.

Somewhere far away, five people sit on a hospital bed with a singular purpose, to bring this madness to an end. Till this moment, however, only Caroline, Anthony, Isabella, and I had been accounted for.

If the Moor standing atop the city wall is in reality Sterling, what does that mean?

Toma steps forward clumsily, his eyes locked with the dark warrior staring down from above. Their silent battle of wills goes on longer than I can say, but in the end, Toma is the first to capitulate. Bringing his red-gloved hand to his forehead, he offers the Moor a solemn salute, a gesture returned immediately by the hand that days before struck him down at the Russian fair. The two of them stand there for what seems an eternity, and then, without so much as a goodbye, the Moor disappears behind a half-crumbled parapet.

Toma, his body finally back under his control, rushes to my side.

"Lady Scheherazade." He takes my hand. "I don't understand. The teacher from *Tuileries* is no more. The egg is destroyed. Koschei is gone. Why are we still here?"

I shake my head, frustration seeping from my every pore. "I wish I knew."

After our final encounter months ago along the Exhibition, I expect Madame Versailles to leap up at any moment and come at us again, but her impaled form does not stir. Even the gentle breeze that sends the falling snow this way and that doesn't so much as disturb the torn lace at her sleeve.

"There's something we're missing," I mutter. "Something important."

"You're Scheherazade the storyteller." Yaga raises an eyebrow. "Can you not speak the boy back to life?"

"You think that didn't occur to me?" I stalk over to the witch, kneel by her side, and caress Antoine's damp forehead. "I may be the storyteller, but even I have to obey the rules."

"And that is my question." Toma makes our circle four, though he remains standing, his eyes vigilant for any further threats. "I have gleaned from what everyone has said that the boy is the one that sets the rules of this world, is he not?"

"That's always been the case so far." I look up into eyes that in another time and place are the last thing I want to see before I go to sleep and the first thing when I awake. "What are you thinking?"

"Just this." Toma strokes his chin in the way Thomas does when deep in thought. "Even when the boy was in command of his faculties, Versailles somehow was able to manipulate the rules of this place to her advantage. Now that he is incapacitated, would not the rules be even easier to bend?"

I raise a shoulder in a subtle shrug. "Unless the destruction of the egg has simply stopped everything and left us trapped in the mind of a comatose boy."

Just like before, Anthony has been traumatized beyond the capacity to respond, but this time, the damage runs far deeper. There's no denying we walk the Exhibition, or at least Versailles' bastardized version of the "Fortress of Solitude" his mind created the last time it couldn't deal.

This time, he was struck down from within his very own not-so-happy place.

That changes everything.

Still, the solution is here.

It has to be.

"He's so cold." Yaga moans, her wrinkled face pressed close to Anthony's pale cheek. "So very, very cold."

Cold.

My mind again casts back nine months. I stand just inside the picture frame leading to Yaga's hut. All the characters remaining that haven't fallen victim to the machinations of Madame Versailles stand assembled around Baba Yaga's strange home, ready to depose the perceived tyrant of the Exhibition.

Little did we know at the time we were fighting the wrong witch.

In the real world, Veronica Sayles was suffocating Anthony, leaving the Mussorgsky-derived dreamscape harsh and cold, as if the very life was being drained from the world. This time, Versailles has succeeded where Sayles failed, but that doesn't begin to explain the abject cold that fills this place. The snow began to fall on the world of *The Firebird* long before Antoine's death and, in fact, started even before I was banished to the Bald Mountain.

Snowfall may be a critical piece of *Petrushka*, almost becoming a character itself by the end of the ballet, but every iteration of *The Firebird* I've watched seems to occur in the summer when the apple tree is full. I had assumed the blizzard that hit Koschei's garden was merely an idiosyncrasy that somehow bled over from the Russian fair.

But what if that isn't it?

Anthony is nothing if not an expert all things Russian, and if I've watched *The Firebird* a dozen times in the last few days, Anthony's probably seen it a hundred. He wouldn't screw up a detail that big, unless the presence of snow in this place is some kind of clue.

His words from our last conversation in the real world echo in my mind.

About how Stravinsky's ballets all end in death.

Koschei's defeat at the hands of Prince Ivan.

Petrushka's execution in the streets of the Shrove-Tide Fair.

And in *The Rite of Spring*, a chosen maiden literally dancing herself to death to bring an end to the cold.

On the day Thomas was admitted to the hospital, Anthony sat in Rachel's room, engrossed in Stravinsky's *The Rite of Spring*. He said watching it was important. So unlike the majesty of *The Firebird* or the quirky beauty of *Petrushka*, *The Rite of Spring*, or what little I saw of it, appeared raw, ugly, primal, the music anything but melodic. But the beauty of the piece doesn't matter.

If Anthony has made such a deliberate decision as to change the summertime world of *The Firebird* to winter, it's for one reason and one reason only.

He needs me to bring the spring.

"Isabella," I whisper. "Rachel. Gather the girls and bring them to me."

My daughter, silent for so long in this nightmare, begins to cry.

"Mami," she gets out between whimpers. "Don't."

"You don't even know what I'm considering."

But she does.

Her tears don't change a thing.

"What are you doing, storyteller?" Yaga runs a ramshackle sleeve across her face to wipe away the tears. "What idea have you hatched in that pretty little head of yours?"

"Yes," Toma draws close. "What insanity are you planning?

One glance at Versailles' still form and the last piece of the puzzle falls into place.

"Everything we see here is the Exhibition. Though warped by Madame Versailles' machinations, this is still the house that Anthony and I built." I bring my hands together before me in prayer, hoping as I have before that

God isn't deaf to us in a place like this. "Versailles may have changed all the rules and brought us to the edge of ruin, but the story isn't over yet."

I throw my head back and peer up into the still lightening sky. "I, Scheherazade the storyteller, call upon the Exhibition to heed my words." Receiving no answer but the echo of my own voice, I lower my head and speak again, the words falling from my tongue as if spoken by another entity, ancient and powerful. "Hear me, Exhibition, and obey."

Silence reigns, but as I part my lips to speak a third time, thunder rumbles in the distance.

Not the answer I was expecting, but it will have to do.

"Hear me, home to Mussorgsky and haven to his many creations." Answered again with silence, I take a breath. "Your halls have been corrupted, your inhabitants tormented, your very foundations shaken by the interloper in your midst. I come today to restore the balance and free the innocents imprisoned within your walls."

For a second time, rolling thunder booms from beyond the walls of the city.

I pray it means something.

Struggling for the next thing to say, my mind flits through a cavalcade of images.

Hannah Abrams, found atop the shelter in the park in the real world and laid out on the stone beneath the apple tree in Koschei's garden.

Elizabeth Baker and Janey Campbell frozen mid-caper the day they were taken.

The dance of the ten princesses in Koschei's garden that nearly led to the horrific deaths of their counterparts in the real world.

And then, my own experiences in the world of *The Firebird*.

Chained to a bed in the topmost reaches of the Immortal's tower.

Shackled to an altar during my banishment to the Bald Mountain.

Hung on the wall inside the courtyard of Koschei's palace.

At every turn since this began, I have faced chains, sacrifice, dance—all components of the grand rituals of humanity's pagan past.

Like the snow, this has to be a message from Anthony.

As the twelve girls, including Rachel Faircloth and Isabella gather round, I know without a doubt what I must do.

"Exhibition, hear me." My eyelids slide closed, as I will the next few words into being. "I call upon you to manifest *The Rite of Spring*."

Baba Yaga squawks in disbelief. "Scheherazade. No. *The Rite of Spring* brings death. You would sacrifice one of these girls to free the rest? If you do that, you're no better than Versailles." She lets out a single cackle. "And you dare call me…"

"The girls will be fine." A tear meanders down my cheek. "All of you will be fine."

Her face shifts from anger to shock and finally to understanding.

"Wait…" The witch inhales sharply. "Are you sure?"

I offer Yaga a solemn nod, and when she answers with the same, Toma steps between us, his eyes filled with panic.

"Another sacrifice?" he asks. "Have we not lost enough today?"

I take Toma's hand. "Insane she may have been, but one thing Versailles said is true. An exchange of essences will no doubt require both significant energy and, in this place, a ritual." I stare again skyward. "And if I know Anthony Faircloth, no other ritual will do."

Toma's face crumbles with emotion. "But… you've already given up so much."

"And yet, my daughter still suffers in this hell. Eleven other innocents remain trapped here as well, pawns in a game of which they know nothing." I peer deep into Toma's eyes. "And the love of my life, not even aware of who he is or what he means to me, lies unconscious in a hospital bed far away from here." Unable to bear his gaze, I look away. "No longer."

"This man—" The Prince takes my chin and gently pulls my eyes back to his. "—has no idea of how fortune has smiled upon his life."

I stroke the Prince's cheek with a trembling hand and then cast my gaze upward at the taunting sky. "Exhibition," I command. "*The Rite of Spring*. Now."

In answer to my demand, the walled city fades into nothingness, and in a blink, our surroundings shift to a simple woodland scene, the ground adorned with a pair of concentric circles marked in white powder at the center of a clearing. A lone bassoon sounds, the unseen player bringing a melancholy melody. Soon, other instruments join in, and for the next several minutes, the cacophony I remember from Anthony's tablet fills the space.

That's when everything changes.

One moment, Baba Yaga sits crouched on the ground with Antoine's unmoving form draped across her lap, and the next she stands alone in the center of the circle in new garb, a deep yellow dress and matching headscarf, both marked at the edges of the cloth with a row of arcane symbols. Beneath her arm where moments before her broom handle rested, she now carries a small collection of sticks. As the music begins in earnest, she launches into a most ungainly routine. Wandering the circle, she stops first by the cluster of terrified girls, then the huddle of witches caring for Tunny and Modesto, and finally Toma. As she twists, jumps, and gesticulates in her grotesque performance, so do they answer in kind.

Soon the entire assemblage comes together in the most bizarre dance I've ever seen. Leaping, stomping, spinning, the dance winds on, and in a flash, everyone's attire shifts to this new paradigm born from the fertile mind of Igor Stravinsky.

Half the girls in burnt orange and gold and half in white and midnight blue, they dance in two circles of six. Though their crude frocks, headdresses, and paired braids are reminiscent of Hollywood's idea of Native American fashion, I have little doubt what I'm seeing actually finds its roots in ancient Russia.

The only man among fourteen women, Toma stands on the periphery of the outer circle across from me, his white, orange, and red garb from *Petrushka* replaced by a long, white tunic adorned with a matching fur hat and cape. The only one other than me not dancing, he looks on, helpless, frozen to the spot much like both of us were inside the Charlatan's booth.

The music strikes me at various times as pretty, frantic, dramatic, quiet, but throughout all of it, an undeniable energy pervades every step. Then, just as the performance hits a fever pitch, the music shifts into a more plodding melody that reminds me of the oxen from Hartmann's realm along the Exhibition.

From the tree line comes an aged man dressed in white robes. The three witches, as young and beautiful as when they still called the *Marketplace* home, surround him. Their raiment appears similar to the girls', though more ornate with tops of white cotton and long skirts of blue and gold.

The old man's flowing white mane and long beard clearly label him as the wise man of the tribe. I recognize the ancient creature, however, for who he really is—another incarnation of the Charlatan, who, in turn, is another aspect of Mussorgsky, the composer and father of the Exhibition.

In this new role, however, he represents a new character. The medicine man, the elder of the tribe, the lynchpin of society since time immemorial.

A name from Anthony's Exhibition echoes through my mind. A character all but forgotten, who shares a face with, of all people, the janitor at Anthony's school.

As the dancers all slow in deference to the new arrival, the Sage falls to his knees to bless the ground with a reverential kiss.

Something wicked this way comes.

Once his entourage has helped the infirm Sage to his feet, the gathered dancers rejoice, their movements even more energetic and crazed than before. Performed solo and in circles of six, the celebration goes on for what seems an eternity. Eventually, all the dancers gather close around the wizened old man and as one lift their arms to the sky as the unseen symphony blasts my ears with a series of orchestral hits.

The very sun in the sky dims for a moment as silence fills the space.

The opening act is over.

Time for the real show.

When the sky again fills with light, I find myself no longer an observer, but a full participant.

I and the twelve girls taken by Versailles' madness now stand around the periphery of the outer chalk circle, facing outward with Isabella to my left and Rachel to my right. Scheherazade's sarong no longer hangs from my body, my clothing now shifted to align with the aboriginal costumes of Stravinsky's third ballet. The burnt orange, bright gold, and deep blue of the girls' previous garb has also changed.

We stand, all thirteen of us, arrayed in virginal white.

As the music swells anew, the thirteen of us launch into an intricate dance of strange steps and bizarre hand gestures choreographed a century ago to connote a pagan ceremony from another era. Our widely disparate movements punctuated by moments of perfect synchrony, we move in time with the peculiar melody, and for a moment, an overpowering peace overtakes me.

A moment that ends far too quickly.

Our feet guided by rhythm and primal instinct, we fall in on the outer circle and begin a game, a strange cross between follow the leader and musical chairs. With every few beats of the quiet music, half the maidens rush past the person before them, weaving in or out as the game requires, and take new positions among the thirteen dancers. I try to keep up, but there is something peculiar about the play of this game I don't understand. We perform two full circuits when, without warning, all the other maidens freeze in their spots and pull their fists to their brows in fake shock. Left with no place to stand, I fall forward and nearly land on my face. A glance up reveals all twelve maidens staring at me with a mix of dismay and relief.

I rise from the ground and both the music and the game begin anew. Another full circumference of the circle, and the maidens freeze in place again. I trip over a root as I try to claim my spot and fall again to my knees. The twelve stare at me, their arms raised in none-too-genuine shock. Worse, where before I found relief in their faces, now only a cold pity fills their eyes, a pity that devolves quickly into mad glee.

That's when the game turns dark.

Before I can take a breath, the one resembling Hannah Abrams jerks me up from the ground and hurls me into the center of the circle. All twelve maidens, including Rachel Faircloth and my own daughter, circle me like rabid wolves. Each of them takes their turn shoving my spinning form from one end of the chalk-drawn circle to the other in an ever-maddening dance, and with every cruel push, one thing becomes increasingly clear.

This game is designed to choose a sacrifice from among the maidens.

As horrifying as it seems, my plan has succeeded.

I am the Chosen One.

Nothing left to do now but wait for the inevitable.

The music shifts to a martial beat and any semblance of compassion leaves the maiden' faces as they cavort around their sacrificial lamb. With leaping bodies, flailing arms, and stomping feet, they block my every escape.

Not that I'm going anywhere.

I stand paralyzed at the heart of the circle, simultaneously terrified and at peace. At one point, ten of the maidens take positions at the periphery of the outer circle as Rachel and Isabella draw close and dance in cruel synchrony on either side of me. Neither compassion nor regret nor even a hint of recognition pollutes the cold dismissal in their stoic eyes. Just the callous stares of two who are thanking their gods they weren't the ones chosen and are performing their ritual as flawlessly as they know how in case fate, in the end, proves itself a fickle mistress.

As the ritual draws on, the twelve maidens' bodies and expressions grow increasingly violent, even taunting and cruel, as hope slips further and further beneath the frenzy of their bloodlust.

My heart pounds in time with the tympani drum as all twelve maidens leap twice with the music, then twice again, and then fall forward at my feet, their bodies pointing in the twelve directions of the clock face. The music gives them but a moment's respite before they again rise to their feet, and fall again, this time facing away from me. Again and again they go to ground, and it's only after the third or fourth repetition that I get it.

The mockery apparently over, the girls now attempt to honor me.

The sacrifice.

She who will bring the spring.

From opposite ends of the clearing come two small clusters of dancers, their familiar faces made menacing by their bizarre attire.

From one side, Toma, the Moor, and the Sage, all in white priestly robes and wearing peaked orange hats with fur rims pulled down across their ears.

From the other, Tunny, Modesto, and Antoine, all dressed in similar garb.

Not one of them acknowledges me as anything other than the sacrifice as the two groups march round me in opposite directions, all in time to the beat of invisible drums.

From the woods come the three witches and Baba Yaga, all wearing hooded cloaks fashioned from the pelts of slain bears. They stalk around me, hunched over like the animals whose skin they wear and even sniff at me, as if attempting to smell my fear.

The twelve maidens break into two groups to sit and watch as the three clusters of once-allies circulate around me in turn, no doubt assuring themselves they have selected an adequate offering to their gods. Soon, the ceremony begins again in earnest, the quartet of witches joining the two trios of men and the twelve maidens in the circulating throng.

The mob circles me like a school of sharks, as if daring me to break their line. The four groups take turns drawing close with threat in their eyes and then pulling away to rejoin the ceremony. If I expect to find one iota of compassion in the bunch, I am sorely disappointed. Of them all, only Toma regards me with even a hint of empathy.

Eventually, all but Yaga and the witches trail off into the woods. The remaining four, each bound in the skins of bears long dead, round me once, twice, three times, and then sit at the points of the compass around the inner circle. The accompanying orchestra hit sends a charge straight to my core. As if yanked upward by a puppeteer's string, my right arm flies into the air and my body assumes one of the basic positions I once learned in ballet.

My turn to dance.

God help me.

The music pounds into my mind, releasing me from my invisible bonds even as it seizes control of my limbs. I leap in time with the drums, my upper body contorting with every fourth beat as if an invisible child were squeezing the life from me. Again and again I repeat the four steps, my heart beating like a jackhammer as much out of fear as exertion. The bearskin-clad witches circle around me in a low crouch, watching my every move, as if daring me to run.

A moment later, I am given the choice to do just that.

My arms and legs freed, I rush terrified to one edge of the circle, but an angry Antoinette blocks my escape. I sprint to the other end of the circle and am stopped by Yaga's snarl. Returning to the center, I crouch and tremble, my legs shaking uncontrollably. As the remaining characters rejoin the dance, I attempt another run, my escape this time blocked by Modesto's leer. Time and again, I rush for freedom and, each time, I'm denied release by a merciless face that once regarded me with kindness. I return for what seems the hundredth time to the center, my eyes darting left and right in search of a weakness in my human prison, but the circle surrounding me remains unbroken.

Nothing left to do now but complete the dance.

Bowing deep, I wait for the music to do its magic. As it takes control, I first run in place like a rodent, then flap my arms like a mighty bird of prey, and then, as the melody fully takes me, I spin drunkenly around till vertigo nearly sends me to my knees.

And then, as another orchestral hit fills the space, I freeze in place as the other maidens did during the game and await the final gambit.

The music from before returns, and I begin to leap and contort again, faster with each passing second, up and down, side to side, to the ground, and back on my feet. The steps and gestures come to me as if I've performed them a thousand times, and all the while, the twenty-two figures surrounding me draw ever closer, their heads bowed as if they are ashamed to let me see their faces.

Time after time, I fall to the ground, beat my fist on the snow-covered earth in lamentation, and then leap again to my feet to continue the bizarre performance. The others all keep time with my contortions, the bacchanalia spiraling further and further out of control as my heart threatens to pound its way out of my chest.

Faster and faster I leap, arms flailing, body trembling, mind frozen. Hot and cold, energized and exhausted, terrified and calm. The music continues to accelerate, and with every passing second, the four witches in their bearskin cloaks draw ever closer.

I push my body to its limits and beyond, my chest burning, my legs screaming, my heart exploding, and then, in one sweet moment of release, it's over. My body falls to the ground, my skull impacting the frozen ground with all the grace of a coconut pitched from a tree. The four witches hasten forward and raise my still form to the sky. A bolt of lightning crosses before my vision, and the sky answers with one last rumble of thunder.

Everything goes black as my spirit steals away. Fear and peace and pain and numbness and joy and sorrow all coalesce at the core of the being the world knows as Mira Tejedor.

Unbidden, a smile finds its way to my face.

And then, with one last breath, everything goes away, and I am alone in darkness.

EPILOGUE

TOMBÉ

From the journal of Anthony Faircloth – July 24th

To whoever may be reading this, my name is Anthony Faircloth, and in the absence of the true storyteller, it would appear it's up to me to finish this tale.

Two days have passed since Mira Tejedor ended the nightmare that had taken over not only my family, but families from every corner of our great city. Mom and Dr. Archer aren't quite sure how much to tell me as they still see me as the victim here, a vulnerable child.

I've read the paper, though. Watched the news.

Everything I've learned makes one fact abundantly clear.

I don't need protection from the world.

The world needs protection from me.

I do take some solace knowing the twelve innocent girls I unwittingly sentenced to my own private version of hell, among them Mira's daughter and my own sister, have all recovered and seem none the worse for wear. I've been able to talk with both Rachel and Isabella, at least briefly—if anyone thought Mom was overprotective before, they should see her now—and it's clear they remember very little of their shared ordeal. I can only hope Hannah Abrams and the other nine recover and similarly have forgotten most if not all the misery I caused.

Dr. Archer as well seems to have come through this relatively unscathed, his mourning over Mira's fate notwithstanding. He refuses to show much in the way of emotion when I'm around, but like the woman who no doubt occupies his every thought, I have a sense for such things. He's hurt, badly, and though I was only another victim of Madame Versailles' machinations, I can't help but feel a part of him blames me.

He can't blame me any more than I blame myself.

Detective Sterling insisted Mom tell me Ms. Sayles passed away in her bed at the nursing home the same day Mira danced *The Rite of Spring*. He hoped knowing Veronica was gone forever might somehow give me peace of mind, and in a small way, the knowledge helps.

But only a little.

This second coming of Versailles may have grown out of whatever remained of Veronica Sayles' influence on my thoughts, but it was still my mind that carried out her plan, created the scenarios that led to all the torment, and left everything in such a sad state. If only I had been stronger, more self-aware, more... anything, maybe none of this would have happened.

That's right. Mom doesn't know, but I remember it all. The garden. The palace. The Russian fair. The Bare Mountain. All of it. Versailles kept me in the dark as she executed her plan, but with her gone from the picture, the floodgates have opened. Every instant of each of the three worlds is now emblazoned on my mind like a movie I've seen a thousand times after having written the script, played every part, and scored the soundtrack.

That last part, quite literally.

I've had a couple of days since all of us woke up from this latest bit of madness to sort out exactly what to do next. After examining every option, I've finally come to a resolution.

Versailles may have been the mastermind behind this theatre of pain, but without me and the things my mind can do, all those girls wouldn't have nearly leaped to their deaths, Dr. Archer would never have fallen ill, and Mira wouldn't be lying in a coma in the same hospital where the twelve girls she just saved all but lost their lives. Though Mom is doing her best to shield me from the truth, I've been able to glean a thing or two from half-overheard conversations between her and Mira's mother.

As best I can tell, it doesn't sound like Mira is doing well at all, which isn't especially surprising. The first time she walked a world of my creation, Mira faced terror after terror sculpted from my obsession with Russian music and folklore. Regardless of the obstacle or the danger, she kept coming back for me, each time at greater and greater risk and, in the end, was forced to slide a dagger between her ribs to stop the madness that had blossomed in my mind.

The monumental self-sacrifice left her incapacitated for the better part of a day.

This time, she followed the storyline of Stravinsky's third masterpiece straight through to its horrible conclusion and literally danced herself to death in *The Rite of Spring*, concluding a path I laid out for her as surely as I created the Exhibition that nearly killed her nine months ago.

If anyone should be lying in a coma, it should be me. Still, regardless of who is to blame, I know if our positions were reversed that Mira Tejedor would come for me. She's already proven herself twice before, and I have no doubt she'd do so again without a second thought.

Can I, the architect of all this suffering, do any less?

ACKNOWLEDGMENTS

As I've said more times than I can remember, writing may be a solitary activity, but making a book requires a team. You would not be holding this book in your hands without the help and support of more people than I can possibly mention in these few pages.

Hats off to my monthly critique group of J. Matthew Saunders and Caryn Sutorus for their detailed reading and recommendations. You always hone my steel to a razor edge and find all the nicks in the blade and for that I am grateful.

To all my friends and fellow wordsmiths in Charlotte Writers, thank you for all the years of unyielding support. I look forward to Wednesday nights more than you will ever know. Best wishes to all of you on your writing endeavors this year.

To Mom, Dad, and Jilly, thanks as always for your undying support and enthusiasm for my dream. I hope you enjoy this book as much as the last one.

To Katelyn and Olivia, watching you grow into two such fine young women has been an education all in itself. No matter what, make certain you follow your dreams. You never know where they might take you.

To Stacey Donaghy, thank you, as always, for being my sounding board, my representative, my friend.

To John Hartness and the team at Falstaff Books, thank you for allowing this phoenix/firebird to rise from the ashes. I believe it has many miles yet to fly.

To Lisa Gus, Eugene Teplitsky, and the team at Curiosity Quills, thank you for all you did to make this book a success in its first iteration.

To Ateendriya Gupta and Amanda Roberts, thank you for your thorough proofreading. Who knew I could miss so many commas?

To Brice Chaplet, thank you for the beautiful artwork on the CQ edition of this book. Your take on the both the Firebird and Petrushka were breathtaking.

To Natania Barron, thank you so much for the beautiful cover art that embodies this new edition of the middle chapter of Mira and Anthony's adventures.

Again, to all my teachers and professors over the years, thanks for the countless hours you put into helping produce the person I am today. A second wave of educator shout outs:

To Evelyn Davis, for starting me off right in kindergarten and for coming to my hometown signing almost four decades later. That was a special moment.

To Carolyn Murphy and Gail Hedrick, for taking turns driving me to school for three straight years and for teaching by example as well as in the classroom.

And now, as I did last time, to thank a few individuals long dead who never even fathomed of my existence.

Without the genius of Igor Stravinsky, this book would not exist. The composer of *The Firebird*, *Petrushka*, and *The Rite of Spring*, as well as *Feu d'artifice* and dozens of other pieces I didn't have room to include, was newer to me than the composers from the first book. I will admit that initially, I wasn't as taken with his music to the degree I was with Mussorgsky or Rimsky-Korsakov. Stravinsky did train under Rimsky-Korsakov, and parts of *The Firebird* show that influence. The second and third ballets, however, each go in a very different direction, and it took some time and many listenings to appreciate them fully. I will say that you really can't truly understand any of these pieces without seeing the ballets either online or in person and watching as the choreography and stories unfold to Stravinsky's masterful orchestration. In the end, I've truly come to love each of these pieces. When you have the time, find a good production of each of the three ballets on the internet—they're out there, trust me—and see what I mean.

I was so happy I got to revisit Modest Mussorgsky's works in this one with one of my favorite pieces, *Night on Bald Mountain*. His genius comes through in every note of the piece and touches me on a level that most music simply can't reach.

Funny thing? *The Mussorgsky Riddle* was never intended to be a series. One and done, as they say. But the same magic that brought the first book brought the second, and as I approach the end of the third and final book of this series, I am simultaneously sad that my time with Mira and Anthony is coming to an end and yet grateful that I found two such wonderful travelling companions to come with me as I explored some of the greatest music ever written. I know that with this second volume in the trilogy, I have left both of them in a horribly untenable situation, but bear with me. I've learned a thing or two these last few years about classical music, to include fugues and ternary form. If you're curious about what happens next, and I suspect you are, then those are all the clues I'm giving at this point. A little research may reveal where I'm headed next.

You can only hear a piece of music the first time once. I hope you found the melodies here compelling, the harmonies sweet, and the rhythm hypnotic. The third and final volume of this series will be out soon enough, but for now, enjoy the brief pause before the music begins anew."

ABOUT THE AUTHOR

Darin Kennedy, born and raised in Winston-Salem, North Carolina, is a graduate of Wake Forest University and Bowman Gray School of Medicine. After completing family medicine residency in the mountains of Virginia, he served eight years as a United States Army physician and wrote his first novel in the sands of northern Iraq.

His Fugue and Fable trilogy was born from a fusion of two of his lifelong loves: classical music and world mythology. *The Mussorgsky Riddle, The Stravinsky Intrigue,* and *The Tchaikovsky Finale,* are the beginning, middle, and end of the closest he will likely ever come to writing his own symphony. *Pawn's Gambit,* the first novel in his The Pawn Stratagem contemporary fantasy series, is also available from Falstaff Books with more to follow very soon. His short stories can be found in numerous anthologies and magazines, and the best, particularly those about a certain Necromancer for Hire, are collected for your reading pleasure under Darin's imprint, 64Square Publishing.

Doctor by day and novelist by night, he writes and practices medicine in Charlotte, NC. When not engaged in either of the above activities, he has been known to strum the guitar, enjoy a bite of sushi, and, rumor has it, he even sleeps on occasion. Find him online at darinkennedy.com.

ABOUT THE COMPOSER

Igor Fyodorovich Stravinsky (1882-1971) was a Russian composer, pianist, and conductor who rose to fame in the early 1900s for his compositions for the Ballets Russes in Paris, the first three of which spanned the opulent *The Firebird*, the romantic *Petrushka*, and the controversial *The Rite of Spring*.

ALSO BY DARIN KENNEDY

Fugue & Fable

The Mussorgsky Riddle

The Stravinsky Intrigue

The Tchaikovsky Finale

The Pawn Stratagem

Pawn's Gambit

Queen's Peril *(forthcoming)*

King's Crisis *(forthcoming)*